TRANSITIONING HOME

TRANSITIONING HOME

by

Heather K O'Malley

2023

TRANSITIONING HOME
© 2023 By Heather K O'Malley. All Rights Reserved.

ISBN 13: 978-1-63679-424-2

This Trade Paperback Original Is Published By
Bold Strokes Books, Inc.
P.O. Box 249
Valley Falls, NY 12185

First Edition: June 2023

Credits
Editor: Cindy Cresap
Production Design: Susan Ramundo
Cover Design By Jeanine Henning

Dedication

To all the Transgender Individuals who are serving
or have served this country honorably despite
the challenges they faced, you are all heroes,

To Monica Helms and Angela Brightfeather,
thank you for encouraging me to tell this story,

To all my friends and readers who gave me
valuable insight as I worked on this,

And as always, to Kaye.

CHAPTER ONE

T he fuck did I join the Army?" grumbled Thomas, eyes tight as he worked to complete his third leg lift, muscles burning. Physical therapy was hard, really hard, what with learning to walk all over again. Despite how it felt, he pushed to make his legs do what he wanted, and his legs fought back. He wanted to walk again, but was it worth this pain? He pondered that often, especially during PT.

His therapist grinned evilly. "Let's go, Sergeant Simmons. Seven more. You can do this."

Thomas glared at the specialist. His muscles quivered with exertion, but he gritted his teeth and made it through his fourth repetition. He let the leg just fall. It felt like there was no strength to control its descent. With another grunt and grinding of teeth, he managed to make five. This part of therapy fucking sucked, and his legs screamed. Maybe he should just quit and lie there. Just give up.

"Only five more. You have this, you can do it, Sergeant. Push!"

Thomas wanted to strangle the blond specialist helping "motivate" him. The bastard made Thomas's life a series of excruciatingly painful exercises designed solely for torture. Maybe this was how the Spanish Inquisition worked. If so, it was a good method for breaking people and surely more successful than not. The specialist even had the gall to be tall and broad-chested, unlike Thomas. All Thomas wanted was to stop and rest, but that pissant little wannabe soldier kept telling him to do these goddamned leg lifts. If it weren't for the fact that he would get in trouble, he might just reach up and break the specialist's neck.

"Three more to go. You're almost there."

Sweat burned Thomas's eyes as he realized he could kill without remorse right now. He could just snap the moron's neck before he had time to react. This whole process was torture, and the specialist was his torturer. Didn't the Geneva Convention speak poorly about the use of torture? Maybe the prick would be arrested and charged with crimes against humanity? It would be fitting. Specialists, especially tall ones, should know not to fuck with short men for fear of getting themselves killed. It would serve this cocky bastard right.

"One more, Sergeant. Push!"

Thomas screamed as he struggled to lift his leg a last time. It felt like fire ran along the inside and outside of his calf and thigh, one big conflagration. Sweat ran down his hair, and into his eyes. After he lifted his leg all the way up, he collapsed to the mat, wrung out. Thomas's breath came in heavy pants, and his thoughts burned away in a white torrent of pain. He wanted to lie there until he died as his leg throbbed in time to his heartbeat, each pulse a new flash of pain. Thomas gasped for air. His stomach churned.

"Good job, Sergeant Simmons. You did really well. That'll be it for today. Let me help you to the table. We'll get some ice for the leg to help with the burn. At this rate you might be able to walk a little by early next week. Sound good?"

Thomas grunted and the physical therapist levered him into his wheelchair for the short roll to the table. The ice would feel incredibly good. He hoped to get through the rest of PT without killing the kid. It would be nice to get out of the wheelchair, but the pain was almost worse than the initial injury.

After twenty minutes of ice leaching the ache and pain, the packs were lifted and Thomas helped back into his chair. He shifted to get comfortable and adjusted his wrist brace. The specialist looked down. "Need help getting back to your ward, Sergeant?"

Thomas shook his head. He didn't want to rely on someone to move him about. He might be stuck in a wheelchair, but he wasn't a cripple. "No. I have the head shrinker. See you tomorrow."

Thomas wheeled along the hallways, moving around walkers, keeping up a decent speed despite his wrist. He was bitter about the whole being in a wheelchair thing, but maybe the end was in sight and he would be able to walk again. If his leg healed right and the physical therapists agreed, he might be able to get back to his unit. Better than being stuck in this POS hospital.

Ahead he spotted the restroom. Good, he needed that. Thomas wheeled into the bathroom, then maneuvered into a handicapped stall, where he struggled from the chair to the toilet. Afterward, he splashed water on his face, which was still a bit gaunt from his time in the desert, and noted that at least he hadn't gotten so mad his eyes changed color. Everyone in his unit said that when his eyes went from blue to green they dove for cover, which they found hysterical.

He ran his wet hands over his hair, which had gotten longer than he usually wore it. He needed a haircut soon to stay within regs since he could run his fingers through the mop. In all honesty, he wanted his hair on the long side and always had, but the high and tight he had in Iraq was a lot cooler. He felt sorry for the female translators with all their hair bunched up under their Kevlar. It had to be sweltering.

He wasn't looking forward to this next bit as he didn't trust shrinks, positive they all worked to find ways to discharge soldiers for being crazy. So what if he had nightmares, or felt uncomfortable because he was unarmed, or there was a loud noise, what was wrong with that? At least things were better than in Germany, when he repeatedly asked for his Kevlar, rifle, and flak vest. He certainly wasn't going to let the shrink know about the other things rolling around in his head. Those thoughts would probably get him dishonorably discharged. No, those thoughts would stay safely in his own head for now as shrinks were clearly the enemy.

The psych receptionist smiled at him. "Yes, can I help you?"

"I have an appointment with Captain Wilson."

"Okay, your name?"

"Simmons 7953."

The woman checked her computer for confirmation. "If you could wait, the doctor will be with you shortly."

He thanked her and rolled to the side. Oh joy, more hurry up and wait.

Ten minutes later, a young-looking captain came out of the hallway with a file in hand. He was wearing glasses and a condescending smile. "Sergeant Simmons?"

"Here sir."

"Come with me." Thomas took an immediate dislike. In his opinion, this was the kind of officer who worked toward getting fragged. "Do you need any assistance?"

"No sir. I'll be fine." Thomas wheeled into a small, very white office and the fluorescents did little to help. This was not a comfortable place.

The captain sat behind his desk and glanced at the computer briefly. "So, Sergeant Simmons, I hear you've been having some nightmares. Want to tell me about them?"

"What do you want to know?" asked Thomas. He wouldn't let himself be caught out by some idiot. He was definitely not as dumb as the officers thought. Contrary to popular belief, not all ground pounders were idiots.

"Well, your chart says probable post-traumatic stress, and the notes support that. We should probably focus on that, so why don't you tell me about your time in Iraq?" The doc leaned back in his chair to come across as relaxed and open. It looked smug to Thomas.

"What's to tell? We got there, fought, and I got injured." Thomas did not intend to make this easy. If the doc wanted to shrink his head and call him crazy, he would have to put up with whatever crap Thomas dished out, especially since he didn't want to talk in the first place. Captain Wilson would earn his pay.

"All right, tell me about how you got injured. Let me know all the details you remember. I'm sure there's something useful that will help." The captain smiled in a way probably meant to encourage trust. It failed and put Thomas more on edge.

If the doc really wanted to know what he had gone through, he guessed he could humor the man. Part of it was straightforward and would in no way give away any of the things that really bothered Thomas. "Okay. Our platoon, along with several others, was sent in to pacify a section of Mosul, as some insurgents were doing their best to drive us out of the city. Things were going well initially, and we moved through several streets safely. We moved deeper into the city and into the problem area, when all of a sudden, things got real ugly…"

❖

"Fuck!" Thomas flinched, ducking lower as several bullets slammed into his sparse cover, bits of sandy colored wall pinging off his helmet. Moments like this made him wonder why he joined. He was an idiot to pick a job where people actively tried to kill you.

His squad was pinned down by a group of Iraqi insurgents safe behind a fortified position farther down the street they crossed as they moved toward their objective deep within the problem area. The people here, especially the insurgents, were holding out against coalition forces, and so they went in to "pacify" the city. Parts were resisting and other parts were just happy not being blown up further.

Thomas hated urban warfare with a passion, as you had to constantly be aware of every direction at once, just in case the enemy circled around. That had happened several times in training exercises and now this was for real, the worst final exam ever with no room for failure. Thomas looked across the gap between himself and a nearby building. He could get better cover over there, if he made the sprint across open ground.

Peterson opened up with the 249 to provide cover fire and get the enemy to pull back under cover. Thomas took that moment to sprint to the corner, his gear shifted heavily as he moved. A few rounds spacked off the ground behind him, urging him ever faster. He slammed his back against the wall and took deep gulps of the dust- and cordite-filled air. Sprinting with a full combat load wasn't easy; in fact, it was like running with a full-grown person hanging on your back. He was glad to be short, for a change, because at five foot five, he made a smaller target and could hide behind things others couldn't. It served him well in training and he was desperately hoping it would help here.

A few more rounds struck the corner, gouges torn in the brickwork. He shifted back, and looked to the members of his unit, slightly scattered behind various bits of fallen masonry, burned out cars, and the small wall of a garden or something. He hoped the Iraqis didn't have anything stronger on hand, because a grenade launcher would make short work of the haphazard cover. Thomas was closest to the Iraqi hard point, making him the one who needed to take out the machine-gun nest. This was not good. A frontal assault would be suicide.

"Medic! Medic!" The voice sounded distant, the world closing in. Air throbbed with the sounds of street-to-street battle, but he felt like a witness and not a participant. He glanced back at his team and saw the medic, Hernandez, scuttling toward Jones who clutched his left shoulder and screamed, blood oozing between his fingers. The air smelled of various things, only some of which were identifiable, each disparate scent in sharp contrast. In addition to dust and cordite, fire and some unnamable thing choked the air, maybe burning tires? Or flesh? This was an utter clusterfuck. They had to get moving before reinforcements arrived.

Thomas took a quick glance around the corner, toward the Iraqi position. Their position was well built up, the corner of the intersection covered with heavy sandbags and a store's facade as overhead cover. None of the grenades had gotten in their position thanks to that metal roof extending over the site. They just rolled to the ground to explode against the sandbags. If Thomas could make it closer, he just might be able to toss a grenade in and turn the tide. He looked down the street alongside his position and spotted a door about four meters away. Maybe that route would play out and he could move closer, either through the building or up. It was the best option available.

He edged along the wall, weapon trained down the street, toward the door, knowing his unit had his back if things got hairy. He reached the boarded-up window, then glanced back at his unit. They were still hunkered down but returning fire and trying to move forward. Once this engagement was over, he was positive he was going to catch flack for this. Thomas spotted the sergeant and called out, hoping to be heard over the din. "Sarge! Sarge!"

When the sergeant turned and looked his way, Thomas used hand signals to let him know the basics of his plan. The sergeant held up a hand telling him to wait. Thomas nervously watched him talk to several others, then send the signal for him to go ahead. Thomas nodded and settled himself. Going into a house alone was a bad idea, all his training reinforced that. There were too many ways this could end poorly, but there was no other option.

His unit provided distracting fire to cover his entrance. They put a lot of brass into the air as he kicked in the door, foot slamming next to the doorknob. Before the door swung in fully, he charged, weapon ready, just as he had been taught and practiced until it was second nature.

At a glance, he noticed it was an electronics store. There were several televisions in various states of disrepair, a few stereos, as well as radio parts scattered about. There were even a few completed TV sets with tags, not that he could read them. There was no movement in the front room. He moved deeper, trying to cover everywhere at once, nervous sweat trickled cold down his back.

Sounds were muted, making the battle outside seem farther away than it actually was. It only cranked up his nerves rather than the opposite. He went through the room-clearing tactics they practiced before deployment, making sure there was no one who could hassle him. As he moved into what seemed to be a storage/supply room, he heard a deep male voice cry out, "Ya raab, sa'edni!"

Thomas spun, M4 aimed at the cowering Iraqi, his heart rate jumping further. The man looked as if he hadn't bathed or shaved in days, and his eyes were wide. The man was down on his knees; he went face down quickly, as if at prayer, body trembling. Thomas ran over and kicked the man onto his back, then scuttled back to cover him. The man's face was a mask of fear, tears rolling through the dust making mud trails. "Are there any more in here?" Thomas yelled. "Are there any more?"

The man trembled, eyes watching the weapon instead of him, hands quaking as if with palsy. Thomas screamed the question again to no effect. The man had no idea what he was saying. Why couldn't people just speak English? The man cried out, "Qif! Qif! Lestu jundi! Lestu jundi!"

Thomas moved forward and toed the man again, forcing him back onto his stomach. Once in position, Thomas dropped a knee into the man's back and zip-tied his hands together, ignoring the groans of pain. Safety was more important than comfort.

He got up and backed away from the man, weapon still trained on his prostrate form, in case he tried something. The man muttered the same things over and over, but Thomas did not understand. Another quick scan of the room showed no doors or windows. Thomas cursed as he looked around the back room, to find something that would help, some way he could get outside and back to the battle. Blocked from sight by boxes, Thomas spotted a ladder leading to a hatch and quickly made his choice.

He slung his weapon, and with a quick exhalation to calm down, he started up. He reached the top, then shifted his weapon again and slowly opened the ceiling hatch with the tip of the barrel. The sounds of battle rushed back to full volume as Thomas peered over the edge, scanning the rooftop. There didn't seem to be anyone up here. He scrambled onto the roof and fully unslung his rifle.

He noticed several insurgents with the same idea, moving hunched over toward his teammates. He took aim and opened fire, dropping two quickly. The other one dropped, and Thomas lost his line of sight. He cursed under his breath and started moving. He scanned the opposite roof, waiting for his target to pop his head up. When the man did, one shot ended that problem.

Thomas low-crawled toward the roof's edge closest to the hard point. He glanced over cautiously, not wanting to expose himself longer than necessary. This was already more forward than he wanted to be without support. The Iraqis' reinforced barricade blocked their view of him. That should keep him somewhat safe as he could act unobserved.

He made out a narrow opening in the cover from this angle, and if he were lucky, he might be able to toss a grenade into their laps. He noticed another group of Iraqis jogging up the street toward the corner, one armed with a loaded RPG. Reinforcements. He cursed and pulled two grenades from his LBV. He had to do this right or the new arrivals would tear everyone apart.

Thomas muttered a quick prayer, then tossed the first grenade into the hard point, the first priority. It arced through the air and seemed like it made it inside. He lobbed the other grenade down onto the group on the street, since the RPG was more dangerous than the machine gun. He hoped he could pull this off without getting shot. Shouts filled the air, and he heard the first explosion, and then a secondary one as the ammunition cooked off.

The second grenade's explosion never registered as his world shattered into pain. He flew backward as his corner exploded into pieces of masonry and fire. Thomas slammed solidly into the rooftop by the ladder, pain rising, and he realized he was screaming. His shoulder and leg were on fire, and he tried to swat out the flames covering his leg. The pain was excruciating and thankfully it died before everything went black.

❖

Thomas blinked his eyes open, head throbbing. He was in a Blackhawk, one of the medevac birds. The moaning he heard was coming from him, and that was not comforting. Thomas could feel the burns and broken limbs, but apparently painkillers were helping.

He was in the middle stack of injured, one above, one below on the rotating rack made to hold stretchers. He turned his head slightly and noted the other side looked empty. A flight medic moved alongside and injected something into the IV he had not noticed. The pain faded even more and he closed his eyes.

The next time he awoke, bandages were everywhere and several places burned, but he no longer cared as meds fuzzed him. He lay there, listening to the rhythmic thrump of the chopper, drifting in and out of consciousness and trying to remember what happened.

When they set down near the field hospital, they rushed him inside and everything was a blur. They rolled over an x-ray machine, and he felt his uniform being cut off along with other pokings and proddings. Someone injected something into his IV and again things went black.

❖

Thomas's lips were chapped, his mouth was cottony, and he ached all over. What the hell happened? His head was muzzy, and he shook it slightly to clear the mental cobwebs. The movement made everything pulse painfully, so he stopped as nausea rose. He moaned, feeling himself slowly grow clearer-headed. Soon a nurse came up, checking on him.

She was pretty. Her dark brown hair was in a braid, and she was dressed in fatigue pants and one of the ugly brown regulation undershirts. The woman had excellent curves, and he smiled weakly. Her breasts were at eye level. "How are you feeling, Corporal Simmons?"

"Like shit. Hurt everywhere. What happened?" His words were slurred.

"You got a concussion, a badly broken leg and ankle, plus a broken wrist, and burns. You just got out of surgery, where they pulled out shrapnel and debrided the wounds. Your bones are set and you're in recovery." Her voice was friendly. "Thirsty?"

Thomas thought about nodding but remembered it hurt, so just said. "Yes, please."

She smiled brightly. "I'll be right back. Don't go anywhere."

Chapter Two

That's all my memories of getting injured." Thomas had reported this part of the story several times. It didn't even bother him anymore, well...for the most part. However, that had taken a number of tellings. At least the event itself and just thinking about it didn't cause him the stress it had.

The captain wrote down a few notes. He looked at Thomas in that slightly superior know everything manner. Thomas was sure this was his normal way of interacting with soldiers, as if he was so much better than anyone who came into his office. The look made Thomas think weasel. "Is there anything else about the whole event you can remember, Sergeant Simmons?"

Thomas shook his head and shrugged. Of course, he remembered more, but it wasn't anything he was going to tell this guy. There were some places in a man's head a shrink shouldn't be allowed. Besides, these were things Thomas was still trying to wrap his own head around, and he wasn't going to bring them up with anyone until he had a handle on it. He needed answers before they drove him around the bend.

❖

Thomas smirked as the nurse walked away, the roll of her hips and butt through the tight seat of her uniform pants held his attention. He found her quite attractive; she had decent breasts that pushed against the brown shirt and an ass that strained against her pants. He liked the way a woman's ass looked and the nurse's was one of the best he had seen in a while. Given, he had mostly seen teammates' rears of late so that wasn't saying much. However, he also felt a little jealous, which confused him. He had no clue why, but the feeling was there and strong. He closed his eyes to figure it out, but his head hurt too much to think clearly.

When she came back, the nurse handed him a plastic cup with a straw. He took it in his one working hand and sipped the refreshing warm water slowly. The cup was heavier than expected though the water made him feel worlds better and helped with the cotton mouth. She checked the machines monitoring his condition and headed off. Thomas sighed, trying to ignore the odd feeling of jealousy he had felt off and on for most of his life. There was no reason for it, and it made his teen years a misery of angst. Joining the Army helped, but now here it was again.

He sipped more water and felt his head clear, which made the ache in his body clearer as well. The nurse returned, since he was moaning. "Are you okay, Corporal?"

"The pain is getting worse and my head hurts."

She nodded, clearly expecting that. "How bad is it on a scale from one to ten?"

"An eight and getting higher."

She nodded and went to get painkillers. After returning and dosing him, she made some notations on his chart, then left. The throbbing faded and he drifted off to sleep.

After lunch the next day, his first non-medical visitor arrived. Thomas perked up when his sergeant walked in. He looked dusty as usual since everything in this country was made of dust. "You crazy dumb bastard, that was the stupidest and most heroic fucking shit I've ever seen. Damn, Rhymer, you saved our asses and got yours shot off in the process. Not the brightest of plans, but it worked."

"Thanks, Sarge, but what else was I going to do? Let y'all die? You know me, always willing to throw myself in harm's way to keep everyone safe." Thomas smiled, amused by his nickname. They tagged him with that moniker thanks to being noticed writing poetry on guard duty. Guarding the airbase back in Kentucky was exceptionally boring; all you did was sit there, stop the occasional vehicle, go through a checklist, and wave them through. So he wrote.

"You impressed the hell out of the LT so he's putting you in for a medal, a big one. Figure you're gonna at least get the Purple Target." The sergeant chuckled. Thomas did briefly, but it hurt his shoulder. "Unfortunately, I had to move someone into your slot to fill the chain. I want to get you promoted and give you your own team to babysit, especially when you get better and return. Top agreed and is working on the paperwork. Dammit, Rhymer, you didn't need to get yourself injured to get promoted."

"Sorry, I wasn't thinking about that. I just didn't want to watch y'all get chewed up by those guys while I had decent cover." Thomas honestly hadn't done anything special. So what if he excelled at stupid stunts to get them out of some sort of bind time and again. He focused on doing the job as best he could, which more often than not got him killed in war games. Better his one death as opposed to the whole platoon.

"Humph, you and your fucking death wish. I swear, sometimes I wonder if you're just trying to get killed with these stunts." His sergeant looked him in the eyes, boring in to dig out an answer.

Thomas didn't look away. This wasn't a new conversation; it was one that usually occurred every time he did something that saved the team but nearly got him killed. It happened a lot more often than Thomas was happy with, but he was only doing what he was supposed to. "I don't have any intention to die, Sarge. I just act and end up getting hurt. I enjoy being alive, honest. It probably has more to do with me trying to measure up to your height than anything else."

"Fine. I believe you, though sometimes I gotta wonder. Get better quick so you can come home. We need you." The sergeant stretched up to his full six-foot-three height, grinning down at Thomas. "Take care, Rhymer."

"Thanks, Sarge, I'll do everything I can to get better as soon as I can. You can count on me. Say hi to Waltrip and everyone."

Thomas watched him leave then lay back. All he had now was free time. The docs wouldn't allow him out of bed, and he was tired of bedpans. It was gross and he didn't want to think about it anymore.

He didn't have anything to read or write with, and even if he had paper, his right wrist was broken and he couldn't write anyway. So all he could do was mull things over and over in an endless round, like why he felt jealous of women, if he really did have a death wish, if his military career was over, and what would he do if it was. He wasn't ready to be done with the Army. He had plans, dreams, but if his injuries were bad enough, they would be done with him. The finality was depressing.

He rolled the whole jealous thing around in his mind, trying to wrap his brain around it. What the hell was he jealous of? Why the hell would he be jealous of women? Thinking back to high school, Clarksville, and his responses to various nurses, he figured it had something to do with the way they looked, but what the hell was that about? They were sexy as hell. But he felt jealous of that? Why? Because he didn't look female sexy? He was a guy; why would he want that? It was stupid and he dismissed it as one too many hits to the head.

Thoughts about wanting to die were even less comforting. When Thomas reviewed his time in the Army, all the times he rushed into enemy fire, threw his body in danger's way so his teammates would be safe, it made little sense. All he could come up with, when he looked at it objectively, was he really did want to die. It scared him to think it was possibly true. But why? Why would he want to die? He was happy in the Army, doing good things, and making a difference in the world. Wasn't he? What could cause him to commit suicide by Iraqi, well, besides that one thing?

The whole notion irritated him, and Thomas hated not having answers. He was used to solutions to problems, not being blocked, as he was good at breaking things down and finding answers. Why couldn't he figure out what the problem was in this case? He had always been able to sort his thoughts before, and now these jealous thoughts and death wishes come up and he's at a loss? Maybe he needed to talk to a shrink?

That made him shudder. He wasn't sure if he wanted to let a shrink get a hold of him, as a shrink might just chapter him out of the Army for being crazy. In a way he couldn't argue, but it held no appeal. Maybe a chaplain? He didn't know and that didn't help.

He wasn't crazy, so he kept those things to himself, even when discussing his nightmares. He knew if he let these out there would be hell to pay. The shrink at the CSH mentioned he might be suffering from post-traumatic stress disorder and that it would be looked into back in the States. Thomas was afraid that diagnosis alone might end his career. When they said he was getting medevaced for more surgery and physical therapy, he was positive things were worse not better.

The flight to Landstuhl Hospital in Germany was long and he slept through most of it. After over a week and a few surgeries to fix problems the CSH had not been equipped for, they sent him back to Walter Reed in Washington, DC, for physical therapy and recovery. Maybe he would get better and could return to his unit, but he suspected he wasn't going to. He missed his best friend, Waltrip, and the guys in his unit, wanting to have their backs like they had his.

❖

Thomas rolled from the shrink's office, happy to be gone from that quack. More prescriptions and he wasn't sure he even needed them. Thomas was stuck with them, because it wasn't worth arguing with nurses. They always won and had no fear of anyone. It was attractive and he flirted shamelessly, despite all of them having rank on him.

He disliked his therapist and hated that he even had one. He wasn't crazy. Sure, he had disturbing thoughts, but everybody had those. Supposedly, there was some sort of treatment for PTSD involving virtual reality, or following a light, or some crap. The captain informed him he would start specific therapy next week. Oh joy, something else to add to the list.

Aching almost everywhere, Thomas glanced at the clock and noted it was almost meds time. They eased the pain, but he didn't like them. The painkillers made him fuzzy-headed and drowsy, which meant all he did was therapy and sleep. They also made his thoughts drift, keeping certain unwelcome topics floating around. Thomas was told it was part of the whole healing process, but he would rather stay up and think clearly than live in this haze. There were things he wanted to work through, but the meds weren't helping.

He didn't want to delay his exploration of these issues. He still felt jealous whenever he saw women around the hospital, even if they weren't extremely attractive, and it exhausted him. The whole issue was depressing and, coupled with his physical problems, made him pull into himself.

It was two more weeks until he could take off the wrist brace and write again. He looked forward to that as he worked through his thoughts better when writing. Between occasional poems and journaling, he had always been able to take his thoughts out and get a feel for them.

Thomas wanted to keep his job and mentioned it every appointment. He enjoyed being a soldier. He was doing something good and patriotic, something that made him proud. It was the kind of thing a man had to do. To escape his little town, he went straight to his local recruiter after high school and joined up. He chose infantry because military police didn't have any slots open. After basic and AIT at Fort Benning, he got to his unit just in time to train up for Kosovo. They had been there from May to November of 2001, and they all flipped over 9/11. In early 2003, they got their chance to show those bastards you don't screw with the US. The ground war started on March 20, they had fought in Najaf on the twenty-ninth of that month, then shifted to Karbala. Once Baghdad was taken, they had been sent to Mosul to deal with the insurgents there. He had been doing so well when they blew him up on the tenth of June. Shipped out to Germany by that weekend and then after a few weeks there over to here at Walter Reed and the worst Fourth of July ever. In all honesty, he had been on the go for years, and double-time for the last six months. He was tired but this enforced rest was maddening.

Time crawled. It seemed forever before he got his first chance to walk. It was aggravating, being supported by two people to take even small dragging steps. Sure, it was a degree of success, but it only brought shame. Finally, his wrist was freed and he could start writing again, though slowly since his wrist was weaker and it hurt to hold a pencil or pen for long. Thankfully, occupational therapy helped so he hoped he could start writing through his problems.

Thomas's PTSD treatment went on, and he took part in a new technique utilizing videos and video games. It was odd but helped, reducing his edginess and anger. Thomas was glad he no longer felt the need to be armed and wasn't scanning the area for possible attack sites as much. It was a start.

After another month of strengthening everything and learning to walk, Thomas heard about the medal thing again. The hospital commander presented him with a Purple Heart and Bronze Star in a small ceremony in mid-September. Thomas walked forward to accept the awards using a cane, standing proudly in his dress uniform as they were pinned on. He'd put in hours every day for countless weeks to manage even that little bit unassisted.

Back in his room, Thomas just stared at the medals. He understood the Purple Target, but the Bronze Star? That was for heroes, not grunts simply doing their job. He hadn't done anything all that impressive, had he? It was something any of his teammates would have done in the same position. It didn't make sense, but Thomas wasn't going to argue. If the Army wanted to give him a medal, more power to them.

His nightmares faded in frequency, and he struggled through jumbled thoughts. The doctors informed him while he might be able to walk without a cane someday, his leg would never take the abuse needed to be infantry. He would be medically retired, sent to his home base, and transition from active duty to civilian life. His life as a soldier was over. He would still have an ID card and be allowed certain privileges, but as a veteran not a soldier. It was the first time he had cried in over a decade.

All through this, Thomas struggled with feeling out of place. He was working out the why of the jealousy, and despite it making little sense, it seemed to be about wanting what women had, the curves, the hair, the everything, to be a woman. That seemed wrong but was the only answer that fit. The death urge seemed to be a feeling that his life wasn't important, with no good reason to live. Both answers were uncomfortable and worried him. He needed more information and figured the internet would be a logical place to turn, since he disliked talking to military shrinks. If he had to leave the military, he would rather be honorably discharged rather than dishonorably for being a freak.

The trip to Fort Campbell was depressing. No one met him at the airfield except the unit orderly when the Air Force medical transport plane dropped him off. The drive to the barracks was in silence as Thomas had nothing to say, wincing at the bouncy Humvee ride. He limped into HQ and signed in with the rear detachment, the guys left home while everyone else fought. One of them had probably been sent to take his place. He signed paperwork and hobbled up a flight of stairs to his room, using the handrail and his cane. At least he had a weekend to wind down before getting up at six a.m. for profile PT and the illusion of a normal workday.

Thomas was surprised how much it felt like coming home. All his stuff was here: books, music, movies, and computer. His gear was piled neatly at the foot of his bunk, shipped home from Iraq. He sat down heavily on his nicely made bunk and stared at the ceiling. What the hell was he going to do now? By the end of October, he would be discharged and had no clue what to do. Did he want to stay in town? There was a college here and the VA might help him pay for school or help him use his G.I. Bill. He could move and go to school if he wanted. He could even go home, but he felt little pull to go back to North Carolina. He needed to make a decision before things progressed further or he would be cut loose with no solution for where to go or what to do.

Thomas knew this wouldn't be easy, considering he planned on making a career out of the military. His twenty-year plan had gotten flushed. He needed to figure out the rest of his life from this broken place. He didn't want to work in business, and he hated working in sales. Food service was right out, as it was gross, and being a cop or fireman was out thanks to his leg. All the career paths he originally had interest in depended on his ability to move unhindered. Thomas figured he could become a teacher, maybe even a coach, as that wouldn't require him to move around as much. He knew enough about several sports and could take classes to make him even more qualified. That could work, he supposed.

If he became a teacher, he would definitely want to teach something he enjoyed, like English or history. In high school he did well in both classes and figured it couldn't be too hard to teach. Most colleges had some sort of teacher training program, so he could do that and start working. It would be a hell of a lot better than living as a disabled vet with no life.

A glance at his clock showed it was chow time. Thomas groaned as he sat up, muscles protesting, thanks to turbulence and the Humvee. With no recourse, he grabbed his cane and hobbled out, moving far slower than before. Hopefully, the food would be better than Walter Reed's, though he doubted it. Hospital food was generally better than the mess hall. At least it would be better than MREs. Then again, a lot of things were better than Meals Rejected by Everyone. He missed actual food, like steak, seafood, tasty things the Army always found a way to ruin. Maybe he would go out to eat soon and get something that qualified as real food. It certainly was a plan to consider.

CHAPTER THREE

"Yes, Mom, I'm staying here and working on my degree. I'm gonna get my bachelor's."

His mother's strident tone was something he hadn't missed at all. "Tom, come home. There plenty of good schools here."

"I know there are good schools back home, Mom, but I want to go to school here so I can see my friends when they return from Iraq." Why wasn't she listening? It wasn't like what he was saying was difficult to follow.

"Tom, you're leaving the Army. It's not like you're going to be dealing with those people no more. Don't worry about them. They have their own lives to worry about and won't have time for you."

He took a few breaths to calm down before answering. "Look, Mom, just because I'm leaving the service doesn't mean my friends will no longer talk to me. That doesn't even make sense."

"You won't have the job in common, so what'll you talk about?" She was trying to be pragmatic, but it made Thomas want to scream. Why was she against him having his own damn life?

"I've known these guys for years, Mom. We've been through a lot and I'm not abandoning them," Thomas said hotly, his grip on the phone causing the plastic to creak.

"Thomas, you need to move on with your life. Hanging around there won't be good for you. All it'll do is remind you of what you've lost. Come home. We can take care of you."

"Fine, whatever. Look, I gotta go." Thomas hung up the phone and groaned, leaning backward in his desk chair. Talking to his mother was an endurance test. She spoke over him and pushed her ideas so hard it was exhausting. Getting out a full sentence was an accomplishment. He was glad they only spoke every couple of weeks—more often and he would likely strangle her. That alone was reason enough to not head back there.

Thomas ran a hand over his freshly cut hair. The high and tight looked good and the razor-cut back and sides looked sharp. He was ready for the tedium of garrison life, sitting around the barracks, doing paperwork, and no training. Thankfully, he was allowed to stay in his desert fatigues and wouldn't have to iron his uniform or polish his boots. That made him very happy, well, somewhat happy.

Thomas stretched, trying to work out his sore muscles, and shifted in front of his computer. He logged on and went to Google, looking at the prompt blankly. How the hell would you even start a search like this? It was embarrassing to think about let alone type.

"Jealous of girls" yielded no workable results. He shifted uncomfortably in his chair and his face burned as he typed in the next. "Wanting to be a girl" wasn't much better, most results having nothing to do with his search. However, one of the links led to something called gender identity disorder, which sounded ominous. Using that as a search parameter led him to the mother lode. His screen filled with reams of information on gender dysphoria, transsexualism, transvestism, and other things that made his head swim. Some fit and others didn't seem at all close. He used the new terms to expand his search and found a large array of personal stories dealing with this… this…whatever it was.

The personal stories made some sense to Thomas, more so than other sites. The glut of information was dizzying. A few times, it was like reading his own thoughts and feelings. Was this what he had? Maybe he needed a shrink after all. It was unpleasant and the possibility of being a freak made him twitchy.

He checked on gender therapists and found a list of specialists across the United States. After finding Tennessee, he looked for someone he could talk to. There were two in the area and one worked with vets. This surprised Thomas. Were there really that many veterans dealing with this? That made him feel less awkward.

He shook his head. Now he had the beginnings of a plan, so he could drop it for now. He copied the doctor's number and decided to call tomorrow for an appointment. Thomas wanted to get rid of this damn problem. He didn't want to feel this way. He shut down his computer and got ready for bed. Hopefully, this would simply be some odd moment of insanity and he could get on with his life, not deal with this gender crap. It didn't look fun and seemed a tremendous hassle. There was even information about people who died because of this crap, either by idiots or suicide. That definitely did not endear him to the whole concept. The fact that people freaked out over genitals to the point of killing themselves was disturbing.

His mind churned over everything, and finally his meds kicked in letting him drift to sleep.

❖

The temporary CO let Thomas begin out-processing so he could attend the informative classes. Getting out of the Army required him to jump through several weeks of hoops, get signatures from the strangest places, and turn in his gear. It did get him into a Veterans Administration counselor though, to talk about his disability and some of the options it would give him.

"I'm saying it's possible for you to go to school on the VA's tab, son. Vocational Rehabilitation can pay for any accredited school in the United States, and you can study anything you want. Hell, last year I put through paperwork for a guy to go to a blacksmithing school in Arizona. We bought his tools and an anvil for him. If they'll pay for that, then you should easily be covered."

Thomas nodded and jotted down a few notes. This had been interesting and helpful. Maybe he wouldn't have to worry about money while in school. That would be lovely, as he wanted a college degree, since no one in his family had one.

"You mentioned something about being medically retired?" the counselor, a hefty older gentleman with a semi-scruffy beard, asked.

"Yeah. I'm getting around a thirty- to forty-percent disability rating by the med board for my leg, maybe more," Thomas said, wondering where this was going.

"Good. You'd qualify for voc rehab with only a twenty percent rating, so you're in there easily. When your medical records are evaluated, you might even go higher. If you make it over fifty percent then the VA pays for your medical expenses forever. So make sure you do that. Put down everything, and I do mean everything as you never know what they'll approve. Every sniffle, every ache, everything."

"Really?" Would they really rate him higher than the med board? "I thought they only cover things that happened in service?"

The man nodded. "True enough, as if you get injured in service the VA will cover that injury or illness. The coverage is piecemeal until fifty percent disability where you get covered for everything. At that point they take care of any and all medical issues for the rest of your life. It's a good deal. Just make sure when you get your medical records you drop them off here to speed up the process and we'll take care of the rest. We want you to get the best you can."

Thomas stood and shook the man's hand. "Thank you, sir. I'll get back in touch."

Thomas hobbled out, leaning heavily on his cane. He was walking more and could tell by his pain levels that he needed rest. However, he still had to walk to the barracks from the parking lot once he returned. He exited the car, looked toward the building and sighed before walking slowly and purposefully. It was only an eighth of a mile, at most. He muttered with each step, "I can do this."

Sweat trickled down his forehead and he wanted to fall over and lie there. The whole day had been grueling, but he was determined to make it to the building, pain be damned. Only one hundred yards away. Surely he could do one hundred yards?

After reaching the steps, he collapsed, breathless and unable to go further. A few minutes later, one of the privates attached to the rear detachment walked out and froze. "Um…you all right, Sergeant?"

Thomas chuckled bitterly, eyes tight with pain and irritation. "Do I look all right, Private?"

"No, Sergeant." The private was at a loss. "Did you need some help?"

Thomas looked up, exasperated. He thought about it and knew he wouldn't be able to make it to his room on his own, certainly not anytime soon. Swallowing his pride, he said, "I need help getting to the second floor."

The private nodded and helped Thomas to his feet, hefting him with some effort. It took a while, but they managed to get Thomas to his room where he collapsed on the bed. The private even grabbed a soda and meds when asked. Thomas drank them down, looking forward to the meds kicking in. The private fidgeted. "Anything else you need, Sergeant?"

Thomas sighed. He hated feeling helpless. It made him feel like a cripple. "Not really. Thanks for your help. I'm not sure I could have made it up here on my own."

The private smiled. "No problem, Sargent. Um…is it true you won a Bronze Star in Iraq?"

This amused Thomas and made him feel a little better, being recognized for something he had done. "Yeah. For actions above and beyond the call of duty or something like that. Basically, I did something crazy and it worked, but I got injured for my trouble."

"What happened?" The private almost bounced, eager to hear Thomas's story.

Thomas humored the kid and spoke about Iraq, the good and bad. It was nice to talk to someone about what it was like. All his friends were still over there and he was lonely. Even occasional emails with his best friend, Waltrip, weren't that helpful. After a while, the private took off to run errands for the first sergeant and Thomas felt relieved, as it let him make a phone call without anyone listening in.

"Hello, Dr. Richards speaking." It was a direct line? He expected to deal with a secretary.

"Yes, hello, sir. My name is Thomas Simmons, and I'm being medically retired from active duty. I'm calling because…I've been having odd feelings and need help getting over them. I heard you were a good person to see." That should be appropriately cryptic.

There was a slight pause on the line as if the doctor was trying to work out what Thomas said. "I see. What kind of feelings?"

Thomas took a deep breath. This was it. If he was ever going to get past this whole jealous over women thing and back to normal life, he needed to take a chance. "Being jealous of girls, because of how they look."

Again, a pause, which made Thomas more nervous. "All right. Anything else you've noted?"

Another risk. He should go for broke, unlike with Army shrinks. "Um…I also may have been taking stupid actions in an attempt to die? At least that's the best I can figure. My sergeant pointed that out after I got severely injured."

"Do you feel that you are likely to take any action to harm yourself or others in the near future?" The voice was overly calm and cautious. Thomas understood. After all, he could be a nutcase.

"No, sir. In Iraq I often took stupid risks for no good reason. I justified them at the time as looking out for my teammates, but I'm not sure they can be. While I recovered, I started thinking about all this. That's when I noted the jealousy. I mean, I've kind of felt it off and on, but never gave it much thought." Thomas wasn't proud of the admission of any of this, but he needed help.

"And you wanted an appointment to see me?"

"Yes, sir. I found a recommendation for you on the internet." Thomas sighed in relief. If he could see someone who specialized in this, maybe he would get better faster.

"I take it you're still active duty?"

"Yes, sir, though I'm being medically retired and will be out by the end of the month. Is that going to be a problem?" He didn't want to wait until he was out of the Army. He wanted to work on things now. Waiting seemed like a bad idea.

"No problem. I have an opening next week, Tuesday, five o'clock. I work late at the VA on those days so you can find me there. Head up to the third floor and check in at the mental health office. Will that work?"

"That would be fine, sir. I'll see you then. Good-bye." He hung up and lay back. Going to see a shrink on purpose would be a little unnerving. But hopefully, this whole problem would soon be a bad memory. He could go to classes, join a fraternity, and live the life of the big man on campus. A girlfriend would be nice as well. After all, he was a certified hero, with medals and everything. Girls got off on that sort of thing.

Thomas daydreamed about college until chow, playing out all sorts of ideas about being the big man on campus. He even managed to make himself walk without a limp, which he knew was impossible. His girl was shorter than him, quite a feat given his five-foot-five height.

He was trying to avoid hiding in his head, but what else could he do? Right now, he simply counted days until discharge from the only job that he ever wanted. Under no circumstances did Thomas want this to happen, but he never saw an infantryman with a permanent limp. And humping a ruck with a cane or moving at a crawl compared to your buddies would never work. All he wanted was for things to be better, to continue being a soldier. He wanted to head back to Iraq, back to his unit, to shoot the shit with friends. He didn't want to waste time filling out forms and being told about the wonderful opportunities in the civilian world. The civilian world could go fuck itself.

Thomas felt groggy and would have preferred to keep daydreaming, but his stomach demanded action. He limped out, clutching his cane. After a short struggle down the stairs, he made it across the street to the chow hall.

He was glad Waltrip and his friends couldn't see him like this. They would feel sorry for him, and he knew he could not endure their pity, knowing he was useless. Maybe out-processing would be the merciful thing. He had seen other people get injured and believed the other person was faking, that if they simply tried, they could do all that was asked. He had done it to others, and now, thankfully, he was being spared those looks and words.

He needed to get off base and do something. Anything was preferable to sitting around feeling like crap. He didn't even taste his food, something he was thankful for, as DFAC food was generally terrible. Hustling the best he could, Thomas changed and took off.

His car was right where he left it. He liked his Mustang; it was a classic, not a Fast Back or a more recent version, but an old ragtop. He struggled to get comfortable and started his car. The loud thrum of the engine made him smile.

Cranking his music, he just started his drive, thoughts drifting as he let the miles soothe him as he drove north to Hoptown. Hopkinsville, Kentucky, was not far, but going there and back was soothing. He turned onto I-24 and headed to Exit 4 in Clarksville, heading to the mall. He pulled into a handicapped spot, the temporary tag hanging in the window a bitter pill to swallow. Maybe he could find some new games to keep him busy. He couldn't do much else, and his wrist was healed enough to endure gameplay.

He limped through the mall, enroute to the game stores, to see what was available and new. There wasn't much he hadn't played in Iraq, thanks to generous donations. He missed the times they relaxed by killing virtual baddies with teammates. It was soothing and certainly less dangerous than a patrol of Iraqi streets. After a while, his leg ached so he sat on a bench.

He watched people, acutely aware of his feelings. There were a lot of girls and as he watched them, an ache grew inside. This confusion pissed him off. He didn't understand this…whatever it was, and he needed to get cured. He knew what he read, but how could that apply to him? He never cross-dressed or such in his entire life. Shaking his head, he struggled to get his mind off it. There was an appointment next week with the doc so that should be good enough. Dwelling only made it worse.

He limped to the movie theater, wanting to get his mind off this. Some sort of action film would be best, to distract him from the rest of this crap. He bought a ticket, headed inside, and lost himself in *Hellboy*, enjoying the respite from thought.

CHAPTER FOUR

Thomas cleaned his gear as best he could for turn in. Needing to spray-paint some things so they qualified as clean was odd, but whatever. It was the Army way. As long as he passed this part of out-processing he didn't care how strange it was. He hadn't received any down checks that he would have to redo so it was another signature on his discharge form. There were still plenty of places he needed to go to get everything signed off. It was tedious.

Thomas checked the time. He had to get going to make it to the shrink's office down in Nashville. He let the duty sergeant know he was going off post. The sergeant barely cared and simply scribbled something on a sheet before returning to his movie. Thomas rolled his eyes, went to his room, and changed.

The drive to Nashville on I-24 was uneventful. He zipped through traffic, thinking how much easier it was to maneuver his Mustang than an armored Humvee. That brought up Iraq. The vibrant sunsets with smoke rising from a village, the dry smell of sand, the familiar weight of his gear. Lost in thought, he barely stopped in time to keep from rear-ending a semi.

He focused on the road and eventually pulled into the VA parking garage next to Vanderbilt. He parked and headed across the causeway between the garage and the VA hospital. Halfway across, his leg began aching, slowing him. Once inside, it took him a while to figure out where to go. The elevator was a nice break and he limped through a maze to reach the office. He smiled at the receptionist. "Hi, I'm Thomas Simmons. I have an appointment with Dr. Richards."

The receptionist nodded and briefly looked at his computer. "I got you checked in. Have a seat in the waiting room."

Thomas nodded and limped down the hall, leaning heavily on his cane. He dropped into a chair, sighed, and rubbed his leg. The plastic seats were standard government issue, familiar after years in service. There were magazines scattered about and he grabbed one. It was not as recent as he hoped and covered entertainment news from three months ago. After flipping through the magazine, he heard his name called.

An overweight older gentleman with short-cropped blondish gray hair had called his name. He had a friendly smile, giving Thomas a good feeling. "Mr. Simmons? My name is William Richards. Pleased to meet you. This way please."

They headed down the government white hallway. Thomas wondered if there were approved colors and who got the paint contract, as it was terrible. Governmental décor really wasn't. The doctor waved him into a room and closed the door behind them. The room had some warmth and signs of actual human touches to the standard-issue desk and chairs. Once they settled, Dr. Richards started things off. "So, Mr. Simmons, if I remember your call correctly, why don't you tell me about these feelings you're experiencing?"

Thomas shifted uncomfortably. He hadn't expected the doctor to jump right to the point without introduction. "Well, like I said I didn't really notice it until I was in the hospital recovering. I guess I've been having these feelings for a while but hadn't really thought about it, you know? I haven't done a lot of thinking about things before, instead I was focused on the here and now. My injuries kept me in bed for a while, or in a wheelchair, with nothing to do but think. That's when I realized I felt this way, and that I acted suicidal, in terms of my actions in combat, you know, death by insurgents. That's the basics, oh, and nightmares."

The doctor scribbled on the yellow legal pad sitting on his leg. He looked thoughtful. "Nightmares? Why don't you tell me about them?"

Thomas shifted, trying to get comfortable, but nothing worked. His leg ached and the lousy chair wasn't helping. A padded seat and something to put his leg on would help. "Well, they're always about Iraq. My nightmares replay several situations or makes them worse.

And thoughts of being in the field come up when I do other things, like driving and they distract me. It's like I'm haunted."

"We'll get back to that. Let's look at this 'jealousy' thing, since that's what's bothering you the most. If I remember correctly, you said you are jealous of the way women look, correct?"

"That's right. I can't make heads or tails of it, but I get jealous of how they look."

"And what is it about how girls look that causes you to feel this way?"

What was it, specifically? There had to be something, right? "I can't think of anything right now. It's everything: hair, clothes, bodies, everything."

"Is it because you don't look like them?" asked the doctor calmly, looking at his notepad as he asked.

Thomas rocked back in his chair. A rush of embarrassment filled him, and his voice failed when he opened his mouth. All he could do was nod in agreement.

The doctor nodded slightly as Thomas failed to speak. Again, he scribbled. "Is it all women or only specific ones?"

Thomas blinked and cocked his head, trying to run through the times he felt that. Were there any common factors? Realizing there were, he looked up, eyes wide in surprise. "Um...yeah. When I feel the most depressed and jealous is when I see a woman with great curves, or long hair, or dressed in a skirt or dress or all of the above. Especially all of the above."

More notes. "And what do you think about that?"

Thomas shifted, sitting more sideways, legs pulled in close together, or at least as close as he could get, as it was more comfortable at the moment. "I...I'm not sure. It sounds like I'm jealous of them, not just their clothes. I'm not sure. I guess that's because...I want to look like they do?"

The doctor leaned back, facing Thomas head-on, one eyebrow raised as he locked eyes. "Are you asking me or telling me?"

"Telling you, I think? But what the hell is up with that? Why would I want to look like a girl? It doesn't make any sense. Can you help me to find a way to get past this and get on with my life? I want this whole stupid thing to go away."

Dr. Richards looked down at his pad, then back up, tapping his lips with the eraser. "I'll do what I can, Mr. Simmons, but you should be aware this could be a sign you're dealing with some degree of gender identity disorder. Add to that this death urge you mentioned and what's clearly post-traumatic stress. This fixation could simply be a way of dealing with the threats to your life in Iraq, a kind of gendered coping mechanism, but that's doubtful as you mentioned on the phone you were having these thoughts before you enlisted. I'll help you deal with this to the best of my ability."

"Gender identity disorder? You mean like those transgendered people?" Thomas's heart raced and his palms sweated. Could he really be one of those she-male freaks? He shuddered in revulsion.

"It's possible, but not guaranteed. There are no absolutes in situations of this nature. However, there is nothing fundamentally wrong with thoughts like these; the identity disorder is what's bothersome. Because gender identity disorder raises issues concerning self-identity and self-worth, you might become desperate enough to end this. You may try suicide, and with these suicidal urges you've been feeling it's a concern. We can get past this. Now, what can you tell me about your parents?" The doctor sounded very reassuring. This redirection helped Thomas calm down.

"My family? My birth mother died shortly after I was born, I can't remember exactly why, maybe cancer. My father remarried about a year later, and so she's my mom as far as I'm concerned. She's great, except for being overprotective and her obsession with me coming home. My dad works a lot, but we have a decent relationship. He was supportive of me joining the Army and made sure to be there when I graduated infantry school. I have a half-brother and sister from that marriage. Both are in high school right now, senior and sophomore respectively." Thomas couldn't think of anything else about his family.

"Is your sister the youngest?" asked Dr. Richards.

"Yes, she is."

"Okay. Now, how often do you have these feelings?"

"Almost every time I see a girl. It makes things difficult. I mean, it's hard to talk to a girl when jealousy is rolling over me, this derails almost everything. It bugs me, unless I keep my mind occupied."

"Have you dated?"

"Yeah, starting in junior high. I had sex for the first time at fifteen, with Sandra Caldwell. I haven't been in a relationship of any kind since Iraq. I want another girlfriend, but I've been so busy out-processing and figuring this out I haven't had a chance to hook up." Thomas had kept his eyes open, but most women he was interested in of late had wedding rings. He wanted someone he clicked with who wasn't already spoken for.

"And why did those other relationships end?"

"Usually because I moved." This wasn't completely true, but it was close enough. The fact he moved was a part of each breakup and not something he was happy about.

"All right. And you aren't seeing anyone right now?" asked Dr. Richards.

"No. I just got back from Walter Reed and haven't had time to look. Sadly, girls don't just fall from trees."

Dr. Richards nodded and sat back. "I want you to make a list of everything that makes you feel jealous about women, and if it is, for example, breasts, don't just say breasts, say what kind of breasts, large or small, firm or saggy? These specific details are important. Also, pick up some magazines and make me a collage with things you associate with women. Make it things that give your jealousy a tug. It could be women, clothes, any object or person that triggers things. Okay?"

"All right. I can do that." Why that and not some technique to help him stop thinking about his jealousy? Shouldn't he be doing some exercise that stopped his fixation on this? It seemed contrary if he wanted things to quiet down. The craft project was odd, but whatever.

"Good. Unfortunately, our time is up for today. Stay on your current medication and let me know if things get worse. I'll make an appointment for next week. The person in the office will give you the time when you check out. Take care, Thomas." The doctor leaned forward and brought up his appointment calendar on the computer.

That hadn't been too bad. All they did was talk. If that was all there was to this it shouldn't be too difficult. He needed to get to work on the lists and the poster thing as soon as possible to get it done as

Thomas wasn't sure how long it would take to find the pictures he needed.

He took his time on the drive back, letting music wash over him. Would learning the "why" help him get rid of the discomfort? Thomas wasn't sure but looked forward to not feeling that way. He wanted to look at girls, not be them. Right?

Rain started, first a light mist then actual drops with purpose. Thomas turned on his wipers as he slowed, well aware that he was too distracted to drive as usual. The last thing he needed was a car accident. The weather made his leg and wrist hurt more. Rain pelted down, almost making it impossible to drive, but it cleared a little by the time he made it back to post.

Maybe a movie would take his mind off stuff. It would get him out of his normal thought patterns briefly. He frowned looking out the window at the still falling rain and didn't feel like getting wet. Thomas got out and made a sort of a hobbled run to the barracks, over muddy, slick grass. After a slight misstep, his good leg slipped out from under him and he fell, twisting in the air, then squishing heavily into the saturated grass bad leg first. He rolled onto his back.

Thomas lay there, rain pelting him in the face while his back, leg, and arm throbbed sharply. He choked down a scream, his stomach churned, and he swallowed bile. After he wiped water from his face, more rain spattered him. The cold wet seeped into his clothes and he groaned, tears filled his eyes from frustration and pain.

With some effort, Thomas rolled to his uninjured side and spotted his cane a short distance away. He stretched out his good arm and snagged it, painfully aware of his weight lying on a now sore shoulder. Thomas struggled to a standing position. His leg pulsed in pain, worse than it had been in a long time. Added to that, it did not want to cooperate, collapsing underneath what little weight he could put on it. Thomas grunted as he hit the ground again, swallowing back his rising vomit. Seeing no other option, he began to low crawl toward the stairs, using his good leg and arm as much as possible. It was agony, but it was the only way to the barracks and out of the rain, since he doubted an orderly would hear him if he yelled. Slowly he dragged himself toward the stairs, scraping his arms and legs on the rough sidewalk, Thomas powered through.

The door opened as Thomas began to maneuver up the stairs. A couple of privates stopped dead in their tracks and stared at him in utter surprise. Thomas sighed and lowered his head. "A little help please."

They rushed over and picked him up in a chair carry, taking him inside and helped him onto one of the ugly pleather couches. One rushed off calling for the duty sergeant. The other soldier asked, "Are you all right, Sergeant?"

Thomas restrained his first response and grit his teeth. "No, I'm not. I may have reinjured myself when I fell. Injuries to my arm, back, and leg. I'm nauseous and dizzy."

The sergeant on duty came rushing down the hall. "Simmons, an ambulance is enroute. You okay?"

"No. I fucking hate rain. I knew I should have worn field boots and brought my damn Gore-Tex." Tears leaked out, and it took focus to control his urge to scream. Was he trying too hard, pushing himself beyond what his body could do? It certainly seemed that way.

The medics arrived and got Thomas on the gurney. He was rushed to the ER for x-rays, then finally into clean, dry hospital clothes. A nurse started an IV and gave him Demerol. After forty-five seconds, the pain faded and Thomas relaxed. "Thank you."

The nurse smiled and dropped the needle into the sharps box. "You're welcome. If the pain comes back let me know and we'll give you another."

He lay back, arm supported by a pillow, and stared at the ceiling. Why did this always seem to happen? He hurt and hated that, also hoped this wouldn't make his recovery worse. His haste may have screwed up his body more.

After a while, Thomas drifted off. He woke when someone called his name. It was the doctor. "Sergeant Simmons? We got the x-rays back. We can see no visible damage, so you probably just wrenched things. We're giving you Vicodin. Take that and hopefully things will relax in a few days. I've written you a profile for a few days of bed rest so please follow that. Take care."

The doctor left and the cute nurse came back with paperwork. Since his pain was creeping up, she gave him another shot of Demerol before the IV came out. Thomas wasn't worried about anything after that. The duty sergeant took him back to his barracks room, carrying him part of the way with help. "I'll have a runner bring you meals and stuff. Don't worry and don't leave the floor."

At that point, Thomas didn't care; he was loopy from the Demerol. He lay on his bed and watched the ceiling move for a while before drifting off to sleep.

❖

Thomas was a girl but wasn't, wearing BDUs that hugged his body, like several of the nurses in Iraq. His team was clearing one of the villages. His sergeant leered and said, "Rhymer, get your cute little ass up on point. The view will definitely be better than Hernandez's lumpy ass. Hustle."

He flounced to the front, almost skipping into position. The jiggle of his tits distracted the Iraqis and they cleared the sector easily. Thomas giggled. "See, Sergeant. I told you my tits would save the day."

The team applauded, Waltrip laughed, and it only got louder when his fatigues disappeared. He tried to cover up, but his arms had shrunk and all he could do was stand there exposed, naked, raw. He turned away, the whistles and hoots grew louder. Thomas ran, they chased, pinched his ass and tweaked his tits. He squealed, more in fear than enjoyment. It embarrassed him and was exhilarating.

He ended up back in uniform, at his class reunion. Still a girl, but his old friends kept calling her a him, or was it him a her? Frustrated, he stormed out, down a long hallway, that lengthened the more he walked. Then he was running, weighted down by a full combat load, a bright light, back in Iraq. Explosions threw debris everywhere, bits of earth smacking into his helmet.

Thomas flanked the Iraqi platoon with two others and they dropped a few M203 grenade rounds onto them. Opening fire, they shot the rest. Blood and smoke and sand everywhere. His face was sticky.

He walked over to a wall with the remains of a mirror. His face was covered in blood, pieces of flesh and gore dripping off. He tried to wipe, but it wouldn't come off. Blood was pouring from his own face.

He started clawing, desperate to scrape it off, his flesh peeled under his nails, and he kept going, tearing his face off faster, screaming as he struggled to tear the blood away.

❖

Thomas screamed, sat up, and looked around the room, afraid something was coming at him from the dark. When he realized that nothing was, he fell back and shook, glancing around. Since most everyone in the barracks was in Iraq, he hadn't bothered anyone. His heart raced, his throat was hoarse, and he was panting as if he had run ten miles. He stumbled to his mini-fridge but felt his body resisting the movement. It hurt to grab a bottle of water. He guzzled it down and grabbed another and rolled it over his forehead. The cool bottle felt nice, and condensation trickled down his face soothingly.

He wasn't going to sleep any time soon so he fired up his computer and filled a Word doc with what he could remember of the nightmare. Then he surfed the net after more pain medication, hoping to get tired again. He went from site to site, the mouse trembled on the screen. They slowed as the panic drained and he exhaled loudly. A while later, he got sleepy again and turned off the computer. He crawled back to bed, desperate to say good-bye to the day.

CHAPTER FIVE

Thomas was in bed again, thinking about his body, his future, his family, rolling thoughts around over and over. It hadn't been difficult getting the runner to grab lots of magazines and catalogues. He simply said he was bored and needed something to read. He had them in a pile on his desk. Going through them kept him busy and his mind quiet. The pull of attraction he had mentioned to Dr. Richards apparently existed, as he had a large number of pages marked. He leafed through a women's clothing section of a catalogue, to mark different outfits he felt a pull from. The jealousy felt like it wanted something, which creeped him out. He wanted bras, panties, dresses, skirts, all that feminine crap? A current of nervous and uncomfortable energy rolled through him as he went through the different pages, taking note of what he liked, and he felt more awkward than ever.

This was screwy. He focused on the collage exercise, trying to get it done. Slowly, he built a collection of clothes and objects. He put them aside. Tomorrow, he would tape them to the poster board. The runner had grabbed it for him, taking it from the orderly room. At least it saved him money and with the unit deployed he doubted anyone would miss it.

He pulled out a pad of paper and started a list of things he felt jealous about. It felt weird, and he kept looking at the door nervously. Embarrassment overflowed. Even thinking about what kind of breasts he felt most jealous over was odd. He sat back and pondered the things that made him feel that way. The first person he thought of was the nurse in Iraq.

She was probably a C in breast size. They were firm and tasty looking. He thought of her nice round ass that filled her BDUs, keeping the seat of the desert fatigues taut with every move that she made. Her hair had been in a thick-looking bun, so her hair was likely long. Thomas never had long hair, as his mother always threw a fit at the idea, and once he left home it was straight into the Army. Long hair drew him like a moth to flame, and he realized all the girls he dated had long hair past their shoulders. What else? Some of the outfits. He listed skirt and blouse outfits, some lingerie. He wrote it all down, trying to keep up with the flow of images.

There was a knock at the door.

Thomas's heart rate increased, and he quickly stuffed the notepad under his pillow. "Yes?"

"Sergeant, you need anything?" It was the runner. "Lunch is coming up and I wanted to see if you wanted anything special?"

"No thanks, just the basic lunch. I have water and Cokes here, so I'll be fine. Thanks." Thomas started to calm. It wasn't easy.

"Okay, Sergeant, I'll be right back."

When there was no more talking, Thomas breathed a sigh of relief. That was disconcerting, like getting caught masturbating by his mom. The notepad remained under his pillow and hidden until the runner returned. He saw no reason to tempt fate.

The food was as expected—fuel. The better cooks had gone to Iraq with the battalion. He washed it down with a Coke and played a video game, losing himself in virtual violence, which was definitely better than the real thing. The more realistic combat games triggered flashbacks so he couldn't play those any more. In a way, he was glad he wouldn't go back, but it also depressed him. He sighed and took more painkillers.

After forty-five minutes, they kicked in. His attention wandered hither and yon, thanks to the meds. He thought over the list and what it could mean. Did he want to look like that? He pictured himself with that nurse's curves and long hair. The image made him smile and also gave him a slowly firming erection.

He kept imagining himself as a girl, in different outfits, wandering around different places at different times. Everything seemed right, fitting, true. Those pictures danced through his mind, showing his feminine face. His penis was almost painfully erect when he drifted off, the drugs pulling him under.

In his dreams, the way he looked switched between a male and female, though he hardly registered it as being different. A few hours later, he awoke but was still groggy from the meds.

He pulled his list from under his pillow and considered it. He blinked a few times to bring it into focus. Thomas added a few more items and figured he had everything he could think of on it. He added severity levels since some things made the jealous feeling worse than others. The page was soon filled with his handwriting, and he tore it off the notepad and placed it under a book on his desk.

Thomas went through more magazines and marked things. There were a lot of items marked and he wasn't sure if it was too much. The doctor hadn't given a limit. He went back to scanning pictures, trying to make sense of what was going on in his head.

❖

"Are you okay?" asked Dr. Richards as Thomas limped into his office.

"Not really. I slipped and fell after our last appointment and got laid up for three days. It aggravated everything but no extra damage. So...that was fun." Thomas felt much better. The extra stretching and physical therapy exercises helped.

"I see you have the assignments done. May I?" asked the doctor, smiling politely.

Thomas handed over the rolled-up poster board and the list. It was a relief to get rid of it, the stress of having it in the barracks was nerve-wracking. "Here you go."

The doctor perused the images carefully, paying attention to several sections and individual items. He set it down and looked at Thomas. "Did you find this assignment difficult?"

"Not really. I've thought a lot about that feeling since it first showed up, so I knew what to be aware of." Thomas shrugged. "I grabbed whatever triggered that in the least little way."

"You have a lot of things on here and a wide variety. I guess I wasn't expecting furniture or pieces of art."

"True. Being reinjured gave me time to lie back and go through a lot of magazines. And there was all that space to fill. I finished what I already had and then needed some more."

Dr. Richards nodded. "What made you choose these pieces of furniture and such?"

"I don't know. They stood out and I marked them to be cut out. I don't know why that feeling arose, it...just did." Thomas searched for some way to explain, but there was nothing.

"Don't worry. The fact you were able to broaden your search beyond simply clothes is good. Now let's go over this list, shall we? It does seem fairly specific and detailed, like your poster. All these things get you to feel jealous and to these degrees?" Dr. Richards scanned the list.

"Um...yeah. I figured you might need to know that in order to do your job," Thomas answered nervously. "Was that wrong?"

"No, not at all. There is no right way to do this, just interested is all. I notice you have some very specific items listed here."

"I thought you wanted specifics?"

"I did, I do, but I wasn't expecting this specific. Thank you. It will certainly make analysis easier. Anything else interesting happen?"

"Besides getting hurt? Not much...though, I've been having odd dreams." Thomas sat back.

"Dreams? Like what?" The ever-present notepad appeared.

"Well, I don't remember much, vague images. Me dressed as a woman, catcalls, Iraq, stuff like that. They're really disjointed. They've woken me up, ready to scream," said Thomas, unable to nudge anything further from his memory.

Dr. Richards look concerned for a moment, brows furrowed. "I think you should start a dream journal. Record your dreams, whatever you remember, and we can look for any patterns. If you can't remember anything, still write something down. Feelings, vague memories, sensations, anything, all of that is valid. It can help build a more complete picture."

Thomas nodded. "Okay. I see the sense of that. Anything else?"

"Well, yes. You've mentioned you get jealous and handed me this list of things that make it worse. Jealousy is often caused by wanting to be in that person's place, or to have something the other person has. It's symbolic of a desire for something else. Why would you want these things?"

"I...um...I don't know. I never really thought about it, but I've been thinking a lot lately." Thomas's mind whirled. He wanted to be a girl? Like for real and everything? Was that what the jealousy symbolized? "Maybe...that's who I want to be?"

"Is that a statement or a question?"

"I don't know?" Thomas focused inward. "It would make sense, I guess, given all of those feelings, but I never thought anything like that before."

"Never? You have never, in your whole life, thought about dressing and being a girl?" he asked, quirking an eyebrow at him.

Thomas recalled his life, running through everything, to see if there was any truth to this. He remembered something and his face flushed. "I had a few sexual fantasies in high school. I can't remember clearly. I've never worn girl's clothes or anything. So, why would I think about this?"

The doctor smiled. "Isn't that the reason you're here, to figure this out?"

Thomas grumbled. Any answer summoned fifteen or more questions. "I know, I'm looking for some sort of explanation."

"Well, what if this is gender dysphoria, what then?"

Thomas rubbed his temple. This was the crux of the matter. "I don't know. I want to stop feeling jealous. It's irritating and distracting. If it means I have to become...a girl...then, I don't know. It's bizarre. I mean, I'm a guy, right?"

Dr. Richards sat there watching Thomas tremble as he continued. "I mean, I can't figure out why I would want that? My life is normal, nothing out of the ordinary. I grew up in a good Christian household. I never felt this until I got injured. Could this have something to do with the concussion?"

"It's not impossible, Thomas, but doubtful. That kind of trauma rarely has effects like this. I think, however, this could be something deep-seated coming out under stress. I think you buried this deep inside, and since it's surfaced, you're going to have to deal with it." He peered into Thomas's eyes. "You can try to hide, but this isn't going anywhere until you face it."

Thomas sat quietly, overwhelmed and a little scared. "I don't want to be a girl. I'm happy. Why can't that be good enough?"

"I don't know, Thomas. I'm here to help you work through this. If we work together, we can get to the root of this and ensure this doesn't bother you again."

❖

Thomas hobbled down Franklin Street. He felt good enough right now to leave his room and do something other than mull over this fucking gender thing. Maybe he would get lucky? After all, there was only so much Rosy could do.

Music pounded against him as he entered the club and sighed in relief. It was familiar. He'd been here several times before deployment. He limped past the doorman and made a beeline for the bar, wanting something strong to shut his head up. The music helped; the beat thrummed through his body. Since it was early, Thomas grabbed one of the few tables. Given that the base was fairly empty, there were almost no soldiers about the city. He drank his beer and listened, letting his thoughts go.

After his third bottle, the place filled up. He watched the dancers enviously, remembering when he could move like that. He watched girls, enjoying the way they moved, the flow of their bodies, the way their hair bounced, and struggled to ignore the jealousy. He growled. He just wanted this to shut up. Was that too much to ask?

After his fourth bottle, a girl came up, blond hair falling to the bottom of her shoulder blades with a little flip at the bottom. She had bright blue eyes and was thin and pretty. "Hey, can I leave my drink here?"

Thomas smiled, feeling really mellow. "Sure."

She set down her glass and skipped back to the dance floor. Thomas watched her all but writhe as she danced. She could move, and good dancers made better lovers. When the waitress came by, he ordered another beer and a refill of the girl's drink. This might be a good night after all.

The girl returned, sweat glistening, hair matted down. It looked good, natural, and Thomas wanted her. She saw the drinks. "Why are there two drinks?"

"I thought you might be thirsty, so I bought you another. Have a seat, rest a bit."

The girl appraised him a moment, shrugged, and sat. "Sure. Why not?"

It was his lucky day. Maybe he would get laid.

"So, what's your name?" asked the girl.

"Thomas. Yours?" The smile he gave her was mostly guileless. Mostly.

"Deborah. You in the military?"

"The haircut give it away?"

She smirked. "Just a little. So why aren't you in Iraq?"

Might as well go for the truth. "Injured saving my platoon and got sent home."

Deborah's eyes went wide. "Like as in you're a real hero?"

"Yep. Got a medal and everything. That's why I'm over here not dancing. My leg got tore up." Thomas loved flirting. It was like stalking prey. If this worked, he would be very happy indeed. It had been far too long, and he really needed this after all the stupid gender crap. Nothing like good old-fashioned heterosexual fucking to get your mind off wanting to be a girl.

"Aw...poor baby. Want me to kiss and make it better?" She smiled before taking another sip of her drink.

"Yes." He grinned.

Deborah stood, came around closer to him, and ran her hand across his head. Thomas closed his eyes in enjoyment. "Let's see if this helps."

She kissed him on the cheek. "Any better?"

"A little bit. Can you help a little more?"

Deborah smiled broadly before kissing Thomas on the lips. Thomas opened his mouth in response, and they began making out. Thomas shifted as he grew hard.

"So, what do you want to do now, Deborah?" asked Thomas with a bit of a leer.

She giggled. "Well, my place is pretty close. Want to come over to my house and you know...play?"

"Sounds like a plan."

They walked the two blocks to her apartment. The alcohol numbed his pain. As they rode up the elevator, kissing and fondling started. He wanted her and hated the fact they weren't already naked. Her tongue was warm and wet on his throat as she kissed and nipped. Thomas enjoyed her breasts fitting perfectly into his hands.

Deborah fumbled with her keys as she tried to touch him and turn the keys simultaneously. Once inside, they stumbled toward the bed, tugging clothes off. Once she was naked, Deborah dropped to her knees and started sucking. The sudden sensation was intense, and he fell back into the pillows. Deborah held on and rode the fall.

She climbed on top to impale herself on him. He didn't mind, figuring his leg would prefer this. The beer numbed him just enough that things took longer. Once they each screamed their climaxes, hers first, then his, Thomas collapsed onto the pillow and fell into deep post-sex sleep.

CHAPTER SIX

Thomas's head throbbed with his pulse. Maybe drinking and painkillers was a crap idea. His stomach churned as something foul died in the desert of his mouth. He wiped the caked sleep sand from his eyes and looked up blearily, lids cracking open. The ceiling was different, as were the sheets. He couldn't recall anything and had no idea where he was, then his brain woke up and he remembered last night.

The sex had been really good. Having something other than his hand and pornos for pleasure was glorious. After his injury, masturbation had been difficult, especially with a broken wrist. His body currently had that sweet sore muscle ache. Now he had to figure out who the girl asleep next to him was. He wasn't sure but thought her name started with a D.

Ignoring the name issue until either she said it, he remembered, or he saw her mail, or something would be best. Telling the girl you banged you had no clue who she was could never end well. After a bit of a struggle to get upright, Thomas limped to the bathroom and emptied his bladder, accompanied by a heavy sigh of relief.

As he shook, Thomas scanned the white-tiled room. Shampoo, conditioner, skin care products, makeup, all sorts of things he didn't understand. They intrigued him, but he was clueless what they did. He knew conditioner made your hair softer, but that was the limit. Thomas found her laundry basket. There, near the top, tucked to the side, was a pair of light pink panties.

Thomas nervously glanced at the closed door, worried someone might see what he was doing, then he picked them up. The material was slick with lace around the legs. He ran his fingers over them, amazed how soft they were. He lowered his hand, rubbed the material over his crotch, and grew lightheaded as he got a swift, throbbing erection. He dropped the panties, forgetting them in a rush of desire.

Thomas woke her by kissing and nibbling her neck, brushed blond hair out of the way, one hand playing with a breast. She awoke with a smile and kissed him, opened her legs, making it easier for him to settle between. She was plenty wet as he thrust, all while thinking about how the panties felt, how soft, how the lace skritched his skin, how it made him feel. Thomas pictured himself looking a little like her as he gutturally screamed his orgasm, thrusting as hard as he could.

She turned to him as he lay there, panting heavily, her eyes a happy glaze. "That was wonderful. Thanks for waking me up that way. You know, a girl could get used to this."

Thomas smiled.

"I definitely think we have to do this again." She propped up on one elbow, appraising his face, blue eyes searching. "Want to get breakfast?"

Thomas grunted, still recovering. His throat was parched and his leg burned even worse than when he awoke. Where had that rush of desire come from?

He thought through everything and realized what sent him over the edge. He was thankful the girl had gone to the bathroom and wouldn't see the look on his face. Why had he pictured himself as a girl as he fucked her? Seeing himself as a girl had thrown him over the edge. After breakfast and coffee, he was determined to head back to the barracks and wrap his head around this.

❖

Thomas popped Ranger Candy and lay back, swallowing them with the last of his Coke. The hot shower helped, but he ached everywhere. He stretched, following the PT directions, but his muscles were too stiff to move easily. Maybe when the Motrin took effect, he could get rid of the kinks. Who knew sex could hurt so much?

He stared at the ceiling. What was happening? First, he picked up her panties and touched himself with them, which was odd and creepy, but picturing himself as a girl while fucking, that was nuts. But what an orgasm!

He hadn't done anything with the image. It was just him as a girl, simply standing there in a light summer dress with a hard-to-understand smile. The image wasn't disturbing, but it was different and it shook him. He closed his eyes and pictured the same image, working out details, and he felt comforted, not aroused. Was this actually what he wanted? He had mentioned it to the doctor, but now was he seriously thinking it wasn't a question? It sounded wrong and peculiar. Nothing made sense anymore.

Thomas turned the idea over as it held some appeal, but was it "change your life utterly" kind of appeal? The kind that made a person follow the idea to the utter end, despite the difficulties? His mind wandered—of being dressed as a girl, going out, having friends, looking and sounding like a girl in all ways. He pictured himself smiling, a lot. Thomas never smiled much in real life so that was odd.

He grabbed his notebook and wrote about the event—the discovery, the feelings, images, how he felt. There was something about this that was important, like something…different, something akin to writing a poem, writing truth.

There were three quick raps at the door. Thomas almost yelped in surprise and reached quickly for his weapon that wasn't there. After a few deep, calming breaths, he replied, "Yes?"

"Sergeant? Do you need anything?" What was with this private? Had he been assigned to him by the rear D first sergeant?

"No, I'm fine. Thanks." Thomas shook his head. Some people were so helpful it bugged him. Thomas waited but there was no reply. He sighed, then cocked his head. A weird realization settled, and he found he couldn't argue. He looked at the mirror. "Maybe I really am fine."

Thomas smiled and shook his head, chuckling. Sometimes things were so amazingly fucked up they seemed normal, like this whole clusterfuck. The idea that he could be a girl was so preposterous it almost made a sick sort of sense. It explained why the thought of looking like a girl wasn't utterly disturbing. He figured it would, but the idea of having long hair, curves, breasts, wearing girl's clothes was almost…normal, as if that was the way things were supposed to be.

In two more weeks, he would be discharged and moved into a new apartment, nearer the college. Come January, he'd start school and his new future. Things were going to be different, and he wasn't sure he liked that. He would be alone for the first time with no meddling parents, siblings, or fellow soldiers in the way and would have the privacy needed to explore whatever. He would still be Rhymer, although not on someone else's schedule. The idea was appealing and scary. If he was exploring if the being a girl thing was real, then being alone would make it easier. He wouldn't have to explain himself until he actually *had* an explanation.

The idea of working through this with everyone watching was unpleasant. He could imagine what the guys would say, and he wasn't positive what his family would say, but he had an idea. Waltrip would laugh for sure. Maybe it would be best not to mention anything until there was a sense of surety. If he said anything, he couldn't take it back.

Thomas wondered what wearing women's clothes felt like. Would they be softer, the same, tighter, looser? He didn't know and wasn't sure what to buy. Maybe he could figure things out by paying more attention to Deborah and what she wore. He could figure out the clothes, makeup and other crap given enough time. Honestly, how hard could it be?

❖

"Incoming!"

The mortar round exploded and chunks of hard-packed earth pelted down. The platoon scrambled for hard cover, trying to keep fragmentation injury down. The Republican Guard unit near the bridge opened up, laying down a heavy curtain of fire keeping them pinned. The LT called for air support as the rest returned fire.

"Rhymer!" Thomas turned and looked at the sergeant.

The sergeant used hand signs to tell him to flank the heavy weapons squad. Thomas nodded and tapped his team on their Kevlar, heading away from the conflict.

Schapiro was on overwatch, covering their backs as Rhymer and Edwards moved quickly down a narrow alleyway. The enemy hadn't thought of flanking yet, but they would, sooner rather than later. When they reached the end of the alley, they scanned the road. They heard gunfire and Arabic voices yelling where the others were but nothing nearby. Thomas wished they had a translator. Who knew if that babble was important? Intel always helped.

Suddenly, there was movement on the side of the street Thomas was watching. A door opened. Thomas opened fire with a three-round burst of his M-4. The bullets tore through the thin wood, splinters flying. A child fell forward, blood gushing from at least one bullet wound. She fell limp, dead, and Thomas screamed.

❖

Thomas snapped bolt upright, screaming. He scanned the room for danger, eyes darting back and forth, groping for his rifle. There was nothing there, anywhere in the room.

His heart pounded in his ears and cold sweat trickled down his back. He ran a trembling hand through his hair and rubbed his eyes, Thomas flipped on a light and limped to his fridge. The water soothed his parched throat as he chugged it. Breath shaky, he ran a hand over his head again. It was so real, so vivid, every detail. He shivered and looked back at his bed. The nightmare had mostly faded, but some images lingered. He smelled desert, heat, and sand. He still saw…he took another deep drink hoping it would wash the image from his mind.

He felt dirty, inside and out. He reeked of sweat and fear. Maybe hot water would help? It hadn't worked yet, but it might help him fall back asleep. He slipped on shower shoes and grabbed his towel. A shower would, at the very least, clear his head.

The water felt good and relaxed him enough to grow tired. He yawned a few times, weariness mounting. The water pounded on his head and his thoughts drifted back to Iraq. He recalled the Suck: camel spiders, IEDs, snipers, heat, dust that got into everything, and more. He scrubbed still feeling caked in sand. He needed the dirt off. He needed to get clean, needed to wash Iraq from him, the grit, the blood.

Thomas began shaking. He remembered the heat from burning buildings, the bark of gunfire, explosions, the heavy thrump of helicopters, Iraqis yelling. Events flashed—fighting in the streets, wounded crying out, blasts coming from doors and windows, laser sights visible in the hovering dust, bodies lying as if tossed aside, pools of blood congealing in the sand, screams, the body of a small child falling lifeless onto the street.

Thomas slowly slid down the tile wall. Scenes of Iraq played over and over, an unstoppable film loop. He was a murderer, a killer, a child killer. A killer. Killer.

Warm water rained down as he cried.

CHAPTER SEVEN

Thomas dragged himself from bed and threw on BDUs. He felt like utter ass. Maybe breakfast and coffee would help? He laced his boots; today was his first meeting with out-processing and the reams of paperwork needed to sign out of the Army to become a civilian. They would go over his file and make sure they had a complete packet—all his medals, promotions, etc. He hoped it wouldn't take too long but didn't care. At this point Thomas just wanted out since he could never do his job again, and he hated that. Leaving was the best thing. He was even starting to like the notion of sleeping in.

Since the 101st was deployed, there weren't a lot of people, which would make this faster. He limped into the office, following a civilian clerk. They went through all the paperwork. The final review of his DD214 would be this Friday. Then he would be a civilian, get his retiree ID before leaving base, and get a new security sticker for his car. Life would be different at that point.

Thomas headed to the barracks. His day was officially finished and he had completed out-processing. He got out of uniform and started working on other issues, like getting furniture and moving into his new apartment. Friday would come soon enough, and he needed to move out before he out-processed, since he had to turn in his barracks key.

He drove to the rental office and got his keys from the nice lady behind the desk. Now he could move in and set up his new home. There were movers coming and delivery people with his bed in an hour since he planned to move in tonight. For the first time in his life, he would be on his own with no one to tell him what to do, where to be, or when.

His new apartment was nice, spacious one-bedroom, kitchen, living room, and dining room just off 41A in Clarksville. The bathroom was handicapped accessible and had a good-sized tub he could get into and out of easily. He checked that before deciding on this place. Thomas was excited. This apartment was his and he would be alone. That was certainly a good thing given everything going on in his head. He wanted time to himself, to get his head straight and figure out who or what he was. This apartment would be safer compared to living at home with his parents or sharing with anyone in a dorm.

❖

Deborah liked the apartment, and she stayed over his first night there. They broke in his new mattress several times, which made his leg throb to the point he needed meds. All the other furniture was new, though not "broken in" yet. Then she was gone and he was truly alone in his place. The quiet was different, which he kind of liked. It was also nice not having to shower where others could see him.

Now, in the quiet and solitude he asked, was he a girl? That question plagued him, and sessions with the shrink weren't helping. Thomas understood it was only four sessions so far and no way anything could be determined yet, but the jealously seemed to be getting worse. It was all he could do not to get upset when he was off base.

The latest assignment from Dr. Richards was embarrassing. He was told to watch a few female coming-of-age films and see if he felt anything in common with the characters. Thomas watched them alone as there was no way he could explain this to Deborah or anyone else. She would never understand, and he didn't want to overcomplicate his life as she would make him miserable with all her questions. The assignment was odd, but realizing he did have similar feelings to the characters was disturbing. Thomas hadn't expected to enjoy any of the films, but he had.

He wasn't looking forward to his appointment tomorrow for a number of reasons. The biggest was that the doc's questions made him uncomfortable. He wasn't used to all this introspection. Doing things was what he was good at, being active, not sitting around and ruminating. Walking and physical therapy were his only forms of exercise now, and he felt like a worthless slug and hated it. He had never been so inactive. Honestly, he wanted to run, climb, rappel from a helicopter, fire his weapon, road march, anything except limp and think, especially not think.

After a quick shower, Thomas dressed in his uniform for probably the last time. The money spent getting the BDUs pressed was worth it, and his boots shone. Thomas liked looking good, he liked looking sharp and professional. He took pride in his appearance, as feeling like a soldier made him feel better about everything.

He regarded the mirror, and his pride faded slowly. For all his professionalism, his drive to be a career soldier all came to naught, destroyed by a damn Iraqi RPG. He clenched the foam grip of his black government-issue cane and frowned, glaring at himself. What the fuck was wrong with feeling good? Was there some reason he didn't deserve to be happy? Was he ever going to stop feeling sorry for himself?

"Suck it up, soldier! Are you going to let this ruin your life?" Thomas growled out to his mirror twin.

The mirror didn't reply. Thomas pulled himself up and did what he could to stand fully at attention. He could manage if he took the weight off his bad leg, letting it hover off the ground slightly while leaning heavily on his cane. His leg and arm might be fucked, but Rhymer still looked like a soldier and would act like one until the very end. He wouldn't slink away like some broke dick.

The radio blared on the short drive, and he smiled as heavy metal music thrummed through his body. He loved listening to something hard when driving. It made him feel manly and that's what he wanted to feel today. He showed his ID and headed for out-processing, hoping this wouldn't take long as he wanted to get back and square things away. Moving into his new life was his agenda now.

He limped slowly inside, clenching his teeth against pain. It was one of the largest buildings on the base, a place where everyone came through when they arrived and left. There was a small line of soldiers waiting to get through so Thomas felt good. This should be quick. He looked forward to finding out how much he was getting as severance, glad it was going to be deposited directly into his account. The money would be nice, but he would prefer to walk without a limp. There was no amount of money to compensate for that.

His name was called, and Thomas hobbled over, trying to walk as erect as possible. His leg burned with the exertion, but he could endure this to do things right. He sank into the chair by the man's desk, glad it had been a short walk. Once he finished, the first order of business would be to elevate his leg and use an ice pack to numb things. "Here you go, Sergeant. Just look this over and if correct, sign here."

Thomas looked over the paperwork and noted everything seemed to be in order. All his awards were listed, including the Bronze Star and all his promotions. It looked like full retirement pay along with his medical discharge. His eyes goggled at the amount. He hadn't expected something in the low six digits when they said severance pay.

He smiled; everything was correct as far as he could tell. He took out his pen, something every soldier carried, and signed his name. The man smiled. "That's all there is, Sergeant. Take this to finance and you'll get the money at the next pay period. Take care and good luck."

Thomas rose, shook the man's hand, and took his file. With that signature, he was a civilian. He had his Honorable Discharge in the folder, and with one more stop he would soon have more money than he knew what to do with. He would have to plan things and not do something stupid like blow it in one shot. Maybe he would use some of it for something nice for himself, like another car, one that was easier to drive? Maybe he should use the money to live on for a while instead of working? Then again, there was the VA, and Vocational Rehabilitation was going to take care of his school costs and pay him a stipend. He would need to make a plan and stick to it to make the best use of this opportunity.

Finance needed his signature on a few more things. This was it. He was a civilian and able to do whatever the hell he wanted. Before he left the base, he needed get his retiree ID so he could shop at the commissary and PX.

The visit to the unit was anticlimactic as no one he cared about was even in country. All he did was shake a few hands and limp away. The ID was equally a nothing. All the importance he tied to this and it was a non-event.

The drive to the apartment from Fort Campbell was quiet, but his mind was racing. Thomas ached and felt drained even after such a short time. He fought back tears as his dream of being a soldier faded in the rearview mirror.

❖

"So, you're a civilian now. How do you feel?" Dr. Richards asked, leaning back.

"I'm not sure. I always wanted to be a soldier ever since I was a kid. I hoped to make E5 and join the Special Forces. And then I got injured. I'm depressed and angry at the way things fell out. I wish I'd been able to stay in, but my injuries won't let me."

"So, what you're saying is your job was part of your identity?" asked the doctor.

Thomas started. He never thought of it that way, but it was too apt. He shifted in the chair nervously as that ran through his head. "Um…yeah. That makes sense. Since the job was part of me, not having it feels as if something is missing, something important."

"Has something always been missing or just since your accident?"

Thomas sat and thought over his life. Had something been missing? Sitting there, he realized there was, but he wasn't sure why. "Yeah. There has been. I think I joined the Army to find something to fill that spot. It sort of worked. I'm so used to feeling out of sorts I never noticed. Now that I'm looking, I can see it."

"Any clue what was missing?" Thomas could tell the question was leading. Delving into his mind was not something he wanted to do, but the doc kept prodding. If he wanted to get to the bottom of this, he would need to spend more time thinking.

"I'm not sure. The only thing that's come up is my jealousy. I mean, I have all of these feelings that don't make any sense and I'm starting to get strange urges. And I'm not sure what to do. I mean, sure, I've wondered what panties feel like, or a silky nightgown."

"Well, why not purchase something?"

"What?! Buy panties and a nightgown?" Thomas was incredulous. He couldn't do that, could he? The idea was simultaneously embarrassing and enticing. His stomach roiled. "I mean, I'm a guy and guys don't wear panties and nightgowns and…and stuff. I want to get past this stupid jealousy thing and get on with my life."

"One of the things that might help determine if this is some fixation or perhaps gender dysphoria would be your response to wearing women's clothes. Why don't you go out and get some panties and a nightgown? Wear them and note how they make you feel in your journal. If it repulses you, get rid of them. There are other avenues we can try if that's the case." The request seemed logical. But he had to argue, didn't he, because he was a guy?

"But…I…I've no idea what my sizes are?" It was a feeble defense and Thomas knew it. What the hell was he going to do? He couldn't just buy them, right?

Dr. Richards considered him with a critical eye. Thomas could almost hear the mental gears whirring. "My rough guess would be size seven for the panties. Maybe a twelve or fourteen for the nightgown. Those are just rough guesses."

Thomas's head spun. "How the hell am I supposed to do this? I mean, I'm a guy, why the hell would I be in the lingerie section? I'll be embarrassed, and what will I say if anyone tries to help me?"

"Thomas, breathe. Relax. This isn't as bad as you're making it. Just act bored, like it's no big deal. The people at the register couldn't care less. It's just another sale. As for people helping, tell them you're buying your girlfriend a present. It'll be fine." The doc leaned forward and rested a hand on Thomas's knee. It was comforting and helped Thomas relax. "So, what about your dreams? Still having nightmares?"

The topic change gave Thomas some relief. He shivered. "Yeah. I keep dreaming about the little girl and the bodies, friend and foe. They…keep looking at me, accusing me."

"What about the little girl bothers you the most?"

Thomas eyed him incredulously. "The fuck? I killed a little girl, Doc. All three bullets of the burst hit her in the chest. I killed her!"

Dr. Richards motioned him to calm down. Thomas sat back, chest heaving, taking deep breaths. "I know, Thomas, you've told me that. What I want to know is what about killing her bothers you. Is it specifically guilt, anger, fear, what? What are you feeling? If we can figure out the specifics, we can figure a way past this."

Thomas breathed deeply, trying to slow his racing heart. He didn't like remembering, however, the doc insisted. "I think maybe all of those. I feel guilty for shooting her, angry at her parents for letting her run outside during a firefight, afraid I might have liked killing her, and horrified. It was one of the reasons I did what got me injured. I wanted to die because…because of what I'd done. I…I don't like to dwell on this."

Dr. Richards sat there patiently as Thomas tapered off. The quiet grew as Thomas sat, hands clasped tightly, eyes focused on the floor, thoughts whirling around the desert and the horror of her body falling. His stomach clenched. The ticking of the second hand was loud in the silence.

"Part of why I feel so bad is I wanted to die…I mean before that. I kept…trying over and over, but it never happened." His voice was hardly a whisper. "I kept throwing myself in harm's way. It got worse after the little girl. You know, I'm only a hero because I lived. Heroes don't kill little girls. I should have died instead of her. It wasn't fair." Thomas sobbed quietly; tears burned down his cheeks. "Why did I live? I…I feel these urges and they're wrong. I feel jealousy, and it's because I want to look that way, be that way. I wanted to die because I couldn't take it anymore. Why couldn't I have just died? She had everything to live for and I killed her!"

The doctor handed over a box of Kleenex. Thomas looked at it blankly for a moment before using a few to wipe his eyes. He didn't want to cry but couldn't stop. "It's not fair."

"Thomas, your dysphoria causes you to crave death to avoid doing something you've been taught is wrong. You've been conditioned to believe things are set in stone, when very little is, especially gender. But is it wrong for you to be whole? If something is drawing you, then maybe you need to explore this, if for no other reason than to understand. Much of what you're going through seems bound up, this jealousy and your PTSD. We can unravel this, but it's going to take time and will take you working hard and being gentle with yourself."

Thomas nodded weakly. He couldn't bring himself to look up. Admitting that he wanted to be a woman was difficult. Shame descended and he shifted uncomfortably, his skin fitting wrong. The doc must think he was a joke, a pansy, a sissy, a fool, a pervert, and he couldn't argue.

"Don't feel ashamed, Thomas. You're dealing with very complex issues, issues most people never think about. These things aren't bad. They're just different. They need to be worked on so you can accept yourself and let go of things that aren't part of who you are or aren't your responsibility." Thomas looked up at the end. Dr. Richards had the same look on his face the whole session. No disgust, no disdain, no loathing, nothing but compassion and acceptance.

"Okay. I'll keep trying." His voice shook. If the doc was right, then maybe he could do this? He felt post-combat: drained, wrung out, and desperately wanting to drink and forget.

The doctor smiled. "That's good, Thomas. I want you to write what you think about girls in general as well as the girl you are when in the nightgown, to see if your thoughts change."

Thomas nodded, finding it easier to look at the floor than lift his far too heavy head. The doctor went on. "Let's call it a day. You dealt with some rough stuff. Go and do something nice for yourself. Doctor's orders."

CHAPTER EIGHT

Thomas collapsed into the front seat with his head back against the headrest. His eyes and face burned from the salt of the tears. He felt detestable. He was a monster for killing a child. There was no forgiveness for that. However, the doc said things just happened and tried to get him to see the situation differently.

His body shook and tears fell again. He had to get out of there. Thomas started the car and drove slowly, having trouble seeing through tears. Pulling over was not an option since he was desperate to get back to Clarksville and isolate from the rest of the world. No one should be tainted by him. He was dirty and doubted he would ever get clean.

After a long and scary drive back from Nashville, Thomas stumbled into the apartment, hobbling so fast he almost tripped. He dropped his keys twice while fumbling for the house key. He slammed the door and collapsed onto the sofa heavily. Why was he so fucked up? Why did he panic and kill that kid? Why did he have fucked up girl urges? What the fuck?

Thomas cried into a pillow, not wanting anyone else to hear his misery. If there was some way to escape everything for a while and get his head straight, he would take it. And go shopping? For girls things? Was he ready? Did he deserve to? He was alive, that little girl wasn't. She died because of him. The weight of that responsibility was inescapable. He killed her because he was afraid of being flanked, afraid of the death he desperately craved. He yearned for death but was too chicken shit to kill himself. And if he did manage to, like it would fix things.

Thomas lay on the couch and wept out the rage, frustration, and shame of everything; he squeezed it all out with his tears. Eventually, exhaustion and crying took their toll and Thomas fell asleep.

Someone shook him awake. Bleary-eyed, he saw what's-her-name standing there looking worried. He couldn't figure out why she was there until he remembered he gave her a key in a moment of weakness. "Hey there, sweetie…are you okay?"

He smiled feebly. There was no way in hell he could tell her what was *really* going on. "I guess. My nightmares are bad again and the images won't leave me alone. It's not easy to deal with, but the VA shrink has me talking things over. I guess it's helping. Today was just overwhelming."

She sat at the edge of the couch and rubbed his back. A pleasant shiver went up his spine, helping him relax. "Aww, honeybear, I'm so sorry you have to deal with that. Anything I can do?"

"Naw, I'm as okay as I'm gonna get." Thomas smiled a little. She might be annoying, but she made him feel good and was decent in bed. She was also okay with the fact he had trouble having sex in missionary position. If he could manage to remember her name most of the time, things would be fine.

She usually showed up horny which suited him fine. He didn't mind being a booty call, because in all honesty, that's what she was. The last thing he wanted was something serious, though there was no good reason to give her a key. But right now, she made him feel good. Wait…he remembered her name. "Deb, could I get a massage? That will make it easier to do something later."

She nodded and moved, letting Thomas slide to the floor. He sat there enjoying the feel of her hands on his back and shoulders. It felt good and worked away the day's stress.

He sighed, the tension fading. Maybe seeing her more often would help him relax? But would she feel like doing this all the time? Could she deal with all the shit he was going through? Thomas wasn't sure and didn't want to set himself up for pain. Maybe he should break it off?

Deborah was nice, but he worried something would go horribly wrong. Thomas knew she would freak over him being a baby killer or wanting to be a girl. Was this what he wanted? His thoughts needed to stop running in circles.

Deborah ran hands under his shirt. He felt the change in her touch, from soothing to arousing. The touch was lighter, more playful, and occasionally her hands drifted under his pants and BVDs. All worries faded when he realized what Deb wanted. He grew hard. His jeans were uncomfortable, and lying on the ground made it worse. He turned over and she straddled Thomas, smiling broadly.

She bent down slowly, and Thomas raised into her kiss. They deepened the kiss as she rocked her hips, grinding against him. Making a cute growling noise, she grabbed Thomas's wrists tightly, holding him on the carpet. She rode him, growling, kissing, biting, nibbling, moaning on him. A deep, throaty groan of pleasure forced its way out his throat. Deborah took his bottom lip and tugged gently. With his last rational thought, he tumbled into the depths of pleasure, senses overloading.

❖

Deborah had left a little while ago, and Thomas lay in bed, gazing at the popcorn ceiling. The sex had been unexpected and nice. He enjoyed her being on top, holding his hands down, restraining him. Sure, he could have tossed her off, but his wrists being held let him submerge into the sensations. He much preferred being pleasured rather than the mix of pain and pleasure of normal lovemaking. He didn't want to delve deeper, as he didn't want to add submissive onto his list of perversions.

Thomas recalled the doc saying he should do something nice for himself. His first notion was food. The steak houses by the mall were good with decent portions. Or maybe something different, like a massage or facial or something like that.

A massage would be best. Deborah's had been nice and made him want more, something deeper, stronger. It might actually relax him enough that he could buy panties and a nightgown and act like it was no big deal, as if it didn't terrify him.

The phone book was under the coffee table, and he snagged it with his cane. Thomas flipped until he found *massage*. He used the rough map of the city to figure out where they were, but that was easy after using military maps, which was good enough. He chose the easiest to drive to and still close to the mall, along Wilma Rudolph Boulevard, so he could shop while still relaxed. He called and made an hour appointment. Maybe this would be fun and give him the courage to face the lingerie section. He had no idea why, but it felt tougher than charging a sniper.

❖

Thomas smiled broadly as he hobbled to his car. A one-hour massage was just what he needed. He could almost feel the relaxed, Jell-O-like muscles he was sure to get. This would definitely qualify as a treat.

Not needing to race, Thomas drove with what passed as leisurely. At least he was close to the speed limit, rather than quite a bit over. He chuckled as he passed a speed trap. He hadn't seen the cop's position, but it had a clear view of all cars heading that way. Maybe this day wouldn't be as bad as he had feared.

The massage place seemed nice enough, though the rainbow flag sticker in the window worried him. He wasn't sure he could handle some gay guy rubbing on him. That was creepy. He could probably handle a lesbian, even a scary bull dyke, but not some limp-wristed faggot. It wasn't like he hated gays; they made him nervous. The thought of two guys making out like he and Deborah had turned his stomach. If they left him alone, he could leave them alone. However, given what he was dealing with…maybe he needed to reconsider?

Thomas sat in the waiting room and flipped through a magazine, waiting. A guy about six feet tall and maybe two feet across at the shoulder walked out. However, some sort of vibe screamed GAY to Thomas. The man walked up and held out his hand. "Hello. I'm Mike. If you're Thomas you're my next appointment. Let's go."

The deep bass surprised Thomas. There was no sign of a lisp, and the handshake was firm. This guy was huge, with muscles on top of muscles. The man's goatee and thick, black short-cut hair looked great. Thomas was jealous of how utterly masculine Mike looked. Why hadn't he turned out like that, all buff and manly instead of scrawny and scrappy? "Uh…yes. That's me."

"Come on." Mike led Thomas through a corridor, past two doors and opened the third. "Please undress to where you're comfortable, lie face down, and cover yourself with the sheet. Once you're ready, I'll come back."

The dimly lit room was dominated by the massage table, draped with sheets. A shelf held a few types of oil and lotions. Ambient music played softly.

Nervously, Thomas undressed and folded his clothes, then placed them on the only chair in the room and leaned his cane against it. He climbed onto the table and awkwardly pulled the sheet over. He lay there a short while before there was a soft knock that was easy to hear in the mostly quiet room. "Ready?"

"Yes," said Thomas, a little unsure. If this helped the pain it would be worth all the discomfort.

Mike walked in and shut the door. "Okay. You said on your form you have a bad leg and shoulder from an injury. Chronic pain as well. I think we might be able to do something about that. Let's get to work."

The oil warmed in Mike's hands felt wonderful as he rubbed it in. Thomas slowly unwound as Mike worked on his feet and up his legs. Mike had strong hands and was able to work out the knots making up Thomas's back. He enjoyed things so much he forgot Mike was gay.

He woke surprised, blinking around the room. Mike was gone and he was alone. His leg didn't ache as much as earlier and he felt relaxed. He rubbed his eyes, waking up more, and then dressed. His limp wasn't as pronounced as when he arrived, which was great. Mike waited by the cash register. Thomas smiled. "That was great, Mike. Thanks. My leg doesn't hurt, and I feel totally loose."

Mike smiled brightly. "Just doing my job. I'm glad I could help. You know…if you could do this regularly, like once a week, it should loosen up your back as well as your hip and shoulder. Think about it and if you want give us a call."

❖

Dillard's was a major mall store and not somewhere Thomas normally shopped. That should add to his not being noticed. He had his list with sizes, and if anyone asked, he had his story. Trying to spot *Lingerie* or *Intimates* or whatever the hell that section was called wasn't easy. He wandered a bit, then spotted the sign and the wall of lace encircling it. He steeled himself. If he could charge Iraqis firing machine guns, he could do this.

The panties were easy and painless, and he grabbed several different styles, fabrics, and colors; he didn't linger, not wanting to look like a pervert. In total, he had eight pairs in his hands. Some cotton, others satiny, and all different styles. He would have grabbed more, but he drew the line at thongs. The idea of purposely wearing butt floss squicked him out. Who would wear that? Surely it couldn't feel good, could it? Thomas didn't want to find out.

Getting a nightgown proved more difficult. It wasn't that there were too many options, but rather he liked too many of them. He lingered longer, despite his growing anxiety. Finally, he chose a black satin gown with spaghetti straps that looked feminine. It had a little lace at the bust line, but not so much it was overwhelming. Thomas thought it was sexy and wanted to feel the material against his skin. He always liked the feel of satin and slept with several girls who wore such nightgowns. It was nostalgic.

Once his task was complete, Thomas tucked his list into his back pocket and headed to the register. He had enough cash for his purchases, but there wouldn't be a lot left over. That was nice, as there would be nothing saying he had been there, no credit card receipt or check, and he could just refuse a receipt.

The salesperson didn't look at him oddly as she rang things up. She looked slightly bored if anything. After she wrapped the nightgown in tissue and bagged all the items, she wished Thomas a good day and thanked him for shopping at Dillard's. She turned to help someone else, forgetting about him immediately.

Thomas was sure people could tell he bought lingerie for himself as he drove home, like there was a sign, and he drove with a growing paranoia. Every driver seemed to disapprove, to judge. He felt exposed, with no cover in sight. He accelerated and wove through traffic as best he could without drawing more attention. Getting back to his apartment in one piece felt like a miracle. There was no sign of pursuit, and he hadn't been shot at along the way.

Hobbling rapidly and checking his six to ensure he hadn't been followed, he made it inside and quickly shut the door behind him. He double-checked, made sure it was locked and the chain latched. With that, Thomas paused and peered through the blinds, opening them just enough to see but not enough to mark himself as a target. Instead of tan, sun-bleached buildings and the sand of Iraq, there were parked cars and Tennessee trees. He blinked, then looked out the side of the window again. Something wasn't right. He wished he was armed. His rifle would make him feel safer. Hell, even a basic sidearm would be good.

Thomas calmed enough to leave the window, so he grabbed a beer. He took a long pull and tossed the bottle cap into the trash. He exhaled heavily, feeling exhausted. He chided himself for believing he had been back in Iraq. He thought he was better, that the PTSD had gone away, or faded so it wasn't bothering him anymore. Clearly, that was not the case. Thomas trembled, panic still there, urging flight, fight, anything but sitting there. He struggled to remain seated and fought the urge to pace and peer outside, scanning for watchers. When it got too much, he forced himself into the bathroom to get his meds. There was an anti-anxiety pill that should help. He took another swallow of beer to calm his nerves.

Thomas quivered, waiting for the meds to kick in. He hadn't felt like this since Walter Reed. Things were bad right after he got back from the sandbox, especially the paranoia and anger. Cold water splashed onto his face eased things, brought him back to the here and now. Doing that a few times cleared his head more, and he stared at his reflection, rubbing his face. He went back to the living room and noticed he had thrown the deadbolt and chain. Thomas sighed, looking at that sign of fear. At least Deborah couldn't get in.

The meds finally kicked in and the edge came off. His heart no longer raced, and his breathing was no longer tight. He let go of the urge to grab a weapon and take up a security position in his living room. "Why me?"

There was no answer, only the sound of traffic outside. He hobbled to his computer and booted it up. He checked email. It was simple, mundane, and calmed his last jangled nerves. He was happy when the jitteriness faded completely. At least that particular bit of suffering ended for now.

After that, he closed the browser and pulled up his journal. Fingers clicking, Thomas put down the events of the day and how he felt. Things had been going well until he left Dillard's and the feeling of being watched, of everyone knowing, filled him and took over. The stress of buying panties and a nightgown probably triggered things.

Once done, he closed the file and limped into the bedroom carrying the bag. He removed the panties and nightgown gently and laid them on the bed. He stood and stared, a slight shiver of pleasure rolling up his spine. Thomas was unsure why, but he accepted it as best he could. Eyes closed, he breathed deeply, and let it out slowly, trying to calm further, following the less irritating advice from his therapist. His nervousness grew thinking about this. Was he honestly going to put on women's clothes? He shook his head to clear it.

Thomas picked up a pair of panties and rubbed the material between his fingers. They were smooth, soft, and Thomas thought of the underwear of various girlfriends. The cotton slid under his fingers, and he paused and drifted into a daydream where he saw himself differently. An image of a female self, pulling the panties up his/her legs, settling the smooth blue cotton on her/his hips. Lost in the image, he undressed and pulled the panties on. The material was warmed by his hands but still caused Thomas to shiver.

He slid out of the semi-dream state and looked down. The material certainly looked and felt different from his BVDs and the colored panties seemed…fitting? He felt good, relaxed. A little awkward with his bulging penis, but basically good. It felt right or, more accurately, not wrong. The growing erection surprised him, though he didn't have the urge to masturbate, but he grew harder. Thomas didn't mind and stood there looking at himself, stunned that he had actually put them on.

With a tug, his jeans slid back up his legs and he was taken aback by the way the panties felt. He could almost feel the denim through the panties; the fabric was much thinner than his usual briefs. Nice but different. He put his other panties away, tucked in the back of his underwear drawer and hid the nightgown amongst his pajamas.

It wasn't a great hiding place, however securing a better spot would require him having more flexibility than he currently had.

Cane held tightly, he limped to the living room. With a glance toward his kitchen, Thomas realized he had no interest in cooking. There had been too much today, and he couldn't bring himself to prep non-ramen food.

He grabbed his keys. There were a lot of options, but he wasn't sure where to go. As he drove, Thomas settled on a mid-level place, good food, not costly, and a step up from fast food. Under the normality of his evening, he forgot what he was wearing under his jeans.

CHAPTER NINE

The credits rolled and Thomas turned off the DVD. He stretched and felt the nightgown slide over his body, making him shiver. The sensation was nice and the movie was enjoyable, which he found less surprising with each chick flick he watched. Maybe this whole screwy gender thing held some truth? After all, he had slept in the nightgown the last three nights and slept deeply, soundly, and awoke refreshed each night. More importantly, he had no nightmares, for which he was profoundly grateful.

Tomorrow was his next appointment, and he printed out the journal entries. It was like the homework he occasionally did in high school. This week had been the most intense since this started, with the flashback and the first time wearing women's clothes. It had been uncomfortable, awkward, frustrating, as well as wonderful, enlightening, and thought-provoking. So much happened that he should be ready to explode, but he wasn't. That was most curious.

Thomas realized he was beginning to accept this as truth. It was disturbing in one way, but he felt great relief in another. Some invisible weight was being lifted, a weight that had been unknown until it faded. Thomas wasn't completely sold on wanting to be a girl, yet he admitted it might be true. This was bizarre and he was at a loss how this could be real.

In the morning, he wasn't sure how he felt. He was busy working on not getting nervous when he heard any vehicle pull up while wearing panties or the nightgown. His paranoia was improving slowly, and no longer caused panic attacks.

Thomas stretched toward the ceiling and sighed. He limped to his bathroom and shed the nightgown and panties. Since it was laundry night, he put them in the hamper with his other pairs. He had one left and was wearing them today. The pink stretchy fabric was nice and held him firm but not tight. Getting a few more pairs was an easy decision, as there was something that made him feel better, calmer, that he couldn't put his finger on. It was just clothes and he had no idea why clothes should affect how he felt about himself. It was odd, like much of his life.

He pulled on a pair of jeans and an old unit T-shirt. He wanted comfort, as his sessions were getting more intense. Anything to help his personal comfort level was a plus. This situation forced him to get more comfortable with his life, and he was flabbergasted at how quickly panties felt normal.

Thomas put his combat boots on. Not his dessert boots but the black leather boots that had grown supple over countless miles of wear. He loved these boots, and if he tossed all his uniforms, he knew the boots would remain. They were the most comfortable shoes he owned. They sucked during Basic, and the wear made the difference. He tied the last boot securely and stood, tucked his wallet into his back pocket, grabbed his keys and cane, and limped to the car.

The drive to the doc's office felt short, even though the trip from Clarksville to Nashville was close to forty-five minutes. He encountered no problems to make his drive more stressful, no traffic jams or accidents, just a nice drive with the sun shining. Thomas arrived early since the Army drilled into his head the need to be early.

He hobbled into the hospital, down the long hallway from the parking garage, and took the elevator. After checking in and finding a seat, he spotted a couple of "chick magazines" lying about, probably for spouses or female vets. He grabbed one and flipped through it. A few articles grabbed his attention. Thomas was a touch irritated when Doc Richards interrupted. Keeping the magazine, Thomas made his way back. He hoped this session would be easy, as he was having a good day and didn't want to be rattled before another massage appointment.

"Morning, Thomas."

"Morning, Doc." Thomas trusted Dr. Richards and almost considered him a friend. Almost. The doc's advice was beneficial to Thomas's sanity.

"How was your week?"

Thomas smiled. "Um…interesting. It was kind of rough and fairly good at the same time. I have journal entries if you want to take a look?"

The doc's eyes widened. He stretched out and took the offered pages. Thomas continued reading the article as the doc scanned them quickly. He was nearly done with the article when he heard throat clearing.

Thomas smiled, waiting for whatever the doc would hit him with, as it was sure to be something. "What films have you been watching?"

"Um…let's see…all the Tom Hanks and Meg Ryan films, yeah most of the Meg Ryan things. The usual date movie kind of things. I can't remember titles. Do you want me to keep track of that?"

"No, just wondering. When did you start this journal?"

"A few weeks ago. I wanted to keep track of ideas and thoughts that cropped up. There've been so many things coming so quickly, it's a way to cope and keep my thoughts straight." Thomas shrugged. "Writing these out lets me understand what I've been thinking. Seeing my thoughts on paper."

"Good idea. So, since you are enjoying the nightgown and panties, what about women's outer clothes?"

Thomas thought, scratching the back of his head. "I don't know. I've been having more PTSD symptoms, as you can see from the journals, so shopping might be too overwhelming right now. I'm not sure what I would buy, and that would increase the exposed feelings."

The doc nodded. "Given everything we've talked about and your responses, I am fairly certain you have gender dysphoria. From what I can tell, this isn't going to go away but rather is a part of you. We've been talking for over a month and I think, in another month or so you might be ready for hormones."

Thomas goggled, unsure what to do. Was he ready? Would he ever be ready? This made it more real, something he would have to deal with. Thomas blinked, trying to make sense of all this. "I…I mean…I…uh?"

The doc chuckled. "Don't worry, Thomas. By the time I send you to an endocrinologist you'll be ready. I won't send you if we're not both sure. Relax. We're going step by step, without rushing. Now, let's not worry about that and get back to now. You like how the panties make you feel?"

This was something he could manage. So long as he stayed focused, he would be okay. "Yeah, I...uh...do. They're really soft and I like how they fit and feel...better than male underwear by a long shot. I'm a bit frightened by the whole thong thing though."

The doc quirked an eyebrow. "Thong thing?"

"Well, yeah. I got lots of different styles and I was so not ready for thongs. Butt floss is a bit scary. I mean...how in the world can that be comfortable, all wedged up in there?" Thomas was confused since he liked how they looked on women and they didn't look uncomfortable, but he couldn't imagine wearing them. Thomas was sure he would walk funny with fabric stuffed up his butt.

"Okay. That's fair. Some women like them, some don't. So, when does school start?"

"Not too much longer, another month or so. I'm looking forward to this. I mean, I have no idea what I want to do yet as a major, but I can spend my first two years figuring that out. And that way I can see what I'm good at before I limit myself to classes in subjects I suck at." Thomas thought this through, several areas interested him, and he had no idea of what career he might want. Things were wide open, and he didn't want to screw that up.

"Sounds like a solid plan." The doc nodded. Thomas wondered if the guy's neck got sore from nodding all the time like a bobble head.

"I hope so. Basically, I want to find a job that interests me once I graduate, since I can't soldier. I want to get on with my life, since the old one is closed." Thomas tried to keep the bitterness out of his voice, but he wasn't successful.

The doc cocked his head and looked thoughtful. "Your old life is closed?"

"Well, yeah," replied Thomas with some heat. "With my leg and arm screwed up, that life is gone. I planned to be career Army. I miss it. I had a place and my life had order. It made sense. I knew who I was and what I had to do. No real surprises and I liked that. Ever since my injury life hasn't made any sense. There's no order, and I don't know what my place is any more. Maybe I want to be a girl? I really don't know. I'm tired of my life being chaotic."

Thomas shifted uncomfortably and the doc made notes. "So, you see this in terms of one life dying and another one arising?"

"Mostly. I think. Hell, I don't know. It's just…my life made sense before and now it doesn't. I mean, why the hell do I get nervous around narrow alleyways? Why do I get twitchy when I see people with Arabic coloring? Why do I have thoughts and urges to be a girl? My life has fallen apart since Iraq and I've no idea how to pick up the pieces."

"Well, that's what we're trying to do, Thomas. PTSD has a lot of insidious effects that make a mess of your life. Basically, what I see is you dealing with several big things: major depression, gender dysphoria, and PTSD. I think we need to get you started on some new meds to help out. This roller coaster needs to smooth out so you can cope better. I think you also need some group therapy for PTSD, and you should attend the local gender support group. I have the contact information." The doc wrote a few things on a blank sheet and turned to his computer, ordering a few meds. "You can pick those up at the pharmacy. It's an antidepressant and another anti-anxiety medication, which should help stabilize things. They'll take about a month to fully kick in, but don't worry. If they don't help, we'll try something else. Keep up with the journaling."

Thomas sighed, more meds. His life felt out of control, and he wanted to get on with life and move past what haunted him. Maybe meds would help. Hopefully, they wouldn't hurt. So long as he didn't feel like his head was full of cotton he could cope. The doc handed a sheet of paper to Thomas.

"Here is the date and time for the next PTSD support group meeting. The address as well. That's in Clarksville. They meet every two weeks. The contact for the gender group is there as well. Send them an email and they'll get back to you about meeting times and such. They meet once a month."

Thomas nodded, unsure what to say. He felt overwhelmed, especially with the gender stuff being real and permanent. His heart sped and his chest tightened, like a growing panic attack. He tried to slow his breathing to stave it off.

"I know things have been a bit crazy lately, Thomas. This is not a bad sign. This just means the big problems are coming out where we can see and deal with them. It'll be okay. Just breathe and be nice to yourself." The doc patted him on the arm in a fatherly way that Thomas's father never had. "I'll see you next week."

Thomas headed toward the pharmacy slowly, winding through the white halls of the VA. He read the magazine as he waited. Thanks to crowds, it took a while so he collected travel pay, which should cover gas.

Mike rubbed the stress out. Thomas's mind grew calmer thanks to the strong hands kneading his muscles. What could he do for more order and stability? Maybe get up at a set time, do some PT, and then go about his day? That would be familiar and keep him in shape, even helping his arm and leg in the process if he did the physical therapy exercises he'd been neglecting. Since he left the service, he hadn't done much exercise and could feel it.

Thomas's thoughts slowed under Mike's talented hands and he drifted away.

❖

Thomas spotted Deborah's car as he pulled into the parking lot. She had let herself in, again. He sighed and got out, holding his keys and the bag of meds. He was tired of this crap but had no idea what to say.

Deborah was annoying Thomas. She came and went as she pleased, and Thomas felt like he was being used. The sex was okay, but he was tired of that. Each time they made out it followed the exact same pattern, with no spark of originality and very little passion. Thomas knew he would dump her soon, but he wasn't in the mood to deal with that today. Right now, all he wanted was to sit on his couch and watch a movie.

Her smile seemed shallow. It might have been him, but he wasn't sure of much anymore when it came to Deborah. He smiled back and dropped onto the couch, feeling worn out. Deborah joined him. "Rough day, sweetie?"

"Yeah. My appointment was rough and I want to veg out."

She nodded and ran a hand over his slightly longer hair. It was growing out slowly but surely and he liked it, though she didn't. "I'm sorry, sweetie. Is there anything I can do? Do you want a massage? Want to go out and eat?"

Thomas was certain he didn't want to go out and do anything with her, but if they stayed in, she would want sex, and with how his hip and arm felt, he would not enjoy it. He endured enough pain having sex with her, given how she liked it. Sometimes being on the bottom got old, and she wasn't creative enough to come up with alternatives. "Just let me rest a bit. Maybe I'll take a nap and we can decide later."

Deborah kissed his cheek and looked at him with hooded eyes, obviously horny. "Want me to join you?"

Thomas gritted his teeth. All he wanted was to fucking rest and this fucking twink couldn't get that. Why the fuck was he still with her? It wasn't the sex, that was for sure. "I just want to sleep. Is that too difficult to understand?"

She looked startled at his tone and scooched back. Thomas was sorry he upset her, but he didn't care like he did a few weeks ago. She replied with a conciliatory tone. "Okay, baby. Do you need a hand getting into the bedroom?"

Thomas almost growled. He wasn't the invalid she treated him as. She constantly tried to make him feel helpless without her, and it irritated the crap out of him. "I can make it."

She nodded and pressed back into the couch, one of the throw pillows held in front of her. Thomas felt bad and wanted to apologize, but no words were forthcoming. Without saying anything, he headed into the bedroom. Muscles that had been relaxed were now throbbing. He unbuttoned his jeans for more comfort and sat on the bed. Maybe Vicodin would help? Thomas glanced over at the collection of bottles covering his night table and spotted what he wanted quickly. He washed the tablet down with a swig from the water bottle he kept there and slid under the covers, staring at the ceiling.

"What the fuck is with my life?" he mused. "I'm angry over stupid shit right and left and it feels like everything's falling apart. What the hell can I do?"

The meds finally kicked in, dulling the pain to a tingly sensation. It was still there, but Thomas's give a shit factor was in high gear. He couldn't care less about anything and he napped blissfully unaware.

CHAPTER TEN

The cane was nice to lean against as Thomas waited in line to see an academic advisor, keeping his weight off his leg. All his paperwork was in, and he had even gotten Vocational Rehabilitation started. This was the last step before registering and school starting. Thomas made a tentative schedule of classes and hoped he could keep it. The way he planned it, he would have enough time to make it across campus between classes, and the walking wouldn't be that bad.

He took a step as the line nudged forward. He had been standing for about ten minutes and was glad he had stuff in the squad pack slung over one shoulder. It wasn't heavy, but Thomas figured it soon would be, with books, notepads, and everything. He thought about getting a rolling backpack, but it would be awkward dragging it behind him with the cane. Besides, he doubted the books and everything would weigh as much as his field pack had. The line nudged again.

He planned on basic classes the first year to get the majority of required courses out of the way and get a feel for school life. Then he could concentrate on what to do with the rest of his life. He planned on a few PE courses to give himself something that didn't involve sitting on his ass and reading. He already talked about the classes with his physical terrorist, and they came to the conclusion they might be good in the long run. He had three scheduled, for three hours a week. Nowhere near the level of activity in the Army, but it was a lot more than lately. He moved closer to the front.

Thomas sighed. The line was packed and his leg grew sore. He looked at the class sheet. Math, English, science, and he figured French might be interesting to learn, since he never learned another language before, except some high school Spanish he promptly forgot and a little combat Arabic. The PE classes took care of another required area, so he would be okay with fifteen credit hours. He hoped the workload wouldn't be too difficult. He never worked hard in high school, which was an eternity ago. He needed to work this time, as he chose this. The line shuffled two steps this time.

He was ready to get on with his life. Thomas felt like things had been on hold and now were moving forward. Things still weighed him down, but he drove on. Deborah bothered him, especially as he delved deeper into this whole gender thing. She was a reminder of who he had been, and he wasn't sure he could cope much longer. He felt different, as if his eyes had opened for the first time. Only three from the front.

They called his name, and he made his way through the collection of desks, like at out-processing, each person was seeing someone different. Thomas thought advising was a joke. The man only seemed interested in verifying Thomas wasn't overloading himself and was following the recommended plan for incoming freshmen. Soon Thomas was out the door and enrolled in school with the classes he wanted, when he wanted them. It was a different feeling, especially since he was the first in the whole Simmons family to go to college. He signed up for a program designed to help students like him, first-generation students. This might be a good thing as he hadn't known anyone back home who had gone to college.

The path toward the bookstore had an incline and Thomas leaned into it, wincing as he walked. It was slow, and standing in line that long hadn't helped. True, parking in handicapped spots was nice, but he was not near his car. Honestly, why the hell was he walking anyway? He looked at something on one of the walls, some poster for a fraternity, when he slammed into the ground. Thomas stared in surprise as some girl tangled up with his legs and cane.

"Oh, I'm so sorry. Gosh, you know I can be such a klutz. Here, let me help you." The girl extricated herself and stretched a hand toward Thomas. She was cute, in a perky Goth way, with shoulder-length red hair with black tips and black clothes. She was petite but muscled enough to actually help, which surprised him. He held onto her tiny hand for longer than necessary.

"Thanks," mumbled Thomas, brushing dirt from his back and legs.

"Are you okay?" she asked, looking concerned. "That was a pretty bad fall, and you, with your cane and all...ouch. Are you sure you're not hurt? Gosh, I would feel really bad if I hurt you badly the first time we met. What if you never wanted to meet me again? Or you had nefarious intentions to sue me and possibly the school because I'm a klutz. And maybe...maybe I should just shut up and let you answer." It was pure babble but cute.

"I'm fine as far as I know."

She sighed dramatically. It seemed over-the-top, but maybe it was just part of who she was? "Oh, good. You know, let me buy you a coffee to make up for the collision. Maybe a mocha, or a latte, or a cappuccino, or some other mixed coffee drink that is really tasty and yum, or you know, maybe even a chai if you like something with more spice and maybe I should stop talking before I just keep running on and on like I always do, and there I go again doing just that, okay, shutting up now."

He laughed. She seemed fun in a screwed-up sort of way. He liked that. Maybe coffee would be good, and he was sure she wouldn't be boring company compared to Deborah. "Coffee would be excellent. What's your name and where to?"

The smile in response was bright, the kind you expected from cheerleaders, not Goth girls. Thomas smiled back. He hadn't done a lot of that lately. "My name's Tiffany, but everyone calls me Tiffi, except some people who call me things like Tiff or Fanny, but I don't mind and I'm rambling again aren't I?"

Her mood was infectious, and Thomas didn't mind as he had had enough glum. She was cute with a bouncy personality that wasn't artificial like Deborah's. Maybe he could make a friend, instead of just his annoying girlfriend. "I'm Thomas, though my unit called me Rhymer."

Tiffany looked puzzled. Thomas could almost hear gears churning she was thinking so hard. Her eyes widened with a eureka moment, "Oh...Thomas Rhymer...True Thomas...from the Celtic legends or Germanic, I can't quite remember, Scottish? Though Thomas doesn't sound German, but what do I know. You know, that's cool and I really like it. Is that like really your real name?"

Thomas chuckled. She was one of the first to ever get the full meaning of the nickname. "Nah...it's something I picked up in the Army. One of my sergeants was pagan and named me that after catching me writing poetry. It stuck."

Tiffany's eyes widened. "You were like in the Army? Like with the fighting in Iraq and Afghanistan and everything for real? Is that where you were injured? Oh, and are you pagan, cause you said one of your sergeants was, but that doesn't really mean that you yourself are, but maybe it does. I mean someone could have led you to the Goddess and not made a big deal and you might be looking for other pagans, and I'm doing it again, sheesh!"

Thomas laughed. "Yeah. I was in the 101st. Got injured and now I'm here. And no, not pagan."

Tiffany grinned. "That's okay, no one's perfect. Hey, let's get going as our coffee is longing for us. Can you hear it? I can hear its lonely cries in the distance, 'Drink me! Drink me!' Let's get going. Paradise Coffee is by the dead mall, but the coffee is really good. You know where it is, right, because if you don't you can follow me or maybe riding with me might be a better plan unless you need to go somewhere before or after. Honestly, I gotta stop."

"Yeah, I know where it is. See you in a few minutes." They parted, Tiffany waving good-bye as he hobbled to his car, parked by admin. It felt longer, as the collision hurt. His leg burned and he gritted his teeth. He had meds, and half a Vicodin would take the edge off and he would still be aware enough for conversation.

He collapsed into his car and took half a Vicodin. He was aware it would take a bit to kick in, but he could make it to Paradise Coffee. It hurt, but not blindingly so. As long as he didn't need to stand, he should be fine. The drive was nothing, thanks to sparse traffic. Tiffany bounced as he pulled up, looking surprised to see him. How many people agreed to meet her then bailed?

Thomas wasn't sure he wanted any of the beverage offerings. He'd never had mixed coffee drinks before. They looked intimidating and girly, what with whipped cream and chocolate syrup. Though maybe that was okay? He settled on a mocha after Tiffany glibly mentioned it was a gateway beverage, which worried him. A gateway to what?

The conversation was nice. They covered a lot as Tiffany bounced about, but it was a good change of pace talking to someone besides the doc about life. Deborah wasn't much of a conversationalist given she was more concerned with her fun. They had nothing in common, which was a problem.

A couple of hours later, Thomas noticed the time and grew concerned. He planned on doing a few other things today, but the conversation was good, the mocha tasty, and he felt happy. Life wasn't all that bad.

Since the conversation was enjoyable, Thomas suggested it continue over dinner. Tiffany agreed but let him know she was in a lesbian relationship with no intention of getting romantic with a guy even if he was a cute hero and interesting. Thomas chuckled. He had no problem with that, as Deborah was too much relationship for him right now. He needed some human contact from someone who was interested in him and not his penis or pocketbook.

The food was good and they kept talking through the meal and dessert. Finally, they said their good-byes after exchanging numbers. Thomas smiled happily the whole way home. Today had been excellent. This was an improvement and a trend he hoped continued.

Thomas changed into his nightgown after tossing his clothes into the hamper, then took his meds, and called it an early night. He was exhausted, but today had been fun and he could get used to this.

❖

"What the fuck!" screeched Deborah, throwing back the covers.

Thomas snapped awake instantly, scanning the room for danger, heart racing a mile a minute. He reached for his personal weapon, but the M4 wasn't there. Neither was his knife. All he found was a red-faced and screaming Deborah.

"What the fuck are you wearing!? Are you a pervert or something?" The shrillness in her voice was a mix of anger and panic. Thomas's heart raced, encouraging him to punch Deborah in the face, and he fought against that urge. What the hell was going on? "Am I not enough of a woman for you?"

Thomas growled, anger rising from the rude awakening and attack as his sleepiness cleared. He did not need this bullshit at stupid o'clock in the morning. He rose unsteadily and glared at her, clenching and unclenching his hands. "What the fuck are you doing?"

"I'm coming to see my boyfriend, not some fucking fairy!"

"I'm not a fairy!" bellowed Thomas, nightgown shifting with his movement. "And what gives you the right to barge into my house at some god-awful time of night and attack me?"

"This key, motherfucker!" She struggled to remove it from her key ring, anger making her clumsy. When it was finally worked free, she threw it at Thomas. The key bounced off his chest and dropped to the floor. Deborah cried furiously, large hot tears rolling down her face. "You gave me that right, you fucking asshole! You said it was okay to surprise you! Well, happy fucking surprise, faggot!"

Thomas's muscles tightened, the hold on his anger fraying the more she screamed. Jolting him from sleep wasn't helping, and he was ready to punch her. He took an unsteady step toward her and then another. She stood her ground, eyes ablaze with accusation.

"Get...the...fuck...out...of...my...house!" The words were measured and menacing, coming from a deep chest rumble. Deborah took a step back and then another.

She stood in the bedroom doorway, glowering. "Fine, you goddamned cocksucker! Fuck you! I hope you get AIDS and die!"

She spun and stormed from the apartment, the door slamming behind her. Thomas roared and drove his fist through the drywall by the bedroom door. It hurt but not enough to drag him from his fury. He wanted something to destroy, and all he saw were his own things, things he didn't want to break. With a snarl, he tore the nightgown off and flung it away, standing naked in the living room. He screamed his frustration at the ceiling.

Powerful throbbing in his leg slammed him back to the here and now, and with the adrenaline ebbing, he fell to the floor. Heavy sobs wracked his body, and tears burned his face. Thomas wasn't sure why he was crying. After his weeping faded, he weakly crawled back to the bed and dragged himself up, the process made more challenging since his leg didn't want to support him. Weak sobs rolled through him, and Thomas curled up under the blankets and ran away into slumber.

Chapter Eleven

A ringing phone woke him. He blearily struggled to find it, hand groping over the nightstand. His eyelids were caked shut, a reminder of last night. He eventually grabbed the ringing nuisance and answered brusquely, wiping his eyes clear. "What?"

"Um…Thomas?" The voice was soft.

"Yeah. What?" Thomas crawled closer to the edge of the bed. He didn't need this shit. Where the hell was his nightgown?

"Thomas, this if Tiffany. I was wondering if you wanted breakfast or something because breakfast is the most important meal of the day, and then I realized you might not be awake so I drove over here but then remembered it would be impolite to just walk into someone's apartment so I'm calling from the door because of the aforementioned breakfast offer. Are you okay?" she rambled softly, with less energy than usual. There was no bounce and that made Thomas sad.

Thomas remembered Deborah hadn't locked the door before slamming it and it was probably still unlocked. Maybe Tiffany would help him cheer up? It's not like he wanted to stay with Deborah so why was he so pissed? Ugh…his head hurt. "It's open."

He hung up and rolled onto his back, staring at the sprayed-on ceiling texture. The front door opened, and he saw Tiffany in the doorway, backlit. She wore a black dress with red flashes of color under a long leather coat, big clunky boots over fishnet stockings, which was practically a stereotype. Her hair was in two pigtails tied off with black and red bows. He grinned faintly. "Hey."

Her smile was fragile. "Hey."

He sat up and made sure he covered his naked body. Hurting and feeling utterly horrible, he was glad for a friendly face. "Sorry, rough night. Breakfast sounds great. Let me shower quickly then we can go."

She nodded and helped him stand, averting her eyes. He was too tired for embarrassment. Once up and cane in hand, he hobbled into the bathroom while she paid attention to his posters. The alteration between hot and cold woke him enough to enjoy the massage function on his showerhead. The pulse worked on the muscles of his back and hip, giving him a reprieve from his earlier pain. He felt more human and less ass. After a quick shave and brush, Thomas almost felt normal.

Memories of last night returned and he sighed. He had wanted to break up with Deborah for weeks, but hadn't found a way to tell her, which was chicken shit. It was over now, and emotionally, he felt raw. He didn't want to face the world, but a cute girl came to drag his sorry ass to breakfast. The idea of a frowning Tiffany seemed incongruous and not something the world should ever face. With a heavy sigh, Thomas headed to his bedroom, towel wrapped around him.

The room had been tidied while he showered. The bed made, and things Thomas hadn't remembered throwing were in their places, or at least close enough for government work. Everything was nice and orderly. He smiled but then realized she probably saw his nightgown, since he had flung it on the living room floor. With a groan of frustration, he cursed his stupidity. He hoped she wouldn't call him a freak like Deborah.

He pulled on a pair of pink panties and tugged up his heavily worn desert fatigue pants, determined to wear something comfortable that wouldn't cling to his hip. After pulling on an old concert T-shirt, he grabbed his cane and winter coat before he hobbled out. Tiffany waited on his couch, a smile on her face. This room was clean and organized as well. It was like a tornado of tidy had hit his apartment. "Thanks, Tiff. Sorry you had to do it."

"No worries, mate. Let's get going because I can hear pancakes calling my name. They're clearly in need of saving if this is what it has come to. If you listen closely, there are some calling your name as well." She bounced up and made her way out of the apartment.

Tiffany drove, wanting to spare the environment the pollution two cars would generate, and the ride was a lot like she talked—frenetic. Type O Negative pounded out of the speakers and Thomas admitted some of it was pretty cool. She weaved through traffic, chatting all the while. It was frightening, like the time he almost got squished by a Chinook during air assault training. He had leapt off the top of the vehicle in order to survive.

Soon they reached the IHOP by the mall. She opened his door and helped him out. He smirked at the role reversal. They chatted about musical preferences as they walked in. Thomas chuckled as she ordered the Rooty Tooty Fresh 'N Fruity. There was something about the name that cracked him up. How could any adult order that seriously?

The food was good and breakfast hit the spot, making him feel more alive; the coffee was a godsend. Conversation was nice and relaxed until they got back in the car. As she pulled out of the parking lot, glancing for oncoming traffic, she casually asked, "So, have you been cross-dressing long?"

Thomas froze. She had seen the clothes? She had to because he was sure she hadn't seen his panties. He answered as best he could, with a simple and direct, "Huh?"

"Well," she replied, completely unfazed, "There's the fact that a really pretty nightgown was on the living room floor and a few pairs of women's underwear were scattered about. There was no guy's underwear anywhere to be seen, so I assume you're a cross-dresser especially adding in that your girlfriend broke up with you."

Thomas couldn't figure out a good denial, and the longer he delayed the less convincing it would be. Deciding to take a chance, he said, "I…I'm not a cross-dresser. I'm transgendered, maybe transsexual, I'm not sure yet. I've never done this before so that's all I had to wear. I'm sorry I'm a slob, but so it goes."

She nodded, not even ruffled, still smiling as she wove through traffic. "That's cool. You know, if you need help with anything give me a ring. I can help you with makeup, clothes, etc. One of my old boyfriends cross-dressed, but things didn't work out because he was a jackass. Thanks to him I realized I was much more into girls than guys and he wasn't a close substitute."

Thomas nodded, shocked. It was unexpected to be simply accepted. Tiffany acted as if it were no big deal, like she dealt with this every day. Maybe she did? Thomas had no idea, as they were in the getting to know you phase. Maybe he should take the chance and open up? She was the antithesis of Deborah. "Thank you. Besides my doc and ex-girlfriend, you're the first to know. And the first who isn't either paid to deal with me or screaming and calling me a freak at two in the morning. Thanks."

"No problem. You know, I think you and I might become good friends, and what are friends for after all but to help each other?" She smiled, seeming to get brighter from moment to moment.

Thomas stayed quiet as Tiffany slalomed through traffic. He thought about Deborah and her response. If she responded like that, how would his family react? After all, Thomas was the macho soldier, the masculine hero of the family, with the fucking medals to prove it. They sent him a letter thick with praise for all he had done for the family name by getting the Bronze Star. He joined the Army to get away from them, to find opportunity since his Podunk county had a lot of nothing. He didn't want to work at the plants, or mill, or anything like that. Would they accept him as a girl?

That he was going to eventually tell them was a forgone conclusion. They were part of his life, and he had no plan to shut them out. He just didn't know what to say. It might be best to defer the conversation until necessary, like if he started living as a woman, or changed his name. At that point it would be impossible to not let them know. They deserved that much.

He shook off his rumination and saw they were almost at his apartment.

"Home again, home again, jiggity jig!" chirped Tiffany, pulling her Miata deftly into the parking space. Her smile was bright and helped cheer him up.

Thomas blinked, recognizing the quote. He turned, surprised. "You know *Bladerunner*?"

"Sure do," said Tiffany. "I love the movie. The visuals are incredible and the story is great and Rutger Hauer is so hot. If only I could find a girl like him...sigh..."

Thomas chuckled. "What's your favorite part?"

"Where the Replicants put eyeballs on that genetic designer. I also liked when Priss met J.F. Sebastian. Very cool. What's yours?"

"I love Rutger Hauer's last speech after he saves Harrison Ford. That was so awesome." He'd never met a girl who enjoyed *Bladerunner* like he did. It made him want to become a cop, and he would have, if the military police had had any open slots when he enlisted.

They continued to talk about sci-fi movies, discussing their favorites and the worst. Thomas stopped brooding over Deborah. He looked around his apartment and realized he needed to get books and school supplies. "Um...hey, you want to go shopping with me, for books. Then we can get lunch?"

"That might be fun. Where do you want to go?" said Tiffany, bouncing and setting her pigtails awiggle.

"I don't know. Maybe you pick, as you seem to know every restaurant in town. It'll be fun, unless you have a hot date?"

"Not to worry. My new girlfriend is busy. My last one couldn't take the way I talked and rambled about things like movies or books or anything else that interested me, like a couple of local bands I've heard who are really killer and have a glorious sound, and I'm doing it again...sorry." She blushed and turned her face away.

Thomas shrugged. "I don't see a problem, Tiffi. So you ramble, that isn't bad all things considered. It could certainly be worse."

"Well, there is that," said Tiffany. "So, lunch...hmmmm...let me ponder before I answer. You want to drive or shall I?"

Thomas shuddered at the thought of her driving again. "Let me drive. We'll get there in one piece and I also have the handicapped plate that lets us get the best parking spots. Sound good?"

Tiffany nodded. Thomas grabbed his squad pack and limped to his car.

❖

Thomas wasn't sure how they ended up at a Thai restaurant by the Cumberland River. He had never had Thai and had little experience with Chinese food. Putting his stomach in Tiffany's hands had him skeptical, as she was a bit screwy. When they walked in, she said something Thomas guessed meant hello. The staff welcomed her. After they were seated, two orange creamy looking drinks were placed in front of them, and Thomas wondered what the hell it could be. It looked like a liquid creamsicle. Tiffany took a straw, stirred the concoction, and took a long pull. She made happy, contented sighs.

The taste surprised him.

Tiffany smiled. "Just relax. I'll order for both of us and it should work out fine. The food here is great. And I won't order anything too weird."

Thomas sipped a little more and sat back. A waitress came up, and Tiffi started talking in Thai. She chattered away with the waitress, and he sat there amazed. He had known a few people who spoke other languages, mostly translator geeks from the 311th who worked with them in Iraq. The waitress wrote things on her order pad and scampered off. "You speak Thai?"

"I speak a bunch of languages. My mom was Air Force and we moved around a lot. We lived in Thailand, Japan, China, and a few places in Europe." Tiffi bounced. Thomas wondered if she knew how to sit still.

"Heh. Except for Kosovo, Iraq, and my time at Landstuhl, I haven't been outside the country, hell barely out of the south. And those trips were all military related and I didn't see the sites. Hell, in Landstuhl I was in the hospital and never saw anything but the building and grounds. So I don't count Germany, since I never got German food." Thomas wanted to travel but hadn't had any opportunities. He had been too busy getting shot at in Kosovo and Iraq. He asked questions about the various places she had been and was surprised that her mother had been stationed in Ramstein before coming to Tennessee.

When their food arrived, Tiffany said, "These are spring rolls. You dip them in this sauce, very tasty. This chicken satay is really good. You dip it into this peanut sauce. Don't worry, it isn't glorified peanut butter."

Thomas nervously grabbed a chicken on a stick thing and dipped the corner barely into the sauce. The taste wasn't that bad, and he dipped more for his next bite. He was enjoying the food when the next dish came out. Thomas wondered if there was a reason for a funny-looking pasta dish and figured there was an Italian involved somewhere. Tiffi laughed at his theory and introduced him to pad thai, as she squeezed a lime wedge over it.

His eyes popped open at the taste. Maybe this stuff wasn't so bad.

Tiffany seemed pleased that she had made another convert. Thomas sat back, quite content, and then was surprised when more food came out. The mango sticky rice with a sauce was incredible. He wished there was more or that he hadn't needed to share with Tiffany. They fought over the last bite, spoons clacking furiously until Tiffi won with a bold feint that allowed her to drive her spoon home. Thomas grumbled as Tiffany smiled in victory.

The drive to campus was less life threatening than the ride to breakfast, especially since he was driving. Thomas never felt his heart leap into his throat even once, until Tiffany said, "So, Thomas, what have you bought for your cross-dressing?"

"I…uh…haven't bought much, just the nightgown and some panties. I'm not sure I want to take that step yet." It was tough admitting this. Sure, he already outed himself, but this was different. He was still coming to terms with this.

She turned in her seat and looked him over, cocking her head. "Aren't you the least bit interested in how you might look?"

"A little, but I'm not sure where my comfort level is. I got so nervous shopping for the panties it triggered my PTSD. Just the thought of people knowing and judging made me lose it. I'm not sure I could actually go out and buy things without that happening again." It felt good to admit this; it made him feel more…honest.

"Well, I could help. That way you can act like I'm the one buying and you're carrying bags. You could have the look of a long-suffering boyfriend, which should make you feel less on the spot. That way we can pick things where you can comment on them and there you go. Good idea or should we come up with another plan?"

Thomas thought for a second. Shopping with Tiffany would have a safety net. It was a good plan and made it more likely. He nodded. "I think that might work. My therapist recommended getting more things, and I'm more afraid of flashbacks than buying."

"All right. Hey, I got an idea. My girlfriend has a computer program that lets her run through various fashion images and play with clothes, makeup, and hair. Let me get a picture so I can upload it and play with it. Please. Pretty please. With sugar on top and other tasty but bad for you substances, like Twinkies and Ho Hos. I just want to see what works to make you beautiful." The look she gave him was so cute he could barely stand it. Having no resistance, he nodded.

She clapped briefly, squealing, "This should be fun."

CHAPTER TWELVE

Email rarely fucked with Thomas's reality, but Tiffany's managed to. When she emailed the picture generated by that fashion program, his reality shook to the core. That girl couldn't be him. There was simply no way. The outfit, hair, and makeup all worked wonders, and what looked out from the digital image was not masculine in any way. He shook, seeing a girl looking back with his eyes. It was creepy, and chills ran up his spine the longer he looked. According to Tiffany, this was him without a hell of a lot of work.

He shut off the computer and hobbled to the kitchen, shaking as his thoughts churned. With changes to his hair, simple makeup, and appropriate clothes, he would unquestionably be a girl. He barely tasted his cereal or coffee as his thoughts were consumed. The shower cleared his head, which he was grateful for. Thomas tried to lose himself in TV, watching shows that helped turn off his brain and allow that image to fade.

When the phone rang, he jumped. He scanned the room for danger; there wasn't anyone there besides himself. He looked at the caller ID and rolled his eyes. "Hello, Mom."

"Hey there, Tommy. How've things been?" she asked with some enthusiasm.

"Not bad overall. I'm registered for classes, and physical therapy is helping me get stronger. They're still figuring out if I'll ever walk without the cane."

"You know we're real proud of you going to college. Both your daddy and I wanted to, but raising our family was more important.

You're the first in either family to make it. Graduate and make us proud." Thomas could hear the pride in her voice, but it sounded like she was heading toward something. "You think you might be able to come visit? I know you're about seven hours away, but your brothers and sisters miss you something fierce."

Thomas sighed. He hated the little town he grew up in and his family's crowded single-wide. The confines made him crazy, and he ran off to the Army to escape. Why would he go back? Hell, his apartment was spacious in comparison. "I'll think about it, Mom. I'm busy with PT and other appointments so I'm not sure I'll have time for that long of a drive. Besides, even an hour drive is rough on my leg. I'll see what I can do. Maybe when therapy is further along, I can visit?"

"Don't you wanna come out here and see your kin, Tom? We figured you might want a party; all the relatives can come by and wish you well for starting college. And it's Christmas. Don't you wanna come home for Christmas?" Thomas felt his guilt meter rising. He didn't want to do this, but she kept twisting the knife, knowing all his buttons. "Becky's been asking 'bout you, wonderin' if you're ever coming home to whisk her off her feet. She's a good catch."

"I'll try. Honestly, Mom, I'm busy with doctor's appointments, physical therapy, and getting ready for school. I'll see if I can make a trip out there next year. Seven hours in a car is really painful, but I'll do what I can. Okay?" Thomas clenched his teeth, fist tightening. His temper was harder to control lately. It was a PTSD issue, but that didn't help when he started getting pissed off.

"Well, I suppose that's all I can ask." She twisted a little more.

The conversation ended after his mother caught him up on all of the family gossip. He rubbed his neck. He needed another massage and was glad his next appointment was soon. Mike could find all the knots in his back and neck. Thomas considered it money well spent, especially after calls with his mother. She made him crazy.

It wasn't that she didn't love him, because she clearly did, but rather the Army changed him and that was before this whole transgender crap. He changed how he saw the world, and that made dealing with his parents difficult at best. To him, they were narrow-minded and not open to anything new. He didn't want to go back to all his crappy memories. His hometown was smaller than some of the villages in Iraq he patrolled, which was sad. They had the same level of poverty, the only difference was the color of the dirt and who was prayed to. Nevertheless, maybe he should head home. They were family.

The apartment was silent except for a faint electronic hum. He had been so tangled in personal things he hadn't realized he was truly alone. It was a little eerie, but he could get used to it. And he could hang out with people from school if he got lonely. Tiffany was great, but a few more friends wouldn't hurt.

The quiet was getting to him. He felt isolated in the apartment since he didn't know his neighbors, so he decided to call Tiffany.

"Moshi moshi...Tiffi speaking." Her voice was chipper and comforting.

"Hey, Tiffany. I was wondering if you wanted to do something. It's quiet and I'm going stir-crazy."

"Sure. That would be awesome because my girlfriend played around with the fashion program and we found the *perfect* look for you and made a list of everything we'll need to buy and have your colors figured out for makeup, and the two of us can teach you what you need to know, and oh, have you thought about getting hair extensions as they'll give you longer hair immediately without the fuss of growing it out first or maybe a wig. I know a couple of places with really good deals, but I heard that having extensions can help your hair grow longer faster and I'm doing it again. Why don't you stop me?"

Thomas chuckled. "Because you were on a roll and I wanted to see how long you could go without breathing. It's...impressive."

"Yeah. Thanks. You know, I learned to breathe through my scalp to make it easier to eat someone out because when you are down there and really enjoying yourself you don't want to move, and thankfully I don't have to go up for air all that often so nothing gets in the way of my dining experience."

Thomas blinked and stared at his phone. Did she really say what he thought she said?

"I know my girlfriends enjoyed that skill and it was useful when I dated boys, but sucking cock made me gag when they thrust and hit the back of my throat, but I don't have that problem with pussy and besides, who likes gagging?" Tiffany rambled again. "So my girlfriend Stacy and I hoped you would call so we could go shopping and get everything you need in order to become the beautiful new femme you are, and luckily enough she's close to your sizes, and colors and that way we can shop for you without making you too nervous though that wasn't why I hooked up with her. She can breathe through her scalp as well. Isn't that cool?"

Thomas nodded, unsure what to say. "Um...cool." It was awkward, but he was getting used to awkward. "As for being close to my size and all...yeah, that should help. Where do you want to meet?"

"How about your place? Your car is bigger and more comfortable for three than my tiny Miata. And that way the bags just go in the trunk and then your apartment, no transferring necessary. See, it's like we thought this out or something, you know...like a plan."

"Sure. See you soon." After hanging up, Thomas put on his boots and got ready. He had meds, winter coat, and his cane set to the side, ready to roll. Looking at all the stuff he was carrying, Thomas realized he needed more pockets. His fatigue pants would work, but they all were in the laundry. Maybe Tiffany could carry them. The threat of a pain flare was slim, but he didn't want to risk it. And the anti-anxiety drugs were a must.

Thomas channel-surfed, hoping to find something to distract him while he waited. After his third or fourth run-through of available channels, there was a honk. He pulled on his coat, grabbed his cane, meds, and hobbled out.

He locked the door and saw Tiffany and someone he assumed to be her girlfriend.

Tiffany had been right. Stacy was nearly the same height, build, and coloration as Thomas, which seemed odd, since they looked nothing alike. Tiffany was wearing a bubblegum pink Hello Kitty shirt, black miniskirt, long leather coat, and was carrying a coffin purse. Stacy was in jeans and a T-shirt like him, with a windbreaker on, her normal-looking purse slung over one shoulder. "Shall we?"

"Can I get an introduction first?" asked Thomas, chuckling.

"Oh right, I forgot that you haven't met. I mean, I was sure you had met, but clearly not. Sorry about leaving you hanging," said Tiffany. "This is Stacy."

"Hi. How are you?" Stacy replied, giving Tiffany an affectionate glance.

"Fine. You're okay with this?" asked Thomas, worried what she might be thinking.

"Sure, why wouldn't I be?"

"I can think of lots of reasons, actually," replied Thomas.

"Well, I don't care. Once I started working with the program, I saw how easy it was going to be to transform you, and I got all into this...project." Stacy shrugged and spread her hands.

Tiffany hugged her and kissed her cheek. "Can't you see why I love her?"

Thomas nodded. Maybe this whole thing would work. They climbed into his car and while pulling out, he asked. "So, what's the first stop on this epic excursion?"

Thomas watched Stacy pull out a list. "Goodwill. We'll go there first to pick up basic stuff and if needed hit Walmart. After that, a beauty store for hair extensions, if you want them. We can pick up makeup there as well because you need to get used to the cheap before you spend real money. Quick and not too painful. We'll need to get you shoes, but you would need to try those on."

Tiffany chuckled. "Can you tell she's a fashion design major? She's really good at this and should be able to find you lots of good stuff. And it'll be things that'll look good on you and in good shape. And she even has a look set up for you that should work with who you are and everything. Stacy is the best. I told you I could take care of this."

The grin was infectious. Thomas was impressed with what Tiffany pulled together. This could take care of what the doc wanted without Thomas having to spend reams of cash in experimentation. He heard women's clothes were more expensive, and hitting Goodwill would save cash. He still had most of his separation pay left, supplemented by VA disability money in addition to Vocational Rehabilitation, but he didn't want to waste any of it on frivolous items. That's how his parents ended up in a single-wide and struggling.

The drive wasn't long, as the store was on one of the three main roads in the town. He parked in a handicapped spot, stashed his drugs in the glove compartment, then got out and limped after them while they chatted animatedly about what they were hunting for.

They grabbed a cart and wheeled down the aisles. Thomas followed like a forlorn boyfriend turned pack mule. That ruse kept his anxiety manageable, though he still glanced around, afraid people knew this was for him.

The girls pulled things from cramped racks, scanned them critically, and tossed them into the cart or hung them back up. First, it was skirts, then jeans, blouses, T-shirts, and finally dresses. They even snagged a few jackets and hoodies. The growing mountain made his eyes bug out; even at these prices, they seemed intent on using all his money. Finally, they made it to the end after Stacy failed to choose between two purses and tossed them on top. He sighed in relief. If there had been more racks, he was sure they would have bought more.

Time for the next part. Stacy placed herself opposite Thomas and started to go through everything again, this time even more critically. She held items out at arm's length, which conveniently enough was where Thomas stood.

It was impressive the way they arranged this. What got him was that he didn't feel nervous or self-conscious at all, since those feelings faded the longer things went. Stacy shrank the cart to about a third less, lost in a world of assessment. Thomas destressed seeing that, but then realized they had two more stops.

Stacy tried on several things and discarded a few more. Then they went to the cash register as he sighed in resignation. He handed over his card dejectedly. The cost was more than expected. Of course, there was ten times the clothes he even thought about getting. His head spun and his heart raced. Were they actually building him a complete wardrobe from Goodwill?

They rolled to the car with the loaded down shopping cart and tossed bags into the trunk. As Thomas started the engine, Tiffi skipped back after she returned the cart. When she got into the car, she lip-locked with Stacy, making him gape in surprise. Thomas got aroused, as it was pretty hot. He shifted his growing erection uncomfortably and put the car in reverse trying to focus on anything but two hot chicks making out in his car.

The shopping process was repeated at another store, only faster. Stacy and Tiffany went through everything, referring to the list, inspecting seams, and everything else. It resulted in an almost identical pile. Having a closet full of women's clothes for himself was not what he had in mind when this quest started. Thomas sardonically grumbled about what his mother might say.

They took a break for lunch, and he realized the pain to his bank account was not that bad. While eating, Thomas got a better impression of Stacy. She and Tiffany cared about each other; something about them clicked. Thomas had been shocked at first with their kissing, but he was growing accustomed to it and there was no question it was pretty. Tiffany and Stacy weren't freaks or dykes. Both were feminine and not butch at all, and one didn't seem like "the man." This confused Thomas so he leaned forward and whispered, "This is going to sound dumb as hell, but which of you is the man?"

Tiffany barked out laughter then slammed hands over her mouth to contain the giggles, looking to see if anyone noticed. Stacy rolled her eyes and pulled a five-dollar bill from her purse before she handed it to a bouncing Tiffi. Tears leaked from her eyes as she kept laughing. Stacy began to giggle watching her. Pretty soon all three of them gave in.

After getting back under control, Tiffany said, "Okay, so the whole binary guy/girl in the relationship just doesn't play out. I mean, sure there are dominant and submissive people in any relationship, but you can manage to have a sexual and emotional relationship based on meaningful balance between the two or more individuals involved, which means you can have almost any number of combinations with only a duality of people. See?"

Thomas sat there with a blank look, not following a third of that. Stacy leaned forward. "There isn't one. Lesbian relationships don't work that way."

That was clearer. He got the fact there was no "man" but still had questions. Thomas was completely in the dark about how two women could have a relationship let alone how it might work, except for porn. "Thank you."

The girls split a desert while Thomas drank his Coke. With the exception of his mother's phone call, this day turned out quite nice. Tiffany's mood was infectious, and it was difficult to stay morose around her. He was too morose most of the time.

Soon they were on their way to the beauty supply store to pick up makeup and hair extensions. If there was anything on that list after this, he had no idea. Once in the store, Stacy was off like a shot toward the hair. There was lots of it, and Stacy found what she was looking for fairly quickly and grabbed a large amount.

Tiffany joined Thomas against a wall watching Stacy go. Stacy filled the basket with different colored bottles. There were brushes, tubes, vials, all sorts of unfamiliar and intimidating items. Thomas wasn't sure he wanted to know what all that was. It seemed confusing and foreign.

After a half an hour running amuck, Stacy headed toward the register. Thomas paid, sighing at the total. It was crazy, all the things they bought, and he was clueless. Where the hell was he going to put all this? With a frown, he pondered getting rid of his other clothes to make room. Was he ready for that?

The drive home was silent, as Thomas was wrung out. He didn't have the same stamina as before. After a short hobble, Thomas collapsed on the couch after taking pain meds to deal with the burning ache. Tiffany and Stacy brought in the bags while he rested. He smiled and drifted off to sleep.

❖

The smell of spaghetti woke him, and he faintly heard Stacy and Tiffany talking but couldn't make out any words. The scent of tomato sauce filled the apartment with garlic, basil, and oregano. Slowly, he sat up, rubbing his sore leg. He felt better. The leg didn't hurt as it had on the drive home and he felt relaxed. He needed to pace things better.

With a groan, Thomas stretched. He wasn't as sore as expected. Pain was a constant companion, and any relief was noted. The angry gurgling of his stomach made him blush. Thomas's hunger built, and the kitchen smells only made it worse. He padded into the kitchen to check on the status of food and froze.

Stacy and Tiffany were kissing passionately, Stacy massaging Tiffany's ass under the skirt. They broke and looked lovingly into each other's eyes, the world forgotten. The change in position let them notice a slack-jawed Thomas staring. Tiffany giggled. "Have a good nap?"

Thomas rubbed the back of his neck in embarrassment. "Um... yeah."

Stacy wiped Tiffany's lipstick from the corners of her lips with her thumb, a reddish tint covering her cheeks. "Dinner should be ready soon. So...when do we want the fashion show? Before or after? Since all that's left is noodles, we should have time for an outfit."

Tiffany nodded and turned to Thomas, desire clearly visible on her face. "Sound okay?"

Thomas flushed, heat spreading to his ears and down his neck. "I...um...you see..."

Tiffany pouted, bottom lip thrust out, quivering slightly, eyes wide and pitiful. He sighed, defeated by cuteness. "All right."

She bounced excitedly at his capitulation, clapping. "Need any help? We picked up a few other items that should help with...things. Something to fill out the bras and some interesting...information from the internet. It's your Christmas present."

He cocked his head. "Like what?"

"Well, you see," replied Tiffany, vibrating with excitement. "I found directions on how to tuck."

"Tuck? Tuck what?" asked Thomas, confused and scared of the implication. Did she honestly mean to tuck that away somewhere?

"Your penis and balls." She was bouncy and excitedly told Thomas, "If you can't figure out the written directions, I found a video that shows how to do it. It was fascinating. I mean, first he took two of his fingers and pushed his testicles up into—"

"Tiffi!" exclaimed Stacy, embarrassed. "There's no need for that."

Tiffany turned and asked, "What?"

Thomas blushed. Stacy sighed in resignation. "Just give Thomas the box and help him get dressed for dinner. Nothing white though. We can get his hair and stuff taken care of afterward if he wants."

Tiffany laughed and gently pushed Thomas into his bedroom. Thomas struggled a little, trying to buy time. "But...but I just woke up and wanted to get something to drink!"

Tiffany stopped and rolled her eyes. "Fine. I'll pick something out for you, because you aren't simply complying, no arguing."

Thomas groaned. "Fine. Fine."

She bounced and clapped. "Yay! This should be fun. Whee!"

Stacy and Thomas watched Tiffany rush into the room ahead of him. They turned, looked at each other, and shrugged. There was no understanding Tiffany.

CHAPTER THIRTEEN

Thomas took the glass of Coke Stacy had handed to him into the bedroom. Tiffany managed to go through the bags quickly and pull together an outfit. Laid out was a brown flowing skirt with a white peasant top Stacy insisted would look good. "Uh…I thought Stacy said no white?"

"We can change your blouse before eating. But until then we can see how this looks," gushed Tiffany, more excited than he was.

A shudder rolled up his spine, heart started to race, though he couldn't tell if it was from excitement or fear. He saw the white bra to the side sitting on a small box. He quirked an eyebrow trying to figure that out. Tiffany continued. "If you want, I can pick another blouse after we see how you look. According to the program, this'll be a good look for you or at least the you that I know, which may not be the real you for all I know, but anyway we thought you would look cute in this and that should be…oh God, stop me."

Thomas nodded, distracted by the clothes. Realizing he actually bought such things shook him, things his mother would have killed him over and the Army dishonorably discharge him.

"Take your pants off. We can start with tucking. After that, the bra and then you just pull things on. Step into the skirt like you would legless pants. Then you're all dressed. We can take care of shoes later."

Thomas wondered what was with women and shoes. Why would he need more than a few pairs? There was no good reason he could think of. He undid his jeans and got ready to drop them, then he paused. He looked at Tiffany, who wasn't moving. "Do you mind?"

"No. Not at all. Besides, do you know how to put on a bra or tuck?" She arched an eyebrow.

"No clue, but if I can take one off, I can put one on." Thomas snapped at her. He frowned, knowing this anger had nothing to do with the situation but rather the stress and anxiety. He closed his eyes and took a deep breath, then let it out slowly. Pulling off his shirt and throwing it against the bed helped burn out some of his anger. The sharp intake of air startled him. Tiffany was pale, eyes wide, and locked on his shoulder. "Wha…what happened?"

Thomas was confused. Was it his scar? Sure, it wasn't thin and pretty and he was very happy it hadn't developed into a keloid. "Remember I mentioned I'd been injured in Iraq? This and my hip and leg were injured from the whole thing. Then there are a couple of bullet holes as well. This was during attacks on some of the troops throughout the region."

"I heard you say that, but this reality didn't register. That looks like it hurts." Tiffany's voice was quiet and flat.

"Well, the concussion from the RPG round knocked me out, and when I woke up briefly, field medics had already started working on the wounds. Morphine is great at chasing pain away if you can take it." Thomas picked up the bra and slipped his arms through the straps. "So, things were cleaned up by the time I woke up. After that, I was drugged to manage pain. It sucked but I'm better."

He wasn't able to get his injured arm far enough back to hook the bra. After some fumbling, Tiffany came up, slapped his hands lightly, and hooked the bra for him. She adjusted the straps and helped settle it better on Thomas. "There you go. I'll show you an easier way after dinner."

She opened the box and pulled out two flesh-colored lumps. They looked like large plastic chicken breasts. "Um…what the hell are those?"

"Your breasts."

While he blinked in surprise, she slipped them into the cups and adjusted them until they sat correctly. The weight surprised Thomas. Somehow, in his mind, breasts didn't weigh anything. Tiffany smiled. "There you go. I'll let you finish. Hurry up."

Thomas looked over the sheet with tucking directions. After reading it a few times, he tried to work it out. A few minutes later, it clicked. A few deep breaths centered him, then he reached down and pushed his testicles up into his body. They slid up with a very odd sensation and some nausea which faded, a milder version of getting hit in the nuts. He then folded his penis back and under before pulling his panties up; the smoothness of his crotch was startling.

After shaking himself from his reverie, Thomas finished dressing. He went to the bathroom and looked. From the neck down, he looked like a woman, with slight curves. From the neck up, he still looked like himself. When he stopped looking at specifics and looked at the full picture, he felt something…shift.

Despite hairy legs and arms, he felt right, like he should have but never had. It was as if he could make out a blurred image in the back of his head he'd forgotten for so long. The colors and look fit him and were comfortable. Was this still him? If not, then who was he?

Tiffany entered and looked him over.

"Huh?" Thomas turned from the mirror when he heard a noise; his thoughts were up in the air. Why couldn't he have just been born without this hanging over him? Why was his life so fucked up? He didn't want to deal with these fundamental questions. But when it came down to it, he liked how he looked and it frightened him.

Tiffi giggled at him. "I was coming to get you. Wow, you look beautiful. That outfit really works. Oh, food's ready."

Thomas nodded. He pulled himself away and hobbled to the living room, using the wall for support. The little dining room table had three places set and the sauced pasta in a bowl. Stacy was seated and waiting. "Nice, I knew those colors would look good. If we add the hair extensions, I think you should pass with a little makeup to change the shape of your face. You look cute."

Thomas smiled shyly, cheeks heating. "Thank you."

Tiffany bounced. "Hurry and change into the other blouse on your bed. Since it's not white there'll be less potential for sauce-ification. Hurry, I'm hungry."

They ate and the conversation flowed comfortably. To his surprise, Thomas enjoyed himself. It was a shock realizing how lonely he was now that there were people here to mitigate that. The apartment was filled with something other than silence. He could not hear the traffic or neighbors talking, all he could hear was chatter and pasta slurping. Tiffany and Stacy helped him feel part of the conversation.

When the topic turned back to him, Tiffany said, "So, now that we know you don't look terrible with minimal work, what should we call you when you're dressed like this? I mean you don't look like a Thomas in that, and when you throw in the makeup and hair no one'll ever know, and if we call you Thomas it won't be right because that will make you stand out and scream NOT GIRL, and I know you don't really want that so we need to figure out what to call you in these cases, though I get how this can be a big deal because names."

"I haven't thought about that. I mean, when I started therapy, I was hoping to get rid of these urges. Now they're part of my life and taking over. I never expected to look like this, so names never occurred to me."

Stacy said, "Okay. We can work on that. I'm sure we can think of a name that fits and isn't odd. Odd names practically scream drag queen no matter how you look."

"Sure. Any ideas?" Thomas had no clue where to start. Names were something parents hung on you, not something you gave yourself. Letting Stacy and Tiffany help made sense as they likely could think of more girls' names than he could.

Tiffany stared at Thomas intently, eyes roving over him. The scrutiny made him nervous. She brightened suddenly and pronounced, "Megan."

Stacy scrunched her face, shaking her head. "No. Given her look, it makes her sound like a twink. Not a bad name, but no. What about Ashley?"

Thomas wasn't sure. It didn't sound right. "I don't know. Um... maybe?"

Tiffany looked thoughtful for a minute, putting more things together. Cocking her head, she regarded Thomas. "You know... maybe we should work with the whole puzzle instead of the one piece. Are you going to use your last name or something else?"

Blinking, Thomas pondered that. There was nothing wrong with his last name, but he was cutting the cord to his old life. This could give him a break from his family, which wasn't a bad plan. Thinking of one thing he did like, Thomas said, "Maybe I should use Rhymer. That way who I am, or rather was, is safe. It's unusual, but that's fine, and it's not like changing my last name is going to be as weird as my first since I won't be called by that all the time. So, a name that goes with Rhymer. Elizabeth?"

Tiffany and Stacy looked thoughtful as they considered. "Nah," replied Tiffi. "Doesn't fit."

"I was thinking Rachel, but Rachel Rhymer sounds odd. Maybe stay away from R names," said Stacy. "What about Kelly?"

The name felt close. "I like it, but what else is there? I mean it doesn't really sing."

"All right. You know, there's always Willow. I mean she was like the hottest character on Buffy and I totally had a crush on her," stated Tiffany. "Maybe that will rub off on you?"

"The hotness will rub off on me? What does that even mean. Besides, Willow Rhymer? That sounds odd," said Thomas.

Tiffany harrumphed, crossing her arms. Stacy looked up from her pasta before tossing out, "What about Melanie or Emily? Either of them work? I figured that if the name felt...I don't know...softer, maybe people won't see Thomas."

Thomas rolled the names in his head. Honestly, Emily sounded pretty good. That or Kelly. Tiffany blurted out, "Sierra!"

"Sierra?" asked both Thomas and Stacy.

"Yeah. There was this really hot girl I knew in high school whose name was Sierra. I mean that girl really had it going on. If you use that name you can be blessed with her hotness." Tiffany nodded wildly.

"Wait, what? Blessed with her hotness?" said Thomas, befuddled by Tiffany's rapid direction changes. "Where do you even get these things?"

"Sure. Sierra Rhymer." Tiffany beamed as if she found the best name in the world. "Throw something in the middle and it rolls trippingly off the tongue."

"No way. Sierra is the letter S in the NATO phonetic alphabet. Just no."

As Tiffany pouted, Thomas thought over the various suggestions, coming back to Emily. There was something about it, but he wasn't sure what. Emily Rhymer. Should he go with that?

There was something about this making him uncertain, uncomfortable, and the muscles in his back tensed. A female name made sense, but was he ready to accept this whole gender thing as real and follow it to the end? Fighting in Iraq wasn't as uncertain as this renaming.

Should he choose or let Tiffany and Stacy decide? Did he want to be responsible for this choice? What if he picked wrong? This felt permanent.

Tiffany and Stacy sat quietly and watched Thomas niggle his way through. He sat there, head bowed, silent, mind speeding, sorting this into a format easier to cope with. Finally, he made a decision. It was basically a call sign. He could live with that, since he wasn't changing his name legally, he could test drive the name. He might not like the gender trouble, but maybe choosing a name would help him move along. He nodded and looked up. "I really like Emily. It fits and is easy to spell."

Tiffany clapped and Stacy smiled reassuringly. "Emily it is then. Now when do you want to do your hair?"

Thomas wasn't sure he was ready for that, as it was a big step. He would go from the short hair he'd grown since leaving the Army to much longer. Suddenly, he would have hair to his shoulders or middle of his back. Hair to his collar would be new, as he had never been allowed to grow it out as a kid. He was used to short hair, and this would be a drastic change. However, if he was going to do it maybe he should do it before classes started to be on the safe side, so it wouldn't seem out of place. He didn't have his school ID yet either, as he had bumped into Tiffany before that. He needed to talk to his doc, and his next appointment was tomorrow. He felt trapped by making a decision and suddenly went numb.

They moved to the living room and Thomas fell heavily onto the couch. Stacy found his liquor cabinet. She poured Irish whiskey into some glasses and handed them around before raising her glass. "Well, since you have a name, I propose a toast. To Emily Rhymer, our newest girlfriend."

Tiffany cheered and Thomas blushed as they clinked glasses. There was a sense of solidity to the statement that frightened Thomas, but maybe, just maybe, he could handle being Emily Rhymer. He sighed, tapped his glass to the table, and took a drink. "To Emily Rhymer!"

Chapter Fourteen

His mouth tasted like death. Everything throbbed, including the sound of his blood pulsing. With effort, Thomas sat up before a wave of nausea hit, forcing him back. He groaned, and the sound vibrated through his aching head. Thomas lay there wanting to die.

He opened his eyes slightly and was thankful the room was not bright. Another wave of nausea hit. Maybe he should get to the bathroom before his stomach revolted? He looked up at an unfamiliar ceiling. Where was he?

He turned his head and realized he was on the couch. What?

He sat up slowly, but the nausea returned and with great effort, he held back a rush of vomit. This was a definite sign. Thomas rolled to the floor. Why was he so miserable? With his head and every joint aching, he high-crawled toward where he knew the bathroom was, at least he hoped it was still there. Vomit in his mouth, he tried not to gag further. He struggled out of his skirt and kept moving.

They drank a *lot* last night, based on the wooziness. However, he couldn't figure out why he slept on the couch. Shouldn't he have been in bed?

The door was mostly closed. He nudged it open before realizing he was only in his panties, still tucked. Had he fallen asleep on the couch topless but still in his skirt? He continued to the bathroom, head down, letting his mind not think.

Inside his bathroom, a naked girl lay on the tiles. Her head was close to the toilet, and he couldn't make out who it was, as that would require thinking. She did have a nice ass though, but that could be either one of them. The cool tiles felt nice, beckoning him to lie down. He crawled closer and made it to the toilet. He flushed, winced at the sound, and nudged the figure on the floor.

He couldn't decide who it was. He looked at the hair, red with black tips, and then blearily glanced at the trimmed crotch, also black. It was a nice view and he was interested, though there wasn't much more visible. He gazed at her chest, and based on the breasts, he surmised it was Tiffany, her hair also a giveaway. He patted her hip and mumbled, "Tiffi…Tiffi…wake up."

A murble. He covered her with a towel. Tiffany made some waking up type noises and shifted back and forth. Thomas felt his bladder urging him on. "Tiffany…please wake up. I gotta pee. If you don't leave, I'll pee anyway."

She moaned but made no motion toward leaving. Thomas crawled onto the toilet seat, moving awkwardly over Tiffany. The tub helped him make it. He sat and let loose. The stream was loud in the bowl, and he sighed in relief. A voice rose weakly from the floor. "Don't forget to wipe, sweetie."

Thomas chuckled then regretted it as his head throbbed. He wiped and began to rise, which he mostly managed before flushing. His head didn't swim but it throbbed with his pulse. He staggered out, using the wall until he found his cane and then headed to the kitchen. He needed field coffee, as would Tiffi. Stacy might but he didn't know. Once the machine gurgled to complete caffeination, he poured a cup and downed it happily. "Ah, nectar of life."

Stacy and Tiffany staggered from the bedroom, making a beeline for coffee. They sat at the table, still laden with dirty dishes, empty bottles, and tipped over glasses. Stacy and Tiffany sat there holding their heads as they sipped. The three of them nursed their mugs, hovering over the extra-strong dark liquid helping bring them to life. The day was not starting well. Thomas glanced at the clock and groaned. "Uh…Fuck! I have an appointment in Nashville. Are my eyes bleeding?"

Stacy tried to shake her head no and stopped, a hand on the side of her head. "Not as far as I can tell."

"Okay." Thomas rose and refilled his mug a third time. He hobbled to his room and pulled out some clothes, eyes still mostly shut. He slipped on new panties and remembered to tuck. Jeans and a T-shirt later, he headed out. Both Tiffany and Stacy still there, huddled over their mugs. "Hey. I'll be back in a few hours. Okay?"

Hands waved weakly in acknowledgement.

Thomas drove to the VA hospital in Nashville, glad for his dark sunglasses. The water helped some, but just some. After painfully working himself free of his car, he limped along the walkway and into the building. Once checked in, he waited, slumped in a chair, trying to rehydrate in the hope it would ease the pain. Maybe he might live after all.

The doc came out and called his name. Thomas collapsed into the loveseat in the doc's office and put his leg up, sighing happily. The throbbing drifted away once his weight was off it. "Rough night?"

"Yes, sir. I got drunk with friends after shopping and such. I even dressed."

"You went shopping? Really?" asked Dr. Richards. "What did you buy?"

"Skirts, dresses, blouses, and some other things. We also got makeup and hair," he said, then drank more water.

"Hair?"

"Yeah, you know, like hair extensions. I'm not sure about that though. I mean classes start next week, and I figure I should decide something so I don't end up with quickly changing hair and have that become an issue." Thomas squinted. "Could we lower the lights?"

The doc nodded, turned on a desk lamp, then flipped off the fluorescent ceiling lights. "Let's talk about that. What's your opinion on the extensions?"

"I'm not sure. Part of me wants it, to see how much long hair would change how I look. Another part of me is afraid. I mean, it's like it will utterly change my world." Thomas grumbled. "I mean, I just wanted these odd feelings of jealousy to go away, and yet here I am with a closet full of girl's clothes, makeup, and hair extensions. Hell, I even have a name."

"What name?"

Thomas blinked a few times, slow on the uptake. "Huh?"

"What name did you choose?"

"Um…Emily Rhymer," replied Thomas. His head hurt too much to keep track of everything. He needed more water and maybe some food.

Dr. Richards wrote that down and looked thoughtful. "So, do I have this right? You're either ready to start or still not sure?"

"Yeah."

"If you weren't afraid of this, I would be concerned you were treating this lightly. However, it sounds like you're thinking things through. I think this worry is healthy and shows you have a grasp of things. This shows me you might be ready to start hormones if you're interested. Getting a new wardrobe? Hair extensions? A name? You're moving pretty quickly at the moment. So long as you are sure, we can continue."

"I'm not sure I want that yet. I mean, I only got dressed in women's clothes last night, and I've no idea if this is what I want," said Thomas pensively. "I mean, I barely understand this." .

"Okay. So, if you aren't yet ready for a big jump, what about this little step? What could be wrong about extensions?"

"I'm not sure why it makes me nervous. I mean, it's just hair and there are lots of guys with long hair. Maybe it's because I've never had anything but a military cut my whole life. Long hair is going to be very different and even though I've wanted it for a while I'm not ready for that."

"But if you don't take any risks how will you grow?"

"I…I…uh…don't know. I guess getting the extensions will work. I mean, it isn't permanent. If I change my mind, I can get them out. Yeah…I can do that." Thomas wondered what he would look like with long hair, especially after last night. If Stacy was feeling okay enough to put them in, then maybe?

"So, have you gone out dressed yet?"

"No. I mean, I just got clothes yesterday and don't have the extensions or anything. I figured doing that later, when I'm more comfortable," said Thomas. The mere thought set his heart racing.

"Are you worried things are going too fast or worried about your safety? You tell me about the things your friends and you do that are filled with all sorts of chances. Are you afraid of getting hurt?" The doctor was silent a moment letting that sink in. "Most people don't care about things that don't directly impact them. You might get some harsh words from small-minded people, but who cares if you have long hair, or dress in women's clothing? Don't let fear make choices for you."

Thomas deliberated. It made sense, a little too much for his comfort. Sure, he heard the same from shrinks at Walter Reed, but it hadn't resonated. Maybe this was something he had to get past, and stop letting fear make decisions rather than take a chance. But he didn't want to get injured again. The memory caused his heart to race and palms to sweat. "You're saying my experiences in combat make me worry about my safety so much I'm afraid to make choices?"

"That's it exactly," stated the doc. "You need to get past that fear. Take a few risks and see that the world does not end."

"Okay. So, should I do the hair and go out a few times before classes start?" asked Thomas, wanting someone else to make the call.

"Yes. I want you to take some risks, to stretch past your comfort zone. Nothing crazy, just things you want to do but are nervous about. Live your life, not simply endure it or let it live you. Do something fun, try different things. Get back to those PTSD worksheets to work through troublesome thoughts. Remember this is like physical therapy, sometimes you have to go through pain to get better."

Thomas deliberated, nodding slightly. If he had played things safe in PT, not pushed through the pain, he would be in a wheelchair. To succeed he had to push past his limits, increase his strength and range of motion. If that was applied to his mental health, then addressing uncomfortable things would help him become comfortable. If he curled up protectively, he would never get better. "Okay. I'll get the extensions and dress more, maybe even go out. Then I can see where to go."

"Good, step by step is how you do anything. All you have to do is take a few small risks, followed by a few more, and soon you'll find you're healed and whole," said the doc. "Go take care of that and look to your friends for help. And think about hormones. They can have a powerful and transformative effect on the psyche as well as your body, but be sure. Go home and get some rest. You look terrible."

Thomas smirked. "Thanks, Doc. I'll take care of that."

Lost in thought, he drove. Could he go beyond his comfort level? He used to believe that whole-heartedly, before getting injured. The Army pushed "No fear" and he learned that on the sports field. He used to take risks all the time and now…maybe he needed to push the envelope to break through.

As he pulled up to his apartment, Thomas noted Stacy and Tiffany's car. Chuckling, he figured they were about as awake and alive as he was. With a twinge of pain, Thomas entered his apartment to find things cleaned and the smell of food in the air, some sort of egg, sausage, cheese, potato thing. He dumped it into a bowl along with a piece of toast. The protein would help, plus the bread and potatoes would soak up any leftover alcohol.

It was good, basic, exactly what he needed. Finally, he started to feel almost human. He got a little more coffee in his mug and flumped onto the couch. He was exhausted, sore, and positive the alcohol played a major role. Maybe he'd take a nap after eating and before asking Stacy to do his hair. He had no idea how to do the extensions, added to the fact his arm would not reach back and up.

He didn't see either Tiffany or Stacy and moved to check the bedroom. He could hear the sound of the shower running and very pleased moans. Obviously, they enjoyed themselves last night and today. At least someone got lucky last night. It amused him thinking his only two friends in the country were a pair of lesbians. He was so used to hanging out and being one of the guys he never hung out with girls he wasn't dating. Now he found people he could comfortably talk to, and they were girls. Life had turned a corner to someplace strange.

He snickered and left the bedroom, and pulled the door shut to give them more privacy. His life was changing so fast it was like riding a tiger. He was holding on with his bare hands and expected to be thrown off any second. In fact, that magnified once he met Tiffany. Prior to that he had been going slow and steady in a direction.

He turned on the television to wait for them to get dressed, sure they would be out soon. The more water he drank the more human he felt. Maybe he would feel like dressing again. He changed channels to some cooking show with interesting food that sounded tasty, and Thomas learned the value of zest.

The bedroom door opened and they walked out looking peaked. Tiffany was paler than usual, obviously still suffering from last night. Stacy looked fine. She smiled at Thomas. "Hey, doing all right?"

Thomas nodded. "I'm feeling a lot better, thanks to sleep, food, and water. Oh, can we do the extensions today? My doc thinks it's a good idea."

She nodded. "I can do that. I have everything we need, so we can get started after more coffee. Want any?"

"Yes, please. Thank you." Thomas thought it was a shame Stacy was a lesbian. There was something very attractive about her that drew him in, and while he hoped she and Tiffany never broke up, Thomas would love going out with her.

He paused as another question blundered through his head, and he frowned.

Stacy looked at him, concerned. "What's up?"

"Well, if I'm transgendered and attracted to girls, am I a lesbian?"

Stacy snickered as she sat. "Well, that's one way to look at this. Thomas, Emily, I think it depends on your gender presentation and sexual preference."

"Come again?" Thomas was trying to get that sentence to line up in his head.

"It's like this, your sexual preference can be for those like you, those different than you, both, or neither, but it's just one facet of who we are. Another is gender presentation. That is, presentation based off various cultural ideas as to what is male or female. Trans people and intersex folks mess up the binary of being only male or female. So, if you align with 'female' then your interest in women would be for those like you, and thus lesbian. If you see yourself as a guy, then your interest would be for the other, making you hetero. Got it?" Stacy rolled this out smoothly, as if she had rehearsed it.

"So basically, if I'm a girl then yes? Okay." He nodded thoughtfully. "That makes more sense. I just don't know what to do. I'm going through this crazy-making situation and I want to date as well. However, most women I know would freak, like my psychotic ex, Deborah. You seem okay with me as does Tiffany, so that supports the lesbian thing."

"I know a couple of T-girls who come by the Lounge, a lesbian bar in Nashville. Maybe some night we can go down. I'd suggest going dressed, as some girls there really detest guys. However, Thomas, Emily, whatever your gender and sexual preference, you should get to know people and get out of the house more often. It would be good for you. You'll pass with very little effort, thanks to our work and in no small part, your body. Now, let's get your hair." With that, Stacy stood, grabbed a dining room chair, and took it into the bathroom. "Come on. Let's get this done because I want to see how you look. I think it'll be cute."

Thomas followed Stacy as she got things ready. He had no idea how this would turn out and the uncertainty made him twitchy. This was scary, another step. He sat down nervously and let Stacy get to work.

CHAPTER FIFTEEN

An IED rocked the Humvee with a whump. The lead vehicle turned askew and tumbled under the force, flipping into the air. The eruption of gunfire was immediate from fedayeen positioned on either side of the causeway. AK-47 rounds slammed into the Humvee, puncturing the thin metallic skin. A few men screamed as hot bullets burned through flesh. The .50 cal started, and buildings, dirt, vehicle scraps, bodies were torn up. Thomas and the others leapt out and began to move from cover to cover, driving closer to the ambush. Staying in the Humvee was suicide.

Thomas used a palm tree for cover. The fight wasn't supposed to be like this. They won the war. Sure, it took more than one hundred hours unlike last time, but still Iraqi units had broken under the might of US forces and the victors began the follow-up mission to rebuild the ravaged country. The 101st worked hard in Mosul, fixing just about everything, to show the Iraqis they were only there to help. Despite acts of goodwill, attacks began. He picked out his next bit of cover and moved under Peterson's fire. The 249 rumbled, keeping the insurgents' heads down, allowing him to make a hunched-over sprint.

Once he thumped into place, he opened fire, dropping one with a center mass three-round burst. The figure spun slightly, weapon toppling to the hard-packed earth. The man was dressed like any other Iraqi he had seen on the streets, with the exception of the scarf covering his face, like a bandit from a western. He supplied cover fire, helping them press forward. His sprint moved him close enough he could hear someone speaking Iraqi. There was no way to figure out what they were saying, as their translator had been in the Humvee that rolled. A quick glance showed at least one medic made it over there. He pulled the trigger on his M4 and nothing happened.

Cursing, he popped the magazine and yanked one free from his LBV. It slammed home and he slapped the bottom to seat it before pulling back the charging handle three times to prime for burst. He spun around the rock to engage when he heard someone to his left yell, "Grenade!"

The explosion was loud and more than dirt fell on the hard-packed sand, more dust filling the air. Thomas rolled from cover and rushed the position.

All that was left were remains, three bodies torn by the grenade. One of the guys to his right yelled, "Clear!"

He parroted. A couple of soldiers congratulated Hernandez on his throw. Thomas scanned the area one more time before returning to the Humvee, the echo of gunfire still rattling his ears. The faces, or rather, what had been left of them, lingered. Would he end up like that?

❖

Thomas woke tangled in his sheets, skin clammy. He was nauseous, a hollow fullness caught in his throat, and his heart raced. Struggling free, he sat up with a groan. He grabbed his cane and levered to his feet, nightgown sliding to his knees, and he limped to the bathroom. He splashed water on his face and rubbed his skin, slight stubble skritched his palm. He gazed at himself and frowned. The circles under his eyes looked darker, but was this him? His heart pounded and he remembered his hair was now just past his shoulders. It felt like him looking back.

The longer hair changed the shape of his face and the look of everything else. He studied himself, breathing slowly and calmly and trying to connect to the foreign reflection. Pushing a strand of hair behind his ear, Thomas closed his eyes and used a relaxation technique from his PTSD counseling. Now that he was actually using them, they helped.

Thomas limped to the kitchen for water. He drank half then refilled his glass. The computer chair creaked under him as he sat heavily. It was five in the morning, and since he planned on getting up in two hours, he might as well stay up.

He opened his email and pulled up the rendered pictures of himself. It was impressive how close the pictures looked like him with this new long hair.

The effect was mind-blowing. He was not used to anything except short hair. This hair had ended up in his mouth several times already, and he kept brushing it out of his face. While it looked good, he was still getting used to it, going from short to long hair with no time to adapt. Tiffany and Stacy laughed as he struggled and made faces when it ended up wildly all over his face. Stacy said he would get used to it and not to worry. Easy for them to say.

His email to the gender support group down in Nashville had a response, giving him directions to where they held meetings. This was an opportunity to meet others dealing with this. The doc mentioned it would be very helpful talking to others dealing with the same issues. Apparently, the group had several people involved in the national transgender scene and wrote articles for magazines. There would be a lot of experience he could draw from.

Thomas sent a reply, planning on showing up at the next meeting, and used MapQuest to figure out where the hell the place was. The program showed it a little off the interstate so it wouldn't be difficult to find. Next weekend he would meet these people to see if they could help. With a sigh, he realized he would also start classes.

He brushed hair out of his face since it drifted over one eye. Maybe he needed a scrunchie-thingy to make a ponytail? That would help until he got used to it and besides, he had seen lots of guys with ponytails. He could play it off and still come across as male, despite so much about him screaming female.

Stacy and Tiffany planned to come by to teach him how to tame it. He wasn't sure how much he wanted to learn; parts of himself rebelled at learning "girly" things. True, it was a feminine skill he should learn, but he wasn't all that interested in it. Taking care of his hair in a trouble-free non-complex manner might be all he could handle, especially with his shoulder problems.

And the whole makeup thing made him uncomfortable. Thomas understood the reasoning behind military face paint, but this? What purpose did it serve? He read a few articles but couldn't figure it out. What the hell was he supposed to do with some of the tools and items mentioned? Plus, putting makeup on in order to look like you weren't wearing any was bizarre.

He turned off his computer and limped to the couch, rubbing his hip. Once seated, Thomas looked across the dark room. What the hell was he doing? Shouldn't he be more worried about finding a wife? Getting a good job, to afford a family? Act like a responsible man instead of a willful little girl? His tight neck resisted attempts to loosen, bands of muscle were tight and he worked them with his good hand, kneading the unyielding knots.

Everything pointed to gender dysphoria. Thomas never thought about things like this before, thought about his life this way. He played football, dated girls, joined the Army, and had done well. At no point had he felt like a girl. Thomas never felt this until getting injured. He was happy as a guy, but the diagnosis matched everything he experienced to a T.

His hyper-masculinity made sense. All through his life, he was unaware he did things that fit a particular framework. Thomas had been an aggressive child from about fourth grade on, in fights thanks to taunts about his height. He got into extreme sports, emulating the stunts on the X-Games. He became a daredevil, which helped in football and the Army. He always went full-tilt at any barrier, flung his body into harm's way without a second thought. The infantry harnessed that and turned it to risking himself for his unit. Was it all just to prove he was a man?

Thomas took another swig of water and stared at the white wall. While so much of him wanted to look away, this was something he needed to finalize.

Was it possible to not be the person you believed you were? To have hidden truth so deeply the lie affected you? The idea seemed strange, but he fit the profile. Being dressed like a girl felt good, as if he wore the correct, properly-fitting clothes for the first time. It was discomforting and surreal to think clothes made such a difference.

Thomas sat there in his nightgown and felt...odd, like he was dressed in what he should have been wearing all along, making his past an appalling and uncomfortable dream. It felt like there was nothing real to hold onto. It would be easier if he were simply delusional after the injury, instead of feeling like his life was in freefall. What the hell was he?

He rubbed his forehead, hoping to work out the headache that usually accompanied these thoughts. He always tried to coast along without thinking any deeper than he had to. Was he trying not to see himself?

He wasn't positive, but he had thrown himself into the purely physical to avoid thinking about uncomfortable things and this whole gender question made him extremely uncomfortable. He wanted to move.

Thomas rolled his shoulders. It was strange how his body tightened whenever he thought about this, to distract him from working things through. The pain wasn't working anymore, as Thomas wanted to figure out whoever he was. At this point, his future seemed more Emily and less Thomas.

If discomfort was to lead him off track, then maybe he needed to go into that darkness and find what was so carefully hidden. Maybe he needed to take that leap into the unknown to find what lurked there? What else could he do except sit there and take it like a man.

He absently brushed stray strands of hair behind one ear. He took a deep breath and exhaled slowly, like they taught in basic rifle marksmanship. After a few breaths, the maelstrom slowed and Thomas could follow one train of thought at a time.

Thomas reviewed everything he talked to the doc about, everything he had done in exploring this and how things lined up. Each time he reached an answer he went through the process again and again, niggling out anything that might disprove the result. Each time the same answer returned: he was a girl. His near suicidal actions in the service, aggression as a kid, the way he treated women as if they were disposable and for his use, hell, especially the negligent way he treated himself all fell neatly into place with the gender dysphoria diagnosis. It even explained his love of poetry and indifference to sports but love of playing. He tried to hide both, one successfully and one not so much, as evidenced by his nickname. With a sigh, he rubbed his eyes, a fullness in his chest building as he fought off tears. There was no denying it.

Part of his mind rebelled, pointing out he had a penis. Thomas was well aware of that, aware of his body in the way only the severely injured could be. You didn't cope with a permanent disability without getting to know your body, discovering new limits. He knew he had a penis, and generally, if you had a penis you were a boy. Nevertheless, the more he rolled this over, the more he realized he was indifferent toward it. It was just there and not something that interested him or that he gave much thought. It only came up when aroused.

He exhaled loudly. "I'm a girl."

That sounded right, felt right. He was a girl and would ride this as far as it would go. He liked the clothes. He was comfortable in what he was wearing. He shook his head; prior to this he would never have said anything like that. With the way things were going, he figured he would have to get used to being called Emily.

That led to another problem, his family. He wasn't positive how they would react, but he figured there was no way they would take it well. Thomas hadn't gone to church since he left North Carolina, but he knew his family were big church goers. Considering their opinion of "faggots and freaks," this might drive them insane. He was becoming something far worse than a faggot. He would be a deviant, and a crime against God. Did he want to lead two separate lives, being himself here while lying to his family? He wasn't sure he could keep all the lies straight.

Thomas...no—Emily—hung his head, trying to figure a way this might be less traumatic. Could there be any way to explain this that wouldn't set them off, wouldn't get him disowned? He loved his family, but he wasn't sure what they had in common anymore. He left to join the Army, to see the world, without any real plan of coming home. Now that he was out, he still wasn't interested in going home and being around family. The thought depressed him. Besides, dealing with this around his folks would be difficult if not impossible, especially if they got temperamental and contrary, and he was sure they would.

That still didn't answer his question. What was he supposed to do? Maybe he should talk to the doc? Or Tiffany and Stacy? They might have some ideas about what to do, having already come out.

He yawned, sucking in a deep lungful of air. Maybe he was sleepy, or his brain was just fatigued. He should have made coffee earlier. He started his coffeemaker and Thomas...no, Emily headed to the shower. The warm water cleared his head. As he washed his hair and shaved, he looked down at his legs. Since he admitted he was a girl, shouldn't he shave his legs? Some of the skirts would look weird with hairy legs.

He lathered up his sore leg and propped it on the lip of the tub with some effort. He drew his razor up his leg. The hair came off but clogged the blade quickly. He repeated this, a small amount of shaving and then a longer time clearing the blades, being careful around his scars. Finally, it was done with only a few lightly bleeding nicks. Running his hand over the leg felt weird, colder, slicker.

He repeated the process on the other leg. His legs looked strange, but better. As he rinsed, he thought of something else. Underarms. He had never met any girl with underarm hair. Sure, there might be some, but the thought of bushy underarms was unpleasant and since he was a girl...

It was awkward but he managed the task without cutting himself. He felt a little weird, his legs and underarms were different in a way he couldn't put into words. It looked cleaner.

Once dry, he wrapped his towel around his waist and got coffee. Today was undoubtedly going to be long, and Thomas was sure the girls had something planned. He wondered if it would involve removing the rest of his body hair? That sounded daunting, and come to think of it, hadn't Tiffany mentioned something about wax and eyebrows? He definitely needed coffee if he wanted to survive.

CHAPTER SIXTEEN

S o, Emily, what do you think?" hollered Stacy, music thumping through the air.

They were on the bottom floor of the Lounge, a Nashville lesbian bar Tiffany and Stacy went to all the time. After they hung out for a few days with Emily dressed as a girl, they managed to drag him out on a Friday night in early January. He was anxious, but not as badly as he expected. All told, it was a regular bar/club with a lot more women. He figured friends helped with keeping him calmer. They were here to keep him safe, and he appreciated that. He leaned toward Stacy and yelled back, "Not bad."

They grabbed a small table at the back, wedged into a corner by the bar. Two bartenders ran full-tilt, drinks poured at a speed that was magical. There seemed to be a mix of lesbians, gays, and a few straight couples all having fun. There were even a few people Emily guessed were transgendered as well. Upstairs there was an oxygen bar as well as a pool room, but he had no desire to climb the stairs with his leg acting up. There was even an outdoor area with tables if talking was what you desired. It certainly didn't remind him of that crap bar in downtown Clarksville where he met Deborah.

The décor was nicer, and there weren't a lot of soldiers vying for the same few women hunting husbands or someone to screw. The fact that there was a large percentage of women helped, as far as Thomas was concerned. He still lusted after women and there was nothing about men that interested him.

They got their first round and talked to each other, or more accurately yelled, to be heard over the pulsing music. Tiffany got Thomas a cosmopolitan, saying, "I thought Emily might enjoy a girly drink."

He shrugged and took a sip. It was surprisingly good, though he wasn't a big fan of cranberry juice, but apparently there was something the vodka did to make it enjoyable. Stacy promised to buy his next drink. Thomas asked what it was, but she just laughed. "Come on, Emily, like I'm going to ruin the surprise."

He shook his head, laughing. He was getting used to being called Emily, since Stacy and Tiffany called him that constantly. The name felt cute and fit more as time went on. Another song started and Tiffany squealed. "Em, come on!"

With that, Thomas was dragged onto the dance floor without his cane. He barely managed to avoid hurting himself on the way out and now had no idea what to do. He looked helplessly at Stacy, pleading with his eyes. She laughed and headed over, carrying his cane. She leaned in and said, "Just move however you want, follow the music. We'll stay close in case you have leg trouble."

Thomas smiled weakly and began to sway, attempting to dance. The movement made his skirt swish about which was nice. He mentally shook himself and just danced to the music in whichever way his body wanted. As a guy, he worried about how he looked and was completely self-conscious. Now, as a girl, he just moved. It was exhilarating. He hadn't let his body move in months, too afraid of hurting himself again.

Finally, thirst and a growing pain pulled him back to the table. He drank deeply which felt good and helped cool him. He shook his empty glass at Stacy, giggling. He wondered where that came from. It was soft, playful as opposed to his usual guffaws. It wasn't worth thinking at the moment. He kept swaying in his seat as he waited for his drink.

Tiffany danced her cute little Goth heart out, pigtails bouncing along. Thomas realized he missed this, missed going out, having fun with loud music and drinks. His body ached, but it was the good ache. Since this place was open every day, he might come himself just for fun. Besides, the exercise would do him good

Stacy tapped his shoulder and he turned. "Hey, Stac."

"Here you go, Emily, sex on the beach. It's tasty."

Thomas sipped, then took a larger drink. She wanted more. Another long pull and half the drink was gone. Stacy smirked. "See. It's a great goodness."

"Thank you so much Stacy." He gave her a quick hug, surprising both of them. "Thanks for everything."

Stacy chuckled and pulled Thomas toward the dance floor. He barely resisted. "Come on. Put your drink down and dance."

Again, Thomas lost himself in the joy of twirling skirt and the elation of movement. After a while, his leg stung in the bad burny way that seared through the alcoholic haze. He roughly made his way back to the table and collapsed heavily into his chair, wiping sweat from his face with a bar napkin. He was out of shape, panting from exertion, and his leg throbbed, but the icy wet of the glass on his forehead helped cool him. He drank deeply and finished it in one long pull, hoping the booze would kill the pain. He waved a server over and asked for another, liking them better than cosmos.

He propped up his leg on one of the chairs, and the elevation made it hurt less. He sighed in relief and watched. Until now, he never understood the whole dancing thing. The sheer excitement in just moving made sense now, and he enjoyed it. The cold drink of diluted remains was nice, and his heart rate slowed. Absently, he rubbed his hip, taking another sip. A warm buzz was going and he nursed it.

"Hi, anybody sitting here?" Thomas turned and stared at one of the most beautiful women he had ever seen. Her brown, vaguely Asian-shaped eyes and button nose were the first things he noted. She had all the curves he could dream of playing with. Dressed in a blue leather miniskirt and a thin, white tank top with sweat marks, she beamed happily.

"Um…no," replied Thomas nervously, unsure if letting her take Stacy's seat was okay. She wanted to talk…to him? Weren't they in a lesbian bar? Wouldn't she rather talk to a woman?

"So…what's your name?" she asked, leaning in to be better heard, her face close to his.

Thomas wasn't sure what to say. Stacy and Tiffany told him to always use Emily when dressed, but what if she liked him, or thought he was a real girl? "Emily."

"Pretty name. First time here?" She continued to smile.

Thomas nodded. "Yeah. This place is pretty nice. What's yours?"

"Leah," she replied, fanning herself.

Thomas nodded. What the hell should he say? Flirting seemed more difficult than simply getting drunk and screwing. Actually, talking to someone and getting to know them was hard. He grasped for anything and settled for dumb. "Come here often?"

Leah grinned. He noticed it touched her eyes in a way Deborah's smile never had. She leaned even closer, to be heard, lips by his ear. "Yeah, almost every night since I live a block away. Um…hey, wanna go outside and talk? It'll be easier than screaming at each other."

Thomas nodded, standing to follow before his leg gave way. Leah rushed up and stopped him from collapsing onto the floor, supporting him with her arms. With his face burning in embarrassment, Thomas said, "Oops. Let me lean against the bar a sec."

She helped Thomas, letting him rest his weight on her and he leaned heavily, taking weight off his leg. Leah smirked. "Too much to drink?"

Thomas shook his head, definitely too much dancing. "Nope, RPG round and masonry."

Leah started, trying to process. She shook herself and offered her shoulder. "Come on, Emily, let's get outside."

After they navigated the tight confines, they grabbed seats at a table in the walled-off patio that was vacated as they walked out. The remains of Ivy climbed up the wooden privacy fence and a few wisteria vines joined them. The air was far cooler compared to inside but the heating units kept the January air comfortable. Thomas closed his eyes and just breathed, sighing as the metal chair was fairly comfortable.

Leah looked at him quizzically. "RPG?"

Thomas giggled at her confusion. Did she really not have a clue what he was talking about? That was novel. He sipped his drink. "Yeah. I got injured in Iraq. Basically, I got blown up and shrapnel from a wall and the RPG, that's rocket-propelled grenade, had to be dug out of my shoulder and leg. Hence the limp."

"You seemed to be dancing pretty well for someone that screwed up."

His cheeks heated and he looked at the tabletop. Leah had been watching him? "Yeah. I had my weight on my good leg so I wouldn't fall on my face. The alcohol dulled the pain which was a great help. At least it was before I went too far. Thanks for catching me. I hate falling over, it's embarrassing. My cane usually keeps that from happening."

Leah seemed confused a moment and looked around. "Hate to break it to you, soldier girl, but I see no cane."

Thomas searched for his cane and then started laughing. "Oh... sheesh...that would explain everything. I guess I'm drunker than I thought. I was sure I had my cane. Guess it's back inside."

"Speaking of, another round?" asked Leah. When Thomas nodded, she waved over a server who was bussing a table. "Hey, Sarah, can I get a rum and Coke and Emily here a...?"

"Sex on the beach," said Thomas, feeling relaxed and happy despite the pain. Things were looking up, what with Leah here. She was hot and interesting. Yet another great idea by Stacy and Tiffany.

As the waitress headed off, Leah asked, "Umbrella drinks much?"

With a shrug, he replied, "Tonight's the first night I've had one. Honest. I usually drink beer or rum and Coke or straight something."

Leah snickered at the protestations of innocence. "There's something about you, Emily, that I can't figure out. I kind of like it."

Thomas instantly grew paranoid and pulled back slightly. Oh crap! Had he been read? What gave him away? "What?"

"I can't figure how a cute girl like you would be here without a date? I mean, someone hasn't scooped you up yet? I find that hard to believe." Her words were teasing and suggestive, and not indicating that she read him. She was playfully trying to draw him out.

Thomas was at more of a loss as he had no idea how to respond to this kind of flirting. He was usually on the other side of this. "Um..."

"There you are," said Stacy, walking out with a still bouncing Tiffany in tow. They had his purse, coat, and cane which gave him a sense of relief. "When we couldn't find you, we got worried."

"No, I'm fine. Leah helped me." Thomas uttered a silent prayer of thanks for his escape from responding.

Stacy shook her head in amusement as she looked between Leah and Thomas. Her eyes took all this in and her smile grew wider. "Yeah, Leah is great at helping people."

Thomas looked confused. "You know her?"

"Yep," said Stacy, with a mischievous grin. "She and I used to date before Tiffi and I hooked up. We ended well, thank the gods."

Leah nodded, looking at them with an amused grin. "We managed to stay friends and look out for each other. That can be rare in this community as a lot of breakups are loud and full of drama. But the community is also small enough that we all become friends again in the end. Except someone here neglected to tell me about the cute vet she knew."

This time Stacy laughed aloud, tears rolling down her face. Tiffany looked concerned as Stacy nearly toppled off her chair. This attracted attention from other tables. After wiping tears from her eyes, she regained composure. She sighed, looked at Thomas as if asking permission, and he gave a confused nod back, then said, "Leah, honey, this is the cute vet I told you about. More than once."

Leah looked confused, thoughtful, shocked, then stunned all in the span of about fifteen seconds. This made Tiffany and Stacy laugh while Thomas smiled apprehensively. He was embarrassed, both for him and her and he shifted uncomfortably in his seat. Thomas planned to tell Leah…at some point. It also seemed like Leah was being mocked, which he didn't like. "Hey…that's uncool, Stacy. Be nice."

Leah stared, her mouth worked like a fish breathing air, eyes wide. It was a bit amusing, but Thomas refrained from laughing. Finally, they stopped, and Tiffany looked contrite. "Sorry, Em, we didn't mean anything mean. What you don't know is that a few months ago Leah here went off on a *huge* rant about some of the members of the local trans support group coming here after meetings. She bitched about 'cross-dressers,' which I believe was her word choice. Some do look that way and their makeup scares me, but Leah here said she could spot a trans girl despite the fact there are several hot girls in that group that I would totally go after if I wasn't attached, or most of them married, or I guess still married though I'm not sure what the protocol for that is in these sorts of situations…"

Tiffany stopped babbling at a touch from Stacy. She eyed Tiffany lovingly before Stacy said, "I made a bet with her. I told her all about you, Em, all sorts of things. And here I find that I win with someone she knew about."

Leah still gaped fish-like. She worked her mouth futilely. Finally, in a hard whisper, she blurted, "There is no way she's a he!"

Thomas's face burned at the backhanded compliment.

Leah looked at him then over to Stacy and Tiffany, who were nodding confirmation. She looked back at Thomas whose smile grew weaker the longer this continued. He had been having such a good time and now felt like he was doing something bad. Thomas felt his emotions roil, tears welling, and he grew shakier. Leah smiled faintly and said, "I don't suppose you've had surgery yet?"

Thomas shook his head, tears welled in the corner of his eyes, then trickled down. "I'm sorry. I didn't mean to trick you or anything. I can go."

As Thomas reached for his cane, Leah grabbed his arm. He turned, looking at her through tears. "Don't. Please. Before these two bitches got here, I was happily talking to the cutest girl here."

Thomas smiled hesitantly, his heart doing something new, a sort of flutter. "Really?"

She nodded. "Really."

With that, Leah turned to Stacy. "Now, you two, git! I had this table first."

Stacy and Tiffany both made amused noises before standing, then left Thomas's stuff. Tiffany turned after a few steps and skipped back to hug him. "Hey, Em, if we're not here try to find a ride home. 'Kay. But if you can't, like say if Leah runs away, just call and we'll come rescue you no matter the time. Gotta support friends. Love you."

Thomas felt better. He wiped tears from his face, hoping his makeup wasn't totally ruined, as if sweating while he danced hadn't worn most of it off. He sipped his drink turning back to Leah, face still warm. She smiled ruefully. "Well, I guess that would explain why you haven't been scooped up yet. Anyway, as I was saying…this is your first time here?"

Thomas nodded shyly, heart pounding in his throat. He wiped sweaty palms on his skirt and bit his bottom lip.

"You need to come here more often, so I can see you again." Leah beamed.

Thomas again found himself in a position he had never experienced. His face heated and cooled with a mind of its own. "Thanks."

"Anyway, let me get to know you more. Where are you in transition?" She put her elbows on the table, resting her chin in her hands, honestly looking interested.

Maybe this wasn't the disaster he thought. "I…I just started really, several months ago. The doc is going to get me an appointment for hormones as the VA doesn't cover them, which pisses me off, but what can I do? They say they're going to take care of all my medical needs and then renege because they don't agree with the diagnosis. So I have to see a civilian doctor and pay for them."

Leah considered him, trying to see past a facade. He shifted like a nervous mouse watching a snake. "Are you sure you aren't a girl?"

Thomas blushed again, mulled the question, trying to figure out what to say. "Well, truth be told I am a girl. I wasn't always sure I was though. I may be a girl with plumbing issues, but I'm a girl nonetheless."

Leah stared into Thomas's eyes. He could tell she was weighing what Stacy said, what her eyes were telling her, along with everything else. She chuckled. "I think I can deal with that."

Thomas was incredulous. "Wha…?"

"I was thinking," said Leah, brushing a stray lock of dark hair behind an ear. "If you look this good now, pre-anything, then I'm really interested in the end result. When I'm wrong I'm wrong. I can hardly believe I'm saying this, but would you like to get some coffee?"

Thomas blinked, trying to connect the dots in his alcohol-rich brain and kept getting Q, which wasn't helpful. "Really?"

Leah chuckled. "Yes, silly, with you. Gods, you're cute."

She reached out and took one of Thomas's hands. Thomas noted they were warm and a little sweaty, either from the drinks or nerves. He had no idea why he was reacting like this. "Thank you."

They talked longer. Thomas told her about the Army and school, and Leah talked about being a sound engineer on Music Row, before Leah stood and held out her hand. With help from his cane and her, Thomas got to his feet. After a quick scan of the dancing mob, they realized there was no sign of either Tiffany or Stacy. With sighs of frustration, they made their way out, hand in hand. Thomas liked it and did not want to let go. Deborah hadn't been the hand-holding type, hadn't been much of anything except a booty call. Thomas had not been aware that he was that type until now.

They walked slowly down the block, chatting happily. Given how unsteady Thomas felt, he leaned heavily on the cane. Thomas liked how this situation was going. Talking with her was like talking with the guys in his unit only better; it was like they spoke the same language. Thomas never found anyone he resonated with the way he did with Leah.

After a block uphill, they made it to a small, well-loved house with a nice garden. There were a few steps up the porch and Thomas grimaced his way up. The dancing had been fun, but maybe it wasn't worth it in the long run if this pain was what he could look forward to.

Thomas complimented her on the house and Leah smiled. "My grandfather got it for me. I pay him the mortgage and don't have to deal with a mortgage company threatening to break my knees if I'm late. I like East Nashville since it has some very cool stores and restaurants. Everything I need is right around me."

She headed through the house to the kitchen, while he followed. The view from behind was enjoyable, as Leah had a lovely ass. Thomas wanted to reach out and touch, but figured it would get him into trouble. She was still talking. "...wondering what it was you did in the Army."

"Infantry. I was up at Fort Campbell in the Five-Oh-Deuce. It was my only duty station, as we shipped off to Kosovo and then Iraq where I got injured. You know, I miss it sometimes." He leaned against a counter, taking the weight off of his sore leg as she started making coffee, looking through several bags of beans before selecting one. He watched her, impressed by the care she was giving coffee.

"Why do you miss it? I don't understand. You were being shot at and could've been killed."

"I miss the camaraderie, feeling that I was doing something to make the world a better place. I miss down time with friends. I mean, I planned on serving at least twenty years and hoped to go Special Forces or maybe Delta. I loved it."

As the coffee started brewing, he realized by the wonderful smell it was high quality, and wondered if there was some secret connection between lesbians and coffee. She started taking mugs down. "How do you like your coffee?"

"A little sugar, please."

She nodded and got about fixing them. She grabbed the mugs and headed to the living room, where they sat on the couch facing each other. "So, Emily, what are your plans now that you're out?"

He shrugged. "I'm not entirely sure. I figured I'd take some history classes and become a schoolteacher or something."

"What are you interested in, I mean really interested in? What do you dream of doing?"

Thomas thought and nothing came to mind. He had been thinking so hard about gender that he had no idea what to do in any other area of his life. Everything had gone into solving this one problem and he was kind of lost. "As long as I can remember all I wanted to do was be a soldier. I planned on going career to ensure I never had to go back to the little town I'm from. Then I got injured, this crazy gender thing happened, and I've been running double-time just to keep up."

Leah leaned over and hugged him. He used the pause as she sat back to sip his coffee. It was very good, better than anything Tiffany had brought him. Leah rested a hand on his knee. "I'm sorry to hear that. What do you plan to do?"

Thomas shrugged. "Take basic classes at first so I have time to deal with this and then figure out a major. I mean, I have no clue what I want to do so I might as well keep my options open."

"Sounds like a good plan. You're pretty smart, Emily."

"Actually, my name is…" Leah leaned forward quickly, putting her fingers on his mouth and shushing him.

"I don't want to know that name. To me you're Emily, the cute girl I'm starting to get into. You're Emily, you're a girl, and that's all." With that, she leaned forward and kissed him.

Thomas relaxed into the kiss as Leah took charge, opening his mouth to her. He wasn't sure what was going on, but she kissed marvelously. It felt wonderful, better than Deborah's ever had, better than anyone else he had been with. His head spun. Was being Leah's Emily that bad of an idea?

She ran her hand along his leg, feeling the smoothness. "You shaved your legs?"

Emily blushed. "Well, I shaved this morning. It hurt, because I cut myself a couple of times, but I like the feel."

Leah snickered. "Emily, you're such a girl."

CHAPTER SEVENTEEN

Emily woke to a strange ceiling. He turned his head and there was Leah next to him, snoring softly. Her face was peaceful and he could watch her sleep all day except nature sent its insistent call.

With a groan, he sat up and stood, using his cane. Emily barely remembered putting it there before bed. He hobbled to the bathroom, relying on the quick tour from last night.

He wiped himself, tucked, and stood, the sleep shirt Leah gave him last night falling back into place. It had a picture of a sleeping kitten and Emily liked it. When he mentioned this last night Leah simply gave it to him. It was now his anytime he slept over. That boded well.

Last night with Leah had been different. First off, there was wonderful kissing that led to mutual foreplay that lasted forever. She took him to the brink of orgasm so many times without touching his genitals that he lost count. He did the same to her, under her guidance. They collapsed after their orgasms crashed through them, tremors shaking them both. It took five minutes before Emily felt like moving, panting heavily, her limbs refusing to move. Afterward, Leah thanked him, and shifted her body weight off, taking care not to hurt his leg. Moving slowly on wobbly legs, she staggered to the bathroom.

While he cleaned up and swapped into the bathroom, Leah got out sleep shirts. She handed one to Emily without looking at his crotch. She blushed before saying, "Could you please put that thing away?"

Blushing furiously, Emily tucked. Once dressed, they crawled into bed. Leah pulled Emily to her shoulder. There had been no nightmares and he felt rested for a change. Smiling at last night's memories, he padded into the open living room and began doing PT stretches.

They were modified Pilates and yoga moves designed to keep his muscles from seizing up. They worked, as evidenced by last night's exertions. He woke with his leg sore, but not with the expected screaming. Emily moved from stretch to stretch, trying to push just a little further each time, holding the pose for thirty seconds. His cane was near, but he wasn't using it since these poses also built strength. The stretching woke him even more, as pain flares worked better than coffee.

He got down on his hands and knees to do the cat stretch, then he moved down and forward before stretching back upward. He stopped with his back arched and heard, "Mmmmmmm...now that's a pleasant sight to wake up to. Morning, Emily."

"Morning, Leah. Could I sweet-talk you into making coffee?" He was jonesing for a morning cup but was in an unfamiliar place and did not know where the coffee lived. Now that she was up, he had no problem asking. Besides, she made excellent coffee.

Leah smiled and nodded, rubbing sleep sand from her eyes. She turned and padded into the kitchen. The grinder sound filled the room as he continued the stretches. Emily smiled brightly; soon fresh nectar from the gods would appear and all would be right in the world.

Eventually, the watched pot finished and he hobbled to get a mug full of dark goodness. They sat in the breakfast nook, looking out at the small backyard garden partially in shade. Emily sipped the excellent java and said, "I have a personal question and I don't want to offend you."

Leah smiled, looking a bit amused. "Go ahead. I knew a lot about you from Stacy, while you know little about me."

Emily nodded and bit her bottom lip. "I don't mean to pry, but I'm trying to make sense of something from last night. You averted your eyes and asked me to put it away. Why?"

Leah's face grew still, and her brown eyes darkened as she looked down at the table seeing something else. In a voice full of old tears, she said, "If we're going to get involved, like I hope you want as well, you deserve to know. Fair warning, it's not pretty. I didn't have a happy childhood. My mother did a lot of drugs, I mean, a lot of drugs. She was a heroin addict and would do anything for a fix. We lived with Goodwill chic, since she sold everything else to buy a hit or three. The summer before first grade, when I was six, this man came into my room and started undressing. I freaked out and called my mom, panicking. He chuckled and said in a voice I'll never forget, 'Little girl, it's time to pay your mama's bill."

Leah's voice shook. "All that summer, whenever she needed a fix, that creepy old man used me. I told my grandparents during a visit and they took me home before calling the cops. I had nightmares for years. Because of that, my memories of seeing a penis are tied to pain, humiliation, and panic. I can't stand them. Even strap-ons bother me at times, though I have gotten better. Therapy helps."

Emily came around the table and hugged Leah. The horror filling him hearing what Leah went through demanded something. She had endured more pain than he had. "I'm sorry. So very sorry."

Leah shushed him, running a hand over his hair, and cupping the back of his head. "It's okay, Emily. That didn't make me gay. I never felt any attraction to boys anyway. And the sight of one of those... things dangling makes me...twitchy. Um...you know...can we change the subject?" She quieted herself with a drink of her coffee. "I'm sorry to lay that on you this early, but if we have any chance of going further you need to know."

Emily's eyes widened. "Wait, you mean, given everything you still want more? I mean I'd understand if you didn't."

Leah shook her head. "I mean that, Emily, but that's why I don't want to know your other name. I want to see you in my head the way you are now, as my girl. If you're okay with that I think we might have something because I thought we really clicked. But the real question of importance arises...what do we want to do today?"

"Well, before we do too much, I need to get home, shower, change, and especially take my meds. Since I had no idea I'd meet someone, I wasn't prepared. That'll be a great start. Besides, clubbing clothes aren't the best lounge wear, so I want to change."

Leah laughed, the specter of earlier fading, and her eyes brightened. "Emily, you are such a girl."

"What did I say?"

❖

Emily felt better after the shower. He got out a pair of blue and yellow flower panties and slipped them on. Tonight was the support group in Nashville he wanted to go to and if they spent the day together, he wouldn't have time to change beforehand. At least he hoped that was how the day would play out. He scanned over everything he owned, trying to figure out what to wear. He figured denim jeans and a button-down short-sleeved shirt would look good, especially with his sneakers.

He worked his hair into a high ponytail and looked at himself. With the eyebrow shaping, Emily comprehended she looked like a girl. The falsies were a wonderful thing, enabling him to wear bras without looking odd and flat-chested. Leah whistled appreciatively when he walked out. He grabbed his meds and downed them. Leah looked him over. "Do you want to take anything in case I want you to stay?"

Emily blushed and nodded. She grabbed her squad bag and filled it. The idea excited him and he hoped things turned out well, as she really liked Leah.

Once seated in the car, Emily asked, "So where to?"

The grin was so wide it was almost frightening. "Can't tell you because it's a surprise."

He chuckled. This might be fun. When he was in the service, he hadn't ventured off base. Ft. Campbell was a tiny city with a mall, fast food places, and things like gyms or a bowling alley. Now that he was living in town, life was different; he needed to know where places were. If it weren't for MapQuest, he would never find anything. He knew how to get to the mall, coffee shop, massage place, school, and several restaurants. He knew where nothing was in Clarksville and didn't like that.

Leah kept deflecting questions as she fiddled with the CD player. He realized he needed to stop fretting and cope; it was a nice day, and he got to be the passenger instead of drive. Emily sat back and chatted about life, what they wanted to do with their lives. They made it to Nashville, then looped around to the other side before exiting the freeway. Emily wasn't sure what the street name was as she had been looking at Leah, but he did spot a sign for Vanderbilt University where the VA hospital was.

The park Leah drove into was huge. As she weaved to the center, Emily figured it might be as big if not bigger than the town he was from. In front of them was a large white stone building that looked Greek with scaffolding around it. As they pulled in front for parking, he spotted two massive metal doors with carvings on them. He had not known Nashville had anything like this.

Leah got out and headed toward the entrance. She turned and walked backward. "Come on, Em. I know you'll want to see this."

"What is it?" asked Emily, looking up at the building.

"This is the Parthenon, a reproduction of the one in Athens built for the Tennessee Centennial Exposition. Like the original, it houses a statue of Athena," replied Leah as she led them down a slight slope and through the glass doors of the entrance.

Leah bought tickets and led Emily upstairs. Before they turned into the main section, Leah moved in front of Emily and said, "You need to close your eyes, and no peeking. I'll lead you where you need to be to get the full impact."

Emily felt a bit skeptical but did as told. Once his eyes were closed, Leah took one of her hands and led him into the room. Emily could feel the difference between the little alcove and this place. It felt a little crowded due to pressure he was feeling, and he kept expecting to run into someone. Finally, they stopped and Leah turned him. This was weird but he wasn't losing anything by playing along.

"Now open your eyes," whispered Leah.

He opened his eyes and his heart leapt to his throat. When she said statue, Leah had not mentioned it being huge. The sight took his breath away as it filled his vision. He stared, awestruck by the level of detail, his mind struggling to grasp what she was seeing. Finally, Leah nudged him, bringing him out of whatever trance he had fallen into. "Isn't she impressive?"

Emily could only nod. She couldn't take her eyes off her. The statue was breathtaking. Words failed and his brain was trying to process. Leah reached out and turned Emily to face her. "Emily, earth to Emily…come back, sweetie."

Emily blinked furiously, mouth and eyes dry, and registered Leah. "Wow. That is…wow."

"They open the doors for her occasionally so she can look out across the city, the Athens of the South. She's absolutely amazing, forty-two feet high, hell, Nike on her palm is six feet. Every time I see her, she takes my breath away." Leah gazed up at the statue lovingly.

Emily tried to decipher the expression. He had only seen something similar at a tent revival in his teens. Almost everyone had been taken up by some sort of rapture with that look on their faces. Emily didn't get it. He could understand a look of awe being directed to this statue, as it was heart-stoppingly beautiful. But Leah's face was something else. This statue meant something more to her.

Leah looked back at him, a secret smile playing across her lips. "This is one of my special places. I come here when I need to think or get away from all the crap that bothers me. I come and sit with her and everything is better. She helps me get perspective on things, as it's easy to feel small, which I need sometimes, you know?"

Emily looked up at the statue again, at the eyes gazing out into the distance. He did feel at peace here, felt a sort of presence filling the space. He exhaled and let the tension of her thoughts about gender, disability, family, school, and everything fade away. "I see what you mean. She's amazing and you're enveloped by the immensity of her presence. She makes you feel mighty and tiny all at once. Thanks for bringing me here. This is so cool."

Leah took his hand again. "You're welcome, Emily. I wanted to share this with you. It's special to me and you're something special."

She pulled his face closer and kissed her, softly at first, then with more passion. They stood there a while before she let him go. There was something about Leah that made him want to curl up in her arms forever. He didn't feel like a guy with her. She liked being held by Leah. The sensation was nice and he really appreciated it.

She took his hand and lead him around the statue, pointing out details of the Aegis, Nike, and the images on her sandals. Emily was awestruck. Given the fact that the back was as detailed as the front, it was a hell of an accomplishment. She showed him the Elgin Marbles replica in the antechamber and explained what they were. They were also impressive, though not as much as Athena. Maybe it was a matter of scale. There was a feel to this place that wasn't as intense in the antechamber as in the main room.

He realized what it felt like. It felt like he was standing in a church, or one of the mosques in Mosul. There was a presence, watching everything, possibly divine. That troubled Emily, as she never thought that particular feeling could be associated with anything non-Christian. Were pagan faiths real? And given Leah's expression, was she pagan? What would his family think of him seeing a pagan lesbian? Did he even care? "Leah…are you pagan?"

She laughed and faced him. Emily liked the sound. "Yes. I'm pagan and Athena is my primary goddess. Why?"

"The expression on your face looking up at the statue. It made me think of people's faces at a revival."

She glanced at her watch then took his hand and squeezed it comfortingly. "I'll talk about it over lunch. Okay?"

Emily nodded and with that, they left the statue, Leah bowing her head respectfully as they passed.

❖

The restaurant Leah dragged them to was small and not very crowded. The place was nice, and he appreciated the large copper brewing kettles up front. Leah sat across from her, looking amused. "So, what do you want to talk about? The pagan thing?"

Emily nodded. "Yeah. I'm not sure I get this whole pagan thing. Could you help me wrap my head around that? Because everything I grew up with is telling me it's devil worship and I'm sure that isn't what you're doing."

Emily gave the cutest smile that she could manage. Leah chuckled. "Okay, okay…I'll tell. Just no more with the cuteness. It hurts."

Emily felt a sense of accomplishment at doing something cute and distinctly feminine. Part of him still cringed, just as it cringed over the clothes. That part was shouting as loud as it could but muffled as Emily grew more used to being a woman. The voice of worry and self-disgust didn't have much of a chance.

Leah sipped her water and sat back. "Well, in between realizing I had sexual interest in girls and coping with the abuse, I recognized my faith felt hollow, like I was cut adrift. Twelve-step programs ask you to focus on a personal relationship with something greater than yourself, and I wasn't sure I could. See, I was raised Southern Baptist, with very defined roles for people, and a strict version of what God's laws of are. I realized the 'queer threat' ministers were harping about was me and wasn't sure what to do. I started reading all sorts of things, trying to find something that connected to me. After a lot of looking, I found a pagan tradition that made sense, that clicked. This faith I had been taught to fear and despise gave me back something I lost. I knew I could turn to the goddess and she would be there. The goddess saved my life."

Emily thought about what Leah said, measuring the obvious signs of faith against his lack of belief. Nothing was drawing him, as far as he could tell. In fact, the faith he grew up in repelled him. He wasn't sure where to begin to deal with something as monumental as this. But would finding faith help? Could one issue help with another? "So, is it okay to ask about what happened last night? You had me pretty confused."

Leah reached across the table and took Emily's hand. "Emi, it was old ghosts."

"But old ghosts of what? You said something about abuse and it threw me." Emily really was worried. That bit last night about not wanting to see his penis was odd and bothered him, like she didn't fully accept him.

"Like I said, I was abused pretty horribly. There were several times when it was more than one person at the same time. Sometimes just seeing a penis can cause a panic attack, so because of that, my sex toys have to have colors and can not be realistic. I'm sorry, sweetie." She frowned deeply. "It wasn't something I said to hurt you, but rather old ghosts."

Emily felt his heart go out to her, to have come through such a horrible past and seem so together was impressive. And the fact that she slept with him, despite her past stunned him to the core. "Nothing to be sorry about. I understand and can live with it. I'm just stunned that with all of that we…"

Leah smiled and blushed. "Well, you're so hot that, you know, I lost myself in the moment. I had a slight problem with things and then avoided looking. I had fun and certainly want more."

"Me too." Emily smiled, truly happy. She actually felt a connection with Leah. Hell, sex with Deborah had been basically partner-assisted masturbation, certainly nothing like last night. Now that he thought about it, most of his other relationships had been that way, all flash and no bang. He never felt like this in any relationship so far and it was strange, confusing, and wonderful. Was he actually falling in love?

They were lost to their own thoughts for a few minutes while scanning the menu. The waitress came up and they both ordered pastrami on rye with spicy mustard. They stopped and stared. Leah broke the puzzled silence first. "That was unexpected."

"You like them as well?" asked Emily despite the obvious answer.

"Yeah." Leah brushed some hair from her face. "I've liked them since eating at a real deli six years ago."

"The Army served them a couple of times, which was a nice change of pace. I was impressed by both those and Reubens. I never had sandwiches like that growing up, as everything was always on white bread. These are much better than bologna and American cheese," Emily replied.

"So, Emily, how far are you going to transition?"

The question seemed innocuous and she shrugged. "I don't know. I just recently accepted I was trans. I mean I haven't been dressing like this very long, like literally barely over a week. This is the longest time I've been dressed, from last night to now. And by the time we're done and I get home, longer still. The more you use Emily the more it feels like my name." Emily wasn't looking at her as he spoke, rather staring over one of Leah's shoulders. "I don't know how far down the rabbit hole I'm going to go. I do know you don't make me feel awkward. You make me feel like Emily, make me feel real. Ever since last night I've been drinking up that feeling, and I don't want it to end. I'm not sure I've ever felt this way in my entire life."

Leah smiled sweetly, melting Emily's heart. "Emi, honey, you're a real girl and I do cherish you."

CHAPTER EIGHTEEN

Um...what kind of store is Outrageous?" asked Emily, nervously standing in front. The windows displayed books, clothes, DVDs, and music. There even seemed to be a coffee bar. Was this a chain bookstore?

Leah stopped and faced Emily. "An all things LGBT store."

Emily's heart started racing and he leaned away from the store. "Wha...!"

"Emi, it'll be okay. I'll keep you safe from the scary queers." Leah teased her. "Besides, I think I have a solution to that problem we talked about earlier."

That caught his attention. He shifted forward, ready to brave a den of depravity if it meant a solution to the sex issue. She continued. "I figure colored condoms would give me a better illusion of your... you know not being a...you know. I'm hoping it works."

He moved next to her, took her hand, and they entered. Whatever she had been expecting from a fag store, this wasn't it.

The place was clean, well lit, spacious, and not at all a scary den of depravity. The employees and customers looked normal. No one was wearing a trench coat. This could have been any independent bookstore anywhere. She followed Leah deeper inside, past books, movies, music, and other stuff to a door that read: *No minors! Under 18 not allowed! We mean it!*

Leah opened the door and walked in. This room was the scary place Emily expected, where they kept the perverted stuff. There was leather everywhere, bottles of lube, and dildos, lots of dildos. There were so many shapes, sizes, and colors it was almost enough to make him run. Give her Iraqi insurgents any day as opposed to this gay stuff he was still trying to cope with.

Leah walked to the counter and waited for the guy to turn. He had been arranging condoms when he spotted her. "Leah! How've you been?"

"Not too bad, Brad. This is Emily, my new girlfriend." Leah looked over at Emily and smiled sweetly.

That made Emily blush and feel melty happy inside. She smiled at Leah's remark. She was someone's girlfriend. Brad smiled back and that made him nervous, as gay men made her uncomfortable. Brad looked her over and smiled. "Nicely done. She's cute. So, what can I do you for?"

"Do you have any of those colored condoms, the really bright ones? You know the ones I mean, with solid colors?" asked Leah sweetly.

"You know we do, girl. Those club boys can't get enough of them. How many do you need?" asked Brad, all business.

"Can I get two boxes?" Leah asked, looking naughtily back at Emily who blushed more. She was stunned Leah was seriously considering that much penetrative sex with him.

"Not a problem. If there's nothing else, Leah, I'll bring them to the register."

"Thanks." Leah led a wild-eyed Emily from the room. Leah turned his face toward her, trying to stop him being freaked by all the leather and porno. "Earth to Emi, come in Emi."

"Gah! That was...I mean...filled with...Gah!" Emily blurted, stunned by what she had seen, what was implied, and Leah's use of the term girlfriend. Her brain was overloading.

Leah hugged her. She pulled back, still holding Emily's arms and asked, "Have you never been to a sex store?"

Emily shook her head and Leah frowned. "I'm sorry, honey. I didn't know or I wouldn't have done that to you without warning. Come here; let's look at the nice safe music."

They browsed through the music, and when Leah found out Emily had no idea who a number of artists were, she grabbed several CDs. Emily protested, but Leah won pointing out that she had just traumatized her sweetie and needed to make amends.

Emily decided she liked this whole sweetie thing. Soon she was browsing books, and saw a few interesting titles. He found the transgender section and stared like a deer in headlights. He felt embarrassed and yet tried to see if any titles grabbed his attention. He picked up a few non-autobiographical books. Blushing the whole way, she carried them to the register where Leah chatted with the saleslady. He put them down and noticed several other books in a small pile. He peered at Leah and her response was, "Required reading."

Emily figured there was nothing else to do but accept it since Leah was buying. He bought his pile, she bought her even larger pile, and they headed out. She gave him six CDs and three books. "This is a good primer to lesbian culture, which you're now a part of."

"Thanks." He leaned over and kissed her on the cheek.

She started the car and drove past the park again before turning toward Vanderbilt University. They went down a few streets, and she parked in a rundown gravel and torn-up asphalt parking area. It looked terrible, but Leah didn't care. She led him to the main strip explaining, "This area has all sorts of nice shops, a great coffee place, and a few nice eateries. We have a few hours to kill so let's browse."

Emily nodded. If they took their time it wouldn't hurt his leg all that much. Besides, he could see the other end of the shopping area, maybe three blocks at most. He could do that.

They wandered up and down the street, trying on clothes at a few places, and browsed at a great used bookstore that was a lot of fun. Emily wasn't sure when he had more fun shopping. It was nice to spend time with Leah, whether talking or not. Maybe this burgeoning relationship was something he should keep hold of, since he wanted a relationship that meant something. It would be a nice change of pace.

He glanced at his watch and realized the time. "Um, sweetie? We need to eat before we head to that meeting."

Leah turned her wrist over to look at her watch. "Yeah...let's grab a quick bite then go."

"Yeah." He nodded. "But where? Surely there's no food in this area."

Leah chuckled, then looked thoughtful. "If I remember, there are a few burger places out that way. We can head over there fairly quickly. That should get us there on time."

They drove toward the meeting. Emily took a deep breath and let it out slowly, heart pounding as he thought about what he was going to say. "Leah..."

She answered without turning her head, dealing with dense traffic. "Yes Emi?"

"I...uh...thank you for helping me cope with this whole dressing thing. Just being around you makes me less nervous about being dressed like this."

"Like what?" Confusion was clear on her face as she glanced at Emily.

"Like a woman," answered Emily, wondering how Leah had forgotten this simple fact.

Leah sighed, heavily. "Emi, you're a woman, so how else would you dress?"

Emily was at a loss for words. Leah made things sound so straightforward, so simple, that it boggled. Wasn't this supposed to be a big deal? "Leah...uh...I don't know. Through all this, I've been so tangled in my own head that I haven't been able to see clearly. Stacy and Tiffany have been understanding and helpful, but you've just totally accepted me. That's been freaking me out, but I've been completely relaxed all day because of you. When you're around I feel natural, normal, otherwise I'm so nervous I can barely see straight."

Leah reached over and rested a hand on Emily's leg. It was warm and comforting, making him feel less jangled. He continued. "I... maybe I...that is...I think that I might actually be able to reach an understanding about this with your help."

"You're welcome, Emi, but I haven't done anything special. I see you as a woman, so I treat you as a woman. Is there a problem with that?"

"I don't know. I mean, I'm still trying to figure this out. With you, being Emily feels so right, but when alone I'm unsure. Everything I've seen and experienced points to me being transgendered, but am I really?" Emily felt ready to cry and Leah pulled off the road and turned on her hazards.

"Emily, listen to me. Don't worry about me, don't worry about anyone else. You have to do what's right for you. It doesn't matter how I see you, how the world sees you, any of that. All that matters is if this is right for you, if this is making you happy and complete as a human being. If it is, then go and don't look back. If it isn't, drop it and run. Then all you need to ask yourself is…"

"If I feel lucky?" teased Emily.

Leah playfully swatted her on the arm. "No, you dolt. Do you feel happy?"

Emily looked thoughtful for a moment as she juggled that question in her head. The more open smile changed, mouth closing, as the feeling rose up inside. "I'm happy. I really am."

Leah brushed her face softly, holding her chin. "Then maybe you are a woman and should just accept that truth."

Emily laughed. "You make it sound so simple."

Leah stared deep into her eyes. "Emily, the hardest part of coming out is coming out to yourself. That's the first moment you're really free of the shame and fear that all of us feel. From there, you at least know who you are. That is the big question, Emily, who are you?"

Emily took a deep breath and let it out audibly, her mind awhirl as things fell into place. Was it really that simple? She'd thought it before, but it hadn't stuck. "I'm Emily Rhymer and I'm a woman."

Leah hugged Emily tight, congratulating her. She shook in Leah's arms, so close to tears, a bit leaked from the corners. Leah made soothing noises, brushing her hair with a free hand. Something inside of Emily broke and she felt drowned in the rush.

❖

Somehow, even stopping for fast food, they got to the meeting early. They shrugged and used the time to finish eating. Leah turned the radio on, and they sat there holding hands, relaxing. It wasn't a bad way to spend some time, and Emily smiled at the feel of Leah's hand in her own.

Twenty minutes later, a green van pulled up next to them. Two women got out and went to the door, moving as if they knew what they were doing. One pulled a key out from a pocket and opened the door. They went back to the van and started carrying several boxes and a cooler. Leah and Emily both got out of the car. "Hi, I'm Emily, this is Leah. This is our first meeting," Emily said, by way of introductions. "Need some help?"

"Naw, we should be fine. There's just this one load," replied the long-haired brunette, the shorter of the two, while carrying the cooler. Once the ice chest was put down, she turned and extended her hand. "Hi, name's Rebecca. This is my girlfriend, Susan. Welcome to the Vals."

Emily took her hand and shook it. Rebecca had a firm grip. This was repeated with Susan, a bit heavier woman with short blond hair and a genuine, open smile.

Leah and Emily helped set up thirty chairs and a few tables. Once done, Susan handed them temporary badges. "Write your name here. Specifically, the name you want to be called."

Emily felt confused. Wasn't that obvious? "Okay. Anything else?"

"Nope. So, get comfortable. People should get here soon. One of the others will introduce you around, so you can meet everyone. Have fun." With that, Susan went back to arranging name badges on the table.

Leah and Emily took seats and waited. Emily grew more fidgety as the clock ticked forward. Leah rested a hand on her leg, which reduced the fidgeting. Leah leaned over. "Emi, if you're too nervous we can go and do something else. It's entirely your call, sweetie. Remember, a bunch of these people go to the Lounge or Chaps, a gay bar not far from here. They have a nice piano bar where you can sit and listen to music. The rest of that place is a club with a drag show and a members-only leather section. So if you want to go, there are things we can do."

Emily nodded, biting her bottom lip. For all that she could accept herself, being around other transgendered people made her nervous and she had no idea why. Maybe this was something to talk to Doc Richards about. The only downside was she already had more than four sessions' worth of big insights since last night. Thanks to the way this weekend played out, she had deeply accepted herself and started to see herself differently. She hadn't gotten a chance to slow down this weekend and process. Maybe the meeting was one step too far? Should she try next month?

A group of five people came in, chatting together and Emily tensed. Her breathing tightened and she struggled to slow it down.

Her eyes darted a little about the room, which Leah caught. "Emi, are you all right?"

Emily swallowed dryly. Her heart pounded and her breathing got faster and shallower. "I…I don't know."

Leah nodded and rose. She held out a hand. "Come on, sweetie. Let's go outside."

She led Emily back out to the parking lot and over to a picnic bench alongside the building. She helped Emily sit and remained standing next to her, one hand running down Emily's hair, as she rested a forehead against Leah's chest. "You looked like you were about to have a panic attack. Is there anything I can do?"

Emily nodded. "A drink please?"

Leah hustled inside and came back with a bottle of water. A few more people entered with a wide array of appearances, some screamed guy in a dress and others she guessed were there to support someone. She grabbed meds from her purse and swallowed the pills down with the water. Leah held her soothingly, murmuring endearments until her heart began to slow.

Leah looked deep in her eyes. "Do you want to do this?"

Emily nodded.

Leah took her hand. "Ready when you are."

Smiling back, Emily squeezed Leah's hand in thanks. A few more minutes of breathing and Emily felt ready to brave the meeting. They walked inside, still holding hands.

There were a good number of people milling about chatting. One tall blonde dressed in a semi-formal gown, walked up and extended her hand. "Hi. My name's Molly, the membership chair for the Vals. Welcome to the group. Let me introduce you around."

Emily shook Molly's hand and asked, "What does Vals stand for?"

"It's a play on the whole Tennessee Vols thing. You know…UT, the Volunteers?"

Emily shrugged. "Sorry. Not into sports. Besides, the Tar Heels are the only team that matters."

Molly started laughing, dabbing her eyes to keep her makeup from smearing. "Oh my God, that was great!"

Emily snickered while Leah rolled her eyes as Molly led them through the throng, introducing them. Emily lost track of names quickly and just smiled and nodded. Molly introduced a few other officers, then excused herself and headed toward the front.

They got everyone's attention and started the meeting. The first part was introductions and business stuff which Emily fazed out since she had no idea who anyone was. After that, a woman stepped up and spoke about wigs, how to wear and care for them. With the extensions, a lot of this was not useful to Emily. The conversation itself was getting to her, and panic rose a little as she felt weird. A couple other members looked bored, and Emily resolved to talk to them later. Things went on and on, covering lots of information Emily didn't need. Leah was going through her planner.

After an eternity on the differences between real and synthetic hair, it ended and people milled about chatting. Emily made her way through the crowd to talk to the bored people while Leah headed to the ladies' room. "Hi, I'm Emily."

"Tara. Nice to meet you." The girl was a little taller than Emily, with dirty blond almost light brown hair. She looked very much like a real girl. Part of that was the cleavage.

The other woman had black hair, a deep voice, and was a bit overweight. She was dressed rather terrifyingly, like someone snatched from an 80s Robert Palmer music video. "Hey, I'm Becky."

Emily nodded. "The topic didn't interest you?"

Tara shrugged. "The programming varies. There is currently a shift toward more stuff for cross-dressers, since that's a good chunk of the group right now. Two years ago, things were more focused on transsexuals. With each new board the types of programming change."

"That makes sense."

Becky asked, "Goin' to Chaps with us?"

"I think Leah and I are going to the Lounge." Emily searched for Leah and spotted her heading that way. "We off to the Lounge?"

"Yeah. Tonight's acoustic night. There are some good musicians in the lesbian community, and this being Nashville, a lot have a folksy, country sound. Besides, I like picking up new CDs. It's a lot of fun. If we get there early, we can get a good table," replied Leah.

Emily nodded. She liked some of the music Leah played for her. She had never heard of Dar Williams or Sarah McLaughlin before, but they sounded good. Melissia Ethridge, she knew and really liked her stuff. "Okay. See you there?"

Tara nodded and smiled while Becky replied, "No. I prefer Chaps. See you later, kid."

They said their good-byes and headed off, both sighing in relief which made them laugh. Emily thought about the meeting. It had been somewhat interesting, but she wasn't sure how useful it would be. She would talk to Tara more before she made up her mind.

"So, what did you think?" asked Leah as she pulled onto the interstate.

"Some of the people seemed nice, but that presentation…wigs? Ugh. I guess I'll wait and see what I think later," replied Emily, absently rubbed her aching hip. "The people might make up for that though. I honestly don't know. I'll see what happens next month before making a decision."

"Sounds good to me. Let's go have some fun and forget about our cares for a while?" Leah prodded her, making sure Emily was up for this.

Emily smiled and rested a hand on Leah's thigh. "That sounds fun. Today has been one hell of a day."

CHAPTER NINETEEN

Emily smiled as she showered. The weekend had been awesome and life-changing. She spent every day with Leah, and it had been wonderful, especially waking up to that smile. That had been well worth the grief of running back and forth between Nashville and Clarksville for clothes. She had classes today and an appointment with the doc so she had to get moving before the day ran away. Hot water felt good on her bad leg and arm, as they ached thanks to walking with Leah.

She opened her closet to figure out what to wear. She would need to wear guy clothes as she wasn't listed as Emily Rhymer but rather Thomas Simmons. They were stuffed in a trash bag in the back of the closet where Tiffany threw them to make space for her new clothes. She hadn't worn any of them since early last week. Since then, she had been in girls' clothes the entire time, not even noticing from Saturday on thanks to Leah. She paused. Had it really only been a week?

So much in her life changed within such a short span of time it made her head spin. It honestly felt more like a month than seven days. She felt like she had been dragged through the mud and Emily was the one who came out on the other side. She frowned, unsure what to wear. The jeans would be all right, but she wasn't sure which shirt to wear. She sighed and shrugged. They were just clothes…right?

Until she dealt with other issues, she would be living out of two wardrobes. She didn't want that, but she was barely into her transition. She was sure who she was, what she wanted, and what she wanted right now was to get things going.

It felt odd pulling on guys' clothes as that wasn't her anymore. Her weekend had been transformative. Dressing like this felt like cross-dressing. She shook her head to clear it. Instead of boots, she wore sneakers, since the weather was nice.

After dressing, she pulled her hair into a low ponytail, like a guy. It looked odd and she couldn't figure out why. She realized that flat-chested and with her hair up, she looked more in-between male or female, androgynous. Emily wasn't sure she liked looking trapped between genders, a no man's land of conflicting messages. Things felt awkward. Emily wanted a dress for the first day, while Thomas would simply grab anything that smelled clean. She gave up; she wasn't going to be happy with what she was wearing because it wasn't firmly in one world or the other.

Emily grabbed her school backpack that couldn't hold what the squad pack could, but did she need all the crap she used to carry? There was no need for stripped down MREs, extra magazines, spare uniforms, weapon cleaning kit, and other assorted items. She headed to her car, leaning lightly on her cane. This would be odd as it was her first real interaction with other people since her big gender recognition over the crazy weekend. She knew she was a girl, deep down inside, despite any claims from biology, like the bone-deep ache of a long road march with full combat load, and she would do everything to live the way that let her smile.

What would that mean for school? That drew her up short. She couldn't dress like she wanted, at least not yet, but she didn't want to continue the lie. In many ways, she was more Emily than Thomas. And that realization was going to crash on campus at some point. Going in Thomas drag during school would be weird. If she could make it out of a war zone in mostly one piece, she could do this.

After an uneventful drive to campus, she managed to snag a great parking spot that provided easy access to all her classes. Having the handicapped plate was a good thing. She felt nervous, watching other students milling about. What would they think? Could they see the girl in the guys' clothes or would they just see a freak?

They probably didn't care one way or another about anyone but themselves, truth be told. With that, she limped toward her first class. She had three on Monday, Wednesday, and Fridays and two on

Tuesdays and Thursdays. This was going to be a heavy start to the week, and she hoped she could deal with it, as it had been a while since she'd put in a full day's work. Once at Algebra class, she grabbed a seat in the front and sat down happily, stretching her leg out.

The room filled in in bits and spurts, early birds like her near the front and the later ones moving toward the back. Emily got out her notebook and made sure everything was ready, that her pencils had lead, and her textbook was on hand. The military had very specific ideas about how one went to classes, and she was following that model. If it worked why screw with it? She was glad the VA was buying her school supplies, as the books and calculator had cost so much she had thought it had been a mistake. One of her books was about a hundred dollars, which was crazier than Tiffany.

The teacher arrived and class began. Emily turned her attention to the young man standing at the front. Each class went the same: the teacher came in, handed out the syllabus, talked about their expectations, and then handed out a metric fuck ton of homework to be done over the course of the semester. This was definitely more schoolwork than Emily ever had before. It was insane. Her whole family had never gotten this much homework, and this was just one class?

The backpack was heavy, but still lighter than the standard load she carried in the service which meant it was manageable, despite her leg. When she went into the field, she humped an insane amount of gear, ammo, food, and other stuff. It had been a serious gut check to hump at the air assault pace. It was a hard pace, almost a run trying to cover twenty klicks in three hours. And when your ruck was over a third of your weight, it was hard to move and react quickly, but she had done it.

Back at her car, she tossed the backpack into the passenger seat and climbed in slowly. She ached everywhere, especially her leg. With the hills the school was built on, it was the longest amount of walking she had done in a good while. She wanted painkillers so badly she could barely see straight so she dry-swallowed a Vicodin. That should take the edge off enough that Emily could make it through her appointment and back home. It should kick in about the time she hit Nashville.

She arrived at the VA early and waited patiently, massaging her hip and leg, to work the pain out as the Vicodin gave some relief. She wanted to go home and soak, since that usually helped. What she really wished for was a hot tub. Maybe three classes in a row was too much.

Eventually, the doc came out to get her. She grimaced as she limped toward the office, leaning heavily on her cane. She fell into the soft chair she used during these appointments. Dr. Richards looked concerned as she stretched her leg, not to mention seeing the dramatic change in her appearance. "Are you okay, Thomas?"

"I'm fine. Just a long day. I had to hike all over campus and my leg is screaming. The pain will fade in a while." Emily shrugged.

"Okay. So how was your week?" As usual, the doc was poised, notebook and pen ready to take down whatever seemed important.

"Let's see, since I last saw you, I got hair extensions, I've been dressing full-time, I went to a support meeting, then a lesbian bar, and I got my very own lesbian girlfriend." All of this rolled off her tongue, as if she had practiced, which she had. She had been looking forward to his response.

The doc started, clearly surprised. "You've had a busy week. So why don't we go over these things. You've been dressed full-time?"

"At first it was awkward, but I got used to it and it felt...right. I wore girl clothes all weekend and most of the week as well, but straight from Friday on. It was...weird to put these on this morning. They feel wrong."

"Okay. So, what about the hair?"

"Stacy did that as well. You suggested it and I agreed. I've gotten used to this fairly quick. I love how I look. It's like I can look in the mirror and see me. Well, a me in progress, but definitely me." Emily struggled to explain in a way that would make sense to anyone outside her own head. "I've felt more...real this past week than ever before. I...I can't really explain it."

The doc nodded but didn't say anything else.

Emily continued. "I...think this is the happiest I've ever been. I mean, I think of myself as Emily, as a girl now, which is weird. I'm fine with this. I'm Emily and a girl."

"You're really okay? Honestly?" he asked, pen flat on the paper.

Emily thought about her answer. Was she really okay with giving up being a guy? With becoming a girl? The thought of living this way forever made her smile. "Yes. I am."

The doc took some notes. "Now, you also said you had a lesbian girlfriend? How did that come about?" he asked, smiling as he wrote.

Emily described the weekend, meeting Leah, meeting with the Vals, and everything. The doc took notes, making some lines of connection on his paper. "So, you had a good time?"

"Yes, I did, a lot of fun. I've thought about it, and I want to start hormones. I want to become the woman I am and take the next step. This weekend was awesome. I actually felt normal, happy, and things felt...good." Emily wanted to get started with the rest of her life.

"I have no problems with that. I figured you'd be coming to a realization like this soon so I arranged an appointment in two weeks. This should help get you started." With that, he smiled at her and held out a business card. "Here's the address. And the appointment time is on back."

She smiled broadly, happy burbling inside. "Thank you. I... thank you."

"Not a problem. There is no doubt you are suffering from gender identity disorder and continued treatment following the standards of care is completely warranted. Now when you start hormones, pay attention to your body. This is not some great cure-all that will fix everything. If you start feeling weird, let me or the endocrinologist know as soon as possible. Hormones are very powerful and can kill you if misused."

Emily nodded. "I get that. I just want to figure all this out, and being stupid isn't a part of that. So, what should I start doing besides hormones?"

"Well, starting hair removal is a good next step. That way you won't have to deal with stubble when you finish transition. In addition, you should look into getting your name changed. That will help with the real-life test. I also think you need to tell your parents. Dealing with your family is a big step."

Emily's heart skipped a beat. "Um...do I have to?"

"Yes. You need to let them know what you're going through. If you plan on living as a woman, don't they deserve to know before some family function?"

Emily was quiet. She didn't want to deal with her family, as she was sure how they would react to this particular announcement. "My parents…are not the most understanding people about this sort of thing."

"This sort of thing?" asked the doc, leading Emily to say more. He scrutinized her.

"My family is very religious, Southern Baptist. The church back home is very conservative even for Southern Baptists and believes everybody should stay in the place God appointed for them. This justifies all sorts of beliefs against different races, genders, and sexual orientations. I've actually heard my mother say AIDS was God's way of smiting faggots." Her voice shook. "If I call them and tell them, I'll be disowned."

Dr. Richards thought for a bit, glancing down at his notes. "But if you transition, won't they find out and be even more upset? Is it worth it to pretend to be Thomas for them?"

Emily conceded the point. She sighed heavily, agreeing to her doom. "Fine. I'll talk to them and see if they'll understand. But I'm not holding my breath."

"I know it might be difficult, Emily, but in the end, you'll know for sure one way or the other. Isn't that better than being in limbo?"

"I'm not sure. My family means a lot to me, and if they can't accept me, I'm not sure what I'll do. And not knowing scares me." It hurt to admit. She was so used to hiding her feelings and her fear, and now that she was letting it out, it shook her.

"I'm sure the conversation won't be pleasant, but I have something that might help. Why don't you have your girlfriend come over beforehand? That way if it's good you can celebrate and if it's bad you can commiserate. You can be together on doctor's orders. I can write a script if you want?"

Emily blinked in surprise. Would Leah do that? Would she sit there while Emily dealt with a family that might want nothing to do with her ever again? "I…sure, I guess. I can't think of how it could hurt for her to be there, and support would be nice."

"Good. I hate to think of you being upset and alone after that phone call. I know this won't be easy, but it has to be done. True friends would definitely be there for you in situations like this. True family would as well."

Emily tried to think of something else, to take her mind off her parents. "I can also call Tiffany and Stacy. I'm sure they would help. There are a couple of the Vals I'm making friends with. When should I tell my school?"

"About what?"

"About the whole transition thing," said Emily, as if it were completely obvious.

"Well, when you get your name legally changed. The school shouldn't care one way or the other since you're not living in the dorms. You're not going to a church-based school, and they would have no reason to expel you over this. Besides, people change their names to all sorts of things for all sorts of reasons, especially in college. There isn't a need to tell them until they need to know."

That made a good deal of sense. It also kept her out of the spotlight, as she didn't want her private life dragged in front of the whole school. Being known as the trans girl on campus would suck, so she would avoid that. "Okay. I can deal with that."

The doc smiled. "Good. There's no need to cross any bridges before we have to. After all, you might decide this isn't who you are and change back, which isn't unheard of. And no, that isn't a good reason to wait. With your family, you can say this is something you're dealing with and move on from there. Besides, if you're ready for something as permanent as hormones you're ready to tell them."

Emily's hopes were dashed. She thought she had an out, until she found her courage.

"Now, I want to see you again in two weeks. I'll make the appointment and they'll send you a letter. Take care, Emily. Oh…if you're comfortable with it, could you show up dressed next time? I'd like to see how you look."

"Sure, Doc, see you then."

CHAPTER TWENTY

Leah moved into Emily's arms, kissing her passionately. After coming up for air, she asked, "How's my best girl?"

Emily smiled blissfully, as the kiss muddled her head. She kept hold of Leah as she leaned against the wall for better bracing, her legs weak for some reason. "Not too bad. I missed you."

Leah moved free, took Emily's hand, and they skipped into Emily's apartment, well, at least as much as Emily could manage. Emily was pensive as she thought about what Dr. Richards said she should do. She snapped her head up as Leah asked, "Sweetie, what's wrong?"

"My shrink said I should tell my folks about being Emily. I talked to Rebecca from the Vals and got some advice from her." Her nervous tremor was obvious. "The thing is, I want you here when I do this, as I'm afraid things might not go well. In fact, I'm fully expecting this to go badly. I'll need your help afterward, as I…I expect this to end in fire."

Leah looked worried, caressing Emily's head gently. She leaned in and kissed her forehead. "I'm here for you, Emi kitty."

Emily smiled at the nickname and looked at Leah. "Emi kitty?"

Leah blushed, looking at the floor as if caught doing something naughty. "Well, I really like how you look in that sleep shirt, the one with the cats on it? I even brought it up so you could wear it again. So, you're my Emi kitty."

The last bit was at a near whisper and Leah was a bright red. Emily had no problem with the nickname. "I kinda like it. It's cute."

"You do?" asked Leah.

"Yeah. If it works for you, it'll work for me."

Leah sighed in relief. "Thank you. I've been calling you that in my head all week and worried you might not like it. I've had girlfriends break up with me because of the nicknames I come up with."

"No. I like it. Honest. It's okay." Emily limped to the couch and sat heavily, putting her sore leg up and wincing a little as she lifted it. Leah brought in her bags while she rested. She decided to stay with Emily this weekend, instead of the other way around, to hang out with Tiffany and Stacy. Emily watched Leah bustle about. She put something into the fridge, then took her luggage into the bedroom, as if she was moving in slowly.

"Hey," Leah called out from the bedroom. "I got you some things."

"Really? Will I like them?" Emily pushed to her feet before heading into the bedroom using walls and furniture in place of her cane.

"I should hope so." Leah was going through her suitcase to dig out what she wanted. "Close your eyes."

Emily looked at Leah for a moment and then closed her eyes. She was unsure what she might be getting. "Okay. Open your eyes."

Emily's eyes widened at Leah holding a very lacy and frilly teddy with garter straps. She gasped and choked out, "That's for me?"

Leah smiled mischievously. "Well, more like it's my present, but I got it for me to wear and you to unwrap. I think it will look really hot on me and maybe on you as well, and it passed the corner test."

Emily smiled. If it did indeed look good tossed in the corner, then tonight might not suck as much as she feared. Sex with Leah was a treat, despite the need to mask her penis as a dildo. "So, when do I get to unwrap this particular present?"

"Oh, sometime later. Depends." Leah teased her. "I also made you a lesbian starter kit."

Emily sputtered. "A what?"

"Lesbian starter kit. You haven't been a lesbian before, and it would be cruel to let you go off into the wild world of lesbianhood unprepared so I made this starter kit. It has music, books, movies, all the important things you need to know as a lesbian." Leah struggled not to smile. "You'll like them."

"What sort of things? Specifically."

"Well, there is the book *So You Want To Be a Lesbian*, which is a lot of fun. Then some music from Dar Williams, Ani DiFranco, Jill Sobule, um...Melissia Ethridge, the Indigo Girls, and a few others. And some movies: *Better than Chocolate, The Incredibly True Adventures of Two Girls in Love*, and more. These should give you a grounding in what you'll need to know to be a great lesbian." Leah grinned broadly. "I thought of getting you *The Whole Lesbian Sex Book*, but figured I would rather give you lessons instead. I'll do everything I can to help you learn."

Emily blushed at Leah's suggestive tone. "Wow. I don't know what to say. I...I mean, you've just accepted me so completely I can barely understand it."

"Well, I'm the one getting something special, which makes me okay with the work needed," stated Leah, looking up at Emily with a soft smile. "You're becoming more and more special to me. Stacy was right. I had been a bitch before, but once I met you...things changed."

Emily felt better. If Leah could accept her, then certainly her family could. Shouldn't they? She was still the same person, so that shouldn't be a problem...right? She had no answers, which was scary. Facing death in the streets of Al Najaf, Mosul, and other places was far easier than telling her mother she was transgendered.

"So, when are you going to call?" asked Leah.

"I was waiting for you to get here and settled before I started. I wasn't about to do this without you." Emily smiled faintly, having heard the concern in Leah's voice. "I hope that isn't a problem?"

Leah came up and hugged Emily lovingly, kissing her cheek. "Not at all, Emi. Not at all. Everyone in this community knows just how hard this can be. I'm just grateful that my Grandparents don't care now. Whenever you're ready, and not before."

Emily swallowed dryly and got a bottle of water. She took a drink to moisten her dry mouth, heart racing, chest tight, like she couldn't quite breathe. The water helped, as did Leah's hand on her thigh, making Emily think about different things, and stop dwelling only on the negative. She took a deep breath, then let it trickle out slowly, slowing her heart. She repeated it a few more times. She picked up the phone, muttered, "Here we go," and then dialed. Maybe they wouldn't be home?

Her mom picked up on the third ring. "Hello?"

"Hi, Mom."

"Thomas? How are you? We haven't heard from you in a while and were wondering what college is like?" Emily's mother sounded happy, so it was difficult to continue. Could she really say this?

"I'm doing fine so far. The first week has just been introductions and basic stuff. Not a lot of homework yet."

"That's wonderful. Are you still with that girl, Deborah?" asked her mother.

"Not for a while now. I have another girlfriend, Leah." Emily looked over at Leah, who smiled back. "She's really awesome and has been showing me around Nashville."

"That's nice. Will you be coming down on your spring break? You know your family misses you." Emily knew this was coming; her mother always asked this any time she got time off.

"I'm not sure. I have something to talk to you about that might affect my plans." Emily crossed her fingers, hoping this would go well.

"Oh? What's that?" Her mother sounded interested.

"Well, do you remember how withdrawn and reckless I've been the last couple of years? I found the reason and I'm working on getting past that. It isn't easy, but therapy's helping." Emily's heart was in her throat. She felt like she had to force the words out. Leah squeezed her leg comfortingly, reminding Emily she was there.

"Really? That's good, right?" Her mother sounded so concerned, so loving, Emily struggled to continue.

"Yeah, it is. I've really been feeling better about my life, which is a nice change. I'm also starting some new meds next week which should help even more." Emily kept dodging, hoping she wouldn't have to have this conversation.

"Well, what's been causing this, Thomas? It worried me, but I never said anything for fear of making things worse."

"It's called gender dysphoria," said Emily, her stomach roiling.

"What?" asked her mom, the tone of her voice shifting from artificially cheerful to neutral. "Gender what?"

"Dysphoria. That's what it's called." Her voice wavered. This wasn't going the way she hoped.

"I'm not sure I understand, Thomas. Why don't you explain?" Emily didn't think she sounded confused. This was not a good sign. It reminded her of the fight after she joined the Army. Her mother sounded just like then.

"Well, basically, from what my doctor tells me, my brain is likely wired differently. The belief is that I'm showing signs of female brain structure and that means my hormones have been fighting my brain structure, making me a little bit crazy," said Emily, hoping the theory and the medical-ish language would help.

"And what does that mean, exactly?" Her mother's voice was harder still. Emily took a drink of water to moisten her dry mouth. This was going downhill rapidly, like she knew it would.

"Well, what it means is…what it comes down to is that I'm really…a girl." Emily winced, cringing away from the phone. She had done it. Now the fallout.

The line was silent. Emily took Leah's hand. Hers was sweaty and she held her breath; the contact with Leah was calming her slightly. After about a minute of silence, her mother replied, "Is this a joke?"

"Um…no, Mom, it isn't." Emily knew who she was, and come hell or high water she was going to stay the course. At least, she was fairly certain she could, right?

"Thomas, how can you be a girl? I changed your diapers, even when you wet the bed in sixth grade. I know how the good Lord made you," declared her Mom. "The good Lord made you a boy, to live as a man and a husband, not to pretend to be something you're not."

"Mom, sex is the body, gender the mind. My mind is female. That's what makes me a girl. The fact they're opposite is making me crazy. That's why I couldn't fit in anywhere. I felt out of place in my own skin and so I withdrew from others. And in trying to prove my manliness I did stupid things that risked my life, like what I did in Iraq. I'm just trying to make sense of my life and live as myself. That's all."

Leah rubbed at the tension building in Emily's neck. In all honesty, this conversation was going the way she feared it would. She knew her mother would not take this well, but it was too late to back out.

"The Lord doesn't make mistakes, Thomas. He made you a man on purpose. All this other stuff is a sign that the Devil is leading you astray. What you need to do right now is get down on your knees and pray to Him to set you back on the path of righteousness." She was building a head of steam, and Emily knew that was not good.

"Mom, I'm not on the path of Satan. I'm still your child."

"If you really were my son, you'd give up this nonsense, instead of parading around like some prissified faggot. When I tell your father, he might just drive up there and beat some sense into you. Thomas, what in God's name made you such an abomination? There is no way this could be who you are." Her mother was pushing every button to get Emily to recant. "I mean, what would your brother say? He looks up to you. You're his big brother the war hero. Don't do this to little Ritchie."

"Please! I'm the cripple who's his big brother! Like hell does Ritchie idolize me. He despises me for things that happened in high school before I joined up, and you know that." Emily growled, clenching her free hand tightly. Why couldn't her mother just listen?

"Thomas! I'll not tolerate that kind of language."

"Sorry, Mom. I have prayed and I'm following the answers given. I'm being true to myself. Surely the Lord wants that? Right?" Emily pled, looking for some way to make her mother understand.

"Maybe I should have made you play football? Put you in shop class. Something. Was that what I did wrong?" Her voice was full of worry, as if she were the cause, as if something she had done or not done was the deciding factor.

"Mom, I played football for two years in elementary, and the Army taught me plenty about cars. I took shop class. I built that clock in the kitchen. You didn't do anything wrong." Emily seesawed from pleading to arguing. Things were not headed toward a good end, not unless a miracle occurred.

"Thomas, how? We raised you boys the same. Ritchie is normal and you...you've become this..." Her voice failed.

"This what, Mom? This girl?" asked Emily, hope fading.

"This abomination!" Emily heard the first sob from her mother.

She was trapped between wanting to comfort her mother and screaming. "I'm not an abomination. I was your son and now your daughter. I'm still your child, Mom, still the same person. I am following the path of truth God has shown me, isn't that what I'm supposed to do?"

The line was quiet again. Emily worried, heart racing, a death grip on Leah's hand. "Mom?"

"No child of mine shall be an abomination. Either give up your evil ways or get behind me, Satan!" The voice was full of steel, with a deep rage Emily only heard on the battlefield, and thankfully never directed toward her. Until now.

Blood drained from Emily's face. Did her mother really mean that? Would she simply kick Emily to the curb because of this? "Mom, you don't mean—"

"Yes, I do." Emily was cut off sharply by her mother. "Thomas, if you can't let this perverted fantasy go, then you're no God-fearing child of mine. You're a boy, and no amount of pretending will change that. God made you a boy and you'll always be a boy!"

Emily growled low, worry and fear turning to anger. She had tried reason so now she had to take the next step. "I'm not a boy! My name is Emily and I'm your daughter!"

The line was silent again in Emily's hand. When her mother spoke, her voice was harder and harsher than anything Emily heard before. "You're not my daughter or my son. I don't know what the hell you are, you abomination, you perverted filth! Don't call unless you have begged the Almighty for forgiveness and have changed these filthy ways and returned to the path of righteousness."

"Are you disowning me? All over whether I'm a boy or a girl? You can't be serious, Mom." Emily didn't want this. She loved her family even though they made her crazy and never understood her.

"I am. Thomas, may Almighty God help you to find your way back from this foul state. I love you, Thomas, but don't call again until you've been healed of this…perversion." The line went dead.

Emily sat stunned, the dial tone loud. She couldn't believe her mother disowned her. Was this some sick joke? Why couldn't her mother make the simple leap and see Emily as her child, desperately in need of her mother to say things were all right? Was there something wrong with her? Was she tainted, cast out by God? Was that why she almost died in Iraq? Her family didn't want her, thought she was perverted filth. If blood didn't want you, who would?

Leah took the phone from Emily and tossed it in the direction of the base. It had started saying "If you would like to make a call please hang up and dial again." Emily was bawling, sniffling wetly, tears burning down her face. Once the phone was moved, Leah took Emily in her arms and whispered soothing words of love and comfort. Emily began to cry harder, sobs wracking her body, howling her pain. She felt abandoned, like the toy nobody wanted, a pet abandoned by the side of the road.

She wept for who knows how long, warm in Leah's arms. Emily clung to her, like she was a lifeline, a rescue from this morass she found herself in. Eventually, the sobs petered out, leaving only sniffles. She looked up at Leah, her heart and spirit so lost. Leah looked at her with understanding on her face as she wiped away Emily's tears and kissed her forehead, repeating over and over, "It's going to be okay, Emi."

Emily sat slowly and moved from Leah's arms. Her eyes and face burned, and she was thirsty. She downed the bottle of water. She looked at Leah. "Can you get me more water…please?"

Leah headed to the kitchen and returned with the water and a wet washcloth. She wiped salty tears from Emily's face. With a faint smile, she placed the washcloth on the back of Emily's neck.

Emily finished the water before facing Leah with a weak smile. "Well, that went as expected. Thanks. I don't know how I could've done that without you."

Leah's smile was gentle and honest. "You would have managed. I believe in you."

Emily's eyes welled up again. "Thank you. It means a lot. I can't believe she said those things."

"Parents say some stupid things when they get too wound up. I actually got thrown out of my house when I came out. They completely flipped. Of course, my girlfriend and I making out in their bed didn't help, but, nobody's perfect."

"Did they ever forgive you?" asked Emily.

"Yeah, they did. It took a few weeks, but my grandparents calmed down. We talked and talked and then went to therapy and managed to forgive each other. If I had trusted them in the first place maybe things would have been different," said Leah, running fingers through the hair framing Emily's face.

"Things got better?"

"Yes. My mother and I are on decent but shaky terms. In fact, when my ex dumped me, she asked if I wanted a guy or a girl, since she hopes I'm secretly bisexual, which I don't know what to make of. I told her about you and said I was getting the best of both worlds." Her comment made Emily chuckle. "But she really wants to meet you."

Emily eyes widened. "She wants to meet me? But I'm nobody special."

"You're special to me and that's all that matters to her."

"Thanks. You really are the best. I've never had a girlfriend as awesome as you."

She chuckled and replied modestly, "I try."

Emily smiled, growing more animated as Leah distracted her. "You take such good care of me. I really appreciate that."

"Thank you, sweetie, but how about we go out to eat? Grab some food, something to drink, come home, cuddle and sleep. I plan on ravishing you tomorrow and Sunday before I head home so maybe we should build up your strength."

Emily smiled, then snickered slightly.

"Why don't you go splash some water on your face. That should help get rid of the blotchiness. Okay? Then dinner is on me." Leah made everything sound like the most normal thing in the world.

Emily rose from the couch and hobbled to the bathroom, using the wall for support. She ran cold water and filled both hands. She lowered her face into that and felt the cold leach away some of her turbulent emotions. She rubbed gently and did it again, each pass soothing her a little more. Emily looked in the mirror as she dried. The face that looked back didn't seem familiar. The eyes seemed off and her face didn't look good, almost as if she were staring at a stranger. She immersed her face in cold water a third time and looked up again.

Emily didn't look or feel as bad as she had; the cold was helping her pull back from the shock. Her stomach gurgled angrily. Prior to the call, she had been too nervous to eat. There were a few buffet places by the mall, which might work, but Emily would have to ask Leah if that was okay. That way she could load her plate up with all the comfort food she could imagine and fill the ache in her heart with food.

After a deep breath, she let it out slowly, breathing like the relaxation exercises said. After another few breaths, she peered deeply into her eyes and said, in a voice full of certainty, "My name is Emily Rhymer. I'm a woman and I'm happy. Fuck them."

CHAPTER TWENTY-ONE

S he really said that to you?" asked Stacy, shocked.

Emily nodded slowly. She was in Leah's arms on the couch as she hadn't been able to leave the house after all. All her nerves and stress rose back up when she made it back to the living room. Stacy and Tiffany rushed over once Leah called. Tiffany was in the kitchen cooking.

"I'm so sorry. I wish you didn't have to go through this. Not everyone's parents are asshats when coming out. Mine just laughed and said they knew," said Stacy.

Emily shifted, uncomfortable with being the focus of attention. "It was also the way she said it, like I was some sort of bug needing to be squashed, like I ceased to be a person."

Leah hugged Emily and kissed her head. "It'll be okay. You have friends and can just relax and recover. I know it won't be easy, as family can cut us worse than any stranger."

Tiffany chimed in from the kitchen. "That's because they installed the buttons."

Emily chuckled. "Well, she certainly pushed all of mine. It was difficult sticking to the truth, as I felt like I had to keep justifying myself. If she hadn't been making me mad, I probably would have caved and told her it was a joke."

"This may be the only time when getting mad is actually a good thing," said Leah. "I'm very proud of you, sweetie. It took a great deal of courage to even make the call."

Emily shrugged; it didn't feel courageous. "But it wasn't worth the effort."

Leah turned Emily's face toward hers and stared intently into her eyes. "It's worth the effort for you, not her. If she's dumb enough to turn her back on her child, then screw her. Her loss, not yours. Just coming out to her is good for you however it falls out. It makes you stronger, and just think, you no longer have any reason to hide who you are."

Emily mulled that over. What was there to get in the way of her discovering this part of herself? Maybe Leah had a point. "Well, there is that. It just hurts."

Stacy rested a hand on her knee. "Emily, everything worth doing hurts in one way or the other."

Emily nodded, having heard a similar sentiment in the Army. The others made a lot of sense and it was difficult countering their points. "You're right. Maybe I should stop worrying and move on?"

"Yay!" Tiffany cried out from the kitchen. The others smiled. Stacy looked at Leah. "So, how are things with you two? Did either of you spend any actual time apart?"

Leah rolled her eyes. "Of course we did, Stacy."

Stacy chuckled. "What, like going to the bathroom? Like this week? Come on, you two seem too cozy for people who met last weekend."

Leah smiled strongly. "Well, yeah. It feels like I've known her a lot longer than two weekends. It's hard to explain. She just feels right."

Emily nodded. "There's just something. It's as if when we met, I'd seen her somewhere before and not in that cheesy way. I've never hit it off so well with anyone, like I've known her for years."

Stacy looked thoughtful as they smiled at each other. Emily remained snuggled with Leah. She thought over the phone call and started to see all the blame was on her mother. She was being true to herself, true to her truth, which was a change, as she usually told whatever lies would keep things from erupting. Emily tried to explain, but her mother wouldn't give her a chance. What more could she do?

Leah was still stroking her hair. Emily liked that, liked how Leah took care of her, made her feel safe, loved, and she needed that, though she'd never been aware of that need before. Being macho, aggressive, and all that had felt odd and a bit unnatural, but that was how she knew to be a man. Her father had been that way, as had every guy she ever met. She didn't miss that.

So much had changed it made her head spin. She was still getting used to the face that looked back. Leah accepted her at face value. She was someone who had never known her as Thomas and had no memories of her trying to be strong and manly. It was liberating.

Tiffany called out. "Soup's on!"

Leah said, "We're having soup?"

Emily smiled at the playful exchange. She felt like everything was right in the world, and after that phone call, she needed that.

❖

Emily looked at the business card again to triple-check the address. This was the place and the time. She walked in, leaning on her cane nervously. The small waiting room had a sliding glass window in front of the receptionist, and there were several chairs against the walls and a coffee table off-center piled with magazines. It was a basic waiting room. She went to the window and smiled at the receptionist. "Hi, my name is Thomas Simmons. I have a three thirty appointment."

The dark-haired woman scanned the list and checked off the name. "I have you. They'll call you back when they're ready. Please fill this out."

Emily took the proffered clipboard. It was weird going by Thomas after being Emily for the last couple of weeks. She no longer thought of herself as Thomas and was fine with that, but hearing her old name was strange.

She finished the forms on the clipboard, handed it back, then grabbed a magazine. She flipped through the articles, more as some way to channel her nervous energy than to actually read them. She was more worried/excited than she cared to admit. Would the doctor say no? Would they say yes? She wanted this to work.

A nurse opened the door and called her back. Usually, the VA was backlogged so she hadn't expected to be seen almost on time. After years in the military and time spent with the VA, this was strange. Emily smiled at the nurse and limped to the examination room. The stress made her leg hurt more than before and she wanted this whole ordeal to be over with.

The nurse quickly took all the usual preliminary information before leaving, saying the doctor would be there shortly which was nurse for "get comfortable."

She looked around the room, hoping the wait wouldn't be long, as her nervousness was growing. About fifteen minutes later, the door opened after a brief knock. "Mr. Simmons?"

When Emily nodded, the doctor extended his hand. It was a strong, firm handshake. "I'm Dr. Jones, the endocrinologist helping you through this. I got the letter from your therapist and he faxed over your medical history. I see no obvious problems with your health at this point, so if you want to proceed, we have several options. You can do shots, pills, or both. Some people do better on one than the other, so we can try things out at first to make sure you're tolerating the meds."

This was going really fast, but if he had gone over her medical records, then it should be fine. "Maybe I should go with both."

The doctor nodded. "A popular choice. You'll get the shots every two weeks. You can come here to the office and the nurse will give you the shot. That simple, yes?"

Emily was confused. The doctor made her think of a used car salesman for some reason, which was disconcerting. She didn't want something this important be dealt with by a smarmy salesman. "Okay."

"Great. I need some labs drawn to provide a baseline and the nurse will come in for that. And after the blood draw you get the shot and your prescription. Any questions?"

Emily nodded. The doctor moved so fast it was almost too hard to follow. Was he related to Tiffi? "Um…yes. Can I get estradiol instead of Premarin?"

"Given that I prefer my patients to use estradiol, that should be easy. I don't prescribe Premarin for the simple fact that I can't stand the idea of what it is made of. The stuff works great for some patients, but I'm not a big fan. Besides, when we test the hormone levels, we're looking at estradiol levels." The doctor made a very exaggerated ick face at the mention of Premarin.

"That works for me." The whole process of starting hormone replacement therapy seemed painless overall and not like she had pictured. She figured there would have been more hoops to jump through before getting approval.

The doctor smiled broadly. "Now there are some things I want you to watch for: rapid mood swings, feeling really out of sorts, nausea, vomiting, and the like. Let me know if you're experiencing anything like that. We might have to stop the HRT for the good of your health if that happens. However, don't fret, if you can't tolerate this particular mix of hormones, we can try a few other combinations before saying it isn't going to work. And if it doesn't work…well, there are always other options."

Some of the side effects surprised Emily. Rapid mood swings? Vomiting? Had she really thought this whole thing through enough? Was she leaping without looking?

"Remember, this is basically going through puberty on purpose a second time, so be aware of that. Now, is there a name you prefer your records listed under? We do that for the comfort of the client."

"Yes, Emily Rhymer." He nodded and made a notation.

"Great. I want to see you back in a month, to check on things. Please let me know any unpleasant side effects. We can always change the meds around, stronger, weaker, different brand, so don't fret. When the nurse comes back, she'll draw blood, give you the shot, and the prescription for the estradiol and the spironolactone. That should get you started. All the directions will be on the labels. Nice to meet you, Emily. Good luck." The doctor bustled out of the office after shaking her hand again.

Emily breathed a sigh of relief. She was ready to cry as she made another way point on this journey. Maybe things would work out? After everything else, good news was nice. The nurse came in with the basket of needles and tubes she had grown to loathe back at Walter Reed. "Ready?"

Emily nodded. It was actually happening. A wave of euphoria filled her.

The nurse drew blood with a minimum of fuss, taking several tubes. It wasn't the best blood draw, but it wasn't anywhere near the worst. She lowered her pants for the shot. Some of the vaccines prior to deployment had hurt worse. The nurse rubbed the area briefly to work the medicine in and put a Band-Aid on the spot. Emily turned to look and saw the Barbie Band-Aid. It made her grin.

The nurse handed her the prescription. "Now, remember, pay attention to side effects. They're not fun and most can be easily dealt with. With the Spiro remember to drink plenty of water. We'll see you back in two weeks."

Emily nodded, wondering if the shot would make her feel different right away. "I'll see you then."

Leaving, Emily felt wonderful, on her path to becoming whole. Her smile was so broad it ached. She didn't care. She paid for her visit, since the VA wasn't covering this, and headed back to school. After classes, she would pick up her new prescription and her journey would continue.

The day lasted forever, each minute dragging like an eternity of boredom. She felt antsy all day, wanting to rush off and get her hormones, which would help her become the woman she was supposed to be. When class finally ended, she limped quickly to her car and drove to the pharmacy, jittery with excitement. She handed in the prescription and then browsed until they called her name.

She walked up to a register and gave her name. The attendant turned and grabbed a bag. The girl in the lab coat scanned them and asked, "Do you have any insurance?"

"No, I don't. I'll be paying."

"Okay. The total is three hundred and seventy-five dollars for both prescriptions. Any questions?"

Emily gasped. "You're joking."

"I'm afraid not. That's why I asked about insurance. That would drop the costs a lot. Do you still want them?"

"Yes," grumbled Emily. She dug through her backpack and pulled out her checkbook. She wrote out the check and handed it over. She took her meds and hobbled to the car, bitching. The cost of her meds was insane. There was no reason for it and was highway robbery. She glanced at the clock and realized she could call Leah. Once she got her, Emily ranted about the meds until she calmed down and returned to her apartment.

Leah took this all in stride. "Okay. But do you have your meds?"

"Yes," huffed Emily.

"Then what's the problem? You have them despite the cost. I don't see the issue. If it's just the cost, why not buy them from Canada? I've heard you can get some good savings on meds from there." Leah's voice was calm and reasonable.

"Canada?" Was that legal?

"Yeah. We'll look into it before you need a refill? That way we can get cheaper meds instead of spending a fortune." It made sense and sounded like a plan. Even though she had a lot of discharge money left, she didn't want to spend it stupidly.

"Okay, we can do that. The cost is insane."

"I know, Emi. But we'll find a way."

"I know…it's just the principle. That and it ruined my excitement over getting my first hormone shot today. I was giddy until this bullshit." It had been nice feeling a sense of accomplishment. It had been as good as taking her first unassisted steps after her injury.

"I'm sorry, sweetie. I'll take Friday off and come see you Thursday night? That means you get me in two days instead of three. Yes?"

"Yes, please. I can't wait to see you."

"Okay. I'll do that then. I miss you, Emi."

Emily could hear the emotion in the words. "I miss you too. So, I get you on Thursday?"

"Yep. I'll head up after work. See you soon, love." Leah hung up. Emily sat there stunned. That was the first time Leah said she loved her. Maybe this relationship was turning serious. Was she ready?

Leah loved her. Leah *loved* her. Emily was certain she loved Leah; she just hadn't gotten her courage up enough to say it. Saying it had killed a relationship before and she didn't want to screw it up by rushing in too fast. And to just casually call her *love*…

She felt warm inside and forgot about the cost of her meds. Leah loved her. *Leah* loved *her*. Emily floated through dinner and took her first pills right before bed. Maybe the day ended up in the positive column after all.

CHAPTER TWENTY-TWO

Emily sat on the couch with her notebook, bad leg stretched out, the other bent to provide a writing surface. She was halfway through a poem and struggling with the next line. The poem glacially worked its way out, and she tried to avoid forcing it. It was about the conversation with her mother, the first lines made that painfully clear, but she wasn't sure if it was connected to anything else.

> Your words tore
> the home I built
> in my heart
>
> I thought you
> might see me
> before your eyes
>
> You surprised me
>
> In your version
> a failure, perversion
> a broken thing

Emily examined the pain she felt. Nothing leapt to Emily's mind as she scanned the lines yet again.

She grabbed her water from the coffee table and took a swig to settle the slight nausea. What was the big question in this? She loved her family and her mom's words stung. She was surprised by her mother's refusal to deal with the new her, but she shouldn't have been. Emily was true to herself and had been taught how important that was by her parents, simply being the person her parents raised. Why couldn't her mother see that?

She looked over the few lines. Maybe...? She picked up her pencil and continued.

I thought Love
might reveal me
your child

You surprised me

That wound
still bleeds

She read it a few times more times. It felt finished, like things connected. Writing was helping her cope: the transition, her family, Leah, her friends, PTSD, being crippled, everything that happened since that rocket-propelled grenade exploded. There were so many things clouding the issue and writing let her sort her feelings and thoughts.

This had worked since middle school when Mrs. Parrish, her English teacher, introduced her to poetry. She read a number of different poems, and something about them clicked. She kept this from pretty much everyone, since it was such a "girly" pastime. Butch men did not write poetry. She read and wrote a lot, using it to reduce the pressure inside.

Emily closed her notebook and limped to her computer, leaving her cane against the couch. She laid the notebook next to the monitor and while the system booted up headed to the kitchen for more water. Since getting on antidepressants and other meds, she drank more. When she asked about it, the VA said it was a common side effect. At least she was going to be well hydrated. The Army certainly harped on it enough.

Overall, she was fine. After nearly a year drinking nothing but water and Army coffee in the desert, it didn't faze her. She drank less than she had in country, but it didn't get nearly as hot here. Her Camelback sat unused in her closet and she kind of missed it. Not being able to hike or run removed its need, but she couldn't throw it away. It had been an important part of her life as an infantryman. Then she remembered Leah bought a water filter for the kitchen sink. She wouldn't use so many plastic bottles and could keep her Camelback. It would save money and be good for the Earth.

Emily frowned as a stray notion started a cascade of thoughts. She hated this, hated not being able to run, jump, climb, do all of the things she had been able to do before getting blown up. Saving her friends had been worth it, that wasn't a question, but the results of that would be with her forever. One moment of idiotic bravery in combat changed the rest of her life.

She sat in her desk chair and went to her email, hoping to distract herself. There wasn't a lot. She had occasional comments on her LiveJournal and rare emails from friends in the unit. But the journal was new and only Tiffany, Stacy, and Leah had her email address besides the unit.

Her unit was due back to Fort Campbell in about three months. It was a long time in a combat zone. She knew she had to tell them about who she was now but had no idea how. How could she explain this so they would understand?

The sergeant sent an email. It was good to hear from him and catch up on the news from the front. Access to email in the field was spotty, and there were a few positive stories about interacting with the locals. What she read chilled her to the core: *Check the news.*

A message that short meant bad news, seriously bad news. It also meant they were not allowed to comment. She opened another tab and brought up her news server. There had been an attack on various units in their area of operation. Knowing what to look for, Emily quickly brought up the story. It showed three members of her unit had died when an IED shredded the bottom of their Humvee. The vehicle tumbled and crashed into a wall. One person had been severely wounded, but the other three never had a chance. They were torn to shreds by the bomb and shrapnel. The screen got blurry. She wondered which friends she lost forever?

Numb, she dialed the dayroom of the rear detachment, hoping for answers. The phone was answered on the second ring. "Delta Company, Second of the Five-Oh-Deuce."

"Hey. This is Sergeant Simmons. I read about the attack on my team. Who got hit?"

"Let me get the NCOIC," replied the orderly.

A minute or so later, another voice came on the line. "Staff Sergeant Waite."

"Staff Sergeant, this is Sergeant Simmons. I out-processed a few months ago due to combat injuries. I saw the news and I'm trying to find out who the casualties are." Emily hoped the staff sergeant would let her know. After all, until her injury, they were her family and she would have died for them.

"Sergeant, you know I shouldn't do this," said the staff sergeant.

"I know, but I don't want to discover it through the news. I want to hear it from another ground pounder." Emily wasn't sure how this sergeant would go about things. It was a risk, as this was a breach of OPSEC. Plus they had only talked a few times and she didn't have a feel for him.

Staff Sergeant Waite sighed. "If I get screwed for this you better come testify. Devlin, Tompkins, and Waltrip were KIA and Stevens was injured. Sorry about that. They're coming home soon."

"Thank you, Sergeant." Emily hung up and began to shake.

She remembered playing spades with them, since it was her team. Stevens was new so had to be her replacement. Waltrip wasn't very good at the game and almost always lost, which was why he was invited in the first place. He had been Emily's best friend in the Army and now he was dead, because of some cowardly insurgent. Rage filled her. She wanted to hurt those responsible. She wanted to go back to Iraq and gun down those who had done this. It didn't matter if it was Al Qaeda or some upset Iraqis, she wanted to get them. But her injuries made her impotent, weak, worthless. She couldn't do anything except sit there and hope her team was all right.

The couch creaked as she dropped onto it. Her body shook. Why hadn't she been there? If she had been there, she could have…

could have…could have what? An IED killed them, not enemies you could defeat. If she had been there, she would have been one of them. Waltrip and the others died in a completely random act of violence aimed at anyone. It had been impersonal and senseless and that was worse.

Emily pounded the couch. Fury and grief filled her until she was drowning. Why couldn't Waltrip have been the one injured and not dead? Why did the fucking new guy get to live? It was unfair. She screamed, muffling it with a pillow.

She hated her injury, hated the fact she hadn't been there. She kept hammering the couch, wishing there was something or someone she could hit that would magically make everything better. What good was a crippled infantryman? She was a useless lump. She had been worth something before and now she was just broken.

It hurt like her brother had died. In many ways, Waltrip had become her brother, and not just in arms. They had talked about all sorts of things, plans for when they got home, women they slept with or wanted to, movies, songs, games, everything. Her own brother, Ritchie, had never been as close to her as Waltrip had. Talking about her transition was a conversation she had feared and hoped for, but now would never be. She wished there was blood, gore, something that could show her pain, some way for others to see how much she hurt. Emily lay there, weakly hitting the couch, weeping, lamenting the injustice and desperately wanting her friend back.

❖

The pounding grew louder. Emily slowly pushed herself upright and rubbed her eyes. The bothersome noise was coming from the door. She snatched her cane and hobbled over, feeling old with her leg on fire. She opened the door and saw Tiffany smiling broadly. "Hey there."

Tiffany's smile and enthusiasm faded as she looked at Emily. She put a hand on Emily's arm. "What's wrong?"

Emily relied on her cane more as she made her way back to the couch. Every joint ached. She felt muffled, wrapped in cotton. Surely she was bleeding due to how much this hurt? "My unit got hit yesterday. Three were killed and one injured. One of them was my best friend."

Tiffany pulled her into a hug. "I'm so sorry, Em."

Emily heard the sincerity and gave Tiffany a half-smile. "Thank you. There was nothing anyone could have done. An IED destroyed their vehicle."

Emily kept talking, noting how flat her voice sounded. Tears trickled down her face along familiar routes. "The explosion tore apart the unarmored bottom of the Humvee. I hope it was sudden because that's no way to go."

"I'm sorry, so sorry. I wish there was something I could do." Tiffany helped Emily to the couch. "Do you want me to call Leah or Stacy?"

Emily shrugged. She was lost in Iraq. Seeing the color of sunrise over the desert, inhaling the dry smell of ever-present sand, hearing the sound of the call to prayer over loudspeakers. She remembered the way parts of the cities were modern and parts seemed unchanged for hundreds of years. She began to feel the heat from a burning car they moved past on patrol. She could hear the crackle of the flames as the upholstery was consumed. Emily barely registered what Tiffany was saying, all she could think about was Iraq, her unit, the life she left behind, the smell of cordite, the crack of gunfire. Various Iraqi faces ran through her mind, other memories arising, the shopkeeper's terrified face, the little girl's surprise.

She shook, uncontrollable tremors rocking her. So much had happened her brain wanted to shut down. She accepted the pills and glass of water pressed into her hand. The water tasted dusty, like the water in Iraq. Everything had the faint taste of dirt, of sand. She cried, carried by memories into the desert.

❖

"This one shouldn't be too difficult. We need to start winning hearts and minds. Until we get Hussein, we have to be wary of him regaining support. If the people support us, then we have less to worry about. So be nice, take good care of the translator, and stay safe. Got that?" asked their lieutenant.

"Hooah!"

They left the fire base and rode to their patrol site, falling into formation as they spread out ensuring no single attack would catch all of them. They could have used vehicles for this, but they wouldn't have been able to really look at things, to see any details that warned of an attack. The translator from the 311th hovered near the LT to provide language support if they had a chance to interact with civilians. This was supposed to be a mercy trip and security patrol, not a tactical strike, but they were still armed to the gills with plenty of reloads.

They ran into a group of Iraqis who seemed interested in what the LT was saying. Some building, hospital, or church had been destroyed during the fighting and they wanted a new one. Rhymer heard the LT say it would be taken care of as he faced away from the conversation, scanning his sector. He could hear the platoon sergeant grumble something about making more work for them. The translator was talking back, sounding more stilted than the others. Something else to isolate them from the locals.

They stayed put for almost forty-five minutes, while the conversation went on, the LT occasionally calling for guidance from the captain. Finally, after an eternity of talking, they moved out and started walking to the checkpoint where their ride was.

The radioman fell as a shot rang out. Somebody yelled the obvious. "Sniper!"

They opened fire on the approximate position, hoping to either flush the sniper or kill him, moving forward in leapfrogs. Rhymer's team held back to provide support for the field medic treating the radio operator. It was a minor wound overall, a clean shot through the meat of his leg. The team scanned everywhere, hoping no one else would open fire on them.

The radio worked, so the translator called for medevac and support. The gunfire finally stopped with sudden silence. It felt unnaturally quiet after the exchange, eerily so. The blood congealed in the dirt and Rhymer couldn't help taking in all the details: blood on the street, heavy smell of cordite, hum in his ears from the gunfire, dry taste of dust, the weight of his gear. He kept forcing himself to look away from the radioman and continue to scan for anything heading their way. Despite the lack of gunfire, his heart raced, and he felt a rush of adrenaline. He wanted to move, feeling exposed.

Waltrip looked over and grinned. "Looks like yet another clusterfuck, eh, Rhymer?"

He smirked in response.

❖

After a while, Emily noticed someone's fingers moved through her hair in a very soothing, gentle motion, and her head was in someone's lap. Something fuzzy was in her arms clutched tightly. This confused her and she lifted her head slightly.

She opened her eyes and sat up, realizing she was in her apartment. Her leg throbbed. Tiffany and Stacy were sitting at the table looking worried. Leah was in her work clothes, sitting next to her, brushing her hair. They looked at her with concern and Leah asked, "Hey, Emi, you okay?"

Emily wiped her face as she thought. Something else was more important than her pain and that was a good thing. "What happened?"

"That's what we were wondering," said Leah. "Tiffany came over to hang out and you were freaking out over something. She got your anti-anxiety meds, then called us. We got here as fast as we could and tried to wake you. We were getting ready to call 911 if you hadn't gotten better in a bit. It really scared us."

Emily thought back over what happened earlier and frowned, memories rushing in. "My…my best friend was killed in Iraq."

Leah hugged her tightly. "Tiffany mentioned that. Sounded like you had a flashback or something."

Emily pondered that. When things overwhelmed her, were they really flashbacks? It made sense, not that it helped any. "I guess so."

Leah leaned in and kissed her forehead softly. Emily smiled weakly. "Thanks for the concern, everyone."

Stacy smiled and shrugged. "Hey, what are friends for."

Emily saw the apprehension on their faces. It was obvious this episode had frightened them. Maybe she should do something to thank everyone? Dinner might be good. And a night out might let her take a break from her grief. Besides, the idea of spending more time with Leah was a good one. She wanted to get away from the pain, get some greater distance, so it would hurt less. "Let me thank you for looking out for me by taking us all to dinner."

Leah smiled at the idea. Tiffany and Stacy looked at each other and Tiffany said, "We don't have anything else planned."

"Thanks. Let's go. I'm hungry." Emily used her cane to lever herself upright.

"Where to?" asked Stacy, as she slung her purse onto her shoulder.

"Whatever you want. I'm buying," said Emily.

Leah looked worried but nodded. "First, go wash your face. I can't have the girl I love go out with tear streaks down her face. People might think I beat you."

CHAPTER TWENTY-THREE

So, how have you been doing?" asked Dr. Richards, settling himself into his chair.

"Not bad. The endocrinologist is happy with my blood levels. My thinking cleared, which is odd. It's sort of, like…as if a fog I didn't know was there lifted. I…feel better is the best word I guess, and I keep being surprised by smiles. For no reason, I smile. It's weird."

"What's so weird about it?"

"It's just that I hadn't realized I never smiled. It's like I was so used to being miserable it never registered. It was the way things were. I guess I buried my gender issues so deep all I had left was my unhappiness."

"Okay. And you feel like this unhappiness has lifted?"

Emily nodded. "Yeah. I'm starting to feel like myself, like whatever was holding me back is gone. I like it. The thoughts clearing thing is strange, but now I understand things that eluded me and it happened suddenly."

The doc returned the smile. "Are you still being only Emily with…Leah?"

"Yes. I'm living two lives right now. I'm Thomas at school, the VA, and any time I go on post. The rest of the time, I'm Emily. It's odd and stressful juggling my life like that. It feels like Thomas is the lie and Emily the truth." She brushed some hair behind her ear. "Putting on guy clothes feels awkward and I don't like it. It's weird, like I'm cross-dressing."

The doc nodded. "I know it's a bit early, but do you want to officially start the real life test?"

Emily sputtered. "B-But I thought I had to be on hormones for at least six months? I've only been on them for two."

"I know. But the meds seem to be going well, and if you're living full-time for the most part, then what's the problem. It's not like you don't already dress this way most of the time. What would change?"

Emily considered that. It made sense and would mean she wouldn't have to remember who she was at each place. "Okay, but what am I going to tell the school?"

The doc smiled. "If you're serious, you'll figure that out. I'll give you a letter explaining things to make the process easier, but you'll have to start this on your own. I guess you should also start facial hair removal and get your name changed, if you're ready."

Emily's heart beat faster. Had she really gone so far and changed so much? "I…uh…I…okay."

The doc chuckled as he pulled up a program on his computer and entered Emily's old name. With the click of the mouse, the letter was printed. He signed and handed it over. Emily took it with trembling hands, her eyes locked on the paper. "So, how are things with your family?"

"I still haven't heard back from them. It hurts, but I have to be true to myself. I'm getting happier and feel more alive, more interested in things. I'm not going back to the way things were before. Personally, I'm tired of feeling miserable."

"Still bothered by nightmares?" asked the doc, changing directions again.

"Yes. Ever since my unit got hit, they've been happening every couple of nights. I haven't zoned out totally since first hearing about the attack and the death of my best friend," said Emily. "The time I spend with Leah makes things easier. Thankfully, I've destressed thanks to my friends. Between reading, movies, hanging out with Leah, and shopping I've been able to cope better."

"Keep working on it. It's good to hear you have several ways to destress. Just try to avoid compulsive spending. You don't need a new problem. Maybe going full-time will help?"

Emily nodded. "I'm just worried about school. I don't know what they'll think and it scares me."

"Don't worry too much about it, Emily. It'll be fine."

❖

Emily looked at her closet, trying to figure out what to wear. It was her first day going to school as Emily and she wanted to make sure people could make the switch in genders without screwing up. She asked her friends in the Vals, and the majority said a skirt and blouse, a dress, something that showed the difference. Leah recommended dressing comfortably, which didn't help. Emily settled on a calf-length denim skirt and white blouse with three-quarter sleeves. She snagged a red and purple vest to go with it that gave the outfit a southwestern vibe she enjoyed. This would do the trick. She knew she looked cute and that gave her courage.

She gathered her school supplies and headed to the car. The patrol pack was worn in and comfortable on her shoulder. She was nervous, making her more aware of her pain. Sighing, Emily strived to get her thoughts under control.

She parked in her usual spot by Harned Hall and sat a few moments breathing deeply and preparing herself. She loosened her death grip on the steering wheel. It was a major step, but in a way, it really wasn't. All she was doing was living her life, being true to herself, and going to classes.

She stepped out and limped to her first class, using her cane, as her nervousness made the pain worse. Somehow, Emily felt disappointed that no one yelled about the guy in a skirt, no one pointed and screamed; in fact, no one seemed to care at all. Emily shook her head. After all the buildup this seemed like a non-event.

She took her usual seat and waited for class, going over her notes. All of her instructors had been sent an email telling them what was going on so it wouldn't be a surprise. The email explained everything, including what to call her, and let her instructors know if they wanted more information to simply ask. She got no replies. Things were unnerving and she hoped no one called her Thomas.

Class went as usual. She got a few confused looks from other students, but nothing major as most were in their own little worlds. She took notes and that was that. As she made her way across campus, people didn't give her a second glance. She felt let down by the lack of response as she wanted some recognition for how major an act this was. Here she was, doing something akin to running into a hail of bullets and no one seemed to register that. Although, ignoring her was better than the alternative.

When classes finished, she headed back to her car. She had assignments she wanted to get started on and homework for tomorrow's classes. All in all, it had been a nothing day, like any other day. At home, she started homework, had dinner, and prepared for tomorrow. If she had been expecting something, she went to bed disappointed.

The next day was more of the same. No screaming, pointed fingers, nothing. Emily felt cheated, but also realized it wasn't a bad thing. Maybe not having a response was the best response and she would go from Thomas to Emily, no harm, no foul.

As she headed back to her car, one of the girls from math class caught up, panting, as if she had run over. "Hey…um…can I talk to you?"

Emily stopped and turned. "Sure?"

"You want to get some coffee? We can talk in the student center, and you won't have to stand." Emily struggled to remember the girl's name, but all she had was that it started with an S, which didn't help. There were a lot of S names.

"Sure." They headed to the student union at the speed of Emily's limp. The silence got to be too much, so the girl blurted out, "So why are you…you know…dressed this way?"

Emily took a quick glance to check if what she was wearing had changed. She looked fine so she was unsure what the question was. "Like what?"

"You know…like a girl."

Emily chuckled. She shook her head as they entered the student union, the other girl holding the door open. "Because I am a girl."

The other girl, Susan—Emily remembered her name—was open-mouthed like a fish. Emily giggled. Susan blushed more and said, "But at the beginning of the semester your name was Thomas. I remember that."

Emily knew she was going to have to explain sometime, might as well start now. As they walked into the coffee shop and waited in line, Emily thought about what she was going to say. She ordered a chai and biscotti while Susan ordered a mocha. Once they had their drinks, they found a booth and climbed in.

"I'm transgendered," Emily said. "I realized I was a girl and now I'm taking action to be myself. That's why, so I can live as who I really am, Emily."

"That's a pretty name. Have you had the surgery yet?" Susan seemed interested, at least enough to ask. This helped Emily relax more.

"Not yet. I have to live full-time for a year before I can, though I'm seriously thinking about it." Emily hadn't realized she had been, but she totally was. It was unexpected and almost threw her out of her train of thought. Almost.

Susan gushed. "Well, you look great. You look like a real girl."

Emily bristled at that. "I am a real girl."

"I…I mean that you, I mean you still have a…" Susan blushed as her words jumbled in the car wreck of her thoughts.

Emily sighed. "Yes, I do…but I'm a girl with a plumbing problem, that's all. Once that's fixed it'll be all good. But that doesn't change the fact that I'm still a real girl right now."

Susan struggled with that. Emily drank her chai, dipping the biscotti to soften the hard cookie. She heard her name and turned. Tiffany was waving by the doors. She quickly ordered and headed over to the booth, then scooted in next to Emily and gave her a big hug. "Hey there, sexy. How're classes?"

Emily smiled. Tiffany looked Goth but was so totally perky and chipper it was almost ludicrous. "Not too bad. No problems to report so far. Susan here is in my math class. She's trying to figure me out."

Susan looked taken aback by the way Emily explained things. Tiffany looked over. "So…where are we?"

"Plumbing," said Emily, wondering where Tiffany was going with this. Sometimes the way Tiffany took a topic and ran with it in strange and unusual directions scared her.

"Right, plumbing. Well, I know lots of girls with plumbing issues. Some can't have kids; some have odd problems with long medical names. If you think about it, gender can't be something of the body because of the vast variation. It has to be in the mind because that's all that's left. So, if gender is in our minds who's to say if someone we think is one way turns out to be the other?" Tiffany bounced as she spoke. Her name was called at the counter and she excitedly chirped, "Oo…caffeine!"

In a flash, she ran over, grabbed her drink, and then slid in next to Emily. Susan was so busy mulling over what Tiffany said she hadn't reacted. Tiffany continued to pontificate, now with caffeine support. "Here's another thing, since you don't have enough to ponder yet. How brave do you think you have to be to do this? To be your gender even if your body doesn't look that way? Emily's a real hero, with medals and everything, but I bet this takes more courage than anything else she's done."

Emily blushed and looked down at her drink. "I guess. But what I did in Iraq took a lot of the same courage."

"I'm sure," replied Tiffany fondly. "You've been living fearlessly, living your life the way you want it to be. Too many of the rest of us just live the lives others made for us, the same grind day after day because someone somewhere thought we needed to live this way. I started living fearlessly in high school. I was called a freak, devil worshipper, and told I was going to hell all because I wanted to dress this way and liked girls. If I hadn't been able to move away from that little town, I may have killed myself."

Emily was startled by that. Maybe Tiffany's involvement in this conversation was a bit much. She reached next to her and rested her hand on Tiffany's. She patted Emily's hand, acknowledging the look with one of her own. "Don't worry about me. I'm okay. And hey, in a lot of ways you're my hero. You faced death and came back; you faced all this confusion and came through. Who wouldn't be impressed?"

Emily felt her face burn. The hormones made blushing far easier. She wasn't a hero; she was just a girl trying to live her life. Lots of people did that. It didn't make her special, didn't make her different from the girls sitting with her. "I…um…"

"Wait…you mean…he…she won an actual medal? Like for real?" blurted Susan.

Tiffany nodded. "The Bronze Star. It looks cool and is for courage under fire. She did something very brave and they gave her a medal."

"Wow. I never met a real war hero before." Susan seemed so sincere Emily was at a loss. "Was that where you got injured?"

Emily nodded, on firmer ground. "Yeah. In fact, my getting injured is responsible for this. When I was in the field hospital, I realized I was jealous of women. That led to here by a winding road. I wanted to get rid of those feelings and get on with my life, but it didn't work out the way I figured. I certainly didn't think that would mean living like a girl."

Tiffany smiled. "But you make such a cute girl."

Emily stuck her tongue out. Susan laughed, dealing with things better. Talk turned to classes and other things. Her second day as a girl was going rather well. They sat and talked for hours. Maybe she was going to have another friend in Susan? Who knew?

Emily glanced at her watch. It was a lot later than she realized and was already dark. They said their good-byes and planned to make coffee a regular part of their days. Emily felt more real somehow for talking with someone not part of her transformation.

She limped toward her car, exhausted, but glad her leg had gotten plenty of rest. What a great day. She made another friend and that pep talk by Tiffany had been unexpected and greatly appreciated. That girl was certainly more than she figured when they first met. It was nice to have her girlhood defended by someone else.

She was almost to her car when three guys came out of the shadows. She recognized two of them from different classes and wasn't sure why they were here. The hairs on the back of her neck lifted and a chill ran down her spine. This was not good. She stopped, ready for anything.

"Hey, faggot!" yelled the guy from English class. He was big, broad, and stood over a head taller than Emily. His words slurred, as if he had been drinking, and was maybe driven by liquid courage. Emily knew she had to deal with this head-on despite her worry.

Emily lifted her cane to ready position, holding it like she had been taught to hold a rifle in combat training. It was all she knew, as her leg would hamper hand-to-hand. There was no way she could run, and a weapon was the biggest equalizer she had. With a well-practiced shrug, she dropped her patrol pack, tossing it slightly away to give her a clear space around her feet. Her heart raced and she recognized the feeling descending on her. It was her game face, her war face, her Iraq face. She tilted her head down, watching her opponents as she asked, "What do you want, Rob?"

"What the fuck you doing in a skirt?" There was actual animosity in Rob's voice. Emily wished someone could fix this before it descended into violence. Three on one was not good odds even if she hadn't been disabled.

"Go home, Rob, and leave me be." Her voice was even, calm and she quickly scanned the quad looking for help.

One of the other guys stepped forward, pointing his finger in condemnation. He was equally large and broad-shouldered and filled with righteous anger. "You know, God hates faggots like you, Thomas."

"Okay…so he hates me. That isn't news. Are we through?" She wished they weren't between her and her car. If she could just get in there and lock the doors, she would be safe. She didn't want this fight.

The third one laughed, face partially in shadow. "See, and you wanted to let the sissy join our frat. Fucking little faggot is probably wetting herself in fear right about now, confronted by real men. She probably wants us, isn't that right, fairy?"

Emily groaned. What the hell had she ever done to them? And now this crap. Her grip on the cane tightened as she fell more and more into her Iraq frame of mind. "You're right. I'm scared. But I don't want you. Are you done trying to intimidate me?"

Rob growled. "Sissy faggots like you should just fucking leave and never come back."

This was coming to blows now. She had no idea how to defuse this and couldn't run. It felt like Iraq, and while she didn't like that, she would do what she had to.

The one she didn't know came in first, while she was distracted by Rob. He threw a wide, curving punch toward her face. Time slowed for Emily as she moved. The fist connected right over her eye, cutting her eyebrow. As the next punch came, she slammed the hook of the cane into his face with a straight butt stroke, textbook perfect. Blood spurted out and he stumbled back, hands to his face. "See boke by dose."

The other kid from class rushed her. She planted her feet and thrust forward. The point of the cane caught his chin instead of his throat and he stumbled forward into her. Emily brought the cane across the guy's face and wrenched her shoulder. The burn flared across her back and down her arm, but she didn't let go.

The guy collapsed to the ground next to her, tangling her legs. Rob came at her screaming, as did Broke Nose from the other side. Her heart raced as she quickly butt-stroked the unknown guy in the forehead, dropping him to the pavement and pivoted swiftly to face Rob.

Rob looked like he was coming with a haymaker. She tried to step toward him with a thrust like she had the other guy. However, her feet tripped her up and she stumbled, missing. Rob's punch to her face didn't.

Emily sprawled back, feet still tangled, catching most of her weight on her sore hip. She screamed in pain and swung wildly to gain some space. Rob backed away before coming in with a kick toward her ribs.

With both hands, she blocked the kick with her cane. Rob's leg hit hard, taking the cane into his shin and shoving her back. Tears streamed down her face as her shoulder burned intensely, and Emily swung at his other leg with the now bent cane. Rob's knee collapsed from impact and he hit the ground with a solid thud and oof.

Emily struggled to her feet. She held her bent cane at the ready, making sure there were no more coming toward her. There was no movement, only groaning. She lowered her cane, glad for its support, but worried about it breaking. What the hell was their problem? She chuckled without mirth, scowling. Idiots. They chose the wrong target for their aggression. She smirked. "Now that's a gay bashing."

Once she covered the short distance to her car, she dialed the campus police emergency line. She locked her doors and waited, safer than out there with them, despite none of them moving. Was what she was doing that offensive? She started at the knock at her window. One of the campus cops stood there looking concerned. "Are you okay, miss?"

She rolled down the window. "No. They jumped me and I defended myself. That's about it, besides the slurs."

Her voice sounded distant, but she knew this was post-combat adrenaline drain. She didn't want to be here, but it wasn't like she had a choice. This had to be dealt with. The officer smiled. "Miss, we need a statement."

She nodded, afraid her voice would shake if she spoke. She followed the officers to the ambulance, hissing in pain with each step, as two other officers zip-tied the hands of her attackers. She figured they would also need a trip to the hospital after what she had done. She felt like she had in Iraq after killing insurgents. She didn't care, and was numb.

The paramedic looked at her eyes and prodded her ribs gently. She took a sharp breath, new pain flaring. "Miss, we need to take you in for X-rays."

Emily nodded absently, tears rolling down her face. She wasn't in Tennessee but back in the desert, going over the bodies of the dead. They lay there, the deep red of blood the only color against dusty clothes. He could see faces, but none resembled the high priority targets they had been briefed on.

"Miss, is there anyone we should call?"

She held out her phone to the paramedic, who took it before passing it to one of the campus cops. Pain rolled over her—hip, shoulder, and wrist—and she began to sob. The paramedic spun back around. "Miss, miss…where does it hurt?"

"Everywhere."

❖

Emily hated hospitals, hated the memories they brought. The doctor gave her some IV painkillers and she watched the clock until a wave of relief filled her. She was happily buzzed and didn't care about the pain anymore.

The doctors were looking at X-rays to figure out the extent of her injuries. From what it felt like, her old wounds were reinjured, and the hits to her face and ribs hurt as well. Leah rushed into the curtained area, crying. "Oh, baby, are you okay?"

She was happy to see the woman she loved but smiling hurt her face. "Hey, sweetie, I gave as good as I got."

The kiss was a nice reward.

The doctor came in, looking at her chart. "Mr. Simmons, I've gone over your X-rays and it looks like you sustained a cracked rib. The blows to your face caused no bone injury, and there is sign of a mild concussion. Your old injuries don't seem more than badly strained, with a slight abrasion on your hip further aggravating your leg injuries. I advise home rest for a few days to let everything mend and then you can get back to your classes. Follow up with the VA in a few weeks. An officer is going to take some pictures of your wounds for evidentiary purposes."

Emily nodded, crying out in relief now that Leah was there. If she went through this alone, she wasn't sure what she would have done. The officer came in and had her pose for pictures, so there was good visual reference of the wounds. They even took pictures of the bent cane and took it as evidence. After that, the campus cop came in with a notepad. He was an older, bald-headed man.

"Okay, can I see your student ID?" he asked. He looked very fit and cop-like despite his age and had a friendly vibe.

Emily sighed. This might end up sucking even more than it did already. She took out her ID and the letter from her purse. From what she could gather, it wouldn't hurt.

The officer read the letter in silence, twice. He nodded and wrote something into his report and then looked back up. "Thank you, Emily."

She let out a breath she had been holding, worried about her reception. "You're welcome."

"Now, why don't you tell me what happened?"

Emily told him the whole story, including drinking coffee with Tiffany and Susan beforehand. He wrote down everything she said, simply taking the information and making no comments. "All right. Now, let me get this straight. You're saying that because you're LGBT these guys accosted you and called you various names?"

"Yes."

"And then attacked you?"

"Yes. The first one to move in was someone I didn't know, then the guy from my math class, and finally Rob."

"And you used your cane to fight back?"

Emily nodded. "I used my cane like a bayonet and rifle. I guess it worked."

The officer smirked. "I guess it did. Okay, I need you to sign this to make it official. We'll let you know how this goes down when we find out more."

"Thank you. But one question, why are you taking this so well? I mean I'm transgendered. I wasn't expecting a lot of sympathy."

The officer chuckled. "My brother's gay. So, I have some understanding of the community."

Emily sighed thankfully. "Are we done?"

It had been over an hour, and she had gone over her statement about three times with different officers. She was wiped out and felt worse than when she headed to her car.

"Yeah. We're done. Someone'll be in touch. I suggest calling your therapist in the morning. Something like this can really mess you up. Good night." The officer turned and left the curtained area, tucking away his notebook.

After another hour, Emily limped wearily out of the hospital, leaning on her new cane and Leah's shoulder. Tiffany and Stacy shot out of their seats when they saw them, coming up and hugging her tightly. Emily burst into tears of relief, as she fell into her friends' embrace. It had been a good day for a while, but the ending left a lot to be desired.

CHAPTER TWENTY-FOUR

Emily started awake, heart racing a mile a minute, skin clammy. She scanned the room for enemies. Nothing moved, and it was silent, except for Leah's rhythmic breathing. Rubbing her face, she limped to the bathroom, wincing with each step. After finishing, she washed down an anti-anxiety pill. Nothing like a little combat to bring everything back.

She headed out to the living room and sat on the couch with her leg elevated and her arm resting across her belly. Did getting mugged excuse you from homework? She figured she would try that for the rest of the week. It couldn't hurt, and she was in no frame of mind to do it. She needed time to get more together and for the pain levels to get manageable. Besides, Leah had the paperwork for her name change ready. Apparently, it had only taken her forty-five minutes to get it all put together.

Since Leah had rushed up here from work, she had the paperwork in her bag. Somehow, Leah managed to get the rest of the week off to care for her sick "cousin." It made Emily feel loved knowing Leah did that.

She limped into the kitchen to get more water. Her mouth felt dusty and she needed to rinse it out.

It was nice having Leah there. She left her car at school then took Emily home for some loving and dinner. The chicken soup was very nice, even if from a can. Leah doctored it quite a bit before giving it to Emily.

The cold water was soothing. She sat and waited for meds to kick in. What made those guys attack her? What had she done? And what the fuck was that whole fraternity thing about, as she had no interest in joining a frat.

Emily rubbed the back of her neck, which was tense and sore. She was tired of thinking about the attack and its implications of a hate crime. The meds made her feel sleepy, so she staggered back to bed and Leah. Maybe she would wake up and feel normal again?

❖

"So, all I have to do is sign this, turn it in, and that changes my name?" asked Emily incredulously. This seemed far, far too simple.

"Yep. That's it. Once you sign, we turn the paperwork in to the chancery court and they process it. Shouldn't take long and then you'll legally be Emily Rhymer." Leah pulled out the papers and handed a few sheets over. "You sign right there."

Emily grabbed a pen and wrote her legal name, Thomas Simmons, for what she hoped was the last time. She could say good-bye to that old life and throw herself into her new.

After signing, they headed downtown to the courthouse. They cleared security, walked into the chancery office, and turned in the paperwork. Emily paid one hundred and fifty dollars, took her receipt, and they headed to get something to eat to celebrate making herself legal.

This made her smile, made her feel like she was going somewhere. Maybe in a year she could get surgery and become complete. She should still have enough money from her discharge for that.

They ate downtown at a place with its own microbrewery that had excellent food. Emily was on top of the world. She was getting her name changed and was with the girl she loved. By and large, her life was better than ever.

Leah asked, "Any ideas about hair removal?"

Emily shook her head. "I can't decide. On one hand, you have electrolysis, which really works but is slow and very painful, and on the other hand you have laser removal, which is faster but has no long-term studies on its effectiveness, so it may or may not be permanent. And when I think about needing to get the surgery area cleared, I cringe. The idea of electrocuting that is just…ewww."

Leah looked sympathetic. "So, waxing and the like won't work?"

Emily shook her head. "Nope. If you don't clear the area you end up having hair grow in there."

They both shuddered. "And in order to clear the face and get rid of my faint shadow, you need to get rid of the hair follicles completely."

"All right. What's wrong with laser for face and electro for… your…you know?"

Emily shrugged. It made as much sense as anything else. Besides, surgery was no place to skimp. Maybe she should look into surgeons? That way she could have everything set when she finished the RLT portion? She would be complete, or more complete than she already was. That had great appeal.

"Hey, since you aren't going back to school until next week do you want to come home with me? You can get away from here and relax. Stay with me until Sunday."

Emily smiled brightly. "That would be awesome. I love waking up next to you. Once we're done let's get my car and head to your place. I'll pack."

As she followed Leah to Nashville, Emily thought about her feelings and what she wanted. She loved Leah and felt sure this would be the weekend to say it. It might be early for some people, but Emily couldn't hold back any longer. Maybe, in time they could get married, especially if they did it before surgery. She would still be technically male at that point, right? That should be enough to make it happen, even here in the Bible Belt.

Leah made Emily feel loved and protected, comforted and feminine. Part of that was that Leah was the more aggressive and dominant of the two of them. Leah joked she had been quite the lipstick when she met Emily and was now becoming more butch because Emily was not very butch at all. She was content, no longer fighting to be male, and that made the difference.

They arrived at Leah's place and Emily joined her to cuddle on the couch. Leah liked to watch the news, so Emily snuggled while Leah watched. That was until the next story. "Elements of the 101st are heading back this week, with the rest of the division coming home in a month. Some of the first forward units will be arriving tomorrow with more groups scattered over the week."

Emily sat bolt upright, eyes wide. "Oh God, what the hell am I going to tell them?"

Leah calmed her down, getting her to relax. "Emi kitty, we've handled everything that's come against us so far. We can handle this. There is nothing we can't do together."

"But, Leah, these are the people I got injured protecting. If they don't accept me, I have no idea what I'll do. Oh gods, why did this happen now?" Emily was sliding into a panic attack.

Leah turned off the TV and held Emily, running a hand over her head. "Shh...it'll work out. All you have to do is be yourself. You're still the person who saved them, with a few...differences. Surely they'll understand."

Emily slowly calmed under Leah's gentle hands. She was on edge, more than she had been in a long time thanks to the attack, Waltrip's death, and one small piece of news. It had to be the hormones and the stress making her so jumpy and overly sensitive. It was like her life was out of control. She wanted to get back to the happy place that was becoming her norm. Really, what was the worst that could happen?

She shuddered at the thought, a number of scenarios running through her head. If any of the guys from the unit came after her, she would be toast. They knew how to fight and could cause serious harm. With her leg there would be no contest. But would they come after her because of how her life had changed? She wasn't sure.

She called it an early night to rest as much as possible. So much had happened and she wanted to crawl under the covers and escape. Emily woke briefly and murmured something vague when she felt Leah climb in later, then she rolled over and rested her head on Leah's breasts, making contented noises. Leah sighed and stroked her hair until Emily fell asleep.

❖

Emily's cell phone rang. She looked at the caller ID and went white, her platoon sergeant. She picked up the phone, trying to keep her racing heart out of her throat. She had changed the voice mail message to Emily, not Thomas, and that might make things get out of hand before she could deal with it. She answered. "Hello?"

"Rhymer?" asked the sergeant. "How the fuck are you?"

"Not too bad, Sergeant. How about you?" Emily hoped the conversation didn't take any funny turns.

"Not too bad. Not too bad. So when can I come over and check how you're doing? The other guys got you a few gifts from the dust bowl."

"Um…not today. I'm in Nashville with my girlfriend."

"Outstanding. How about this time next weekend? Would that be good?" He seemed interested in seeing her, or more to the point, Thomas. She wanted to see him as well, as she missed her unit, but the thought scared her shitless.

She looked over at Leah who shrugged. Emily swallowed. "Sure. Do you want to come over Sunday?"

"Sounds like a plan. See you, Rhymer." The sergeant hung up.

Emily looked at Leah, on the edge of tears. "What the hell am I going to say?"

Leah hugged Emily. "We'll think of something. Besides, you're going to see your shrink before the weekend, so don't stress too much."

❖

"Are you all right?" asked Dr. Richards.

"For the most part. A black eye and a cracked rib are all I got. It was three drunken assholes picking a fight with the wrong girl."

"And your nightmares?"

"Back. I thought I was doing well, then my unit got hit, I was attacked, and now my unit's coming back. It hasn't been a good couple of weeks. I'm stressed out of my gourd and twitchy." Emily shifted uneasily.

"Okay. So, what can we do about your unit?"

Emily rubbed her forehead, feeling a headache build behind her eyes. "My sergeant is dropping by Sunday."

The doc peered closer. "And who is he going to see?"

"Um…me."

"That's not what I meant. Is your sergeant going to see Emily or Thomas?"

Emily thought about the question. It would be easier to say Emily and actually be Thomas, but she no longer had any guys' clothes except uniforms, which she just couldn't let go of. After a deep breath to center herself, Emily replied, "Emily. I haven't gone through all this to turn tail and run now."

The doc nodded. "What are you going to tell him?"

"I've no idea. I mean, I guess I can tell him what's been going on and hope he understands. I have no idea if that'll work."

"I think that might be a good idea. Being honest may be the best you can do. If he really is your friend he'll see you despite what you look like and will remain your friend. I'm not saying it won't be difficult, but perhaps it's for the best."

Emily swallowed nervously. The thought of seeing him again after so long and so many changes made her skin crawl. Maybe she could call in sick to her life that day? She realized it wouldn't work as she used that once on the sergeant. She had even called in dead once to no effect. She was screwed.

The session ended due to an emergency calling Dr. Richards away, for which she was grateful. She sighed…there was no real option except to answer the door, talk to the sergeant, and hope for the best. Sadly, it was the best idea she had. Her only hope was the truth would be enough.

She walked to the lobby. Leah was reading an old issue of *National Geographic*, hair hanging down one side of her face. Something about that made Emily smile. They headed off for lunch and to find some way to relax. Tomorrow was a spa day, which Emily looked forward to. If she was lucky, it should calm her down enough to not scream.

CHAPTER TWENTY-FIVE

Emily paced as best she could, hobbling across the floor. She was not looking forward to this, but it was important. Odds were this whole situation would go downhill rapidly once the sergeant arrived. The door was unlocked and she sat, trying to remain calm. There were two beers on the coffee table, one already open. Emily had a few sips to settle her nerves. She desperately wanted to drain it. This wait was making her crazier, and the beer wasn't helping.

Leah was at a nearby diner waiting for her call. That would be a good safety net, if she didn't call in twenty minutes she would be heading over. Emily looked at the clock again, watching as time seemed to move faster. The sergeant was bound to be here any second because he was always prompt. It was like the man never heard of the concept of being fashionably late…ever.

Sure enough, there was a quick rap at the door. Emily took a big swig of her beer, hoping for a little liquid courage. It was now or never. She exhaled slowly and called out, "Come in."

It wasn't just the sergeant; nearly half the platoon poured in. Emily almost fainted at the sight. This possibility had never occurred to her and scared the crap out of her. Silence hung heavily. No one had any idea what to say; everyone stared at each other awkwardly. Emily grabbed her cane and stood, then stumbled backward. "Um… hi. This is a surprise. Have a seat where you can and let me grab some beers from the fridge."

The guys followed along, too confused to do anything else but obey orders. The beer idea was to buy more time. She limped into the kitchen cursing under her breath. "Shit, shit, shit, shit."

The sergeant followed her into the kitchenette, whispering harshly, "Rhymer, what the fuck is going on?"

Emily turned and whispered right back, fear shifting to anger. "I was going to tell you what was going on and then you show up with fucking everybody. If you want to know what the fuck is going on help me pass out the fucking beers and let me explain."

The sergeant was taken aback, as was Emily, who had never talked like that before. She and the sergeant came back and started handing out beers. Between them they managed to get them passed out quickly. Emily stood in front of the TV, leaning heavily on her cane, too scared to sit. She smiled weakly and nervously began. "Okay. I guess y'all deserve an explanation. This was not some sort of joke on the sergeant, even though that would be easier to deal with. I meant to explain things to him before I saw y'all. You beat me to that."

She took a swig of her nearly empty beer. Had she really drunk it that fast? "I'm transgendered. I had no idea until that RPG knocked me ass over teakettle and I had all that time to sit and think. I'm getting treatment and this is who I am, a girl. Really, no shit. And this is serious. I'm on meds and my name change should be done Tuesday. So, questions?"

Hernandez raised his hand uncertainly. "Um…Rhymer, wha'the fuck?"

Emily sighed, hadn't she just explained that? She rubbed her face and said, "Hernandez, what part of I'm a girl are you missing?"

A few people snickered, breaking the tension. It faded as they realized neither Emily nor the sergeant were laughing. Emily continued. "I'm a girl, I've always been a girl and did a great job hiding it from myself. That's one of the reasons I was such a dumbass, risking my life all the time. I hated myself and wanted to die. I took chances that had a high probability of killing me and justified it as saving all of you. Now I'm living my life as who I am. I hope you guys can accept that."

"And what if we just kicked the shit out of you?" Robertson asked.

Emily glared; she didn't need this. She hadn't invited them, just the sergeant. "Is that what you want to do, Robertson? Kick my ass for being different? Fuck, that's not even original. Here I thought you guys would be different than fucking civilian pogues."

The room quieted quickly as her words registered. The sergeant spoke up. "Wait, what?"

"A few days ago, I got jumped by three drunk frat boys. Three on one. Real fucking fair." Emily was pissed. Were they no better than those asshats? She wanted to scream and strangle them.

"Whoa, hold on, are you saying some civilian limp dicks jumped you because of this?" said Peterson. This caught everyone's attention, since he was the only guy to never use the F word for everything.

Emily nodded.

The room erupted. Several of them were all for going back to base and loading up for a "visit" to all the frat houses on principle. Emily was flabbergasted. She stood there totally befuddled, tears leaking as she heard the team argue and plan different ways to strike back. Suddenly, a voice thundered, "At ease!"

All sound instantly died, and everyone snapped into "at ease," including Emily. All faces turned to the sergeant. He growled out, "I want to make one thing perfectly clear; I do not approve. But you saved our asses and got a fucking Bronze Star for courage under fire. I do not understand what the fuck you're going through, but you've goddamned earned the fucking right to do whatever the fuck you want. No one messes with one of us. Ever. If you ever, and I mean ever, need someone to curb stomp these fuckers, call us. We'll happily do that for the honor of our platoon."

All of them bellowed out, "Strike!"

Emily stood there overwhelmed, starting to tear up. Of all the outcomes she expected, this option never even made it onto the chart. "I…I don't know what to say. Thank you."

"Say you'll go out with me Friday night!" Kurtz called out from the back.

Emily laughed. "In your dreams, Kurtz. Besides, my girlfriend would kick your ass."

There was lots of laughter and things degenerated to a small party. The platoon drank several toasts to Rhymer, their big damn hero. Peterson came up and sat next to her. He looked nervous and wiped his palms on his slacks. "Rhymer, um…since you said you have…um…changed. What should we call you?"

Emily smiled. Peterson was always so nice it astounded her that he became an infantryman. "Rhymer works, as will Emily. My full name is Emily Rhymer. So, you guys all had a hand in picking my name."

That passed quickly and soon toasts to Emily Rhymer were heard, including one from Kurtz that went, "To Emily Rhymer, prettiest damn girl in the infantry."

Emily blushed. The guys had brought their own beer in case a party happened and one had. Emily texted Leah, asking her to come home since she could use support. After she put away her phone, she noticed the sergeant sat down next to her. "I've no idea what to do with you, Rhymer."

"What do you mean?" asked Emily. He was one of the few people whose approval mattered and she hoped things weren't going bad; this couldn't be easy.

"If you didn't look so fucking natural, I think this situation would be easier. But you honestly seem happy, which never happened while you served. What the fuck should I do with you?" The consternation in his voice was clear.

"Well, you could still be my friend. I know you might not agree with this, let alone understand, but if you could accept it that would be enough. Acceptance is not agreement or condoning, just acknowledging this is the way things are." Emily had her fingers crossed, hoping this would work. The others might be swayed, but the sergeant was someone who always thought things through. He said it was a reason he never got promoted.

His brows were furrowed. She waited, ignoring the grunts in the apartment having fun. After a while, he nodded slightly. "I can do that. You took the heat for us more than once so I guess I can put up with some discomfort."

They shook on it and a wave of relief rushed through her. Her platoon, guys who meant something to her, were not going to desert her over this. Emily smiled. "Thanks. That means a lot."

She heard a few guys say hello and saw a slightly worried Leah enter. She looked over the horde hesitantly. Emily called out, "Leah! Over here."

Leah came over and sat down next to her. Emily gestured. "Leah, this is my platoon...well, most of it."

Leah waved, unsure what else to do. Someone brought her a beer. She looked at Emily who shrugged. "I guess it was a surprise. It certainly surprised me."

After a while, things wound down. The guys left in small groups to do heavier drinking elsewhere. Soon Emily and Leah were alone in the apartment, looking at the mess of beer cans and food. Leah looked at Emily. "I take it that it went well?"

"I guess." Emily was still confused but feeling positive. "I have no idea what the hell just happened. I was so afraid and then so relieved that my mind is awhirl."

Leah looked affectionately at her. "It's okay. I guess it turned out all right then?"

"Yeah, it did. Getting attacked turned things around, apparently. Since the platoon always pulls together, that pissed them off. I only hope it doesn't fade. The last thing I want is them to get pissed." Emily trembled a little.

"Well, love, I don't want to, but I have to get going. I need to get home and get ready for work in the morning."

"I love you," said Emily in response. "I wish you could stay. I don't want you to go."

Leah smiled down at Emily. "I don't want to either, but I have work and you have school..."

"Do...do you think we might...you know...move in together?" asked Emily.

Leah stopped picking up her purse and turned. She smiled, so Emily knew she wasn't in trouble. "That...would be great. We've been together for a few months so we beat the usual U-Haul timeline. We can look into it and talk it out over phone and email to figure out where we want to live if you don't want to stay at my house. Sound good?"

Emily smiled. "Yeah, okay. It's just that I love being with you and this whole being apart thing sucks, a lot."

"Yeah. You concentrate on schoolwork, and I'll work on the housing thing. And then we can move in together."

Emily stood and hugged Leah tight. They kissed and Emily was sad they had to part. Getting a place together would make her more content. After the last couple of days, she really didn't want to deal with being apart anymore.

They said their good-byes and Emily watched Leah drive away. She cleaned up her apartment and went over her classwork. She was going to classes tomorrow and wanted to have something ready to turn in. She sighed heavily as she sat at the dining room table and got to work.

❖

In the shower, Emily noticed new aching spots. Her breasts were budding and tender to the touch. They also itched a little. Running the poof over them made the skin feel raw. She looked down and could see slight swelling. She giggled and bounced. She was growing breasts. It was really happening.

She beamed as she toweled off. This was awesome. Both she and Leah were wondering when it was going to happen. And now it was. She was so excited that she was bouncing like Tiffany. Today should be a great day; after all, she was changing. She almost had boobies.

After parking in her usual spot, she got a little twitchy and nervous. The attack kept replaying itself. She realized she would feel more comfortable if one of the guys from the platoon were there, or Leah or Tiffany or someone. She walked away as fast as she could, gripping her cane tightly. She was scared being alone, especially at the moment.

She sat in her first class and noticed the absence of her attacker. That made her feel better. It was odd. As Thomas, she never felt vulnerable but rather invulnerable. Now she felt exposed, her ability to go unscathed gone. She realized that big, muscular guys made her nervous. This was new and she didn't like it. Since the attack, feeling vulnerable was ever-present, which made sense, but she wasn't sure how to move on. She didn't want to live in fear. Did every girl experience this?

She pondered this. Was there a sense of vulnerability in being a woman? Jars were harder to open, and she couldn't carry as much, which was disconcerting. The hormones were doing a number on her strength. Being physically weaker was tough to get used to. It added to her sense of weakness, making her more cautious. How come no one mentioned that as a side effect?

This was a side of hormone replacement that hadn't been discussed in any of her research. It was unnerving, but she doubted if reading about it would have conveyed the experience. Being weaker, when added to her injuries, annoyed her.

She noticed her clothes were tighter this morning. Apparently, she was gaining weight, which didn't make her happy. Of all the stupid things to happen this was the most irritating. She could barely manage to exercise enough to keep her metabolism high enough to avoid weight gain, thanks to her injuries. Just her luck.

She limped to the coffee shop after class. Tiffany and Stacy were supposed to meet her there. Maybe they would have a few ideas on losing some weight. Maybe she could try yoga, Pilates, swimming, or something. She wanted to keep in shape, knowing she would never be able to run ten miles in an hour again, but she wanted to do something. Being inactive was grating on her.

CHAPTER TWENTY-SIX

Emily woke and stretched. She ached all over and had ever since the attack. Stretches were helping and encouraged her to keep up with physical therapy. She swung her legs over the side, grabbed her cane, and limped into the bathroom for morning necessities.

After breakfast, she headed to class. Today, she was officially becoming Emily Rhymer. Thomas Simmons would pass away nice and legal with hardly a sound. It was a bit sad that Thomas was leaving, but she was absolutely positive about spending the rest of her life as Emily. She giggled, excited at the renaming.

Emily was relaxed, energized, and ready to take on the world. She fidgeted during classes, wanting nothing more than to get her name change instead of taking notes on things that barely interested her. Once done, she hustled away.

Waiting in the chancery court office for ten copies of her name change documents, Emily bounced. She could barely sit still. She wanted her new driver's license and hobbled out of the office quickly, papers in hand. A new picture, a new name, and a new license. She concentrated on not speeding, even though she was so excited that she wanted to break some land speed records getting to the DMV.

Waiting for her turn, she hummed some pop songs and a few jodys, liking the rhythm of the marching tunes. In a short while, she was called up. She gave the woman a copy of the name change and her old driver's license. The woman was not very surprised, which shocked Emily, who thought the DMV might not be familiar with this. She chided herself. Of course they would be used to this, as there were transgendered individuals all over the place. A few keystrokes later, the woman finished.

It was a short wait for the photo and then she had her new ID. She had a huge smile in the photo, which was funny considering in the old photo she had short hair and a near frown. Emily bounced out with this tangible proof of her changes. She felt more real. She called Leah, who seemed distracted. "Hello?"

"Leah, guess what, guess what?"

"Um…lobsters are attacking?" replied Leah, not really focusing.

"No. Sheesh! I got my new driver's license. I'm legally Emily," she squealed.

"That's awesome, sweetie. Do you want to come down and celebrate?"

"Yes. Oh, yes. I'll buy a drink to try out my new ID." Emily was beside herself. Her life was going well and that was new.

Emily checked her list of who needed copies of the name change document. It was longer than expected and she was glad Leah suggested grabbing a lot of copies. She changed into something nice for dinner and grabbed her kitty sleep shirt and a change of clothes, planning on staying the night. There were a few places in Nashville, like the VA and Social Security where she needed to go to change her name, and staying in town would make that easier.

Emily called to share the good news with Stacy and Tiffany. They gushed over her, almost as excited as she was. Tiffany squealed for a bit.

Emily did homework waiting for Leah to get off work. There was a lot of homework and it was crazy-making, especially as she felt overwhelmed by the rest of her life. It was hard to focus on class when the insanity beckoned. She glanced at the clock and smiled. Time to go.

The drive was easy and pretty; the trees were starting to bud by this point. Emily relaxed and enjoyed the radio playing softly. Things had been crazy ever since she got blown up and yet, despite all that, she was happy. For so long, she had been miserable to the point of invisibility. Misery had been her world and colored everything. Now she could see clearly, and looking back over her life it was obvious. There were too many events explained by gender issues. Even her belief this could be cured was part of that pain, part of her attempt to deny the truth. She wanted the difference to be excised, to make her "normal," but it would only be burying the truth again.

She had no idea happiness came from accepting what she feared, and was happier now than ever before. It was unnerving sometimes. She kept expecting things to turn bad. When this insanity started, Emily had no idea what lay on the other side. What she had been so afraid of had been her path to happiness.

She wove through East Nashville and made it to Leah's house. Emily cherished time with Leah and wished it could continue without having to drive all the way to Nashville. True, her place was near the Lounge, but was that enough of a reason to stay in the area? Besides, it was a bit cheaper to live farther out. But Leah owned this place, so did it make sense to move? Being able to wake up with her girlfriend every day would be worth whatever trouble she had to go through.

She hobbled inside. Her leg ached, as it did every time she drove over an hour. Maybe if she got a better car she wouldn't have to deal with that. She would look into it. Maybe there was something that could be done to make the car easier to drive. She could ask the VA, because they were supposed to help. It was a shame she bought a car to defend her illusory manhood. Maybe a better car would work instead of a new house?

Leah met her at the door with a hug and a kiss. That helped Emily forget about her pain as she lost herself. The moment stretched, and Leah helped her to the couch. "Do you want an ice pack, heat pad, something?"

"No, I should be fine with some rest. The car's vibrations hurt after a while. But I'm here now, so it's all good. Any luck on the place hunt?"

Leah shrugged. "Some. There are a couple of houses that don't seem too expensive that I can look at this week. They're around the midpoint between us now, so we'll both have to drive. Is that going to be okay, you know...with your leg?"

Emily smiled, not bothered in the least so long as it meant she could be with Leah. "Living with you will make the drive worth it. Besides, I sleep better with you than alone. I want to live with you. You mean everything to me."

They kissed and Leah hugged Emily tightly. This was what she needed, and she got her wish. Leah murmured into Emily's ear. "Hungry?"

"Getting there," said Emily. "Why?"

"Cause I was going to make dinner." Leah hugged her again. "So, I was waiting to see if you were hungry before I got the last of the prep done."

"Oh…okay. I'm getting there, so…please food me." Emily looked at Leah trying to give herself large puppy dog eyes.

Leah laughed, hugged Emily one more time, then kissed her before getting to her feet. "I'll call when it's ready?"

"Please. I wouldn't want to waste away." Emily tried to look pitiful. Leah laughed, making Emily smile again. She would do anything to get a response like that from Leah; dignity didn't matter.

Emily watched Leah head into the kitchen and then lay back looking at the ceiling. Life was turning out better and better, so much so that it was odd. She never had an expectation of her life being happy, and now…now it was easy to think about a future with meaning, filled with something other than guns, violence, and hiding from herself. It was unexpected, but she could live with it. She was starting to believe she could grow old with Leah and have a tomorrow. It was a completely different paradigm.

Looking around Leah's house a bit more critically, she smiled. It was a nice old place with wood floors, plenty of character, and a garden in the back Leah enjoyed working in. It screamed Leah in so many ways and was homey. That she was willing to leave this place for her meant a lot, but was it worth it to leave such a great home? Besides, if driving her Mustang hurt maybe she should get a new car instead?

"Hey, Leah!"

"What?" she yelled back from the kitchen.

"I was thinking, what if I got a new car instead of us getting a different place?"

There was no sound from the kitchen.

"Leah?"

"Are you serious?"

Emily smiled. "Yeah. You said your grandfather gave you this place, so why not stay? I can get a car that won't hurt as much to drive, maybe even have the VA help me make it easier to drive."

Leah hustled into the living room and kissed Emily soundly.

"You like?" Emily asked.

"Yeah...I like."

As Leah bustled back to the kitchen, Emily's thoughts turned to surgery. Her mind was awhirl over the transition, but she wanted to think it through carefully. Gender reassignment surgery would cost over eighteen thousand dollars. Add to that the cost of hair removal, airfare to get to wherever the surgeon was located, and the cost to stay a week or two post-surgery, and the money added up. It would be a huge dent in her severance pay, but she could pay for surgery and still have money. It would be rough but worth it, but the cost was staggering. She could get a fairly decent car at that price.

She wasn't sure which surgeon she wanted, as several were pretty good with prices in the same range. They were scattered over the country, as no one did this in Middle Tennessee. Emily wanted Leah's input, as Leah would play with it the most. She knew the sites to look at that could be an after-dinner plan. For now, she was going to take a short nap and hope the pain would go away.

❖

"You want to what?" asked Leah, blinking a few times.

"Let's go shopping for vaginas," said Emily, enjoying the confusion.

"Um...how exactly are we supposed to do that? EBay?"

"Well, we can try eBay if you think that's a decent option, but I was looking at a couple of surgeons' sites and we can pick one. That is, of course, if you want a hand in picking something pretty for me," said Emily.

Leah blinked and then everything clicked. "Oh! Oh, yeah. Let's do that."

Emily giggled and they headed into Leah's office. They kissed while the computer booted up. That was a much better use for the wait time than sitting there looking at the pretty lights. Leah got onto the net and looked at Emily. She rattled off the first surgeon's website. They went to pictures and looked at the surgeon's results, making appreciative noises, and taking notes on things they did and didn't like. The biggest problem was that the pictures were post-surgery and the patients hadn't had a chance to heal, so it was pretty rough. However, there was still plenty of good stuff there to make decisions.

Emily looked at Leah. "So, what do you think?"

Leah replied without taking her eyes off the screen. "They look really good. Have any more?"

"Yeah." Emily rattled off another site and they repeated the process.

After checking five different surgeons, Emily asked, "So…who did you like the best?"

Leah looked thoughtful and clicked on different tabs. It took a few minutes and some photo close-ups before she finally answered. "I like these two best. They look the most natural. If I saw them, I would definitely think they were homegrown and not aftermarket."

Emily chuckled. The image of homegrown and aftermarket vaginas was funny. She pictured rows of vagina plants being harvested and chuckled. Leah looked confused. After Emily shared the joke, she laughed as well. "Kitten, you are so odd."

"True, but you love me for that."

"Well, there is that." Leah leaned in for a kiss. "Besides, you made me smile, and I like that."

"Really?"

"Really. Would I lie to you?"

Emily thought about it a second, prompting Leah to act affronted. Emily snickered. She never felt so accepted or alive, even with her family. She could get used to this.

CHAPTER TWENTY-SEVEN

The pain was intense. Emily's eyes watered with each zap. She waved off the technician and regained some equilibrium, blinking back tears. Thankfully, they had saved the upper lip for last, but it hurt so much it was beyond rational understanding. Emily did everything she could to not flinch, so as to avoid scarring her face. Emily took a deep breath, lay back, and motioned for the technician to finish.

When the torture was done, they gave her aloe vera cooling gel and some antibacterial ointment, in case she needed it. The idea that her face could get infected due to laser was strange and something she didn't want to experience. She sighed and picked up a tube of face-numbing gel for the next session. There was no way she was going through that again without numbing.

Emily's face felt swollen and hot, like a bad sunburn. Once in the car, she turned an air conditioner vent onto her abused face and sighed as cool air raced across her. Zapping her face hurt more intensely than most of her injuries in Iraq. Of course, getting knocked unconscious probably had something to do with that. Yesterday's pain was barely remembered in the face of today's.

The transformation had started. Her facial hair was doomed, but not having to shave again was appealing. That made her wonder, was it still a transformation if you were becoming yourself, becoming more authentic rather than less? Wouldn't it be more like excavating? Not a transformation but a revelation?

Emily shook her head. It was a stupid train of thought, and she didn't want to exert that much effort. There were more important things to deal with, like thinking up ideas for the house. Decorating was much more important in the long run since she was moving over the weekend, after her last final.

Emily headed back to her apartment; happy it was one of the last times she would do that. Tiffany and Stacy were coming over to have dinner and a movie. Thankfully, those two wouldn't be that far from their place, so there would be plenty of chances to visit since the last thing she wanted was to lose friends.

Her face felt really tender and she struggled to avoid rubbing it. They told her rubbing would make things worse, aggravating the pain and letting bacteria get onto the skin. She drove on, wanting to make it home to take a nap. This new pain wore her out, and if she was going to be of any use to anybody that evening, she needed a nap.

She made it home after what seemed like an hour, rather than twenty minutes, and hobbled to her bedroom before falling onto the bed. She grabbed the covers and rolled in them like a burrito before coming to rest on her pillow.

❖

Emily danced with Leah, following her lead. They were wearing white wedding dresses, the mood light, happy. They laughed, kissed, and danced. All was right in the world. A faint whistling sound grew louder and louder, a familiar sound. Someone screamed, "Incoming!"

Emily and Leah dove behind a pile of sandbags. The explosion shook the earth violently, sending up clouds of dust and coating everything. She grabbed her M-4 and pulled on her helmet. Somehow, Leah had gotten separated from her. She had to find her before the insurgents did.

Her platoon advanced onto the enemy site, firing and moving, perfectly following infantry protocol. Her dress was dirty and torn from the occasional low-crawling needed to avoid enemy gunfire. Off to one side, she heard moaning.

Her team broke off and moved toward the sound, weapons at the ready. They came across another platoon from her battalion, or rather what was left of them. While the rest of her group took overwatch, she knelt next to one of the wounded, staring at the gut wound. Her mind was blank. How did you dress a wound?

She just stared as it oozed dark blood. She reached down and touched the pool. It was warm, slightly sticky, and clung to her, covering her hands. A bandage, she needed a bandage.

She wiped her hands on her wedding dress and opened the first aid kit she had. She rummaged through it, looking for a bandage. All she could find were large bottles of 800 mg ibuprofen and one Scooby-Doo Band-Aid. She pulled out the Band-Aid and checked it against the size of the wound. It was way too small.

She heard pounding growing louder and louder, the pounding of artillery. She covered the soldier, more blood smearing her dress, and she screamed for the medic.

❖

The pounding finally woke her. Emily glanced at her alarm clock blearily and realized it was probably Tiffany and Stacy. With a loud groan, she worked herself free of the tangle of blankets, vague recollections of a dream fading the more awake she became. Something about wedding dresses and a firefight, of white and red, which didn't help. She shook her head to clear the cobwebs.

She looked out the peephole and saw Tiffany and Stacy. She rubbed her eyes to get the sleep out as she let them in. She limped back to the couch and fell into the cushions.

"Long day?" asked Stacy.

Emily nodded, holding back a yawn. "Yeah. The laser hurt like hell, and then I had funky dreams. I don't feel any more rested than before I lay down."

Stacy looked concerned. "A nightmare?"

"Not really. At least, I don't think so. I didn't wake up screaming or anything, just exhausted," said Emily. "I'm fine."

"We can stay in if you want?" said Stacy, eyes flicking over to Tiffany. "After all, we don't have to spend our money on movies. We have DVDs galore and there are several delivery options available."

Emily was torn. On one hand, she was exhausted physically and mentally and wanted to stay in. On the other hand, she didn't want to upset her friends by canceling plans. She hadn't been out to the movies for a while and was looking forward to this. "I'll be fine, honest. You guys drive, that way I can keep resting. Deal?"

Stacy nodded. "Deal. Grab your coat. If we hurry, we can make it to the restaurant early and get to the theater on time."

Emily snagged her purse and they set off with Stacy driving, so no Tiffany death slaloms. Tiffany complained to protect her dignity. Dinner was salad with chicken, as she was fighting rising weight. The endocrinologist assured her that weight gain was normal, and exercise and diet changes would help, but she felt hungry all the time and was losing the battle against her weight. She already went up one clothing size and that was growing tight. Soon she would no longer fit into the clothes Stacy and Tiffi got her and she would have to get new things. If only there was something she could do for exercise, but jogging and bicycling were out and she didn't know enough alternate exercises to help.

They finished their meal and headed to the mall theater. Emily still felt off, but figured it was just exhaustion. The movie was an action-adventure horror film she was looking forward to. It was supposed to be good and had already been out for a while. Emily enjoyed horror films, although most American films were boring. Stabbity, stabbity just wasn't all that scary. Sometimes she liked to get her scare on, and there were precious few films that did it anymore. The Japanese ones were good though. Tiffany and Stacy knew this, as Tiffany was a big fan of horror and had been sharing films.

Partway through the film, something leapt out onscreen and Emily screamed in terror. She flung herself into the aisle and bolted from the theater, heart beating a mile a minute. She had to get out. Things were bad, very bad. An employee was in her way and got bowled over as she fled, hobbling faster than ever. Once outside, she managed to avoid getting hit by a car as she rushed deeper into the parking lot. She hunkered down between two cars, letting her heart slow as she searched frantically for her weapon but couldn't find it. She couldn't kill the thing if she didn't have her weapon.

She felt lost and confused. Where was the Blackhawk going to set down? Where was her fire support? Her heart pulsed, her leg burned with pain, and her head spun. What the hell was going on? With a heavy sigh, she collapsed against the side of a station wagon, too tired to keep going.

As her heart rate slowed, Emily calmed and started to think clearly. When she realized what had just happened, she groaned, unable to figure out a graceful way to get out of this fucking mess. Someone called her name.

It was Tiffany, her voice frantic. Emily timidly stood, leaning her weight against the car. She waved at Tiffany and limped to the center of the parking lane. Tiffany rushed up and hugged her fiercely. Face burning with embarrassment, Emily returned the hug. Tiffany asked, "Are you okay?"

"Yeah. Sorry. I guess with all the stress I had a flashback. God, I feel so stupid. Where's Stacy?" asked Emily, using Tiffany for support. Tiffany took it all in stride.

"I guess she's still talking to movie theater people. You know, you scared the shit out of everyone with that scream and the way you left. I honestly think it was scarier than the film. It even got a couple others to scream at an unscary part. Stacy's explaining what happened. It's all okay." Tiffany smiled and hugged Emily. "Anything wrong I need to know of?"

"Just injured pride. I feel like an idiot."

"Don't worry about it, Em. It isn't like you decided flashbacks would be cool and wanted them all the time. I mean all the hip veterans are doing it. I'm sure Stacy is spinning some story about how you were injured in the line of duty and hadn't expected to flip out. It'll be fine," said Tiffany. "Lean on me, we'll head to the car."

Emily nodded, face burning. She leaned heavily on Tiffany, her leg painful as adrenaline faded. She began to cry, tears trickling down her face as she struggled to muffle her sobs. The pain flare felt like acid melting her flesh. Emily hoped Stacy would get there soon, as she needed the pain meds in her purse. Her cane would be nice as well. The pain was so intense she was ready to vomit. She spotted Stacy heading over.

They helped her to the car and Emily took pain meds with a bottle of water. The water was warm and tasted faintly of plastic. Emily lay back and sighed. Stacy looked anxious as she watched Emily. "Do we need to go to the ER?"

Emily shook her head, wiping some tears. "No. I just need to get home and ice my leg. That and pain meds. There isn't much an ER can do."

"What happened?" Stacy was trying to make sense of this whole misadventure.

"When that thing jumped out on the screen it triggered a flashback. I'm sorry and embarrassed," said Emily. "I think I need quiet time away from people."

They headed back to the apartment while Emily called Leah to distance-cry on her shoulder. Tiffany kept a hand on Emily's shoulder. The car was quiet with the exception of Emily's slight sobs.

CHAPTER TWENTY-EIGHT

Emily felt weird as she woke. Something was off and she wasn't sure what. As full wakefulness reached her, she realized what it was. She had a fat lip. Emily thought back over yesterday to figure out what could cause this. She limped into the bathroom and looked in the mirror, hoping for an answer. Her lips did look swollen, but there was no obvious place where she could have been hit. The skin of her lips and mouth looked perfectly normal.

Figuring there was nothing she could do, she got in the shower and started her day. Leah got her into scented soap and body spray, and she discovered she really liked several scents. Smelling good all day was nice, and not like sweat and cordite that Thomas was much more used to. She grinned realizing that there needed to be another shopping trip soon, which sounded fun.

After stepping out of her shower, she pulled on a warm, fuzzy robe Emily wanted to burrow into. Leah had laughed when Emily opened her present and responded to the feel. The ability to like soft things was nice and Emily reveled in it.

She made her way to the kitchen, looking for breakfast. She toasted an English muffin and made a pot of coffee. She checked her planner to see if anything was pending. There was an appointment with Dr. Richards that afternoon but that was it. She also had to get new bras, as hers pinched. The chest strap was biting into her now that she was getting heavier and her breasts were growing. She was almost a full A cup. That made her giddy. Her breasts were growing!

Thankfully, her clothes and panties still fit even though they were growing snug.

The trouble was the weight gain. She had never gained weight as fast as she was currently, ever. She'd always been rail thin. She was already ten pounds up with no sign of it slowing. It irritated her and she was desperate to figure out why. True, the weight had a nice effect on her curves, providing fat to pad her out, but it was still disconcerting.

Emily finished breakfast and dressed, trying not to stress about her weight or her fat lip. It didn't work. She filled a ziplock bag with ice and put it on her lips. Hopefully, that would reduce the swelling.

The cold wasn't doing anything. Frowning, she returned the ice to the fridge. There were several ice packs in there, as she used them frequently. She shook her head, then headed to her car. Maybe she should call Leah and get her opinion?

After a few rings, Leah picked up. "Hey there, Emi kitty, what's with the early call?"

"Well, one, I love you, and two, to talk about something odd."

"Odd how?" asked Leah.

"My lips. They're swollen, like I have a fat lip."

"Is that why you sound weird? Did you get hit in the mouth or anything? Bitten by a spider? Molested by aliens?"

"I don't know. Nothing happened before I went to sleep, and I woke up with them this way. Nothing woke me, which those things would have, and my tush doesn't feel molested, so no alien abduction."

"Do your lips look…fuller?" Leah asked.

Emily glanced into the mirror. They did look a bit fatter than she remembered. It wasn't like she looked at her lips all the time. "Yeah?"

"I don't think this is anything to worry about, Emi kitty. It means your lips filled out, making you much more kissable." Leah purred the last part.

"Oh…really?" asked Emily, suddenly very interested. The fat lip didn't seem so bad anymore, and she looked forward to the difference.

"Oh, yes. I definitely have to take your new fuller lips out for a test drive. Just to make sure they're up to code. Purely scientific research you understand." Emily smiled when Leah lusted after her. It made her tingly.

They chatted, discussing the move that weekend. Before next semester they would be living together, and Emily would wake up every day to Leah's smile. The crazy sex might cut into study time, but she was all right with that.

Emily drove to the mall, wanting to purchase some nice bras. Plain ones were okay, but she really enjoyed cute lingerie. It made her feel intangibly better, and besides, Leah thought she looked hot.

She parked close to the good lingerie store. She had bought some things from there before and Leah loved her in them. That night had been wonderful, as she never orgasmed that many times in a row in her whole life.

Before transition, she'd have one, maybe two orgasms, then pass out. But now, things were changing. Her body was much more sensitive than before; there was no comparison. She never liked anyone playing with her nipples before and now she loved it. Her breasts were heading toward a B cup, making her extremely happy. They were still growing, as evidenced by the tender knot under her nipples that hurt if anything hit them wrong. She looked forward to larger breasts.

Now she felt different things. She shuddered when Leah licked her neck. Her ears being nibbled made her moan. Her skin burned under Leah's touch, and the first time Emily orgasmed without ejaculating, she cried. Now, she had one peak experience after another after another, each growing stronger until she erupted into the colored condom Leah insisted she wear. It was a small price to pay to help Leah play with her. Though, of late, her erection was not as big or as hard as before HRT.

At the end of the month, she had an endo appointment and he should be able to answer her questions. It was odd, to be sure, but Emily enjoyed their sex life even though it was different from the mount and thrust from before. It was different, and her body felt alive under Leah's touch. She also gave as good as she got and learned to make Leah moan as loud as Leah made her. Emily felt good about that, knowing her lovemaking skills changed for the better, because she was paying more attention to her partner, and that made everything better. The similar bodily responses helped as well, as she could guess what would feel good for Leah by what felt good on her.

Emily shifted herself before leaving the car. All those happy thoughts of Leah moaning gave her a chubby, and getting hard while tucked was…less than comfortable. Thankfully, her tight panties held her down. Tucking the way she learned seemed less scary than some techniques on the internet, like those involving duct tape. Pushing her testicles up and folding her penis back was simple, easy, and gave her the look she wanted, provided her underwear was snug enough.

Retail therapy was not always a bad thing. Emily avoided thinking about her last trip to the mall and how she freaked out at the movie. Her face burned with embarrassment. Thankfully, nobody noticed. They were all too busy running from store to store. She loved passing well enough to be anonymous.

This helped her support the local economy. She still had a tidy sum in her account drawing interest so she wasn't too stressed over money. After all, she had a big purchase in the near future. Between her pay for leaving the military, disability, and her Vocational Rehabilitation stipend, she was not hurting for cash. She was saving for surgery, using the money from being injured for a great purpose. Nothing like having the government ultimately be the one to pay for surgery.

That made her smile as she lugged her bags to the car. One of the security guards was helping, being nice to a disabled woman. Emily highly approved, since she didn't have to carry as much. She looked at the time and realized she would have to speed through lunch to make her appointment. She sighed and got fast food, hoping this wasn't one of the reasons for her weight gain, but it probably was. She needed to deal with this.

❖

"Good afternoon, Emily, how are you today?"

"Fine, Dr. Richards. It's been a pretty good day so far, except for my fat lip." Emily took the comfy chair.

"Fat lip?"

"I don't know. I woke up this way. Leah says my lips may have just filled out and that's what I'm feeling. I don't know. It feels like I'm talking funny." She shrugged.

Dr. Richards made a notation. "What do you think about that?"

"About what? My lips filling out? Well, it's cool and annoying, you know? I really have no idea why this is happening only that it is."

"That's okay, Emily. Hormones are powerful and their effects differ greatly from person to person. Just be open to whatever happens and remember hormones take time. After five years, breast growth stops, mostly, but the hormones will affect you for the rest of your life."

Emily nodded. This was good information, as some of it was new. "Oh…okay, that makes sense."

"So, any regrets? You've had a lot of things happen and that can make anyone a little skittish."

Emily thought about it. There certainly had been both good and bad. The attack had been bad, but the assistant district attorney treated her well when taking her deposition. He had been forthright and stuck to the events and nothing more. There had only been a few questions about her transition and those were mostly in building a timetable. Overall she felt happy and at peace. "None at all. Well, maybe I shouldn't have just attacked blindly back in Iraq and ended up getting injured, but this has been good for me."

The doc smiled. "Good. Anything bothering you?"

Emily frowned. "The trial is coming up and the ADA is trying to decide if I need to testify. If I take the stand, who I am will be on the news, in front of everybody. All of middle Tennessee will hear about the tranny vet who was attacked. I…I'm not sure I want to expose myself like that."

"You're afraid of exposure? Of everyone knowing?"

"Well, everywhere I'll go people will say 'Hey, look at the freak!' I don't want that! I just want to live my life."

"Do you think you could have them keep your name out of the news? I mean, you are the victim, and the law does have several ways to protect victims."

"I don't know. I can ask, but I'm afraid. Leah says it'll be okay and if we go on vacation after the trial, I'll fade from people's memories before we come back." She shrugged, unsure of the plan but would go along.

"Leah sounds like a very smart woman."

Emily smiled. "She is. I don't want the strain of the trial to affect us. I move in this weekend. In a little bit, the trial will be coming up and I don't want the stress making me snap and have her realize I'm not good enough for her."

"And how exactly are you not good enough for her?" asked Dr. Richards.

Emily choked up. "I'm not a complete woman. I'm broken. I freak out, feel like crap, and my family hates me. What's there to love?"

"Emily, what makes you think you're broken?"

"Well, look at me. My leg and arm are messed up. I'm broken!"

"Emily, you're not broken, just disabled. That isn't a bad thing. Things in your life have to change, that's all. Being disabled is about managing your pain and bodily restrictions. How does that make you broken?"

"I guess it doesn't, but I feel bad not being able to do the things I used to. It hurts to be weak and trapped by my body. I feel…helpless." Emily sniffled, barely managing to hold back welling tears.

"Things change, Emily. Take a look at yourself and tell me they don't?"

Emily snickered. She certainly had changed since she started. There was no denying that. Going from Thomas to Emily was an enormous change.

"Now the whole 'freak out' thing, is about your PTSD and occasional flashbacks, correct?"

She nodded. "I feel bad and embarrassed. I know it's not my fault, but isn't there something I can do? I can barely stand them and I feel awful afterward."

"You are doing something, Emily. I'm not just treating your gender stuff you know. You've been doing fine. You're going to have times where these things crop back up due to new stress. It's all part of the healing process. And the feeling like crap? Part of that is likely depression."

Emily nodded again. Dr. Richards's words made her feel better, if for no other reason than boosting her ego.

"And as for your family, you were honest and they made their choice. I wish I could say it'll be happy endings, but a large number of families never cope when someone goes through transition. They get trapped in the memory of who the person was rather than the reality of who they are. This happens to people with other issues as well. Sometimes you lose those you love by being true to yourself. Sometimes family can't deal. Sometimes family wants you to stay the messed-up person you were because they wouldn't have to change in response."

Emily took it in, realizing she agreed. "And the being whole thing?"

"Emily, if you have surgery, you'll be whole physically. So, where's the problem? As for mentally, you're working toward that. That's a process that may take your whole life, but you're on your way."

"I guess you're right. Maybe I'm being foolish?" she asked.

"No more than any other person in love and worried about things."

Emily smiled. It was nice to be normal.

"Oops...looks like our time is done. Take care and I'll see you in two weeks."

Emily stood and said her good-byes. Maybe it was time to do something about her relationship, something more.

❖

After they were done with the move and had put away most of her things, Emily struck. She took Leah's hands in hers, dragged her into the living room, and got down on one knee, making Leah gasp.

"Leah, I love you with everything in me. You make me happy and fulfilled in a way no one else ever has. I can't stand being apart from you. Leah, will you marry me?"

Leah stood there, blinking at her. "But...what...huh...is...is that even legal?"

Emily laughed. "Who cares? I love you. I want to spend the rest of my life with you, and since I'm still technically male, through no fault of my own, we can legally get married. I looked it up and everything. According to what I read, what's important to Tennessee is the person's sex at birth, not what they are now. That's honestly what it says. So regardless, to this state, it'll simply be a man marrying a woman."

"Do…do you really think we can do this?"

"Sure. Amazingly enough, it's completely legal. You still haven't answered. Will you marry me?" The suspense was killing her and her heart throbbed quickly, almost choking her.

"Yes. Yes, I want to marry you, Emily." They hugged, kissed, and made out on their shared living room floor.

CHAPTER TWENTY-NINE

Leah and Emily pulled into the county clerk's office parking. They had all the paperwork needed, plus a little more to be safe. Emily was as prepared as possible since the last thing she wanted was a misadventure. From what she read, all they had to do was walk in, show their driver's licenses, and fill out some paperwork. Leah managed to find a Unitarian Universalist minister willing to perform the ceremony, so all they needed was the certificate.

They leaned over and kissed. While walking in, Emily held Leah's hand. The plan was to get there early in the hope they could get this over with before lunch and married that afternoon. Emily was nervous but one hundred percent positive she wanted this, looking forward to being wife and wife. The whole idea amused her to no end, as she had never expected to be a wife. Leah had said she never expected this either, as it wasn't legal. Emily almost giggled in pure happiness when they looked at each other.

There was a bit of a line. Three other couples were in front of them, and as they shuffled forward, another showed up behind.

The woman behind the counter looked bored, scanning things briefly as she typed. When they reached her, Leah handed over the application and her driver's license. Emily handed hers over as well. The clerk took them and started to fill things out in the computer, when things registered. "Um...these are both ladies' names."

Emily sighed in resignation. "Yes."

The woman seemed to grow confused as she looked at the licenses and back up at them. "But...but...that's not legal here."

Emily tapped her driver's license. "If you look right there, you'll see this is all perfectly legal."

The woman picked up Emily's license and inspected it. She looked at Emily, the license, Emily, the license, then over toward another employee for help. It was clear a circuit had blown. "Um… let me get my supervisor."

She hustled off, leaving them standing there amused.

A short while later, the clerk returned, supervisor in tow who jumped right in. "You can't do this here. This state doesn't allow same-sex marriages."

Emily shook her head and replied calmly. "Right there on my driver's license it states I'm male. According to the state code annotated, that's all you need to present in order to get married. That says I am male."

"But you aren't a male. I can clearly see you're a woman," said the supervisor. The original woman looked sheepish.

Emily grew frustrated. This was not supposed to be a fucking interrogation. What was so difficult? All she had to do was look at the licenses and type things into the computer. Leah rested a hand on her arm then asked politely, "What do you need in order to confirm Emily is male?"

"A birth certificate or a doctor's note stating there are male genitalia and no surgery altered them," she replied.

Emily opened the folder, pulled out her birth certificate and name change form and handed them over. The supervisor scrutinized them and narrowed her eyes. "I don't have the authority for this. I have to check with my superior."

They waited silently, trying to figure what the problem was this time. They had all documents needed and were in accordance with the law. After a few minutes, the woman returned and handed back their paperwork. "I'm sorry, we cannot give you a marriage license."

Leah and Emily looked at each other and then back at the supervisor. Leah spoke, voice growing sharp. "Why not?"

"My superior said I'm not to issue you one."

"Why? There is no legal reason for this, as the criteria listed in the state codes have been met. Let us speak to your superior." After more huffing, they were led to another door. Emily could feel people staring. The name on the door read, *Mitch Tyler, Vice Clerk.*

Mr. Tyler was an older gentleman, with thinning gray hair and glasses. He had a scowl etched on his face as he looked at them. They stood before his desk and Emily politely said, "Good morning."

"I told her we're not going to have any of this here," he replied.

"Um...Mr. Tyler, you do know this is perfectly legal according to the Tennessee state code, correct?" asked Leah.

"What you fail to realize, miss, is that I can make this decision. I'll not have any of this. The buck stops here." Tyler looked angry.

"So, even though we are legally allowed to get married, according to the Tennessee state code annotated, you aren't going to let us?" asked Leah.

"I'm the one who makes the final decision. Me. If I decide you can't get married then you can't because I say so." Tyler glared at Leah.

Emily looked at the man's nameplate and thought about what it said as Leah battled over their right to get married. Something clicked when Tyler claimed "the buck stops here." She looked directly at him. "The buck doesn't stop with you though."

Leah and Tyler both shut up and turned to Emily. "It says right there on your name plate, *vice* clerk."

"That's right. And this ends with me."

"But being vice clerk means you aren't actually the county clerk, only his or her assistant. Since you are being so aggressive and refusing to follow the law, we want to speak to your boss, the actual county clerk."

Tyler turned his glare to her. "I'm the one who makes this decision. I'm the final person you talk to."

"No, you aren't. Let's speak to the county clerk." Emily stood firm. She knew the chain of command, and this was clearly time to go over someone's head.

Mr. Tyler stormed out in a huff. Leah smiled. "I'm sorry, sweetie. I was so pissed about him not following the law I got stuck on that and didn't notice."

Emily beamed at her. "Don't worry, love. One of us caught it and that's all that matters. Are we a great team or what?"

"Is this guy a jerk or what?"

"He's a total asshat. I can't believe he isn't following the law."

"I know. It's odd." She quieted as Tyler walked back in. He looked smug, as if he just won. "He isn't here. His secretary told me he's out."

Emily smiled. This really had become a whole chain-of-command issue and she knew how to use the chain in a way this guy wasn't ready for. This fool probably thought he was dealing with stupid people willing to give in at "insurmountable" challenges. "Then can we speak with their secretary?"

He scowled and gestured for them to follow. It was a short walk to the actual county clerk's office. Tyler made a motion to enter, turned, and left them, grumbling the whole while. The secretary was on the phone and gestured for them to sit. Emily and Leah complied, patiently waiting. It was a few minutes before she finished and turned to them. "What can I do to help you two?"

Leah took charge, which Emily didn't mind. Leah liked to be in charge. "Mr. Tyler wasn't being helpful so we asked to talk to the county clerk. When he said the clerk wasn't in, we asked to speak to you."

She nodded. "So, the situation he mentioned?"

"Yes. Emily is transgendered and has legally changed her name. Since she hasn't had surgery, she is therefore legally male. We have her driver's license, which is all that is required for a marriage license, but the problem is apparently the license will have two girls' names on it." Leah laid everything out. "They then asked for a birth certificate, which we showed them, along with name change paperwork. That got us to Mr. Tyler, who said no for no apparent reason, even though we have complied with the law and every request. So, we wanted the clerk's assistance in this matter."

The secretary thought about it for a short while. "The clerk isn't here. He's at a doctor's appointment. I can't call and talk to him until he gets out, which is in an hour. Leave me your number and I'll call once he checks in. Now, you did say you have the name change forms, birth certificate, and driver's licenses?"

They nodded and Emily handed over the small stack of paperwork. The woman looked over the documents carefully and took notes. She handed them back with a smile. "I'll call you as soon as I've talked to him."

Once outside, the cursing began. Emily growled angrily. "Motherfucker. That asshole is pissing me off. The sanctimonious prick! I should kick his ass!"

Leah laid a hand on her arm to calm her. "Let's get some coffee, maybe some breakfast, then we'll wait for the call. It'll be okay. No need to act all butch on account of that asshat."

Emily grumbled. They drove to a place near Vanderbilt hospital, in a pet store-turned-restaurant that served food plus the black nectar of life. After they ordered, Emily and Leah found a free table and sat. Leah sipped chai while Emily had her coffee and they both ate bagels happily. The food helped Emily calm down more. "This whole thing is making me crazy. Why is this so difficult? I mean, so I have a girl's name, so what? I knew a sergeant who changed his name to the letter Y and another who took his wife's last name when they married. You can change your name to Motorboat and that's fine, so what the fuck?"

"It's the gender thing, sweetie. People get crazy about things outside the norm. This is the buckle of the Bible Belt. The Southern Baptist Convention has a huge building only a few miles from here. Sometimes you have to remember these things." Leah paused to sip her chai.

"What? I mean, I grew up in a very religious community. I was very religious until my senior year. But I don't see where religion should get in the way of the law. The law is clear on this."

Leah patted Emily's hand. "I know, but let's not get worked up unless things don't work out. We can fight then. I'm just sad. I thought Nashville would be less psychotic. Maybe Clarksville would have been a better idea."

Emily sat back and drank more coffee. She had almost had the chai as it was very good and she enjoyed the flavor. She had gotten into those thanks to Tiffany and her near addiction, and apparently, it was contagious.

Leah's cell phone rang, and they stopped everything. Maybe this was the call that would fix everything. Leah answered on the third ring. "Hello?"

Emily couldn't hear the other side of the conversation. It made her crazy not knowing what was being said. "Yes, thank you for calling back. What did the clerk say?...Okay, but this is the county we live in....Why not? The whole thing is in the state law codes.... Yes, we read them. Even if she had surgery, the fact that she was born male would be enough according to the law as written. You saw the birth certificate....Uh-huh. Okay. I'll wait for your call." Leah hung up and took a sip of her drink. Emily vibrated, wanting to know what was going on.

Leah finished and said, "The clerk wanted us to do this in Montgomery County, where you got your name changed. Basically, I don't think he wants to deal with this and is trying to pass the buck. I pointed out we currently live here and want to get married here. The secretary asked about the records and surgery. I mentioned the documents she saw and she's going to call him back. Hopefully, we don't have to wait long."

Twenty minutes later, Leah's phone rang again. "Really? That's wonderful. Please thank him and we'll be in there in a few minutes."

Emily looked at her and she beamed at the growing smile on Leah's face. "We won?"

"We won."

They hugged, then kissed. No one in the coffeehouse seemed to care. They sang along with the radio as they drove to the county clerk's office and nearly bounded in and to the back of the line. They pointedly didn't look into Mitch Tyler's office as they passed.

The wait wasn't long, with only one couple ahead of them. Soon they were again up at the front. This time a different woman was waiting. "Ladies, please have a seat. I need to go over the paperwork and then we can do this."

They sat down and waited. "Okay, first things first, let me see your driver's licenses."

Leah and Emily handed them over happily. The woman examined each carefully, obviously checking to see if one was fake. Since neither was, she soon handed them back. "And now the other paperwork?"

Emily handed over the stack of paper. The woman looked carefully at her birth certificate and checked the raised seal. Then she turned to the name change documents and their raised seal. When she seemed satisfied, she looked up. "Okay, all your paperwork is in order. You need to sign the book and we can get this done."

While Leah and Emily signed the huge book with pairs of names all through it, the woman took their application and began typing. "I don't know what the problem is. I mean y'all are going to have the right to get married in a few years or so anyway. I mean people are just people, that's what I say. So, it really shouldn't be such an issue, but this is the Bible Belt and people here don't do things like this. Makes 'em grumpy."

Leah and Emily smirked. The woman kept talking as she typed, running on like Tiffany. "But don't worry, in ten years or so, everything'll change and y'all can get married without hassle. It's like with Black folks back in the sixties. There was the same fuss about marrying whites. How it was unnatural and such. Now look at things. So, don't worry about it."

The woman finished and printed something out. "Look this over for any mistakes. Let me just take care of this."

She took out a sheet of parchment with the marriage certificate and began to write their names. Her hand was apparently shaking a little as she did and was finally able to complete one on her third try. She laughed.

Emily smirked as she scanned the printout. The paperwork looked in order and nothing was missing. She shrugged and Leah quickly scanned her own portion. She pushed it back to the other side of the counter.

They woman quickly finished and printed two copies of the official form. She put one copy in a large envelope with their certificate and kept the other. As Leah and Emily stood, the woman noticed something and looked away. She took a deep breath in and paused before asking, "Um...honey, I know you're proud of 'em but could you cover them up until you're out of here?"

Emily looked down confused until she realized the woman was talking about her breasts. "You want me to cover up?"

"Could you? I know I'm being silly, but it's my job and I don't want you to draw attention to the fact that things are different than they seem. And please don't put this in the paper. I don't want to lose my job." The woman was really nervous about that.

Emily smiled. "I can do that. And we won't tell the newspapers."

The woman looked relieved. Emily and Leah left, Emily's arms crossed over her breasts, as if that would hide the fact she was a girl. Once outside, they started laughing, especially when Emily uncrossed her arms and thrust her chest out. It continued all the way to the car. They looked at each other and grinned. True, they would have to race to the church to make it on time, but they managed to get this taken care of.

Leah started the car, saying, "Come on, Emi kitty, let's get married."

CHAPTER THIRTY

Emily rolled over in bed and smiled at her lightly snoring wife. It was funny, as a guy, she hadn't planned on marrying for a long while, and now it was the most normal thing in the world. Leah was wonderful and fit her better than anybody. Honestly, she had never been happier and that took some getting used to. She felt blessed and wasn't sure by who, God, Athena, or someone else. Sometimes she thought her face should hurt from smiling, since as a boy those muscles weren't used often.

She lay there, watching Leah, the bathroom nightlight casting enough illumination to identify some features. Brushing a hand down her back made Leah sigh contentedly. Emily wished the moment would last, but she knew it wouldn't. Tomorrow, she would testify in the trial against her attackers. She hoped she wouldn't have to, but the defense hung everything on a trans panic defense. The defense was alleging that she hit on them and when they realized the "truth" they freaked and attacked her.

The district attorney was disgusted by the ploy, but glad that Emily could produce a large number of character witnesses. Between that and the hard evidence, the district attorney was sure it would be an easy case. Maybe her sergeant would be able to get those idiots to shut up and take their punishment when he talked about her character. Maybe not, since they were dumb enough to jump her in the first place. The DA planned on pointing out how brave it was for three strong, well-built men to attack a disabled woman. If she had been armed with more than a cane, they would have been taken care of permanently. She had done what she could and made the right choice.

Emily rose and pulled on her robe to cover her naked body. She hobbled to the living room and sat on the couch. It was comfy with a lap quilt over her legs. She was too nervous to even contemplate sleep. She was busy planning her outfit, wondering what she would say, and running the event over and over, to make sure the details were set. She hadn't been afraid until afterward, just like in Iraq. Emily being a war hero apparently would be another card played. She wondered how the defense attorney planned to counter that.

Her mind drifted back to infantry training at Fort Benning with the bayonet. It was interesting, and pugil sticks had been fun. They spent some time on it but not nearly as much as other things. The rest of basic was a blur of running, waiting, marksmanship, and basic tactical training. Her time with her training unit, the 198th Infantry Brigade, had been great. She never worked so hard in her life. It turned her thoughts to might-have-beens.

She had hoped for Ranger school and maybe Special Forces. Her career had been moving forward, her Ranger packet already approved, and she had simply been waiting on a class date to rotate out of the desert. Maybe if she had gotten picked earlier, she wouldn't have gotten injured? But then she would still be hiding from herself and would never have met Leah. She would still be her miserable old self, trapped in a male identity that chafed.

Emily sighed, realizing she was doing that a lot more. If she hadn't gotten injured, she wouldn't have figured out the whole jealousy thing and gotten this whole fucked up gender roller coaster started. She wouldn't wish this on anyone, even her attackers. Gender problems were too painful. She was different from the infantryman who yelled, "Blood! Blood! Blood makes the green grass grow!" Thankfully, her old teammates decided getting severely injured allowed her a few personal quirks. Saving a bunch of their lives certainly figured into that as well.

Emily remembered telling her sergeant about the court date and registered what that would mean. She shuddered at the thought of a room filled with a bunch of infantrymen in Class A uniforms, looking like recruitment posters. Maybe she should skip the trial and head for Rio?

She yawned, a wave of sleepiness feathering over her. When she yawned again, the corners of her mouth tightened under the strain so she stumbled back to bed. After a quick bathroom break, she dropped her robe and climbed into bed and slid up against Leah's naked back. Emily shifted her testicles, grumbling slightly, as the maneuver pinched them. As soon as she was able, she planned on eliminating the need to tuck. She looked forward to that. With those happy thoughts, she drifted off to sleep.

❖

The wait for the verdict had been tense, though it had not taken very long. It had turned out one of the campus cops had seen things go down but had been too far away to intervene. Considering the glut of evidence and the over-the-top character witnesses Emily had, the jury had not been sequestered long before the guilty verdict was passed. And she had managed to dodge the majority of the potential fifteen minutes of fame between the DA taking care of her and the school wanting to avoid the bad press. She could sleep again without nightmares and managed to start eating normally.

With the stress of the trial over, Emily turned her focus to the details for hair removal and the surgical procedure. It was fascinating and disgusting. She barely looked at the accompanying photos, as they made her a bit sick to her stomach. She had seen blood before, both hers and other people's in Iraq, so that wasn't the issue, but this... this was different. This was something more intimate and intentional. She was going to do this, was going to pay a man to cut into her, and irrevocably reshape her body to make it look like it should.

She looked at the pictures and her mind pictured each step happening in excruciating detail. She reviewed the risk sheet, and it made her nauseous. She wanted this, but the process seemed nightmarish. To be fair, most surgeries sounded horrific. What was she going to do?

She swallowed dryly, focusing on the end result. That helped clear her head and settle her stomach. After surgery, she would have a vagina, her very own vagina. She would be complete, whole, in a way she could not express. She could look in the mirror and see Emily, not some Emily/Thomas hybrid dangling there. Her penis spoiled her appearance and made her think she was not a girl. She hated that, hated that damned image, how after every shower it was thrown in her face, taunting her. Her mind knew what was real and true, despite her body being off. Her body wasn't her truth. She could fix that. With a bit of help, she would become complete. All she had to do was clear her groin of hair and then surgery before her reflection would be all her.

She could not bring herself to talk about this with Leah, knowing her issues with men. She was unwilling to aggravate them. In a way, she was afraid to let Thomas go, to let her "before" pass away into an unhappy memory. She didn't hate being male; it had just been uncomfortable and ill fitting. Because of that, she felt disconnected, out of sorts, and now she was in her own skin…all except for one last part that refused to cooperate.

Maybe she should talk to Dr. Richards. He might be able to understand. If she could get past her worry and fear, things might get better. That would be a good thing as stress increased pain levels. Her body was marred by her penis, and surgery was the way to end the dissonance.

She shook her head to stop her dwelling. Emily headed to the kitchen for a drink. Leah was working late and Emily had the house to herself. She limped to the living room and fell onto the comfier of their two couches. She grabbed the remote and turned on a cooking show, feeling lonely. She paid attention to how things were prepared, desperately trying to expand her cooking skills from ramen and warming cans of beefaroni to actual food. Leah helped her learn, but TV gave lots of good instruction. Some of those chefs explained things clearly, which was probably why they were on TV in the first place.

The Italian food looked wonderful, and she paid attention to the tips, not sure when she might cook this, but willing to learn. It looked tasty and she had become fond of tasty. So much had changed. Her life took several radical turns after getting injured, and all of this insanity, hormones, confrontations, and realizations were for the best. Despite that, she sometimes felt more like Thomas and less like Emily, but those moments were few and far between. She was Emily at heart.

Thinking back to Army life was like remembering a dream. So many things seemed surreal, like they were another person's memories.

She recalled all the events, but they had faded, shoved aside under the plethora of new and wondrous sensations and experiences of her second puberty. She faced feelings and body shifts that nothing had prepared her for. She was undergoing a radical transformation.

She looked over at her framed Army discharge and the shadow box holding her Bronze Star. She earned that. Without thinking, she had gone beyond what was normally expected of any soldier. She served her country and did her best with what she had. Who could ask for more than that? All she wanted was happiness. She found it and pursued it regardless of whatever worries chased her.

She twirled a finger through her hair, a recently developed habit. Her thoughts roamed, wandering between past, present, and future, as she tried to come to terms with what her life had become. Lost to thoughts, she started when Leah slid next to her, brushing a strand of Emily's hair behind an ear. "Hey, love. Dinner's ready. Hungry?"

Emily pulled out of her reverie, surprised to see Leah. Her stomach growled at the mention of dinner which made her feel herself starting to blush. Leah laughed. "I'll take that as a yes. So, what have you been in here pondering?"

"All the gender crap. It keeps resurfacing. I wish it would just go away," Emily grumbled. "I mean, this isn't the only thing I am, yet it's become the most important right now and I don't like it."

Leah pulled Emily to her feet and walked into the dining room. "Well, that makes sense. I mean, you've been going through transition for a while, all things being equal. So, it's important, right there, all the time. If it's still bothering you in a year or so, maybe three-plus, then it might be something to worry about. Right now, it makes sense."

"You think so?"

With one hand, she brushed Emily's hair back. "Yeah. I do. You're still becoming you. Some things have changed, but nothing has made you anyone but yourself."

Emily hugged Leah and they shared a deep, soulful kiss. "Thank you. I have no idea what I'd do without you."

Leah smiled. "Tell you what…let's not find out. Okay?"

CHAPTER THIRTY-ONE

Leah looked concerned as Emily gingerly tottered toward her, waddling lightly and as wide-legged as humanly possible, leaning heavily on her cane. Leah rushed over. "Are you okay, love?"

"Electrolysis...testicles...bad idea." Emily teared up. The electrolysist came out kneading a chemical ice pack and looking sympathetic. "Hold this there for a while and the swelling will go down. She did fairly well for a first session. That area is one of the most sensitive parts of the body. I'm sorry it hurt. But that section is cleared. We'll use sedation next time to make it more bearable."

They thanked her and headed out to the car. Leah smirked at Emily in a half commiserating, half amused way. Emily delicately got into the passenger seat, holding the ice pack to her aching crotch, not caring about how obscene it looked. Emily wanted to go home to tend to her injured genitalia. Leah said, "She said the first session would be the worst, and that's over with."

Emily faced her, thankful for the ice pack. "I know, but that really fucking hurt and only an eighth of the area got covered. I'm not sure I want to do this."

"So...you want hair growing out of your vagina?" asked Leah, watching the road.

Emily shuddered. "Okay. I don't want that because ewwww. I'll keep doing this, but it effing hurts."

"I know, baby." Leah patted her thigh. "I've had electrolysis as well."

"Really?" asked Emily.

"Yeah. I had some dark hairs between my breasts, around my nipples, and under my chin. I saved up and had it done. Oh my God, electrocuting your breasts isn't a recommended activity. But it took care of the problem."

"I just want this to be done. It hurts so bad. Why me?"

"Because you want an innie instead of an outie," said Leah. "And just think, once this is done, we can get you a surgeon and be ready to go."

Emily cocked her head. "What…you want to go shopping again? We already found someone."

"What? I like vaginas. It's not my fault they're pretty."

Emily chuckled and grinned weakly. "Yeah…I'm fond of them as well."

"Well, good…otherwise you might have an issue with me."

"Never. I love you."

"I love you too, Emi kitty." Emily blushed. The nickname always made her feel warm and fuzzy.

"So…you promised me lunch?" said Emily, her stomach getting mighty feisty.

"Yeah…I did. Sushi?" Leah had introduced Emily to sushi three months ago and Emily loved it. She preferred it to cooked fish, which was disturbing. It was odd, but the more she ate it, the more she got used to it, and the tastier it became. She discovered lots of new things with Leah and couldn't be happier.

They headed to Leah's favorite place. Lunch was fun and Emily's burning crotch eased. They toasted to that with their green tea. Emily had enough distance from the pain to realize the humor.

Emily checked her email once back home. She scanned the previews, seeing if anything had importance. An email leapt out at her, and she quickly opened it.

Emily started grooving in the desk chair. This news was just so great she had to move. Emily turned and spotted Leah, watching her with one hand covering her smile, freezing mid dance. Her blush burned her face something fierce and she hid her radiant cheeks in her hands. Leah grinned. "I love you."

Emily turned her face away. "I got a letter back. Dr. Stuart in Arizona says I'm on the list. Once I get my letters, surgery is a go."

Emily bounced, forgetting her embarrassment. Leah rushed over and hugged her. "That's awesome, sweetie. What do you need for the letters?"

Emily scanned the email again. "Well, Dr. Richards writes one and gives me a consult to see someone for the other. That's it. Well… besides the very, very painful hair removal portion of the event."

"Okay…so we get you more appointments. Once we plan a date for surgery, I can get us a hotel and plane tickets. That'll be awesome." Leah bounced as well.

Emily beamed. "Yes! All my plumbing problems will be gone."

Leah poked her in the arm playfully. "Yeah…Super Clit will be gone."

Emily blushed, swatting Leah playfully. "Stop that. That sounds odd and pornographic."

"You got me," admitted Leah. Things devolved to an eventual romp in the bedroom, upsetting no one.

❖

"Well, you have both letters. The rest should be easy," said Dr. Richards, handing over the two envelopes. "So…who are you going to for surgery?"

"Dr. Stuart in Arizona. Leah and I like his work. There were a number of other people's work Leah and I looked over, but in the end, we decided on him. Dr. Bowden in Colorado was a close second, and the former NASA flight surgeon in Pennsylvania third." Emily happily took the envelopes and put them in her purse. She had the last things necessary to finish. Her plumbing could get fixed once and for all.

"So, Emily, you have no doubts?" asked the doc.

"I'm nervous about the surgery. I mean, it's pretty major. I'm positive I want this, but nervous about having it. Does that make sense?"

"It does. I would have been worried if you weren't a bit skittish. This is a major surgery, and it's good to see you thought things through."

"I did have you to help me through all the twists and turns. Thank you for that, by the way."

"Well, you're not getting off easy. I'm still going to monitor you because of the other things going on with you. The sessions will be like normal, and we can work on the rest, like your family and PTSD."

"I understand and am certain I'll need to talk to someone about all of this stuff. It isn't like surgery is going to make my other problems go away, now is it?" Emily would still have various things to mull over after surgery, some of which were on the back burner.

"That's true. Many people think having surgery will solve all their problems, that their lives will become magically better. They never do. Life is just life and the problems you have today will still be there after surgery. It isn't like surgery cuts out the problems."

Emily nodded. "Yeah. I can see that. I want surgery because every time I look in the mirror, get dressed, use the bathroom, it's there, making me feel tense and incomplete. I have enough trouble remembering that being disabled is not the same as being crippled without that making me feel useless."

"Why is that, you think?" asked Dr. Richards.

"Seeing my penis reminds me of the genetic screw-up that caused this. The whole fucking plumbing problem seems the last toe hold of the person I was." Emily shrugged. "I'm a woman, yet I have something saying I'm not. It's bothersome."

"Does your penis make you any less a woman?"

"In my head it doesn't, but my guts…I'm not sure. As long as I played a guy, I thought my penis defined me, that it constrained my actions, my genitals controlling my destiny. Now…now I'm stuck thinking my penis overrides everything saying woman and other people believe that as well."

"Well, surgery should take care of that. I'm sorry it bothers you. Hopefully, this will correct itself post-surgery. If it doesn't, we'll work on it." The doc scribbled more notes then glanced at the clock. "I guess I'll see you again in a few weeks?"

"Sounds fine to me. Thank you."

"No problem, Emily." Dr. Richards pulled up the appointment schedule. Once they agreed on a date, Emily left the office.

She limped to her car, thinking about the letters, about her body, about everything. Her thoughts were a jumble, but the last keys she needed to unlock herself were in her purse. These letters would allow her to totally become Emily. It would horrify her family and she didn't give a rat's ass. They forfeited their right to an opinion.

Leah would be happy once this was done. The colored latex condoms gave the illusion that Emily's penis was a dildo. Surgery would fix that, and Emily would not have to camouflage herself to sleep with her wife. Not that she minded, but she looked forward to being penis-free and wondered about post-surgery sex.

Most articles mentioned the very good chance for her to experience orgasm post-surgery, that a constructed vagina would function like a natural one. If some gynecologists couldn't tell the difference, then maybe things would be okay. Hopefully, Leah would like her vagina. Maybe she would see herself in the mirror instead of this halfway thing. Maybe her panties would fit better. She could only hope.

As she headed out of the VA, her stomach growled. Leah was working late again so maybe she should go to Music Row and meet her for dinner. Emily could drop by the LGBT bookstore on Church Street. Maybe she could pick up some more music. Leah's taste in music was great, and Emily enjoyed Ani DiFranco, the Indigo Girls, and Melissa Ethridge. Go figure, the sound engineer had good taste in music.

There was a nice Indian restaurant nearby Leah had introduced her to. Her life changed so much after meeting Leah, so many things Thomas never saw, never conceived of, never heard or tasted, and now Emily was immersed in a world far richer than the one she left behind.

Despite the madness and chaos of transition, Emily was content. She could smile walking down the street, at any odd moment. It made her heart swell and burst with happiness. All because she noticed how she felt about a nurse's ass and how tightly the BDU pants fit. Emily laughed at the absurdity. If she knew who the nurse was, she could send a thank you card, but doubted Hallmark made something saying, "Thank you for helping me realize my gender dysphoria."

She drove singing Melissa Ethridge at the top of her lungs. Was a change in gender responsible for her relishing life, for the sense of freedom she gained letting go?

As she drove to the bookstore, that problem absorbed her. Was there something inherently better about being a girl over a guy?

Was there something about this gender that was superior? Maybe it had less to do with that and more to do with truly connecting to herself? Maybe in becoming Emily she came alive? Maybe that was the difference, regardless of gender. Men, women…so long as they connected to themselves, all was good.

She browsed the bookshelves, mind wandering over this idea. She could see one of the owners moving about, tidying the DVDs. He seemed happy and content. Was the trick simply finding yourself? Was it just a matter of paying attention to who you were at the core? Could anyone get there without going through something traumatic?

She stopped, holding a CD by Disappear Fear and trying to work this out, which made her head hurt. She'd never delved into metaphysics before. Was this all some way to connect to yourself? What the fuck was the whole point anyway?

Maybe she didn't need an answer. Maybe just being centered and living was enough? She shrugged and took the CD to the front. She drove to Centennial Park, the new music helping her relax. Once parked, she sat there, her thoughts a maelstrom. She shrugged, deciding she needed to visit the Lady.

She paid her fee, walked up the stairs, and stood before Athena. The air felt heavy. Whether this was a statue of an actual goddess, present or not did not concern her. A feeling of peace poured into her. Visiting the Parthenon had calmed her several times before, especially during the trial and the sentencing. Nevertheless, she came to find true quiet.

She felt the stillness of a placid lake, of a church. Her thoughts settled and were clearer. She discovered herself through this… misadventure. The gender insanity was incidental to the greater trial, facing herself and becoming who she was inside. Discovering the gender she showed the world didn't reflect the inner truth that had driven her to find that. The support group was filled with people trying to find their way, and people like Tara and Becky who were going through the same thing she was. Maybe it was about the self?

That made sense. She discovered all this through figuring out who she was and why she felt jealous. It hadn't started as a gender thing at all; it just ended up that way. Her thoughts stopped whirling.

She glanced at her watch and realized she needed to call Leah, to head off for dinner. She had spent enough time letting her thoughts drift.

Emily thanked the Lady and headed out before making her call. She got Leah's voice mail and left a message. They had something to celebrate so she hoped they could go out. Those letters would enable her to push up the surgery date. She now had the money and the letters to make her dreams real. With one layer of craziness out of the way, she could focus on other internal stuff, like her PTSD.

Emily stopped ruminating to turn to the important topic of filling her stomach. She went over places in her head when Leah returned her call. Emily grinned. "Hey there, sweetie."

"Emily, what's up?" asked Leah.

"I wanted to celebrate, so I stayed downtown after my appointment. I got my letters. Surgery is a go." Emily bounced in the driver's seat as she told Leah.

"That is awesome, sweetie. Where do you want to go? Fondue?" Emily thought about the fondue place on Second Street. It was supposed to be good and quite romantic. The place certainly had the possibility of being fun.

"Sure. Sounds like a plan. Do we need reservations?"

Emily could hear Leah thinking. "Maybe. Give 'em a call and see if we can get in. If not, someplace else?"

Directory assistance gave her the number. She was excited and things were looking up. Emily held up the letters and smiled. This would make things happen faster and her life could move forward. Maybe she should start planning the traditional, pre-surgery weenie roast.

CHAPTER THIRTY-TWO

Emily struggled back to consciousness, wading through molasses. The anesthesia made her thirsty and her stomach jumpy. She looked around the recovery room, trying to make out anything, but nothing came into focus. She blinked slowly, trying to sort out what she was seeing.

Everything seemed fuzzy, the edges of the world frayed. A shape in light green headed her way, a voice coming from a distance but growing closer every moment. "Emily, welcome back. Would you like some water?"

Emily nodded, feeling drained and parched. The ice chip was cool and soothed her raw throat. As she lay back, the faint beginnings of pain started to rise. She grimaced and the nurse handed her something. It was a white object with a red button and a cord coming out the bottom. "When the pain comes back, push this button only once. It'll help."

Emily did so and a rush of numb moved through her body and the massive pain nestled between her legs. Her head was clearing from the anesthesia but was still morphine-muddled.

It was done. She was complete. The surgery was over and all was good. She lay back in the bed and cried in happiness. She drifted off to sleep.

When she next awoke, she was in a hospital bed, legs spread slightly, held open by several ice packs. She had an IV and the morphine drip. Leah was in a seat next to her, flipping through a magazine, one of the most beautiful sights she had seen. The stirring was enough to catch her attention and Leah looked over. "How's my best girl?"

"Sore," murmured Emily. The pain crested, but with a push of a button, it faded. She closed her eyes and sighed.

"The doctor said the surgery went great. Everything should be fine and no complications." Emily nodded sleepily and faded back into slumber.

By early evening Emily was more coherent and was able to have some broth and Jell-O. Emily was completely giddy, though the drugs were helping. "Wow. It's really done? Wow. Really? Wow."

Leah giggled. "Yes, you silly girl, it's all done. You have girl bits now, well, actually, all you have right now is a mountain of gauze and packing material. We can take a look at the new you when all that comes out. So, worth the pain?"

"Definitely. I hope you'll like it."

"Emily, you dork, I love you for you, not your genitals. Sheesh! Some people," she said, ruffling Emily's hair. "You're beautiful, sweetie, and this has changed nothing."

Emily smiled then grimaced as the pain returned, and she pushed the button. She smiled as things faded away.

❖

"Well, let's see how everything turned out, shall we?" said the surgeon lightheartedly, as he moved to remove the bandages and packing material from Emily's new vagina. "Things may be a little tender, but everything should be okay."

Emily had been off the morphine drip for days and was quite glad of it. They were staying in a nearby hotel and all she did was lie about with bags of ice on her crotch. She was nervous and excited wondering what she would look like. This was the unveiling. She could feel the bandages as they were removed, with a few pieces of the gauze sticking to her skin, tugging slightly. She couldn't see, as the angle was terrible, but she certainly could feel.

The surgeon stared at her crotch intently, which made her feel oddly vulnerable and exposed. She wanted to cover up, but the surgeon was making sure everything healed correctly, so she fought that urge.

"Okay, the sutures look good and everything seems to be healing well. I'm going to remove the packing and see how that turned out."

It felt odd, the shifting and tugging of the packing material inside her. It was a sensation she had never felt nor imagined before. It felt like a clown scarf with material being pulled out forever. Twenty-four feet of gauze explained some of that. The stirrups were awkward, her bad leg ached from the position, but it was necessary. Finally, the sensation stopped, and she sighed in relief.

Then she felt probing, something inserted. Emily wasn't sure how she felt about that, but it was new and needed to be endured. "Everything in here looks good as well and is healing up nicely."

Emily nervously asked, "Can...can I have a look?"

The surgeon turned a friendly smile at Emily. "Sure. I think we can manage that."

The nurse handed a hand mirror to the doctor. He took it and looked Emily in the eyes. "Emily, are you ready? Be aware you're swollen and pretty raw looking. It will look different when all that goes down in a month or so."

She nodded, biting her bottom lip in apprehension.

He angled the mirror so Emily could see the surgical handiwork. The area was raw, swollen, and the suture lines an obvious vivid red. She could see the clitoris, the vaginal opening, urethra, labia, everything, after the doctor helpfully pointed them all out. Everything was changed. Everything was right. It was so beautiful she began crying.

The nurse held Emily's hand. The surgeon lowered the mirror and removed Emily's legs from the stirrups gently, ensuring she didn't endure excess pain. Then she helped her sit, so pressure would not be put on her tender groin. The surgeon smiled and said, "The nurse is going to show you everything you need in order to take care of your new vagina. Pay attention. I'll see you again before you leave to make sure everything is healing nicely. Congratulations, Emily."

Things hurt and ached in a new way more irritating than anything else. She was used to pain, but this was a new hurt. The nurse pulled up a seat. "Okay. Ready for post-op care?"

Emily nodded, glad for something to take her mind off the pain. "Do I need to take notes?"

"You shouldn't have to as it's very simple. First off, you need to wear maxi pads for about four weeks as there will be some leakage as things finish healing. You'll need to use a betadine douche occasionally to ensure everything inside is kept clean. Wipes will be necessary to clean around the surgical site and after any bowel movements. You really don't want to get infected. You'll also need antibiotic ointment to keep the area safe and free of infection for a few weeks. And the last thing, get an inflatable doughnut to sit on. That area is going to be tender for three to four months and sitting will be more comfortable."

"Now to keep yourself open, you'll have to dilate daily. This will guarantee the success of the surgery, so not doing this would be bad. You'll have a series of dilators to use, of varying sizes. You need to insert these and leave them in for at least fifteen minutes, constantly applying pressure. This will keep the area open, ensure you have good depth, and keep your body from closing up as you heal. Just so you know, it is unlikely to close up entirely, but don't test it. If you want an open vagina, you'll do this several times a day." She smiled at Emily and cocked her head. "Any questions?"

"So, are these medical dildos?" Emily kept from laughing. When she read about this process that was what struck her most.

"In a way, yes." The nurse chuckled. "But don't worry, they're very boring. They look like medical supplies and aren't sexually exciting at all. Just make sure you lube them enough before use. It would be very painful to insert one without the benefit of lube."

Emily nodded. "I got it."

"Okay. You can rest for a week in your hotel and then come back for a final checkup before your flight home. I'll get the dilators." The nurse walked from the room. Emily sat there and reached down to explore tenderly. The area was smooth, hot, and she wasn't an outie anymore. She started crying from joy and Leah hugged her.

Leah held Emily as she cried the loss of Thomas and the joy of fully becoming her. The nurse came in with a large brown bag filled with supplies and printouts explaining everything. She waited until the crying subsided before handing it over. She smiled gently at Emily. "I have to show you this. And once done, you can head back to your hotel. Ready?"

Dilation was very peculiar. Feeling something enter her was uncomfortable and muscles spasmed around the dilator, and she grimaced in discomfort. The nurse explained as she gently applied pressure. "Okay. You need to get the dilator inside and then you sit with it inside, pushing on it. That will ensure your vagina is properly stretched and open. Keep going until you reach the largest dilator you can tolerate then wait for everything to stretch and get used to its new shape. That's all there is to it. You'll do that at least five times a day to start. Don't worry, as time goes by you won't need to dilate that frequently. That's explained on the printouts."

Emily paid attention to everything, aware this was important. She filed it away while she endured the dilation example and clean-up afterward.

Emily grabbed her panties and slipped a pad in like she had been shown. She pulled them up, consciously paying attention to the not tucking. Her eyes teared and Leah kissed her cheek. "It's okay, Emi kitty. You made it."

A giddiness welled up inside at the realization she was changed. Now completely Emily, the last vestige of Thomas surgically eliminated.

The return trip was exciting as Emily shifted on the doughnut with each turn, hissing in pain. Her body movements on the doughnut gave her uncomfortable sensations making her be more cautious and she offered thanks to all the deities in heaven that Tiffany wasn't the one driving. By the time they made it to the elevators, her knees were weak. She stumbled into the room, nearly tripping on her cane. Leah caught her and with little extra effort, steered Emily to the bed, where she crashed face first onto the mattress.

Emily slept deeply, wrung out from the pain, dilation, moving around, and the car ride. The emotional roller coaster flipped her from happy to depressed and back fairly quickly. All she wanted was sleep.

She grumbled when Leah woke her with drugs and orders to dilate, then refilled the ice packs for her crotch. It was awkward and painful, but she managed to get the smallest dilator inside with slow steady pressure, wincing occasionally as things stretched. Emily lay there and dozed, not bothering to remove the dilator. Leah called for room service, as Emily was not ready to head outside for meals yet.

Emily was dozing and heard Leah call a few people, letting them know how her healing was going. She and Leah had also made a blanket email she sent to everyone. Emily fell back asleep.

The next few days followed the same pattern of sleeping, eating, dilating, and taking warm sitz baths to keep herself clean. This had to be absolutely boring for Leah, staying cooped up in the hotel, but she kept telling Emily that she didn't mind as she could see Emily's happiness. Neither were interested in Arizona and both had brought a few books, prepared to deal with anything.

The final checkup was routine, as Emily had been good and followed the post-op orders like clockwork. She got new dilation orders and new directions for care. The flight back to Nashville was miserable. Any movement of the plane hurt, and planes were not well known for smooth flights. Despite that, Emily returned to Tennessee a changed woman, grinning her head off.

CHAPTER THIRTY-THREE

Dilating was annoying. It hurt, was uncomfortable, messy, and bugged her.

The sarge just laughed when Emily bitched about it to him, finding the whole issue hysterical. He had taken it upon himself to get Emily to exercise more, since she was gaining weight, and not just in the building of curves sort of way. Emily didn't do much except sit around and occasionally walk when absolutely necessary, which was not helping her fitness. Her leg and shoulder made it painful to exercise, giving her a convenient excuse.

The sarge didn't care. He started coming over and dragging Emily out on walks through the neighborhood, which while not overly strenuous made her bitch the whole time. Strength training was easier, though she resumed her desperate hatred of sit-ups. She had been happy being free of them when she left the Army, and now the sarge did all he could to get her back into shape. Leah thought the whole thing was funny.

The walking helped Emily recover, so she begrudgingly thanked him. She was healing well, and her endurance and strength were coming back as was her flexibility, so maybe jars would no longer thwart her. Leah walked with her whenever she could.

Emily noticed other changes. With all the exercise and her recovery, she realized that even though she was disabled she wasn't crippled. She could still do things, still manage something other than sitting like a lump on the couch watching cooking shows and lamenting her fate. She learned a lot about cooking but had done little else except surf the Net.

Emily looked forward to the nightly walks with Leah. They were good exercise and it was pleasant just spending time with her love. Between classes, and other fun, Emily opened up more and fit into her body. And her vaginal healing was going nicely. Ten weeks after surgery, her dilation was becoming less painful and awkward, and she was almost to the largest of the dilators. She still squeed happily whenever she saw herself naked in the mirror. It felt like a dream she was awake in.

Today she had to go downtown to pick up paperwork allowing her to change her legal documentation. Emily dressed nicely and headed into town. During the uneventful drive, she sang along with the radio, feeling alive.

Emily was going to pick up ten copies with her name change, to make absolutely sure that she had all possible copies needed. Last night, she typed out the letter to get her birth certificate amended back in North Carolina. Once she had the change in gender paperwork, she would mail it off and correct her birth certificate. Becoming Emily would be completed, the last legal traces of Thomas vanishing.

Finding parking by the court building was tough, but she found a handicapped spot after circling two times. She was antsy. Emily wanted this whole thing to be over, to be herself legally and completely. There were several paralegals in the chancery court office dropping off and picking up documents as she entered. This additional wait increased her twitchiness. After twenty minutes, it was finally her turn. She grinned and said, "I'm here to pick up paperwork for Emily Rhymer."

The woman nodded and found the form after a short search. "Would you like any copies?"

"Um…yes. Can I get ten copies, please?" The woman nodded and walked off, taking the paperwork with her.

Emily wanted to hold it in her hand, proof she legally was the woman she projected to the world, that she was no longer a man, if she had ever really even been one. She fidgeted, impatient for her proof.

When the clerk returned, Emily was beside herself. The woman handed her a stack of stapled papers and rang it up. Emily could not have cared less about the cost at that moment. These pieces of paper were priceless. She was legally a woman.

But first, one last task for today.

The line at the DMV wasn't horribly long. She waited with her driver's license, paperwork from the court, and the amended information form. Her wrist ached from all the writing, but it was worth the pain. After what seemed like forever, Emily reached the counter. She smiled at the woman and handed over the paperwork.

The woman smiled back then looked confused going over the packet. She glanced up at Emily then back to the paperwork, confusion only growing deeper. Emily felt butterflies begin flying in formation in her stomach. They couldn't refuse to give her an amended driver's license, could they?

"Wait one minute, please," said the woman as she stood and headed into a side office, taking the paperwork with her. Emily wondered what was going on, getting more nervous the longer it took. She had legal documents showing she was who she said she was, so what was the problem? She wanted to get this taken care of, then head home.

After another painful eternity, the woman returned. She sat in her chair and looked at Emily with an apologetic smile. "Sorry for the wait, Mrs. Rhymer. We had to check the documents and regulations. I've never done this before so I wanted to make sure everything was correct. Now, would you like a new photo?"

Emily looked at her old license. She had changed a lot since then and the woman looking back wasn't her anymore. The face was familiar but not the same. The picture would be from her first legal day as a woman instead of when her name changed. She liked that. "Can I get a new picture, please?"

"Certainly. They'll call your name and you go over to B6. Have a nice day." With that, she handed back the paperwork and Emily walked away. This was really happening.

She was in a daze when called. Her picture looked fairly cute, and Emily couldn't stop smiling. When she was handed her card, it took everything not squee and jump around like an idiot. She made it outside and into the car before her happiness burst out. There were a few stares, but she was too happy to care.

Food. She needed food to celebrate properly. She headed toward Nashville, since she could hit the Social Security office afterward. According to Leah, there was a nice Thai place a few blocks from the Social Security office. She was speeding along, beyond happy, singing Indigo Girls at the top of her lungs.

The siren and flashing lights in her rearview scared the shit out of her. She pulled onto the side of the road. How fast had she been going? She was fairly certain she hadn't been speeding...had she?

Emily watched the cop swagger to the car. She had her license and registration ready. She smiled nervously as she rolled down the window. "Yes, Officer?"

"License and registration, ma'am."

She handed them over, wondering if there was a code letting the cop know she used to be male. Maybe when they looked her up in the database? Gods, she hoped that wasn't true. "There you go, Officer."

"Do you know how fast you were going, Ms. Rhymer?" asked the officer in that condescending, doubtful voice traffic cops always had.

"Um...no, Officer. I was singing along with the radio and thought I was at least close to the speed limit, wasn't I?"

"You were going eighty-three in a seventy. I'm going to have to write you up."

"Yes, sir." Emily was bummed. She hadn't gotten a traffic ticket in a long time as she was a very conscientious driver.

The traffic cop wrote the ticket and Emily fidgeted. She hated waiting for things like this. She had been antsy in the Army and real antsy before any air assault operation, whether it was repelling out of a chopper or hooking up gear for sling loading. At least then she would be able to explode into action at the correct time giving her some relief. There was nothing she could do now but wait.

Finally, the police officer finished and handed her the ticket. She looked down at it and noticed her sex marked female. Her emotions soared. In its own strange way, this ticket proved she was a woman. She bounced in her seat and headed off, careful to keep her speed from going too high.

❖

It had taken Emily time to set everything up for this. She had placed candles everywhere but had waited to light them until Leah had called to say she was on her way home. Emily was dressed in nothing but her skin and positioned herself just right on the couch. She knew her grin warned of the mischief she had planned. It had the desired effect as Leah froze in the doorway, eyes going wide. "Beloved, guess what?"

Leah swallowed. "What?"

"I'm a real woman. My speeding ticket says so," said Emily.

Emily held in her snicker as Leah blinked. Emily was well aware that statement didn't make any sense. "Huh?"

"I'm legally a woman and the first use of my new driver's license was to get a speeding ticket. And you know what else?" Emily stretched, arching her back and thrusting her now full B-cup breasts out. "It's also been enough time. Tonight, my love, tonight you get to break in the new me."

Leah smiled and moved forward, closing the door with a kick of her foot. She dropped her briefcase and purse to the floor, and headed toward Emily. Once Leah reached the couch, she took Emily in her arms and kissed her.

They kissed for a while, and Emily scooted over so Leah could have some couch to perch on. Emily broke the kiss. "Someone is far, far too clothed. We need to correct this."

Leah quickly began to shed clothes and fling them about. Emily took in the sight of her stripping. Her heart was beating stronger, and she felt complete and happy. Once Leah was naked, she reached over and lifted Emily, making her eep in surprise. Leah smirked at Emily, and carried her through the house to lay her on the bed. She licked her lips in desire. "Now the fun really begins."

Emily moaned as Leah sucked on her breasts, licking circles around the areola and flicking the swelling nipples with her tongue. Emily ran her fingers through Leah's hair and arched her back, trying to get closer to Leah's mouth, to force more of her breast inside. After a light nip on her erect nipple, Leah kissed her way from Emily's breasts down to her vulva, gazing hungrily at her closely for a second, long enough for Emily to grow shy and bend her legs to cover herself, embarrassed by the naked hunger.

Leah grinned and peeled Emily's legs open. She lowered her head and reached out tentatively with her tongue, gently flicking Emily's clitoris. The sensation was so new and electric it stole Emily's breath. She clutched the sheets and writhed under the building wave that crashed through her, flashing to fill her whole body with tickly lightning. She moaned, spurring Leah to lick and suck more vigorously.

The scream of pleasure ripping out of her was a surprise. Emily twitched, a wave rolling up and down her body, making her weak, lightheaded. Leah didn't stop, holding her hips tightly. Emily realized Leah had a finger inside her and was thrusting back and forth, gently curling the tip. That felt amazing, a haze of pleasure, as different and new places were singing their existence, those feelings fading into and through one another. She gripped the sheets, yanking one of the fitted corners off. All she could do was thrash under Leah's tongue, screaming, rising higher and higher, panting in newly experienced pleasure. Finally, the wave crashed and Emily collapsed limply, totally spent. She weakly pushed Leah with her hands, shifting away from that devilish tongue, the sensation far too intense now.

Leah crawled up alongside Emily and kissed her soundly. She gazed deeply into her eyes. Emily had trouble focusing and mumbled a barely coherent, "Love you, Leah. Thanks."

Leah hugged her tightly, their bodies spooned together as one. "I love you, Emily. Thank you."

CHAPTER THIRTY-FOUR

S o, Emily, how are things going?" Dr. Richards asked warmly.
"Awesomely. My paperwork's changed. I'm waiting for
my amended birth certificate to finish everything else. All is good."

"Glad to hear that. So now that you've had surgery, what do you
think has changed?"

"Everything and nothing. I mean, sure, between my body and
legal status things aren't the same, but other than that, I'm not sure
anything else has. You know what I mean?"

"I think so. Why don't you go over it?" Emily knew she was
being led, but that was all right. She admired the way the doc guided
her through the labyrinth of her own thoughts, helping her find herself
despite wanting to get rid of her awkward feelings.

"Well, I know my body's different and legally, I'm female. And
I've noticed different thoughts and feelings looking at my body. I feel
like a huge weight has been dropped and I can see myself clearly,
without the whole penis thing distracting me. I like being able to pull
my panties straight up without having to tuck. I like how it doesn't hurt
like when tucks go awry or some testicle skin slips under the leg band
or something anymore. That really sucked. I like how I can go into a
women's room and not feel paranoid someone is going to see a penis.
That was unnerving. I mean, honestly, peeing in peace shouldn't be
a worry. I try on clothes without feeling something similar. I mean,
in a lot of ways, how I move changed. I can walk easier in my skin."

"I see. Anything else changed?"

"Well, sex is fantastic. That's changed, and Leah is happier. You have no idea how thankful I am for that. I feel closer to my friends, like I held back from truly committing to the friendship, worried about what they thought. That's gone. I'm a real girl, so no more stress. That's about all I can think."

"Okay, so what stayed the same?"

"I'm still the same person I was before going under the knife, mostly. I have the same debts, quirks, stupid sense of humor, friends, shrink, car, problems. So not a lot has changed in that sense, but it feels like the world has shifted under me."

"You've gone through a powerful transformative event. Not only transition but surgery can change your whole world. You changed incredibly through this process, so it's understandable it feels like everything shifted. And since your problems didn't go anywhere while you transformed, not much changes there either. This whole process can be overwhelming."

Emily nodded. "That makes sense. And yeah, this has been overwhelming, added to flashbacks and what not so it's been an... interesting ride. I'm still changing and the hormones are still doing their work, so I guess I'm wondering what's going to happen from here. I mean, at times, this seems so unreal, like it's someone else's life."

"That's perfectly normal. Like I said, this has been a trying time. You've had a lot of things piling on, and yet you keep standing up and moving on. That says a lot about your character," replied Dr. Richards. "You're becoming yourself, which can be frightening. Most people are terrified of who they really are and would rather do anything else. They would rather pretend than honestly see themselves. You've done that. You've seen yourself and become your truth. That's a tremendous accomplishment. So long as you keep seeing yourself and don't try to hide, you'll be okay."

"One thing I decided early on is that I wanted to be the real me, whoever that turned out to be. I was so sure I was male, but..." Emily smirked, gesturing to herself. "Everything I was sure of in my life turned out to be false. My fear of my old unit, the acceptance of my mom, all of that turned out to be nothing. So, yeah...I've changed, just not in the ways I wanted or expected. And a lot of the credit goes to Leah. She loved and accepted me like no one else ever has, making all this easier. She's my pillar of strength."

Dr. Richards nodded, taking notes. "You're right, having someone love and support you makes a huge difference. I'm happy you found someone who loves you for you. You really have blossomed."

Emily blushed, embarrassed by the compliment. "Thank you."

"Not a problem, Emily. So, other than that, anything new on the horizon?"

"Not that I'm aware of. Life is going well, which I hope continues. Classes are great and I hope to get good grades."

"Good to hear. Well, that's it for our time. You have a good month and we'll talk later."

❖

Emily returned home and began cleaning. She started a load of laundry and took a load from the dryer to the bedroom to fold and put away. She smiled folding Leah's panties, like she did every time she thought about Leah's body.

Once the laundry was done, Emily tidied the living room and bedroom, making sure there wasn't a huge mess anywhere. She struggled to stay one step ahead of the mess that could overwhelm the house. It was a constant battle, but her time in the Army taught her quick and efficient cleaning. It was a skill she was quite thankful for learning.

She headed outside and watered the garden. Leah loved flowers and Emily was growing to relish working in the dirt. The results of that labor were tangible, and she planned on a vegetable garden next year. She could grow food and herbs for their cooking, which was a pleasant idea. She headed inside for a mug of tea.

This was a Leah habit she picked up and discovered tea was a wonderful way to wind down. As she gazed out the window at the backyard, she thought about her life, about everything that had happened. It seemed almost dreamlike, like some fractured fairy tale. So many wonderful things had happened and some fairly crappy ones as well, but she wouldn't change a thing. The attack was something she would prefer to never go through again, but that was the exception rather than the rule.

So, was this life a dream and was there any way to tell? She pinched herself and it hurt, but she recalled pain in some of her dreams, but were they before or after Iraq. She had no clue what the answer was and nothing to go off of to find that date or details about the dream.

Emily sipped, feeling warmth travel down her throat. It soothed and warmed her nicely. This didn't seem like a dream. Her life was so different than before that stupid rocket-propelled grenade changed things utterly. Couldn't all of this be simply the fevered dreams of an injured soldier?

Emily didn't know. Just how radically could a life change before questions like this occurred? Her life was altered fundamentally, so much so she was afraid this might be a dream. Was she going to come to in a Blackhawk, strapped to a gurney? Was she going to wake up in the CSH, post-surgery? Was she still Thomas and her whole life as Emily some morphine and anesthesia fantasy?

She heard the front door open, and Leah call out, "Emi kitty, I'm home!"

Warmth filled Emily, heart pounding with joy from Leah's voice. If this was a dream, did she want to wake up? Did she want to return to being Thomas? Did she want to forsake all her happiness for what she had before?

Emily knew her answer was definitely no.

About the Author

Heather K O'Malley is a fifty-plus-year-old transgender lesbian who has been writing stories since fifth grade, lots of stories. Along the way she joined the Army, got injured, traveled the world, learned a number of languages, failed epically, found true love, went to a lot of schools, got a master's in English, was an activist, taught, learned several martial arts, figured out how to cook, tried most everything, and became a proud grandmother. It has been exhausting.

Books Available from Bold Strokes Books

A Degree to Die For by Karis Walsh. A murder at the University of Washington's Classics Department brings Professor Antigone Weston and Sergeant Adriana Kent together—first as opposing forces, and then allies as they fight together to protect their campus from a killer. (978-1-63679-365-8)

A Talent Within by Suzanne Lenoir. Evelyne, born into nobility, and Annika, a peasant girl with a deadly secret, struggle to change their destinies in Valmora, a medieval world controlled by religion, magic, and men. (978-1-63679-423-5)

Finders Keepers by Radclyffe. Roman Ashcroft's past, it seems, is not so easily forgotten when fate brings her and Tally Dewilde together—along with an attraction neither welcomes. (978-1-63679-428-0)

Homeland by Kristin Keppler and Allisa Bahney. Dani and Kate have finally found themselves on the same side of the war, but a new threat from the inside jeopardizes the future of the wasteland. (978-1-63679-405-1)

Just One Dance by Jenny Frame. Will Taylor Spark and her new business to make dating special—the Regency Romance Club—bring sparkle back to Jaq Bailey's lonely world? (978-1-63679-457-0)

On My Way There by Jaycie Morrison. As Max traverses the open road, her journey of impossible love, loss, and courage mirrors her voyage of self-discovery leading to the ultimate question: If she can't have the woman of her dreams, will the woman of real life be enough? (978-1-63679-392-4)

Transitioning Home by Heather K O'Malley. An injured soldier realizes they need to transition to really heal. (978-1-63679-424-2)

Truly Enough by JJ Hale. Chasing the spark of creativity may ignite a burning romance or send a friendship up in flames. (978-1-63679-442-6)

Vintage and Vogue by Kelly and Tana Fireside. When tech whiz Sena Abrigo marches into small-town Owen Station, she turns librarian Hazel Butler's life upside down in the most wonderful of ways, setting off an explosive series of events, threatening their chance at love…and their very lives. (978-1-63679-448-8)

Broken Fences by Jo Hemmingwood. Former army sergeant Seneca Twist has difficulty adjusting to civilian life until she meets psychologist Robyn Mason and has a place to call home. (978-1-63679-414-3)

Never Kiss a Cowgirl by Ali Vali. Asher Evans dreams of winning the National Finals Rodeo in Vegas, and Reagan Wilson wants no part of something that brings back the memory of what killed her father. (978-1-63679-106-7)

Pantheon Girls by Jean Copeland. Cassie Burke never anticipated the detour life was about to take when a meeting with a prospective client reunites her with a past love and reignites the star-crossed passion they shared twenty years earlier. (978-1-63679-337-5)

Roux for Two by Aurora Rey. For TV chef Chelsea Boudreaux and hometown boy Bryce Cormier, love proves as tricky as making a good pot of gumbo. (978-1-63679-376-4)

Starting Over by Nance Sparks. Jennifer has no idea if she can mend Sam's broken soul after the sudden loss of her wife, but it's never too late for starting over. (978-1-63679-409-9)

The Accidental Bride by Jane Walsh. Spinsters Miss Grace Linfield and Miss Thea Martin travel to Gretna Green to prevent a wedding, only to discover a scandalous passion—for each other. (978-1-63679-345-0)

Three Wishes by Anne Shade. A magic lamp, a beautiful Jinni, and a cursed princess make for one unbelievable story. (978-1-63679-349-8)

Undiscovered Treasures by MJ Williamz. For Cyl and her friends Luna and Martinique, life's best treasures often appear when you're not looking. (978-1-63679-449-5)

Curse of the Gorgon by Tanai Walker. Cass will do anything to ensure Elle's safety, but is she willing to embrace the curse of the Gorgon? (978-1-63679-395-5)

Dance with Me by Georgia Beers. Scottie Templeton mixes it up on and off the dance floor with sexy salsa instructor Marisa Reyes. But can Scottie get past Marisa's connection to her ex? (978-1-63679-359-7)

Gin and Bear It by Joy Argento. Opposites really can attract, and as Kelly and Logan work together to create a loving home for rescue cat Bear, they just might find one for themselves as well. (978-1-63679-351-1)

Harvest Dreams by Jacqueline Fein-Zachary. Planting the vineyard of their dreams, Kate Bauer and Sydney Barrett must resist their attraction while battling nature and their families, who oppose both the venture and their relationship. (978-1-63679-380-1)

The No Kiss Contract by Nan Campbell. Workaholic Davy believes she can get the top spot at her firm if the senior partners think she's settling down and about to start a family, but she needs the delightful yet dubious Anna to help by pretending to be her fiancée. (978-1-63679-372-6)

Outside the Lines by Melissa Sky. If you had the chance to live forever, would you take it? Amara Rodriguez did, and it sets her on a journey to find her missing mother and unravel the mystery of her own heart. (978-1-63679-403-7)

The Value of Sylver and Gold by Michelle Larkin. When word gets out that former Boston homicide detective Reid Sylver can talk to the dead, the FBI solicits her help on a serial murder case, prompting Reid to assemble forces once again with Detective London Gold. (978-1-63679-093-0)

When It Feels Right by Tagan Shepard. Freshly out of the closet Marlene hasn't been lucky in love, but when it comes to her quirky new roommate Abby, everything just feels right. (978-1-63679-367-2)

Lucky in Lace by Melissa Brayden. Straitlaced stationery store owner Juliette Jennings's predictable life unravels when a sexy lingerie shop and its alluring owner move in next door. (978-1-63679-434-1)

Made for Her by Carsen Taite. Neal Walsh is a newly made member of the Mancuso crime family, but will her undeniable attraction to Anastasia Petrov, the wife of her boss's sworn enemy, be the ultimate test of her loyalty? (978-1-63679-265-1)

Off the Menu by Alaina Erdell. Reality TV sensation Restaurant Redo and its gorgeous host Erin Rasmussen will arrive to film in chef Taylor Mobley's kitchen. As the cameras roll, will they make the jump from enemies to lovers? (978-1-63679-295-8)

Pack of Her Own by Elena Abbott. When things heat up in a small town, steamy secrets are revealed between Alpha werewolf Wren Carne and her human mate, Natalie Donovan. (978-1-63679-370-2)

Return to McCall by Patricia Evans. Lily isn't looking for romance— not until she meets Alex, the gorgeous Cuban dance instructor at La Haven, a newly opened lesbian retreat. (978-1-63679-386-3)

So It Went Like This by C. Spencer. A candid and deeply personal exploration of fate, chosen family, and the vulnerability intrinsic in life's uncertainties. (978-1-63555-971-2)

Stolen Kiss by Spencer Greene. Anna and Louise share a stolen kiss, only to discover that Louise is dating Anna's brother. Surely, one kiss can't change everything...Can it? (978-1-63679-364-1)

The Fall Line by Kelly Wacker. When Jordan Burroughs arrives in the Deep South to paint a local endangered aquatic flower, she doesn't expect to become friends with a mischievous gin-drinking ghost who complicates her budding romance and leads her to an awful discovery and danger. (978-1-63679-205-7)

To Meet Again by Kadyan. When the stark reality of WWII separates cabaret singer Evelyn and Australian doctor Joan in Singapore, they must overcome all odds to find one another again. (978-1-63679-398-6)